Immaculate Connection

Immaculate Connection

by
Kay Illingworth

Strategic Book Publishing and Rights Co.

Strategic Book Publishing and Rights Co.
12620 FM 1960, Suite A4-507
Houston, TX 77065
www.sbpra.com

ISBN: 978-1-612024-701-0

Book Design by Julius Kiskis

20 19 18 17 16 15 14 13 12   1 2 3 4 5

Dedication

For my husband, Colin, and all our kids.

And God said, "Let there be light," and there was light

—Genesis 1:3

You can't have a light without a dark to stick it in.

—Arlo Guthrie

Here's to God in its many forms

*Special acknowledgments
and genuine thanks...*

To my dear friend and mentor, Heddy Kyte, for her love
and hard work all these years.
Allan Markin, Francie Greenslade, and the group of 2005

To my family. You know who you are.

1.

Holy mother of God! How much longer? The young woman huddled in the back seat of the luxurious Delage DR70 Saloon was terrified.

They'd driven for hours along the tiny country roads under a jet-black sky. The summer storm, relentless in its attack, wouldn't give up its assault on the car and pounded it mercilessly. The wind wailed and moaned like a crazed woman wandering alone, lost in the foothills to time, her tortured soul crying, "Don't do it, don't do it!"

It was the third car she'd ever been in and if she had anything to do with it, it'd be the last. She didn't trust 'em, not one bit! It was a fine-looking vehicle—she gave it that much. The deep purple body framed with chrome had been polished to perfection, and the smell of the new cream-coloured leather seats that cocooned her added to the car's overall opulence. *A nob's car!* she thought to herself. *Whoever it belongs to must be upper crust.*

She glanced at the chauffeur and couldn't help but notice how big his head was in comparison to his skinny frame, and how white his skin looked beneath his black cap. *He looks more dead than the spirits I talk to,* she thought absently. *I wonder why he won't take that daft hat off in the car?*

Turning her attention away from him, she stared out through the window into the black night. *How many demons hang around out there in the darkness, waiting for the opportunity to slide into our minds and crush our souls into theirs? Or are we already possessed*

I

by thoughts and beliefs that we deny? Thoughts and beliefs that live underneath the surface and subtly dictate our existence? We'll never be free to love each other, to raise this child—our child! No! I can't give him up—I can't do it! If I love this tiny life that I have in my belly now, how will I feel when I hold him? Will I be able to hand the tiny bundle over like one of Angel's puppies? She smiled at the thought of Angel. *I hope she doesn't fret too much while I'm away.*

Her heart skipped a beat as she thought back to the moment when Dr. O'Riley had looked into her eyes and told her she was pregnant. Expressionless, she'd stood up to leave. *Pregnant! By Jesus! By Jesus! I can't be!* Everything drained from her, everything except the new life inside her. She felt her legs give way just as the doctor's strong arms reached out and stopped her from hitting the floor.

But she was used to the idea now. She'd never once considered abortion. Anything but that! *There must be a way I can keep this child—we can keep this child.* The wind rocked the car from side to side. Its piercing howl sliced through her. *NEVER! NEVER!*

She was tired, weary with defeat. Despair stuck its claws into her shoulders and clung on, pecking, gnawing, eating away at her. She had no fight left. She thought she'd cried herself dry, but still the tears fell from her swollen eyes. *Yet there was hope, wasn't there?* She could see the rain sheeting down in the dim beams of the headlights, like tiny sparks from a firework.

He passed her a linen handkerchief. She felt its cleanness soil her nostrils. *Clean, clean, everything had to be clean just like him.* She wouldn't look at him, couldn't look at him, the man she loved, the father of the child she would birth but couldn't keep. *What was so bad about their love? All love is pure, isn't it?* But not theirs! Theirs was a love of mystery and secrets that not another mortal soul knew about. *Imagine if it ever got out.* The people would lynch them; their families would disown them. He'd stand trial, be persecuted, and cast out like the Devil himself. And the child, labelled a bastard. Worse—blamed for the folly of his parents. What chance would he have if she kept him? None! He'd be spurned, ridiculed. "The Devil's child" they'd call him, the narrow ones who sing alleluia to some fancy God in a fancy building.

She could never give him the life she wanted him to have. She wanted him to be educated, have the best, not live a life of toil and slog like she did. Not be dragged up in a cesspit and called names by a narrow-minded community. A community that would take his purity and spit on it with the same saliva they chewed their holy bread with.

But what about the love only I can give him? Could he get that from another woman who'd not felt his kick in her belly? *Who are these people, anyway? They're obviously wealthy. I mean, who can afford a car like this—brand new, with a chauffeur?*

Influential, he'd told her. *"They can give the child a life we can only dream of, Maggie."* His words in her head—she'd lived them over and over again. He'd arranged everything: the family, the journey, even the story they'd concocted.

"Why do we have to go to France?" she'd asked him when he first told her of his plans.

"Because Dun Laoghaire isn't that big a place and these things have a way of turning up when you least expect it."

"These things," she'd whispered, looking up at him, wide-eyed.

"You know what I mean."

Oh, I know what you mean

Yes, he'd arranged everything—everything but her feelings. Thinking back, she knew she'd been naïve. She'd begged him to run away with her so they could be together with their son. She'd known her baby was a boy from the moment the doctor had told her she was pregnant.

"We'll get by—you're not poor."

"If only it were that simple, Maggie. What about your husband, the Church, the people who know us? What if we were found together?"

"You're yellow," she'd screamed at him. "No backbone—a bloody hypocrite like the rest of 'em. You'll let someone take this child from us just to save face and then sing praises to God on Sunday mornings. Well, the lot of you can rot for all I care. They can have you. By God, I regret the day I ever met you!" But she hadn't meant it! Not one word.

She just wanted to wound him, make him suffer.

The pain on his face registered in her soul. "No, Maggie! Don't talk like that. I love you…my life, it…it's nothing without you."

He'd dropped to his knees, wrapped his arms around her middle, wept into her belly. His tears soaked through her clothes. She'd tried to push him away but couldn't. Instead, defeated, she'd closed her eyes, wrapped her arms around his shoulders and pinned him to her. What would her life be like without him? No love. Just hardship, misery, and abuse. He was the only thing that made it bearable.

"Please, Maggie, if only things were that simple," he'd repeated between sobs. "If only they were that simple."

And the morning he'd told her about the wealthy family desperate for a child, it was as if she'd stopped breathing. A piece of her had died that day. She'd clutched her belly, closed her eyes, and collapsed into him. "I can't, I can't do it, please don't make me do it. I'll tell Patrick the baby is his, nobody will ever know—"

"Maggie; it would have to be the Immaculate Conception. How can you even think that?"

"Miracles happen! I could convince him it'd happened when he was drunk, that he doesn't remember—"

"No! He'd never believe you. When was the last time the two of you got together? Drunk or not, Patrick's no fool. It doesn't take a mathematician to work out the dates even if the baby came early, and what if the baby is the image of me? It's not possible, Maggie. He'd kill you and the child if he ever found out."

"You're right," she'd sobbed, with her head still buried in his chest. But then something changed. She stopped crying and backed away from him with a determined look on her face. "There's one condition before I give up this baby." She removed the necklace he'd given her five years before. "This necklace—our son must have it. Promise me that much." She slipped it into his huge palm and closed his fingers around it. "Please."

He looked at it for a moment. Not a traditional crucifix, not for Maggie. A Celtic cross, eighteen karat gold, unique in its design; he'd had it specially made. Their initials were inscribed on the back of it, visible only through a magnifying glass. A spiral pattern etched around the outside represented their love and all its complexities. In the centre, three tiny rubies set in the shape of a triangle represented the trinity, and the diamond in the middle of them was *his* Maggie. She was more precious to him than anything else in his world. "Why, Maggie? This is yours. It represents our—"

"I know," she cut in, "but he's the third piece. Promise me!" she said, holding his face in her hands. "He must have it! I can feel it! Promise me! Promise me!"

"Of course, of course. I'll see to it." He knew better than to argue with one of Maggie's feelings. They had an uncanny way of always being right!

He was a powerful man, her lover. He could pull strings, get his own way, make everything look okay on the outside. It had been so easy for them to make up this cock and bull story about her being ill and having to go to France to be cured. He'd even talked to Dr. O'Riley and asked him to back them up, explaining that Maggie had fallen victim to vulnerability in light of her unhappy marriage. The doctor promised to turn a blind eye, nothing more. If Patrick asked him, he couldn't lie. Dr. O'Riley had no time for the man. He knew Patrick made Maggie's life hell—he'd patched her up enough times. If the bastard thought she was pregnant with another man's child—God knows! They'd find Maggie dead that's for sure and he didn't want that on his conscience.

He even saw to it that he'd accompany her. After all, he was an honourable figure in the community. Who the hell was going to suspect anything? And even if they did, they wouldn't dare open their mouths without solid proof.

She'd hidden her bump for as long as possible and even now at twenty-seven weeks she was only just beginning to show. Time had gone by faster than ever. She didn't want to let the child go and her feelings told her the child didn't want to leave. He preferred to stay hidden inside his mother. Safe.

Holy Mother, is this journey ever going to end! she thought, just as the chauffeur brought the car to a standstill outside a huge pair of wrought iron gates.

He jumped out into the savage night holding a crumpled newspaper above his head with one hand while he fished for a key from his trouser pockets with the other. Realising the key he needed was on the bunch still in the car, he ran back and cut the engine. French profanities flew into the night and joined with the rest of the storm as he yanked the keys from the ignition and ran back to the gates. He found exactly which key he needed and shoved it into the heavy padlock to free the gates from the thick iron chains that held them. His curses accompanied their loud squeaks and clangs as they swung open. Within seconds he'd manoeuvred the car onto the driveway, jumped out, and slammed the gates shut. When he finally made it back to the car, his dark suit stuck to his skinny frame like a second skin. He reminded Maggie of a shiny black pebble that had just been washed up out of the ocean. She used to collect them when she was on the beach in Dun Laoghaire.

"*Merde! Merde!*" the chauffeur muttered under his breath. He threw the soggy newspaper onto the floor of the car and removed his hat and jacket.

David leaned forward and opened the dividing window. "*Le chauffeur, combien plus long?*"

"*A peu près vingt minutes.*" The chauffeur eyed him through the rear-view mirror.

"*Merci, Monsieur,*" David said, closing the dividing window.

"What did you say?" Maggie asked.

"I asked him how much longer; he said about another twenty minutes."

"Twenty minutes to drive up the driveway!"

He smiled and wondered what her reaction would be at staying in a house that was almost as big as the village she'd left behind. "The chateau is vast, surrounded by hundreds of acres of land."

"How do you know these people?"

"I don't know them." He looked uncomfortable. "They are go-betweens, if you like."

She glared at him disbelievingly. "So you have no idea who the people are who want to adopt my baby? You led me to believe that you knew the parents, or at least you had an inkling about them. They could be anybody! What if they're a pair of bloody lunatics?"

"*Our* baby, Maggie!" he snapped. As soon as he'd said it he checked on the chauffeur who was puffing on a cigarette, oblivious to them. *Thank God for the dividing window.* It never occurred to him that the man might not speak English. "The couple are British and wealthy. They've tried desperately to have a child for a number of years. I'm told they are thrilled, absolutely thrilled, to be expectant parents."

"But if you don't know these people, who put you in touch with them?"

"I have acquaintances in high places, people who owe me favours. I made a phone call to the Archdiocese of Dublin and told him about your, um…your plight."

"*My* plight!"

He leaned into her, gripped her arm roughly, and hissed through clenched teeth. His head shook with every word. "Yes! I could hardly tell him of my involvement, now could I? Do you think I feel good about all this? The heartbreak I'm causing you, the, the, the, lying, the deceit? It goes against everything I stand for. Do you think I don't feel it—I'm not suffering as much as you are? That I wouldn't give anything to hold this baby in my arms with you at my side and declare my love for the both of you?"

She dug her nails into his hand, and tried to lift him off. "Let go of me!"

He looked manic and dug his fingers in harder. "I'm sick to death of listening to you! You make me out to be some kind of monster with no feelings." His voice got louder. "All I've ever thought about is you…the baby," he said, with a vicious nod.

Angry, she pulled her arm away. Her face was filled with disgust. "No! All you've thought about is yourself!"

The chauffeur stared at them through the mirror with a puzzled look on his face. Maggie shot him a defiant look, a look that told him to carry on driving and mind his own business.

"Maggie, how many times must we go through this?" He rubbed at his temple.

Over the months she'd imagined a million happy family scenarios until reality turned up and crushed them. No child. A part-time David. A full-time Patrick.

He put his arm around her, wanting to make everything better. "It'll get easi—"

She threw him off. "Don't say that! Don't even try to convince me it'll get easier! You really have no idea, do you? You have no idea of what I'm going through." She broke into uncontrollable sobs.

He tried to hide the defeated tone in his voice. "I do. I'm as broken as you are—"

"No! Not nearly!" she hissed. Her anger picked up pace. "If that were the case you wouldn't care about the thoughts of others. That's what being pregnant does. I can't expect you to feel the same way I do. You haven't felt him move inside you. You can't feel how dependent upon you he already is. If you could feel that you'd never let him go, especially to complete strangers." For a moment she felt the fight in her belly. She turned to him with fire in her eyes. "I won't do it, David! I won't give up my baby!"

He took her hand and stroked the top of it gently with his thumb, closed his eyes, and lay back into the soft leather. He let out a weary sigh. "Maggie, what do you propose we do? He has a chance at a life we can't possibly give him. Ask yourself this question—do you want this child brought up in love or in hate? Because if you keep…if we keep him, he'll live with our shame and our guilt for the rest of his life. Is that what you want for him, Maggie?"

She shook her head from side to side reflexively, trying to clear it. "I hate you for making me do this," she wailed. "I could have some time with him! Be a friend of his parents, an aunt, any—"

He felt her pain scrape his insides out but he kept his emotions hidden. "Be rational! The adoptive parents have insisted that the child be raised with no knowledge of his adoption and they prefer their identities to remain unknown."

"What about the hosts at the chateau?"

"They are strangers, as I explained earlier—friends of a friend of a friend, if you like. They know only the bare facts, the facts I gave to the archdiocese. They have no idea who the adoptive parents are."

"The necklace, how will he—"

"I'll make it a condition," he interrupted. "I promise you that." *It's the least I can do.* "They can say it's a gift from his mother; that way they're not lying."

"But if they don't want him to know anything about us, what makes you think they'll abide by any bloody condition?" She placed her hands on her belly.

"I'm told they're devout Catholics. I'll tell them that I've made a promise to his maternal mother that he be given the necklace at an age when he can appreciate it. They won't refuse," he said adamantly. "Besides, the necklace *is* a gift from his mother. They don't have to mention which one!"

"David—"

"Yes?"

"Can you arrange to take my—our baby to them? I don't like the idea of some stranger taking him."

"Yes, yes, of course. I feel the same way." He leant forward and picked up his briefcase. Flipping the two locks, he reached in and removed a small black velvet pouch. He untied the gold thread that fastened it and took out the Celtic cross. "Here." He placed the cross in her palm and closed her hand around it. Surrounding her hand with both of his, he lifted it to his lips and kissed the top of it. "Maggie, let's bless this cross so that our child will someday, somehow, know who we are. Let's bless this cross so that he knows how much love we hold in our hearts for him."

They closed their eyes and held the cross between them. "Aedan, my little miracle," she said. "May your life be blessed with love and only love."

David was crushed inside. Yet he held back the tears and the torrent of emotions wanting to explode. "Dear God." He had to breathe a few times before he could carry on. "Bless our child. Smile upon our child. Surround him with your love, and ours. May he one day know my heart and the heart of his mother, Maggie O'Connell." He bent down and picked up the briefcase again. This time he took out a small glass bottle.

"What's that?" David had always been intense. But in this moment his eyes drilled into hers with something she'd never seen in him before.

"Holy water. I am taking the liberty of christening my own child with his mother by my side. For once in my life I'm not going to listen to reason, rules, or morals, and I make no apologies for the child I've fathered. This child is mine. I accept that and I'm not ashamed of him, Maggie. The only thing I'm ashamed of is the heartache I've caused you. That, and the hypocrite I've become. I have no right to your love or to be serving the Church—"

"Shh…" she whispered, covering his lips with the flat of her hand. "Let's not spoil the moment with questions about your morals or calling. Let's pretend we're two simple parents at a simple christening with our baby." She leant forward and held her lips against his for a moment. She felt the pain and the sadness that smouldered inside him reach down into her. *How cruelly I've treated him these past months, with no thought of his feelings or what he's going through.*

He unscrewed the small bottle and tipped some of the holy water onto the index and middle fingers of his right hand. He dabbed the water on Maggie's forehead, chest, and shoulders, then crossed himself. Finally, he tipped another small amount of the water into his palms, rubbed them together, and placed both hands gently on her stomach. "I christen our child Aedan David Sullivan-O'Connell…" He'd barely gotten the last word out when he felt the baby kick hard against his palms. They looked at each other startled, and started to laugh and cry at the same time. David wouldn't remove his hands and the child inside her wouldn't stop kicking. It was too much for him to bear. He'd tried to stay strong for her but he couldn't endure it, not another minute. Father David Sullivan put his head on the swollen belly of his lover and sobbed, "I'm so sorry, so sorry…"

His stomach ached with the emotions pulsing through him. His heart had grown dark and felt as if it had split into a million little pieces, every piece a shattered reminder of the guilt he carried. A guilt that crawled through his bones, swam through his blood, and dissolved in his spirit.

Stroking his hair, Maggie looked down at the bowed head of her lover and smiled a sad smile. She turned her head to look out the window. It was still black outside.

2.

The storm weakened. Within minutes the wind howled itself out of existence and the rain became a steady rhythm.

Chateau Saint Esteve surfaced high in the distance, its towers just about visible in the heart of the clouds. As Dawn broke, the cold morning mist hung low and smoked its way around the grounds like a mystical dragon on guard. The tall trees that lined both sides of the drive flipped leaves at the small car in an aloof manner as it passed by.

Maggie opened the car window and was greeted by the odd twittering from the birds and the sounds of small animals as they scurried through the undergrowth. *Everything is coming to life.* She stuck her head out of the window into the fresh morning air. The healthy smell of grass and flowers replaced the stale air in her nose and lungs. She lifted her head to the sky and inhaled deeply. The cool rain dotted her face and neck like kisses from an elusive lover. She inhaled again, taking in the smell of heavy foliage as it renewed her body.

She sensed the amused spirit of the chateau as it watched her read its past. The heartaches and joys, the madness, the wars, the sickness and healing; she could feel it all. Yet despite everything, it had held on to its beauty. She felt a small measure of relief trickle through her. At least her son would be introduced to the world in one of the most beautiful places it had to offer—but then again, something wasn't quite right. Something formidable lurked beneath the surface. Her instincts niggled at her but she ignored them, brushing them off as nerves.

The sound of gravel crunching underneath the tyres jolted Maggie out of her reverie. The chauffeur gave two sharp honks on the horn and brought the car to a gentle stop outside a small cathedral door at the rear of the chateau.

As soon as Maggie stepped from the car, the strangest feeling came over her. A feeling of being home. Like she knew the place inside out. She shuddered visibly. Was this place beautiful or was it a façade for evil? She felt confused and put it down to nerves. *Am I being tricked? What's going on with this place?*

As they walked toward the chateau her feelings were a mixture of pleasure and apprehension and caused the butterflies in her stomach to breed and birth all at the same time. This, coupled with the fact that she hadn't eaten for a few hours, had the natural sounds of her stomach working overtime—the chauffeur turned quickly. Maggie wanted to laugh out loud at the look of surprise on his face.

She flushed with embarrassment. "Pardon me—hunger pangs!"

"*Bruyant, pour une telle petite dame*!" he laughed, as he took their cases from the boot of the car and placed them on the gravel.

"*Oui, oui, très fort*!" David and the chauffeur shared a private joke.

"What did he say?"

David smirked. "He said, 'Goodness, Maggie, we'd better get some food inside you.'"

"You're lying!"

"He said you're very loud for a small woman!"

She sucked in a breath. "Huh! That's even worse!"

"You'll have to get used to the French. Very liberated. Not as stuffy as their neighbours across the pond!" He took her coat and placed it with his on top of the suitcases.

They stared at the thick wooden door as it groaned open, and caught the eyes of a short, plump, older woman. She stared back at them with a knowing look on her face. Her dark hair was scraped back into a neat bun apart from a few grey wisps that hung down at the nape and temples. "*Ahh monsieur, la madame! Vous arrivez enfin.*" Angelette couldn't help but notice how much in love the young couple were. He looked older…by at least ten years.

"*Bonjour, madame, je m'appelle…*" For some reason he dropped the "Father" from his introduction. "David Sullivan. *Mon ami*, Maggie O'Connell."

"*Bonjour, Monsieur.* Angelette Bertrand." She offered both cheeks and, as was the custom, David planted small kisses on each of them. She turned to Maggie and took her hand.

Maggie read her instantly. *She's lovely.* She could see the iridescent pink of Angelette's aura as it sparkled around her. "Pleased to make your acquaintance, madame," she said, smiling. "I'm sorry, but I don't speak any French."

Angelette was stunned! Her emotions did their best to break through the calm demeanour her face portrayed. She kept hold of Maggie's hand. *My God, it's her!* "It's you, Marguerite!" she murmured under her breath.

Maggie eyed her hand. Angelette's grip had tightened slightly. "Pardon, madame?" She turned her head sideways and raised a hand to her ear.

Angelette calmed herself. "Excuse me…it has been a long day. Not to worry, Maggie O'Connell, I speak very good English. Please, call me Angelette." She linked her arm in Maggie's. "Come." They walked through the kitchen into a sitting room that was situated off a long hallway at the front of the house. David followed behind.

"You must be hungry," Angelette said, ringing a small bell. Almost immediately a butler appeared, carrying a tray of freshly baked croissants, some jam and butter, and a pot of coffee. He set them down on the table in front of them.

"*Merci*, Maxime." Using a pair of silver tongs, Angelette placed the croissants on the small plates provided and poured the coffee. "Do you take anything with your coffee, Monsieur?"

David looked at his watch. "I'm feeling quite tired all of a sudden." He contemplated whether it would appear rude if he skipped coffee.

"Monsieur, if you would rather go straight to your room I won't be offended," Angelette said, as if hearing his thoughts.

He put his hand to his mouth and stifled a yawn. "Yes, I think I would prefer to get some sleep—I'll skip coffee, thank you, madame."

"Please, call me Angelette. 'Madame' is so…err, formal." She turned to Maggie. "And you, Maggie, do you take anything with your coffee?"

Maggie had never seen such opulence and found it hard to take in. The French Renaissance surrounding her was amongst the finest architecture in the world. The grand fireplace was hand-carved out of limestone in Baroque design; the high ceiling, hand painted, depicted scenes of kings at war on their stallions. Some of them lay bloody and dying. The angels at their sides waited for their tortured spirits to give up the fight and release themselves into the afterlife.

Maggie saw them all—the past residents of the chateau in all their finery. Beautiful ladies dancing with handsome partners, grand balls, music, pain, sorrow, and debauchery. And the cruelty inflicted by the past aristocracy, and even some of the servants in supervisory positions over the lesser staff. But there was a child who, unknown to herself, held a tiny spark of light in the chateau despite the torment she suffered at the hands of her superiors. To this day it was this child that had enabled the chateau to hold on to its heart.

Angelette repeated her question, bringing Maggie back into their company. "Oh…yes, milk and sugar, thank you. Sorry, Angelette. I'm just a little overwhelmed by the chateau. I've never seen anything like it." *It's her, Angelette. She's the child I see.*

"You see them, Maggie O'Connell…no?"

Maggie looked puzzled. "See who?"

"You are like me. You see dead people…and more!"

Maggie was shocked at Angelette's frankness. Communication with the dead was rarely spoken about so openly. She looked at Angelette with a blank expression on her face. Her mouth was open to speak but her mind struggled to find the words to fill it. Nevertheless, she couldn't stop herself from smiling at the unmistakable twinkle in Angelette's smoky brown eyes. It was clear she'd purposely wanted to shock her guests.

David immediately made an excuse to leave. Talking to the dead was the work of Satan. He'd warned Maggie about it time and time again. What's more, he didn't want his child harmed by such talk. Satan moved in many ways, ways that ignorant people couldn't even begin to imagine. Before they knew it, they were in his clutches having their souls sucked out. "Madame Bertrand, thank you for your kindness but it's been a long journey." He found it hard to hide the contempt in his voice. "Maggie, I'm sure you must be in need of rest."

"Oh…I…not really. I'd like to finish my croissant," she lied. It wasn't often she got to talk to people about this particular aspect of herself.

Angelette picked up the small bell and shook it gently. "Maxime, please show Monsieur Sullivan to his room." She looked at David. "Don't worry about Maggie, Monsieur. She is in good hands." Her tone was pleasant but firm.

"I don't think holding conversations with the dead is fitting for a woman in Maggie's condition, Madame Bertrand," he said arrogantly.

"Oh! And what condition is that Fa—Monsieur David?" she asked sarcastically. "Are we talking about pregnancy or the condition forced upon her by a bigoted society?"

David flushed, never taking his eyes off Angelette. An embarrassed silence on his part followed. He cleared his throat and bowed his head abruptly. "Madame." He turned to Maggie. "Maggie." He took his leave and followed Maxime out of the room. He clenched his fists into tight balls. It took everything he had not to drag Maggie with him, but the last thing he wanted to do was air his grievances publicly. They'd only just arrived, after all.

Angelette turned to Maggie. "I'm sorry, Maggie. I hope I didn't embarrass you."

Maggie smiled. "Don't worry about embarrassing me. I can hold my own if I have to."

Angelette took a bite of her croissant. "Yes, I can see that." There was a moment's pause before the two women broke into quiet laughter.

Maggie leant forward and picked up her coffee. "He means well." It was obvious to her that within minutes of their meeting Angelette had realised that David was the father of her baby.

"I'm sure he does, like the rest of the religions. They should stop forcing their opinions on everyone else, especially when their own hearts don't believe."

Maggie eyed the golden crucifix around Angelette's neck and raised an eyebrow. "And you a Catholic!"

She shrugged. "It's a role I play." Her eyes were warm and twinkled with everything life had to offer. "There are many." Their backgrounds couldn't have been more different—in this lifetime, at least. But there was something between them that transcended time. It was as if they'd known each other always. "Maggie, what did you see? You see the spirit of the chateau, no?"

Maggie hesitated.

"Please—do not worry about upsetting me. I am interested to know and compare our information."

Maggie closed her eyes and looked inside the space at the front of her forehead. Within a few minutes she was transported back in time. A past life at the chateau played out like a black and white movie. "I can see it all in my third eye…Caresse, you were known as Caresse. I can see you hundreds of years…around the seventeenth century, I think. You were a servant girl here at the chateau." Maggie grimaced. Her tone changed from gentle to alarmed. "You lived in fear. The lord you worked for was a monster! Lord Adolphe! Yes, yes. If I didn't know better I'd say he was barely human! You went through every form of abuse imaginable from a tender age…yet you remained kind and gentle, and held no resentment or bitterness in your heart towards those who persecuted you. There was something so special about you. You were here to teach the higher-ups and the rest of the servants, and make them see that there was another way, a kinder way…you and someone else…a lady."

Angelette was excited. "Yes! I have seen this life, too!"

"You were raped repeatedly by the lord and eventually fell pregnant to him. But the lord's wife was kind…yes…it was her…the other lady. She took care of you and the child. She believed it was her husband who had fathered the baby, a boy, but didn't dare say a word in fear for her life…and yours. She tried to convince him to have mercy on you and the child, but he wouldn't. He said he wouldn't have such behaviour going on amongst his servants. He blamed one of the stable hands for your condition." Maggie hesitated, a puzzled look on her face. "There's something about his wife…the lady of the chateau?"

"Keep digging! Try to hold the connection, Maggie," Angelette encouraged.

"The lady of the chateau secretly arranged for you and the baby to stay with some friends of hers in Toulouse. Once the baby was born you would go into service, as would the child when he was old enough. She lied, explaining that your husband had died and you needed food and shelter. She gave you some of her jewellery and told you to hide it in a safe place." While in trance, Maggie spoke perfect French as she relayed the words the lady had spoken all those years ago. "Eventually you will be able to sell it and set up a home of your own for yourself and the child.'

"You broke down and sobbed uncontrollably. You'd never been shown such love, such kindness, by anyone before. But the lady saw something in you that you couldn't see in yourself. She said it was you who held light in your heart and that you couldn't even begin to know how much you had taught her."

Angelette leaned into Maggie. "Yes…you see clearly, but there is still a piece missing, Maggie?"

"I…I'm…it's the lady, I know her—"

"Yes, yes," Angelette urged.

Maggie caught her breath. "My God! She's me! I mean, I'm her—oh, you know what I mean!" She opened her eyes and grasped Angelette's hands. "I was once the lady of the chateau and you were my servant! But why have we come back? Why must our lives be drawn to the chateau again?"

Angelette chose her words with care. She realised that Maggie hadn't yet been informed about the soul group they belonged to. She was still very young. When the time was right, Maggie's spirit guide would be the one to tell her. "There are many reasons. I don't know all of them. But I do know that you and I have some unfinished karma to deal with."

Maggie knew that she had to find out why she'd been brought to the chateau again and that the answer lay within the past life she'd witnessed just a few minutes earlier. She felt overwhelmed but understood it was important, not only for herself but also for Angelette. "What if I can't find out what it is?" she asked, panic-struck. "I'll let us both down."

Angelette smiled and glanced sideways. She could see Maggie's spirit guide, an Indian brave, as he mingled within her aura. He was a handsome man, strong, well built. His dark hair was tied into a long braid that hung down the centre of his back and his tanned skin was flushed with red undertones. He wore traditional dress—long pants and jacket made from buffalo hide and moccasins trimmed with coloured cotton and beads. He was beautiful yet every bit the warrior. Angelette was well aware of the protective energy he gave off. "Ahh, all the good mediums have an Indian guide. The chief with you, he is very funny, no? I feel his strong sense of humour!"

"You see him!"

"Of course! I am like you, remember? But I am seeing him only as an image in your aura right now."

The thought of White Eagle put a huge smile on Maggie's face. Within an instant, he was by her side. "Oh, he's funny alright!"

"Now I see him clearly. He will help you." Angelette noted that White Eagle was even more handsome in the flesh...so to speak! "Ooh, la, la!" she joked. "A good-looking guide!"

White Eagle nodded and took Angelette's hand. "A pleasure, as always, to meet a member from the same soul group—again! When was the last time?" He lifted his chin in the air. "Hmm, must be a few hundred years ago now!" He looked into Angelette's eyes and winked. "I must compliment you on your youthful appearance, madame!"

Angelette laughed out loud and looked down at his hand which was still clasped around hers. He felt like a physical being. "Ahh...a master manipulator! You have the power to manipulate realms, so when in the physical you appear to be physical!"

He shrugged nonchalantly. "Just a little trick I picked up along the way," he joked.

Angelette stared at him intensely. "A very advanced trick, to say the least!" she whispered. Her expression told him she was under no delusions as to how far up the scale he was.

Turning to Maggie, Angelette's eyes glanced at the small round bump in her stomach—*GALAXIAS?* Her heart thumped against her chest as the word invaded her mind. *NO!* She swallowed hard. *Stay composed!* she scolded herself, burying the word again. She didn't know where it came from or why it was tormenting her thoughts and dreams. During her lifetime she'd fought off demons; she'd been to the inky depths of her own darkness to the extent that she thought she'd never get out of it, but the thought of facing him again... He terrified her more than any demon ever could. *"Why? Why so scared of the light? Your light!"* a voice way off somewhere in her mind asked. She dismissed it, relieved to hear Maggie's voice.

"Well, then! What's the reason I'm here?"

White Eagle shook his head, his expression nonchalant. "Come on, Maggie, you know better than that! I can't simply give you the answers. Work them out for yourself. I would be interfering with your growth if you weren't allowed to find your own answers and make your own choices. What good is an interfering guide?"

Maggie opened her eyes wide. "You should know!" she retorted. "You're always damn well interfering!"

White Eagle's hearty laughter made the chandelier above them turn slightly. Its crystal droplets tinkled gentle musical notes and reflected in the sunbeams that had broken through the clouds and moved in through the patio doors. A rainbow of colour splashed throughout the room.

"One day, Maggie, you will understand what is interfering and what is not! Now back to the question of why we are here."

"But I have no idea!" She leant forward and picked up her coffee. "As far as I know, I'm here to give birth and that's that!"

"Not true, Maggie! You have an idea but you deny it."

She raised her eyebrows. "There you go again. Telling me what

I know and what I don't know!" She took a large gulp of coffee but somehow missed her mouth. "Damn! Now I've missed my mouth."

"God knows how!" White Eagle joked under his breath.

"Corny! Couldn't you come up with something a bit more original?"

Angelette was amused by the banter between them. She raised one eyebrow as she passed Maggie a serviette but didn't utter a word. Irritated, Maggie nodded her thanks, wiped her chin, and rubbed the top of her bodice.

White Eagle walked over to the windows. "I've got all the original I can handle putting up with you!" He pushed the curtain slightly and gazed out. "When you first arrived at the chateau, what did you feel?"

"What did I feel? I don't understand…what do you mean?"

He turned and faced her. "Think, Maggie! Try to remember your feelings as you became wrapped up in the essence of the chateau."

She closed her eyes and lived the experience again—she rolled the car window down, felt the rain on her face and the freshness of the air. She remembered being aware of the spirit of the house watching her and the unmistakable feeling of being home. "I felt the house…its beauty—"

"And?" The look on his face said, You know what you felt!

"I remember feeling that the house was very beautiful despite… there was something evil…something that terrified me but I denied it, put it down to my frayed nerves because of all the upheaval." She trailed off, suddenly feeling weak, drained of everything, even life! She felt dizzy, nauseous, her mind in a fog. Anxiety tainted her voice. "White Eagle! I feel sick!" She couldn't understand what was happening. She tried to stand but her body felt weighted like she'd lost control of it. White Eagle and Angelette faded into the background, their voices—everything—now in slow motion.

"WHITE EAGLE!" she screamed in absolute terror, but her voice seemed slow and heavy and, just like her body, she couldn't control it. It didn't seem to belong to her anymore. She felt like an overwhelming force had jumped inside her, kicked out her spirit, and captured her soul as a trophy. She fought as if her life depended on it—it did. But she couldn't win. The evil that held her didn't fight at all. It merely toyed. She was no match for it. She felt herself drifting farther and farther away, backwards somehow, until only a foggy piece of her consciousness remained. It was there but paralysed, numb.

They'd all been caught off guard. It had taken mere seconds for the room's cheerful, light-hearted atmosphere to change into one of terror and darkness. The air, now icy cold, was infiltrated by a smell that could only be described as raw sewage, but ten times worse. The entity poked and jabbed in every corner, sniffing and hunting for life to feed off. But there was one life in particular it wanted.

Angelette jumped up and backed away from the couch. "NOOOO!" she screamed out, her face contorted with fear. "IT IS HIM! HE'S COME FOR HER! DON'T LET HIM TAKE HER AGAIN!"

White Eagle flashed Angelette a warning look. His voice was quiet but firm. "Angelette, don't let him have *you* again! We both know he's here for Maggie, but he won't stop there. If you make it easy for him, he'll take you as well!"

"I don't fear for myself…but Maggie—she doesn't know! She has not enough exp—" She faltered, trying to find the correct English.

"Experience! I know!" White Eagle's patience was being tested. He moved forward. "Maggie, I want you to listen," he commanded. "It's very important."

Angelette leapt in front of him and grabbed Maggie's arms. "MAGGIE, COME BACK, COME BACK!" She was horrified by how quickly demonic transformation was taking place. The eyes staring back at her were no longer a beautiful shade of emerald. They were a deadly shade of black.

"ANGELETTE! GET OUT OF THE WAY!" He grabbed both her arms.

Maggie whimpered, "Am I dying? Why is this happening to me? Help me…please, White Eagle—"

Almost demented with fear, Angelette wrested her arms free from White Eagle's grip and shook Maggie violently. "MAGGIE, YOU CAN'T GO! YOU BEAT ADOLPHE ONCE AND YOU CAN DO

IT AGAIN!" But it was useless. Maggie had already gone. Angelette was hysterical. "WHITE EAGLE, SHE ASKED FOR YOUR HELP. STOP THE EVIL BEFORE IT IS TOO LATE!"

White Eagle had no choice. Angelette's emotions were out of control. He had to stop her. If Maggie shot back into the physical world now the shock of it could kill her, meaning it would take an all-out battle with the dark forces to get her soul back, a battle which he couldn't fight alone. With a violent back swipe of his arm, he released an unseen force towards Angelette. She flew backwards through the air at record speed and landed safely in a chair on the opposite side of the room. His tone changed from firm to threatening. "Stay there until you calm down. We're in a dangerous situation and you're not helping. I know how hard you've worked to get this far but make no mistake, you're at risk of losing it all." He emphasised his words. "I will take you down if I have to."

Wild with fear, Maggie's head moved from side to side, her arms and legs flaying at thin air. Small, pitiful moans escaped her throat but every now and again she let out a loud, anguished cry that was barely human. Her wavy red hair was drenched in sweat. Its thick, healthy texture now gone, it hung around her face in thin, wispy strands.

White Eagle raced over, took her head in his hands and rolled it about as if giving her an examination. Her eyes had rolled back inside her head, and bruises and scratch marks were appearing all over her body, one after the other. He needed to act now or he'd lose her.

The deep, thunderous chimes from the grandfather clock rang out through the chateau. He turned and watched the solid gold pendulum swing from side to side, a knowing expression on his face. It was time to leave. The vibration from the chimes flooded through him, shaking him out of one existence into another—one much more deadly.

There are a few places where linear time plays a part—Earth, and underworld, when a soul is about to be snatched from the light to join the dark ones.

3.

In an instant, White Eagle left Earth's atmosphere and entered the unbearable realm of the underworld. As soon as he arrived, the evil curled around him in an effort to march in and devour his soul. He felt as if he'd ended up in some kind of present-day hell stuck between the past and the future—although this was subject to whatever the Dark Lord determined it to be. *He could make it look like paradise if he so desired. Don't forget that!* he reminded himself.

Made up of infinite fragments—some physical, some not—White Eagle now battled his human aspect. Master Manipulator was one thing but he was in unfamiliar territory, and fear was a powerful dictator. The weaker elements were soon consumed. Fears he thought he'd put to rest aeons before now crawled through him like focused ants. In the spirit world, also known as the astral realms, where he was stationed most of the time, fear existed only as a reminder to those who chose to experience it now and again, more often than not for reasons pertaining to growth. But in the underworld, fear meant life. It was the survival instinct. He didn't enjoy the sensation one bit.

His breathing was loud and heavy as he struggled to take in air, and sweat oozed through his pores making his skin look wet and shiny. There was something inside the silence that was so alarming. He looked back, sideways, up, down. All was still, yet seemed to be moving. The only sounds to be heard were the crunching of his feet in the undergrowth and a few flies buzzing around. He picked up his pace and called out to Maggie. His voice echoed through the dark mountains that loomed over him. He noticed how dead they were. Buried in dead trees—a front for imprisoned souls. Their stiff fingers, like lifeless

24

branches, reached out for salvation against a red and black sky, and made an eerie reflection in a filthy lake not too far off in the distance. It was covered in oil and strewn with rubbish of every description. Litter, plastic, old tyres, and cans littered its banks. Rats ran amok, making their homes in rusty old cars and broken-down buildings. On the opposite side, the enormous towers of an old mansion lurked up into the callous sky to cast a threatening shadow over any visitors.

The air was damp and heavy with a permanent stench of raw sewage that burnt his nose as he tried to close it off—demons! He was surrounded by them. Their beady red eyes followed him through the darkness. When they tried to come within five feet of him, the light he carried struck out like a gleaming sword and scorched their repugnant flesh. But he didn't get complacent. He knew these were just the foot soldiers. They were no match for him but their leaders were every bit as powerful as he was. Some were stronger.

"Maggie, Maggie," he called out through the disturbed silence. *Calm down, calm down.* He knew that if he couldn't keep his fear in check, the battle to get Maggie back would be like nothing he'd ever encountered. He was aware that the evil that held her knew more about her power than she did. *Why didn't you discuss it with her sooner?* They'd touched on it, but not to the extent necessary to deal with what they had here, and so far Maggie had preferred to keep her own knowledge buried, even denied. White Eagle was crushed. *She was in my care—what the hell is she doing down here?* "MAGGIE! MAGGIE!"

At last he saw her. He had to look twice to make sure it was her. Transformation was happening fast. In no time at all she'd changed from a beautiful young woman into a ravished and demented shadow of who she really was. Her creamy complexion was now yellow and wrinkled, and her eyes were black and empty. Her wavy red hair had turned grey and chunks of it had fallen out. She moaned quietly to herself and she scratched at her skin, causing it to flake and uncover large open wounds.

Drawn to the old mansion, she stumbled up the rocky path toward it in a hypnotic trance. But every so often she'd get hysterical and start to claw through the tumbleweed and nettles when they blocked her way. Possessed with an intelligence of their own, they'd engulf her, stab at her, take seeming pleasure in slicing through her flesh and paving the way for the demon to burst out of her.

White Eagle knew she was being sucked in by the power of the dark energy that ruled there. He ran over to her and shook her hard. "Maggie, Maggie!" But she couldn't hear him. "Maggie, let him go. It's the only way you can release yourself from the curse." But she just kept walking, confused and alone in her own bitterness. For a moment she turned and stared at him through manic eyes but she couldn't see him. His light was already protecting him , but it didn't yet repell her as it had the demons.

White Eagle was devastated. He'd failed her. He stroked her hair, slid his fingers across her cheek tenderly, but he spoke with a desperate edge in his voice. "It's up to you to break the curse, Maggie. Face your fears; they serve no purpose—they're a coffin for your soul."

They had dealt with this entity, the dark lord in the past and been able to quell it but had never been able to get rid of it. White Eagle acknowledged that it had gained strength and evolved phenomenally since their last encounter. It was one of the underworld's prominent leaders, not the ultimate ruler, but high in the ranks. It had followed them through aeons, waiting for the chance to claim their group. If it ever succeeded, Earth would be dragged down into the underworld until Galaxias—their home planet and supreme power throughout the solar systems—could build up enough strength to retrieve it. The misery and mayhem suffered by those unfortunate enough to go down with her would be indescribable. Earth also occupied a position in the universe that was essential to communication and to the well-being of the rest of the galaxies—not to mention the universe and the countless other universes that existed beyond this one, their planets all teaming with life. The situation was potentially catastrophic.

Damn it! What a bloody mess! White Eagle thought about letting his mentor, Roman, and NeilA—two of the leaders of Galaxias and both prominent members of G.U.N. (Galactic United Nations)—know of his position. He brushed if off. He would first try to get Maggie back without alerting them.

Unknown to him, G.U.N. were well aware of the situation and had already lined up a galactic presence above Earth and throughout the rest of the universal nations. They were more than concerned over White Eagle's failure to warn them as soon as he'd arrived in the underworld. In his panic he'd broken the golden rule: never go into the underworld alone! However, he was relatively new to the post of spirit guide—just a few hundred years or so in Earth terms—and this was his first major cock-up. For this reason they would make an allowance.

They'd ensured the safety of the baby Maggie carried for the time being, but it was time to remind White Eagle of this fact. They couldn't allow any thoughts of the baby to be transferred through the underworld. Ironic as it seemed, they had to make him think in order to stop him thinking. The thought they sent sliced through him like a guiletine .

The baby! White Eagle's eyes looked into Maggie's abdomen more effectively than any X-ray machine. The baby was fine. From that point on, he stopped thinking about him. It was too risky. The dark forces had plenty of ways to slip into a mind. All embryos were pure and could be influenced one way or the other. They also had the distinct advantage of being able to experience life both in spirit and in human form. Such an advantage gave them phenomenal power, and an embryo that was destined to spread the ways of Galaxias throughout Earth, if tainted in any way by the dark, was capable of causing mayhem yet to be seen. The dark had tried many times to steal a light-one while in embryo form, but so far their attempts had failed. If they got wind of the child while Maggie was going through transformation, they'd speed up the pregnancy and see to it that she gave birth within seconds.

The power of any light-worker at the hands of the dark was unthinkable, but this child was a power beyond power. With both Maggie and David—two prominent Galaxians—contributing to his genetic makeup, he had the potential to bring Earth and the rest of the galactic nations under his rule. But it was the connection between NeilA and the child that was the issue. *What would happen? The*

*Originator's power could match NeilA's but could it overthrow it—
stop thinking about it!* White Eagle scolded himself and turned his
attention back to Maggie.

He walked by her side, called her, shook her, but it was hopeless.
She struggled through the undergrowth, intent on making it to the
mansion where the Dark Lord resided, his hypnotic power drawing
her in. She was deteriorating rapidly and White Eagle knew that if he
didn't act immediately and place her in a seal of protection it could
take aeons to get her back, leaving her power, and the child's, at the
mercy of the underworld.

They came to a crevasse in the mountainside. Maggie stopped, not quite
sure which way to turn. Exhausted, she sat down on a large boulder and
looked up the mountain at the dilapidated mansion. There was still a way
to go. The path spiralled upward and was covered in thorny undergrowth.
All the while she rocked to and fro, whimpering pitifully.

"Maggie." White Eagle whispered gently, in the hope that she would
hear him, see him. But she remained oblivious. He drew his knife from
the leather holder on his belt. The ornate handle was encrusted with
chrysoberyl and black sapphire crystals for spiritual protection. Its blade
was made up of the finest silver to enhance and store the energies of the
stones. The silver would also draw out any negative energy and mirror
Maggie's soul. This would strengthen her awareness of her spiritual
body and, hopefully, her soul, before it was too late.

Reaching into the holder again, he took out a small piece of sage,
placed it onto the knife, and focused his attention directly on it. Within
moments it began to crackle and glow red in the darkness. He picked
it up by the stem and wafted it about in the stale air. The demons
screamed out. Their cries sounded like the twisted squawks from a
million crows as the sage purified the area around them. White Eagle
knew that he had to get Maggie into the seal of protection quickly,
before the demons' ruler arrived. White Eagle never faltered despite
the thousands of demons that stood about, eager to make a grab for his
soul. They chipped away at his energy in an effort to drain him of light
and fill him with fear—then they would have him! But his relentless

determination spurred him on. He would protect Maggie from their badness at all costs and the seal would buy him some time.

Using the sage, he traced a triangle around Maggie then drew a huge circle around the triangle. The area cleansed, he pointed his knife and reinforced the shapes around her to seal in the protection. The blue-silver after-image of the shapes flared off the blade and lit up the blackness. All the while White Eagle chanted from the back of his throat in his native tribal tongue: "Hi, hi, hi emotions are hi, low, low, low protection is low, moon, moon, moon, may your energy cocoon, the soul of Maggie who walks in fear. Sun, sun, sun, light up her heart, bring her home and out of the dark."

Maggie was instantly calmed. She remained seated on the boulder inside the seal with an empty look on her face. The process of demonic transfiguration had been arrested for the time being.

Exhausted, White Eagle sat down outside the seal, breathing heavily. Sweat poured from him along with his energy, which was in need of replenishment. He looked at Maggie. "How the hell did we end up in this, this, cess pit!?" he whispered, his voice full of torment. She appeared more peaceful but was in no way free from the clutches of evil that held her in its grip. He shook his head in an effort to unravel some of his mangled thoughts, unaware that he was being possessed by them. Dejected, he started to lose himself in them just like Maggie. He moaned pitifully. A tortured look burnt into his face. *I can't believe I've put the one thing I'm supposed to protect in the worst possible danger…*

Determination. The demons weren't short of it. Most of them had gone quiet but one of their leaders, Llution, preyed upon White Eagle's feelings of guilt and self-pity—it was easy to fall back into old ways when caught off guard. Llution knew this. White Eagle was in his territory now. He pulled out all stops and slyly gnawed away at any power White Eagle had left, hissing thoughts into his head, one after the other. *"How did you lose her? Aren't you supposed to protect her? It's your fault she's where she is. If anything happens to her it'll be on your conscience forever! Foreveeeeer!"*

4.

White Eagle knew that Angelette was right. Maggie had little experience in handling power like this. He should have spoken to her sooner, made sure she was in with a fighting chance, but instead he'd dragged his heels, preferring to wait until she was older before teaching her how to deal with such evil. The same evil that now, unknown to him, was manipulating his own thoughts, making him believe that he wasn't good enough and that he was responsible for Maggie's downfall. An intelligent, powerful evil was weaving its way through him like it had Maggie.

It waited patiently on the sidelines. What a prize! A power like Maggie would strengthen its position in the universe considerably. But a power like White Eagle to feed off would make it and its brothers capable of causing mayhem in this universe and beyond. Then there's the rest of their group, one of the most potent collections of souls there is. How many other Galaxians will they send in to search these two out? *What an accumulation of strength! Oh, yes! Come to me, White Eagle. Our plan to rule creation draws near…sooner than expected. Galaxias and the Galactic United Nations are about to disintegrate back into the dust where they belong.*

White Eagle remained crouched on the floor by the seal. "Maggie, it's me. Why can't you hear me—"

"TOO LATE, WHITE EAGLE!" The deep, menacing snarl had an undertone that hissed like Medusa's snakes. "She's mine! Just like the millions of feeble-minded imbeciles you see around you. Soon she will sit by my side and take on the same appearance as the rest of the creatures you see here. Then again, I might preserve her beauty depending on how...," he toyed, "...how...subservient she is." His mighty laughter ploughed through the underworld.

White Eagle jumped to his feet. "Evolus! We meet again." Uneasy, he looked around. Evolus was nowhere to be seen. The thoughts started to charge and do battle in his head, sending frantic images of loss, death, destruction of Earth. He ploughed them with new ones: *No fear! No fear! No fear!* He was already finding it hard to breathe. Evolus was too powerful, far more evolved and experienced—*No fear, White Eagle!*

The Dark one, smirked in the shadows, and emitted a sound between a gurgle and a purr from deep in his throat. "Yes, but never under such circumstances. It seems you kept your little sidekick in the dark. Thank you. You have made my job...So. Much. Easier."

White Eagle appeared calm but he was still fighting to keep his fear in check. "Evolus, do you realise just who you are playing with— who the power is here? You can never win. Why don't you give up and join the light? Release yourself from the torment you live in."

Evolus sneered. His irritation seethed at White Eagle's admirable courage—nobody questions Evolus! Incensed, his voice throbbed with disgust and hissed through his kingdom, causing a series of small shockwaves to play out in the distance. "Do YOU realise the power *you* are dealing with, White Eagle? Do you really think Galaxias can hold on to their pathetic leadership for much longer?"

Maggie cried out, her face twisted in horror. "Evolus...," she whimpered. "No! Please, no!"

White Eagle spun around. Relief registered all over his face. *At last!* The first step. She'd acknowledged Evolus. His words came out fast. "Maggie, face Evolus! Release him from your curse!"

Maggie stood up, threw herself against the seal but it pushed her back. She wasn't ready. She screamed out, "RELEASE EVOLUS? NEVER! NEVER!" Her whole body trembled in terror.

White Eagle jumped through the seal and dragged her to him.

"Don't you see? Until you release him from your curse you remain his prisoner. You give him a piece of your spirit! You add to his power!" He looked into her eyes. For a split second he saw her soul pass over her shrivelled face and reveal her inner beauty. "Maggie, I won't let him have you!" Several small tremors rocked the foundations below them as the love in his voice ripped through the underworld.

The demons screamed out. Evolus commanded, "SILEEEEEENCE!"

Desperate, Maggie's soul did break through as it fought to stay with the light. But when the daunting voice of Evolus pierced her yet again, she pushed it back into the fear she'd kept it buried in for aeons.

Evolus raged. He couldn't believe the audacity of White Eagle. His anger exploded, causing the small tremors to grow steadily toward a full volcanic eruption. "YOU THINK YOU CAN COME HERE AND CALL THE SHOTS? TALK OVER ME? MAGGIE WILL BE MINE! MY SEED WILL GROW INSIDE HER—MY SEED INFUSED WITH THE POWER OF THE LIGHT!" He spat the words out and he blew on the seal of protection.

It remained firm but was beginning to show cracks as White Eagle despaired at the news Evolus had just delivered. *His seed!* The fear lunged, attacking him from every angle. If he let it take over, the seal wouldn't be able to help him or Maggie.

This was all Evolus needed. He remained in the shadows clinging to a massive tree that jutted out from the mountainside about thirty feet above where White Eagle stood. His tone changed from aggressive to almost seductive. His demonic breath blew through White Eagle like a poisonous windstorm. "Fear is the power!" With ease, he stretched his reptilian tongue, using it to dig out a colossal hole in ground. "The more fear, the more power!" His words echoed through the mountains. "Your magic already shows signs of weakness. Do you really believe that your pathetic tricks can match mine?"

Black energy with an intelligence of its own erupted from the pit accompanied by a horrible screeching sound. It sucked White Eagle out of the seal and shook him violently, then threw him full force into the terrifying vacuum. Down, down, down he went, his heart beating to the sound of Evolus's eerie laughter. He thrashed, kicked, and screamed like a trapped animal. Frenzied, he fought for his soul. But it kept falling through empty space, hunted down by demons that wouldn't let up. Relentless, they hounded him, tormenting his mind in an effort to twist his essence into theirs. *No!* He couldn't give in. He had to save Maggie and the baby. Oh, the dark ones were clever. They were slyly moving in on his life-force. "MAGGIE!" he screamed out in the darkness. His voice rebounded back and forth off the sides of the pit, loud then low, low, then loud. "MAGGIE! STAY WITH ME! DON'T LET HIM HAVE YOU…"

His courage filled him with strength, bringing him to a sudden stop! Suspended in the blackness, he carried on screaming and kicking until he realised he'd stopped falling. He turned around in midair searching for something to cling to and spotted a long, thin root jutting out of the dry, cracked earth that made up the walls of the pit. He made a grab for it and latched on with one hand but was unable to steady himself. Swaying from side to side, he slammed dangerously into the sides of the pit before he reached out with his feet and dug his heels hard into the earth. At last he came to an unsteady halt.

He looked around. A soft, blue-silver light crept in through the top of the pit high above where he clung to the root. It mingled with the blackness and exposed a mass of tangled roots all around him. They were all dead. All except for the one small root that he clung to—*hope*. It was still there. It had carried him this far even though he wasn't consciously aware of it. His breathing jagged, he took a few moments to compose himself. Instantaneous thoughts hit him again as he realised that he'd seriously underestimated Evolus. "STOP!" he shouted in the blackness. He had to keep the demon's thoughts away from his mind.

He looked up toward the top of the pit and realised that the blue-silver light was the afterglow from the seal of protection combined with Maggie's energy. She was getting stronger. She must have heard him. Somehow he'd got through. "MAGGIE! MAGGIE—"

She had heard him! A small voice in the chaos calling out to her. "Maggie! Maggie!" It wouldn't give up. It was so full of love. Love for her, even Evolus?—*EVOLUS!* "NOOOOOO!" She screamed, throwing herself against the side of the seal again. She still wasn't ready. But that small voice wouldn't give up. It nagged and nagged. "Release Evolus! Release his soul from your hatred—"

"RELEASE EVOLUS? NEVER! NEVER! ANYTHING BUT THAT!"

But the voice in her head got louder as it became more intense, more urgent. "Maggie, you can't deny who you are forever. Let the memories surface. Live the experience again until you can face it with love. Don't you see? Burying Evolus keeps him more alive than ever in your heart. He owns a piece of your spirit!"

It was a long way up. White Eagle tried desperately to levitate to the top but Evolus was in control. He'd put a cap on White Eagle's life force, draining him. It would take him a while to recover. It was like being hung over after a night on hard liquor. He wrapped the roots around his wrists and slowly made his way toward the top of the pit.

Maggie's mind was in torment, bogged down with demons coming in, going out. In an effort to stop them, she lifted her palms to her temples and pressed hard on both sides of her head. *Dear God, will they ever stop?* And then she remembered something. A thought that struck out at random and stood out amongst the others—*White Eagle.* She could see him in her third eye. *White Eagle...Angelette...* It all started to flood back. *The chateau, the baby—*

"NOT THE BABY!" White Eagle, Roman, and NeilA caught the thought frequency as it left her mind and stopped it from drifting through the underworld. Maggie clutched her stomach. Instinct told her that thoughts of the baby must stay locked in her mind. But it was this thought alone that got through to her senses. The mother of all instincts fighting inside her—Maggie was ready to face and do battle with anything that got in her way. Her love would protect the life she carried at all costs. She closed her eyes and faced herself; she turned up at her soul's doorstep. There was no cover-up here, no pretence, no secrets. Not at this level. She took a deep breath and put her hands together, pointing her fingertips against her third eye. She felt her emotions take off from her solar plexus like a flock of startled birds—*Oh, God! The thoughts in her head! Evolus—Lord Adolphe! A lady in the chateau...his wife—me! Oh my God!*

Too painful for her to even think about, she tried to block the thoughts, send them back, but the mother instinct—it wouldn't let up. She felt the fear, intense, furious, rage against her. She did her best to block it. But the voice in her heart said, "NO! DON'T BLOCK THE FEAR! You must face it! FACE IT!" She felt her power break free—*Holy mother! I hold that power?* Up until now she'd had no idea of who she was, preferring to keep her true self buried. But the moment hit her full force. She took a huge breath of pure, fresh air before she left the seal. "God," she whispered in the silence. "Whatever it is I must face, I will face." Slowly she opened her eyes. "I'm ready..."

Calm washed over her. The tide of fear inside her went out on a tide of courage coming in. She felt heat—some kind of presence—creep up from her toes to the top of her head. Her inner beauty opened up like a lotus and nurtured every part of her. The seal of protection disintegrated and merged with the light that already shone fiercely around her.

"I'm ready..." A black and white hologram that resembled a silver matinee screen with no picture appeared and hovered to one side as if waiting. "I'm ready," she whispered for the third time. The hologram slowly opened up from the centre and changed into a kaleidoscope of colour and life. Maggie saw one of her past lives being played out like a 3D movie and stepped into it. It was as if she had never left.

5.

In Maggie's past life she was Marguerite, lady of Chateau St. Esteve, and Evolus was the main influence that governed her husband, the evil Lord Adolphe.

Desperate for a son, Adolphe demanded sex from his wife as often as possible. And so when the servant girl fell pregnant to him and Marguerite did not, Adolphe was enraged. He saw to it that some of Europe's most prominent doctors examine Marguerite, but despite their best efforts the couple remained childless. It just didn't happen, and for good reason. A child from a union such as theirs would hold a myriad of powers, and the dark forces had already foreseen such a child's future. Dictators had come and gone but this child could rule the universe and its influence could penetrate countless others. Galaxias, the army of light, could never allow that to happen.

What Evolus didn't realise was that the young, abused Caresse was also a light-worker. Unable to get past her role of servant girl, she was to be used to satisfy his sexual needs as well as Adolphe's, and nothing more—the physical need was stronger than ever in the demons. They would often jump in and possess a human for nothing more than sex before vacating the body of their unsuspecting victims. Such was the level of his thinking, or lack of it, that when Caresse got pregnant, Evolus didn't believe that either she or the child she carried was worth a damn. He focused everything he had on Marguerite. She was the one with the power, the so called light-worker. That's why she had chosen to be born into French royalty and was lady of the chateau, not just a mere servant. Marguerite would be the one to bear his seed. *The servant girl and her spawn must die.* Oh, his hold over Adolphe was strong enough, but one never knew: a child might stir something inside him, weaken him, and Evolus couldn't risk Adolphe awakening at soul level.

Unknown to Evolus, Galaxias worked diligently behind the scenes. They had plans of their own for the child Caresse carried. His life purpose was already mapped out. He would become a great leader who would bring about significant world changes to aid the mass consciousness on Earth, and eventually ascend into the higher dimensions. It seemed that the battle for Earth between the dark forces and the army of light was a never-ending one.

At soul level, both the child and Caresse had consented to the events that would map out their futures long before they'd incarnated on Earth. At human level, however, this was a secluded memory.

Galaxias had hoped that the lack of interest shown by Evolus as to the child's welfare would make their job of protecting him a lot easier. But they were wrong. The situation was getting more fragile every day and the longer it went on, the more chance there was of Evolus finding out just how powerful the child was. Their plan to distract Evolus had worked well so far, but the outcome of the last remaining days was yet to be seen.

☙

Shadowed by Evolus, Lord Adolphe had his suspicions about the relationship between his wife and the servant girl, who'd simply left the chateau with a stable hand about whom nobody seemed to hold any knowledge. Adolphe started to ask after her well-being. When the news reached him that Caresse was living with friends of Marguerite, he wasted no time in contacting them. He was informed that Caresse had already left their service and was doing very nicely by herself.

His anger at his wife's betrayal burned his insides like a small volcano until it became almost impossible for him to repress. But still he bided his time, preferring to make his wife suffer by playing mind games. He let her know that he wasn't pleased about something but let her ponder what it was for at least two months. He asked questions with a casual disinterest about the whereabouts of the servant girl and her child, and got a sick satisfaction from the terror in Lady Marguerite's eyes.

One night after dinner, he ordered her upstairs to the bedroom. Dutifully she followed him, trying hard to quell the revulsion that crawled through her.

The bedroom was cold and still. Not a sound could be heard yet there was something terrifying in the silence. Marguerite felt her whole body start to tremble. She swallowed hard. The only light came from a full moon right outside the window. She stared at it, blocking out the world around her. *How beautiful you are*, she said telepathically.

The room held many riches and was filled with original art from all over the world. Expensive tapestries adorned the wood-panelled walls, and priceless ornaments stood atop antique furniture, many of them gifts from royalty and influential families. Rembrandt's *Philosopher in Meditation* hung over the hand-carved marble fireplace—but there was no fire in the grate, only the dusty grey smudge of old ashes.

In the centre of the room stood a huge four-poster bed dominated by heavy velvet, and surrounded by curtains made from elaborate red brocade that was hand-stitched with real gold thread. The frame and headboard were carved from the finest wood, and the bedposts were grand and sculpted. It was beautiful. But to Marguerite it symbolised terror and torture, depravity and dominance, and was by far the ugliest thing in the room.

Her favourite pleasure lay in a rust-coloured Persian rug woven with gold, positioned at the side of the bed. Its pattern was an assortment of coloured geometrical shapes. Every morning when she rested her feet in its soft, warm pile, she would look around at the cold stone slates of the bedroom floor and remind herself that there was spirit and warmth in even the most remote places. She'd sit and gaze into the rug for hours, finding peace as she travelled inwards with its patterns.

Despite the wealth the room exhibited, it still reflected the coldness of the heart that dominated it. Lady Marguerite had used cunning tactics to obtain the few items in there she enjoyed.

Her husband crept up behind her and started to unbutton her dress. She cringed inwardly at his touch. "I'd like to block out the moonlight," she lied, knowing that if he thought she wanted the curtains drawn he would make sure they remained open.

His voice was sharp and deep. Marguerite often wondered why it sounded grotesque, as if it belonged to some monster living inside him. "No! Leave them! The moon lights up the room. I like to look at what I'm doing." He moved in front of her. His silhouette was outlined on the wall by the window and loomed above hers. He dragged her to him, tearing at her dress. He loved to see the fear in her eyes; it made the experience much more exquisite. His voice was edged with a touch of anger. "You don't enjoy me, madame!" The blue light of the moon made his face look even more sinister.

She smiled. Her face masked any sign of revulsion. "Of course I want nothing more than to please you, my lord."

"Then please me you will." He unbuttoned his trousers. His erect penis sprung out, desperate for relief. "Kneel." He grasped both sides of her head and pushed her down roughly.

She averted her eyes and kept looking at the moon. At least her mind was free. He couldn't touch that, couldn't change it. Couldn't make her do anything there that she didn't want to do. There she said what her voice was unable to say, and she couldn't find anything good to say about him—but she should. Focusing on his badness only brought more of it to her. But how could she focus on his good if he didn't have any?

She let her mind roam, then joined it in a world far more beautiful than the one she endured here. But unable to hold the vision, she flashed back into the present moment. Her eyes turned away from the moon and she saw their shadows on the wall performing the vile act she was being subjected to. Not able to stomach the picture, she quickly averted her eyes back to the moon. *Help me, please. Get me out of this hell that I endure—*

He grabbed a handful of her hair and dragged her up. She didn't fight as he pulled her along like a rag doll before pushing her onto the bed. He rammed his mouth down on hers, opened her lips with his, sucking, attacking with his tongue. Impatient, he ripped at her bodice like a ravenous predator until her breasts spilled out into his hands. He stopped for a moment, admired them, brushed his thumbs across her nipples, then brought his face down on hers and breathed all over her. The smell of alcohol and stale smoke made her gag but she stifled it with a cough. He fumbled beneath her skirts. Repulsed, she spread her legs wide and begged him to take her. If he thought that she didn't want him he'd subject her to unspeakable depravity, and the sooner this was over the better. He plunged deep into her. With every thrust she winced in pain but wrapped her arms around his neck and moaned in fake ecstasy. She never took her eyes off the moon...*Help me...Please help me...*until he withdrew.

He rolled off her. "Pour me a drink," he grunted, pulling up his trousers. She immediately got up, walked over to a small dresser underneath the window, and poured him brandy from a crystal decanter. She toyed with it for a moment, admiring the colours that reflected off it in the moonlight.

"Madame, my drink!" She jumped visibly at the order. He stormed over to her, yanked the small brandy glass from her hand, downed its contents, and threw it at the fireplace. It shattered into a thousand tiny pieces.

Her breath was loud and jagged. "Sir...plea..." She inhaled deeply but couldn't seem to fill her lungs with air. "I...would you like another drink?" She picked up the decanter.

He studied his fingernails. "Yes, I would." He was calm again. Too calm.

She turned over another small brandy glass. Just as she was about to pour, he lunged forward, snatched the decanter from her hands, and knocked back its contents in a few hard swigs. She watched his Adam's apple jerk in time to his gulps. As the liquid passed down his throat, she wondered what it would be like to plunge a knife into it. Would the light golden liquid spurt out all over the room mixed with his blood? Terrified by her thoughts, her heart beat her back into some sense of normality. She flinched. How could she think such thoughts? *Am I as bad as he is?*

He slammed the decanter down hard on the dresser. The brandy dripped from his mouth. "Madame, is there something you'd like to discuss with me?"

The look on his face turned her to ice. She couldn't move. She opened her mouth and caught her breath. *He knows!* All these weeks he'd been playing games with her. Letting her think that something was wrong one minute and everything was fine the next. But she'd always known deep down that he'd found out about Caresse and the baby. "I…discuss…?" Her voice trailed off. She trembled in front of him but didn't dare look away.

"Don't lie to me, madame. I think you've become accustomed to doing that, don't you?" His lips curled and twitched. He gently stroked the side of her face with the back of his hand. "Have I not given you everything?" He looked around the room and then back at her. He searched her eyes, penetrating behind them in the hunt for her soul.

The rage in his eyes had the ability to sap the life out of her. She felt sick with fear. His voice became distant. She couldn't even remember his question. "I don't feel well," she said weakly, in the hope that he'd leave her alone.

His voice sounded calm, kind even. "Marguerite, why do you make me punish you? All I ask for is some loyalty, obedience." He flipped the back of his hand hard across her face, sending her reeling against a mahogany bureau. The books and rarities, including a copper candlestick from the upper tier, crashed to the floor beside her.

She looked up at him, her eyes wide with fear, blood running from the corner of her mouth. "Sir…I'm so sorry th…that… I deceived you. Please forgive me. It will never happen…agai—"

He relished the moment. The pleasure in his voice ran out of control. "Oh, I know it won't happen again, my love, because your little friend is dead! And so is the bastard she birthed! It was they who paid the price for your betrayal!"

His words drew every ounce of fear out of her, and in that instant all she wanted to do was kill him! "NOOOOO!" Her strangled cry was barely human and could be heard throughout the chateau. She jumped to her feet. "Not even you could be so cruel!" She pounced on him and dragged her nails down the side of his face. He grabbed her wrists and laughed out loud as she kicked and flayed against him.

"She screamed for mercy as I throttled the life out of her, madame." He dragged Marguerite against him, stuck his face in her cheek. "But first I took her hard, again and again, before her breath ran out." He took a gold locket from his pocket. "Recognise this?" He shoved it into her hand and pressed it into the centre of her palm so hard that a perfect replica of its pattern was left there.

Marguerite felt her soul deflate. It was one of the items of jewellery she'd given to Caresse in the hope that she might find some peace. She held it to her chest and closed her eyes. "Caresse, my dear, may you be at peace…and your child."

She turned to Adolphe. The look in her eyes made him cringe before her. There was something different about her. It was as if she'd been inflated with a strength, a superior force. The words came out of her in a slow dark hiss. "Adolphe, I curse you." She threw her head back. "With all my heart and soul, I curse you, Adolphe."

Her words felt like a physical force in his gut. He was incensed by her disrespect but it was nothing compared to the fear that moved him. He squashed his hand into her face and pushed her back against a dark olivewood crucifix that hung on the wall behind her. It crashed to the floor.

In that moment, Marguerite decided to die rather than endure another minute with the monster she was married to. "Adolphe, I curse you with misery for the rest of your life and beyond!" she screamed at him. "May you never leave the hell that you have created for yourself!"

An unnatural gust of wind howled outside the French doors. They rattled violently, ready to burst open at any moment. Adolphe turned and looked at them with a worried expression on his face. He could have sworn he saw the moon drop from the sky as if on a piece of elastic and stop dead outside the doors. But when he looked again it was back—high in the black sky, rolling backwards through the clouds. Something wasn't right…a strange atmosphere crept beneath the surface.

Marguerite, on the other hand, knew exactly what was happening. Her spirit guide, Celenadus, had arrived. She stood waiting for her in the corner of the room, adjacent to the French doors. Marguerite knew it was time to return to spirit. She smiled. Her present lifetime flooded back to her—her choices, why she'd made them. The reason for her pain, her life path, the soul group that she, Caresse, and the child belonged to. She held her stomach gently.

Celenadus spoke softly. "Make your choice, Marguerite. Will you stay and bear his child?"

The tone of her guide's voice touched something deep inside and released the pain and the emotions that she'd long since buried. She felt them lift off her like a lover as he withdrew—and realised, indeed, this was exactly what it was. A part of Adolphe had already gone. Marguerite was overwhelmed with a sense of freedom, an unimaginable, indescribable freedom, a freedom that she could never achieve on Earth. She wept and wept, as she let go of everything she'd endured in her lifetime.

Celenadus was patient but they would have to leave soon. There was no time where they were going but Earth was ruled by time, which meant that the white hole waiting to transport them to the spirit world was bound to Earthly hours when on this side of the veil.

Marguerite smiled at her guide. "Celenadus, do you really have to ask such a question?"

"I do have to ask, my dear, even though I already know the answer. It is one of the fundamental laws of the universe. You could change your mind in the closing minutes—seconds, even—and decide for a host of reasons that you are not ready to return home or to your next incarnation."

Marguerite was adamant. "To subject myself to another moment with him is unbearable, but to subject my child to a father such as this is unthinkable."

Celenadus fanned her hand lightly toward the French doors. They flew open with a force that didn't match her action. A carpet of moonlight unrolled from the doors to Marguerite's feet, and a breeze, gentle at first, kissed life into the room.

Even though she was about to die, Marguerite had never felt so alive. The breeze was insistent and came off some kind of power. She felt it move through her, around her, tickling her skin. Yet it also seemed to be coming from inside her? It whispered quietly at first as it caressed her, steadily getting louder and stronger as it built its crescendo. Apprehensive yet excited, she waited.

Suddenly she felt a pulling inside—a feeling in her stomach that wanted to get out. It was as if she was coming out of herself through her solar plexus, and there was a sound like rushing air passing by her ears. As the feeling got stronger, she felt the fear that she'd clung onto throughout her life lift away like an overcoat being pulled over her head. The joy, the relief, the love…she'd never felt anything like it. The breeze went wild. It flew at her in short, sharp bursts. She felt dizzy, out of control. This was it…death! And she couldn't wait for the sweet release, the peace, the freedom it would bring.

She stumbled with the force but managed to remain on her feet, then she looked over at Celenadus lit up by the moonlight. Her long, golden hair flapped around her face. Marguerite smiled at her guide, lifted her hands into the air, and screamed out, "I'M READY!" Fear could no longer touch her. It was a remnant of a past memory, or so she thought.

Celenadus was concerned. "Marguerite, you must release Adolphe from your curse. Do not enter the spirit world with such karma left behind on Earth."

"I'll never release him! He deserves to suffer eternally!" she said defiantly.

"No, Marguerite!" Celenadus urged. "We must never give up

hope on anyone. Your curse chains you to the dark vibration. Release it before it's too late. Release it with love."

Marguerite knew that her guide was right but she could find no love in her heart for Adolphe, and such was the power of her curse that only love would have the strength to override it. "I'm sorry, Celenadus, but there is no love in my heart for Adolphe, only revulsion." She couldn't hide the disgust in her voice.

Celenadus managed to hide her concern and put on a calm front. She knew that Marguerite was unaware that the dark still had a hold on her. "Look at him as a soul living an experience—not as Adolphe living that experience. Somewhere inside him there is good, Marguerite. You know that. He is testing you!"

"The only thing I see when I look at him is a monster without a soul. A monster responsible for the death of a young mother and her child. A monster responsible for the misery of every life it touches."

Adolphe was terrified. He looked over towards Celenadus, but could see nothing. "HOW DARE YOU DISRESPECT ME, MADAME! LOOK AT ME WHEN YOU TALK!" His voice ripped through the room, antagonising the breeze. It changed tempo and overruled his voice. He raced over to the doors and tried to close them but the force threw him backwards. He landed on top of the olivewood crucifix and lay there for a few seconds, dazed. The look on his face was a mixture of fear and confusion.

Celenadus knew that she had little time left to convince Marguerite. Adolphe picked up the crucifix, lifting it menacingly. "We all make choices, Marguerite—there are reasons for them all. Don't concern yourself with the choices of others, only your own count." She spoke calmly but quickly. "The child whom Caresse birthed still lives. Adolphe was disturbed before he could harm him. The child will go on to provoke an uprising of the French people. He will fight against the atrocities committed by the Church and be recognised as one of the greatest leaders of all time. You and Caresse did your job well. Along with many other groups, you helped to protect Earth from the dark ones. Don't spoil it by leaving a curse with Adolphe. You will do untold damage to your growth. Don't give him that power."

But it was too late. Adolphe brought the crucifix down hard on Marguerite's head. She never felt the blow. Her spirit had left her body moments before he landed it. She stood with Celenadus, watching her own imminent death. Oh, the release from her misery on Earth was hard to describe. It was like waking up from a terrifying nightmare. Celenadus grabbed her hand in an effort to get her away from Adolphe as soon as possible but Marguerite looked back one last time. Shocked, her spirit form pulled away from her guide's hand and walked slowly towards Adolphe.

She looked into his crazed eyes and was astounded at the sheer hatred, the viciousness he held in his heart as he beat her physical body with the crucifix. Oh, he'd always been cruel but this went beyond that. This was an execution. A demonic execution.

"NEVER!" Her face took on the same distorted look as his. "I'LL NEVER RELEASE HIM!" She swore out loud to herself, lost her power to hate yet again. She jumped back into her physical body and looked up at him. She had to do it. Make him suffer like he'd made her suffer all these years. She looked into his eyes and spat the words at him. "Adolphe, not only do you murder me but you murder the child inside me—your child! I'd rather die than bring a baby into the world with a father such as you."

Adolphe stood poised above her. Just as he was about to land the fatal blow on her skull with the crucifix, he stopped.

"Go ahead—finish me, Adolphe," she said weakly. "The cross is made out of olivewood, the symbol for eternal life; but then I don't expect an illiterate such as you to know that. Do you think it is by coincidence that you hold it in your hands? Question coincidence, Adolphe; learn from it. Everything is choice. I have consented to my own murder—don't forget that! You can't harm me in death, nor the child I carry."

Overcome with fury, Adolphe threw the crucifix at the floor with a force that should have snapped it in two. But it remained intact. The golden figure of Jesus flared in the moonlight, and not a scratch could be seen on the beautiful woodwork.

"YOU CARRY MY CHILD BUT HAVEN'T SEEN FIT TO TELL ME? MY CHILD, MADAME! HOW DARE YOU! I WON'T LET YOU DIE UNTIL I HAVE HIM!"

Marguerite let out a small sigh. Her words were filled with contempt. "Even now you think you can control me? Control my death as you did my life? This child will be brought up in the spirit world surrounded by the love of many fathers and mothers. Oh, don't think for one minute he won't know you, Adolphe. You will be used as an example of how not to behave!" she hissed.

Celenadus looked on helplessly. A single tear rolled down her cheek. "Marguerite!" She held out her hand. "Come!"

Marguerite smiled at her guide, took her hand, and walked through the French doors toward the moon.

Adolphe watched his wife smile and lift her hand. He witnessed an expression of calm and peace take over her face. He thought she was crying out to him for mercy and forgiveness. He crouched down, put his arms underneath her back and knees, and carried her to the bed. He pressed his fingers underneath her chin. He could still feel a faint pulse.

Over the coming months he paid doctors from all over the world in an effort to save her life. He promised them riches beyond their imagination if they saved her and the child, but condemned them to a life of hell should they fail.

≍

In the remaining months of Lady Marguerite's life it looked as if she had suffered an unbearable death but this wasn't the case. Her spirit chose to come and go at will from her physical body, just like walking in and out of a room. It was her spirit that controlled everything and it certainly didn't choose to experience any more suffering. That had ended when Celenadus entered the bedroom and death became Marguerite's ultimate choice.

In the spirit world, Marguerite underwent much counseling with Celenadus and others who specialised in past life trauma and karma break-up. All she needed was a tiny spark of love to release Adolphe from her curse, and release herself from the hate in her heart. She tried hard. She travelled between the two worlds in search of some compassion, something to ignite that tiny spark. In the spirit world it was easy enough, but as soon as she was back in her physical body Adolphe's energy would bury her in haunted emotions, making it easy for hatred to take over her heart again and again. Eventually she gave up and left behind a powerful karma that she would one day have to face and clear.

≍

Adolphe's agonized screams rang out through the chateau as he stood at his wife's side and watched the last of her breath leave her body. The child he'd so desperately wanted had gone.

He went on a crusade of destruction and violence. His terrified servants fled, never to return. From that day on he never left the chateau, preferring to drink himself into a state of non-existence. He died alone, with bitterness and misery as his only companions apart from Evolus, who would snatch his soul as soon as it departed Earth.

Evolus was furious. He couldn't believe that he'd had two Galaxians in his clutches and the light had managed to steer him away from influencing any of the embryos they carried. But at least he had some retribution. He'd gained a substantial amount of strength from the so-called Lady Marguerite, and her curse.

6.

*I*t took a few moments for Maggie to comprehend what she'd just been through. She clicked her fingers. Her voice was weak with shock. "Enough!" The hologram snapped shut and disappeared.

The fears that consumed Marguerite—or Maggie in her past life,— were so strong that as soon as she and David had arrived at the chateau the buried memories from her previous lifetime as Marguerite had resurfaced and enabled those old fears to punch a hole into her present lifetime yet again. The energy that overpowered her in Angelette's sitting room had played on her weaknesses like a puppet master controlling the strings of his marionette. Only it wasn't strings it was controlling. It was the raw emotions that were still there. Emotions Maggie had suppressed for hundreds of years.

Now, finding herself in the depths of her own soul, Maggie was faced with two choices: Release Adolphe from her curse, which meant she would take back a piece of her power from the dark—Evolus. Or carry the curse and remain in the dark with him. All she had to do was convince her soul that she had genuine, unconditional love for Adolphe, and for Evolus! To get out of the dark, she had to find love for her enemies?

Alone with her thoughts, she tried hard to fathom her feelings towards Adolphe. They were a mixture of rage, sadness, bitterness, and pity, and though she tried hard to deny it, a tinge of hate still stabbed an icy tentacle through her heart. She knew that she was only hurting herself by carrying such hatred within her, lifetime after lifetime, but she still could not bring herself to feel love for Adolphe. She could pretend to love him, say it in her mind even, but it wasn't enough. At soul level it was all about feelings. True feelings. What was in her heart couldn't be denied. Not here. "But how do I find love in my heart for someone I loathe?" she whispered to the darkness.

Was it really Adolphe's fault that Evolus had wormed his way into him? A quiet voice echoed through her mind. *Of course! Nobody had forced Adolphe to drop his morals and behave in the way he did. Greed, lust, power, control—they'd all been his main focus. He'd made it easy for Evolus. Yes! Adolphe had only himself to blame. He was responsible for his choices. He had no feelings for those around him and the suffering he'd caused them—*

True enough! But what about their choices, Maggie? Could Adolphe have been used as a scapegoat so his so-called victims could evolve to the next level? What did they gain from the experience? Perhaps they should be thanking him!? What about their sacred contracts, their free will? Why were those closest to him in the position they were in? Were they forced into it? If so, by whom? And what of Adolphe…is he not the biggest victim of all? Are there really any victims? There may be countless reasons as to why such souls set themselves up in certain positions…to benefit themselves, mankind, the universe perhaps? An experience affects us at many levels. It's our reaction to an experience that counts. A reaction to a situation is more important than the situation that caused it.

Maggie's mind was in turmoil. She shuddered. *For God's sake! Why can't I forgive him? It's not like I'm still living Marguerite's life!*

But she was. Marguerite's fear had lain dormant, but it hadn't disappeared. As soon as Maggie arrived at the chateau, the memories stirred. The fear resurfaced, and Marguerite fought her way into Maggie's life!

Maggie closed her eyes and wiped her fingertips across her lids. She was beginning to understand that she was part of a powerful soul group that had evolved over many lifetimes on Earth as well as other planets throughout the universe. Some of the members she already knew. David, Angelette, and of course, White Eagle, her connection between worlds; there were also many she had yet to meet. The purpose of the group was to guard Earth from the dark forces. David and Caresse interrupted her thoughts. *Well! I'd never have guessed it!*

In that lifetime, David was the child Caresse had given birth to in her role of servant girl. Starting in his late teens, he'd put his heart and soul into fighting against the atrocities committed by the Church, and was instrumental in bringing about significant changes. His influence led many of the French people to freedom, and their victory reverberated around the world.

Maggie was taken aback. *And him such a devout Catholic!* She'd often wondered why his love for her had superseded his love for the Church. *No wonder he's questioning his calling! Well, at least now he's seen the Church from both sides. The light works in mysterious ways, it does that! But who better to work for the Church than someone with knowledge of its pitfalls and its pluses?*

She smiled to herself at the thought of David's reaction if she were to tell him what she'd found out, then it suddenly hit her that Angelette had been his mother in that particular lifetime! The mother he had never known. *He'd be thinking I'd been at the Guinness if I was to come out with a tale like this!*

Her thoughts drifted to Celenadus, who turned out to be White Eagle.. He morphed into a female persona when communicating with Marguerite because she had opted for a female guide in that particular incarnation—

"MAGGIE!" White Eagle's voice interrupted her thoughts. "MAGGIE! MAGGIE!" He was frantic.

In a frenzy, she looked around. "White Eagle! Where are you? I'm trapped in the underworld!" Her eyes settled on the huge hole in the ground.

"I know where you are!" Exasperated, he dug his hands and feet into the tangled mass of roots with perfect precision as he made his way up the walls of the pit. "You're not trapped. You know what you have to do." His energy grew stronger the closer he got to the top.

Maggie was deflated. "I have no love in my heart for Adolphe.

How can I force love into my heart, White Eagle? It's impossible—"

"Love me or not, YOU WILL BEAR MY CHILD, MADAME!" The quiet then booming voice of Adolphe, through Evolus, hurled itself at her like a bowling ball and knocked her to the ground.

Desperate to reach her, White Eagle climbed as fast as he could toward the shaft of light at the top of the pit. He could feel fear like a physical entity race up behind him and he started to doubt once again whether he and Maggie would make it out of there—*Come on! Come on!* He tried to quell his fears, urge himself to go faster, but Evolus still had a hold. It was like one of those dreams where you have to run but can't. He couldn't get his legs to speed up. "Maggie, you know we have to fight. Evolus is an instant away from fulfilling an important mission for the underworld. If you give in to him now you'll help him to achieve it."

Maggie screamed out. "NOOOOOOO! Evolus, I won't help your evil destroy Earth. I'll never bear your child. Never!"

Evolus fumed. Boulders and debris fell from the sky, past Maggie, and into the pit. Maggie was still flat on the ground. Instinctively, she brought her hands up to her head and curled into a foetal position.

White Eagle stopped climbing to duck out of the way of a huge rock as it skimmed past him. It was so close that the hair on his head wafted in the after-breeze.

Dust was everywhere, swirling around on Evolus's breath that was like a strong wind on a stormy night. Maggie felt the particles burn her throat and lungs. Coughing and choking, she tried to catch her breath. With clenched fists she rubbed her eyes and stumbled to her feet. "EVOLUS, YOU COWARD! ARE YOU TOO AFRAID TO LOOK ME IN THE EYE?"

Evolus smirked. He was amused and impressed by her plucky manner. His voice was polite, toying. "Afraid! A coward! Maggie, please. I'm glad you can't hear my thoughts. Looking into your eyes is the last thing on my mind. I can't wait to take you around your new home and introduce you to your new bed, my queen." Evolus unfurled his wings and dropped down from the darkness above her.

She saw him for the first time. "OH!" The word hissed on her breath as the air left her body. Shocked, she stood stock-still, staring with her mouth open. By this time every ounce of breath seemed to have left her lungs even though her chest pumped hard and fast. He was the most beautiful man she'd ever seen. His skin was tanned and flawless, apart from the dark stubble on his chin. His hair was black and tousled, with a healthy gleam to it. His stunning face was captivating, intense. She looked at his lips and wondered what it would be like to feel them pressed against hers, but it was his eyes that she couldn't escape from—the colours changed from amber to green, to blue, to blackish brown—

He held her gaze. "Aha! You like dark, soulful eyes the best—then that is the colour they'll stay." He cocked his head, "For now." His voice was like peaceful, classical music. It filled her body, her mind. She felt like air, like the beautiful voice was blowing right through her. She was instantly calm. She just wanted to look at his face, listen to his voice—

He held out his hand. "Come!" he commanded. She walked, trance-like, into his arms.

He pulled her against his chest, brushed her lips with his. There was something menacing about him but she couldn't stop herself. She kissed him back, her mouth hungry for his. She hung helpless in his arms while he gently kissed her face and neck. His scent was intoxicating, addictive. She lolled her head to the side to savour his mouth on her skin. Slowly, gently, he brushed his hands over her chest. Small moans of pleasure left her lips. He opened her blouse, slipped his hands inside her bra, kneaded, brushed, and stroked, before exposing her full breasts. She couldn't stand it, the pulse, the charge, racing through her body. Wild with passion, she screamed out, "I want you!" Her heartbeat was frenzied; she could hear the blood rushing through her veins. Her breathing was heavy with desire as her trembling fingers started to unbutton his shirt.

He held her wrists. "Patience, my love." His cunning smile bared perfect white teeth. He ran his tongue along her breasts, fastened his lips on her nipples, teased and taunted.

She collapsed into him. She couldn't stand it any longer. Her whole body burned with need; she'd never wanted anyone so much. She gasped, her expression full of seduction, "I want you now," she demanded.

"MAGGIEEEEEEE!" White Eagle was near the top. He raced the last few feet in a frantic attempt to stop Evolus—the thought of him soiling Maggie! Wild with anguish, he jumped from the pit and eyed the situation. "HE'S NOT REAL, MAGGIE! HE'S TRICKING YOU!"

In the split second Evolus was caught off guard, he morphed back into his usual form. The roar ripped from his throat and tore through the underworld as he ran at White Eagle. "You will die for this!" Saliva dripped from his fangs. His words were a gurgling, vicious snarl. He lifted his hand ready to crash down and rip White Eagle's soul right out of him.

"EVOLUS!" She yelled his name to stop him from landing the blow.

Evolus turned. White Eagle ducked behind the trunk of a huge tree.

She'd never seen anything so hideous. Filled with fear and revulsion, she screamed and staggered backward. She tried to run but her legs were like two heavy weights and seemingly didn't belong to her anymore. Her body trembled as Evolus eyed her like a piece of priceless art, a possession he'd just purchased. His huge fangs dripped thick, yellow mucus all over the floor as he circled her. "Do you really think I will let you go again, my dear?" he snarled.

"Don't back off, Maggie. You have to release your curse. Do it!" White Eagle fumed. "Do it now, Maggie! *NOW*, DAMMIT!"

She tried to calm herself. "I can't," her voice cracked in fright.

Unsympathetic, "*DO* IT!"

Her eyes flickered from White Eagle, then stared at Evolus in horror. She had to try, had to find Adolphe in there somewhere. She thought about the lifetime when she was Marguerite, his wife. They'd grown up together. As children, they'd been inseparable. Adolphe had been a lovely little boy who had grown into a fine young man. She loved him in the beginning but he'd tossed her love away. What was it that imprisoned his spirit and fused him with…with this creature before her? And then it struck her. Power! Adolphe wanted to control everything: wealth, people, the worlds that he lived in, the worlds that he didn't—she already knew that. But he'd failed to realise that it was power that controlled him, and not the other way around. In effect, he was powerless! But his insatiable need for power made him vulnerable. He was an easy target for Evolus, who'd possessed him in his early twenties knowing that one day Adolphe would become Marguerite's husband, the light-worker he was desperate to impregnate.

She sighed. A small voice drifted through her mind. *When will they ever learn? Love is the only power. When love fills up a heart to bursting, only then will you become a force to be reckoned with. A heart full of love is indestructible, eternal.*

She swallowed hard. Her voice was a mixture of weariness, pity, and fear. "Evolus, don't you see that your need for power is what creates…," she looked around, "…this hell? I can't understand why you don't want to live in peace."

Evolus stopped circling her. Something about her tone had reached him, and he didn't like the idea of being questioned any more than he liked the idea of being pitied. He pushed his face into hers. "Why do Galaxias exist? Do they not wish to hold all power?"

She turned her head away, gagging on his breath. It was stale like death. "They exist in the hope that one day the dark will join the light, Evolus," she said between coughs.

Evolus screamed out his indignation. "Then why doesn't the light join the dark? Why do I have to join them? Who says I'm dark and they're light?"

"Can you let go of all control—of all your power, Evolus? Galaxias do nothing without first consulting G.U.N.—but they could! They don't have to involve G.U.N. in any of their decisions but they respect the harmony of all existence. They all work together as a safeguard for creation, following specific instructions from the elders from many nations. There is no power struggle behind any of their decisions, only love. Love is the most potent form of power, which is why Galaxias hold the supreme position. Until you realise that, you will go on craving the one thing that can only ever be found in your heart."

A thought bounced around in her head, desperate for attention. *Love! Love! Love—Love!* She had been void of it when she'd cursed Adolphe. She had to accept that a piece of what was hidden in this vile creature before her was, in fact, hers! *How could I have done that to Adolphe? Not only do I let him down, I let myself down, and our purpose.*

At last, she realised that the power Evolus lusted after was the same power that she'd craved in that single moment when she'd cursed Adolphe: a desperate need to have power over him. A power that made her feel good through its viciousness. A power that saw Adolphe crumble and disintegrate into pain and misery. She'd revelled in it.

Shocked at her own bitterness, Maggie felt her heart shrink inside her chest. She couldn't believe how much hatred she carried for the man she'd once called her husband. Oh, she knew it wasn't her curse that had brought him here. It had little or no effect on him, but it had brought her down to this level! Her curse had hurt her much more than she cared to be aware of. She now understood that the only way she could be free was to release Adolphe not from Evolus, but from herself, and likewise, Adolphe had to release her. He died in misery but not because she'd wished it on him. His own bitterness at the woman who'd let him beat her mercilessly before telling him she was pregnant had seen to that. If he had known beforehand, he wouldn't have touched her!

Maggie caught her breath. It was as if she had inhaled love and exhaled hatred. She looked at Evolus. "I'm sorry," she whispered. "I release you from my hatred, Adolphe. May you go in peace…and love."

But Adolphe needed to hear her.

⁓

White Eagle, Roman, and NeilA were ecstatic. This was a big day for G.U.N. and Galaxias. One of their key workers had taken back a piece of her power.

White Eagle lifted Maggie high into the air, spinning her around and around. "Maggie, do you realise what you've achieved for yourself and for G.U.N.? More importantly, what you've done for the dark?"

"G.U.N.?" she said, puzzled. "For the dark?"

"Yes, for the dark." He beamed at her. "You have brought love into their world." He looked around. "These demons now have a reminder. What a trolley!"

Maggie let out a small chuckle at White Eagle's attempt to use some of the popular slang of the day. "Now you're on the trolley," she corrected.

"I am indeed—"

"ENOUGH!" Evolus's voice shook the ground below their feet. A small amount of debris and a spattering of dust rolled down the mountainside.

White Eagle gently placed Maggie back on the ground. "We'd better get out of here." He took her hand, pulled his knife from its holder, and traced a triangle around them both. The blue-white after-image flared from the knife once again. The triangle remained fixed around them. Its three corners symbolised White Eagle, Maggie, and the light. "Think only loving thoughts," he ordered. "Not the flaky kind!"

"Flaky kind?" She looked puzzled.

"You know, such as love and light, and what a beautiful place the world is!"

"That's flaky?"

"Very! Especially given our predicament."

"I don't know what you're going on about, then! What do you mean?"

"Just think about what you love. You know, like how you'd love to be out of here sipping a cup of tea! Bring on the damn tea!"

A curl of nausea swished about in Maggie's stomach as she let doubt become the dominant force in her thoughts. *We might not make it—we might lose Earth to the dark. Evolus isn't going to stand back and let us walk out of here. Where is the light? Why is nobody helping us?*

"Magic, magic!" The sarcastic voice of Evolus jeered. He blew the triangle softly. It sidled away slowly, like wisps of smoke being enjoyed by two lovers.

"Maggie, lighten up the thoughts! You're letting fear get the better of you again! Face him!"

"That's easy for you to say—I'm scared, White Eagle! Evolus has only played with us so far." She closed her eyes, wishing everything would just go away.

White Eagle was angry. "You've just won a crucial battle with him—don't weaken now! Do you want to be trapped in this hole until God knows when, or do you want to get out of it? What is worse: being stuck here or fighting trying to escape from it?" He put his hand on her stomach and raised his eyebrows. "Make your choice, Maggie," he said, under his breath. "Will you stay and bear his child?" His breath was jagged as he thought back to the moment hundreds of years before when, as Celenadus, he'd asked Marguerite the same question; at least then he'd had the choice of taking her to the spirit world. If Maggie lost herself now they were all screwed. He'd have to leave the underworld without her and the battle for Earth would begin. "Maggie, please! Open your eyes—"

"QUIET!" Evolus waved the back of his hand. His power sent White Eagle crashing into the side of the mountain.

A sickening sound like skull against rock made Maggie cringe. She knew that her guide couldn't be injured in the physical sense, but the influx of energy that had hit White Eagle's subtle system could have critical repercussions. If his chakra system was seriously affected he would need a specialist in energy manipulation from the higher realms to treat him, to help him recover the intricate balance between each chakra. Depending on the damage, the procedure could take years. She had to act quickly. If he didn't get the adequate spiritual attention soon, he would become vulnerable to energy manipulation from the dark forces and if they got a hold of him he would be dragged backwards—everything he'd been through, his evolution, would mean nothing! He'd lose it all, and end up a savage back at the beginning; yet he'd still hold within him the power he'd accumulated so far. A thought struck her that maybe this could have happened to Evolus? Maybe there's a beautiful soul buried in him somewhere?—*My God! Power to be used against our Earth, the universe—No!* She wasn't about to let that happen.

She ran over to White Eagle and cradled his head in her arms. "Come back! Come back now!" She held him for a few moments more. "Don't go. Don't lose what you've worked for." Her tears dropped onto his cheeks. She closed her eyes and sent out a small, rushed request to the universe. *Please help me heal White Eagle.* Within seconds she felt the familiar warmth of a healing presence surround her. Waves of energy rippled through her body accompanied by a slight breeze that itched and tickled her skin. She focused on the pleasant sensation that flowed in through the top of her head and made its way down to her heart. She saw the electric, white-blue essence leave her hands and mingle with the silver-grey, smoke-like form of White Eagle's etheric body. "I won't let you down," she whispered.

White Eagle slowly opened his eyes to see what he could only describe as an angel—Maggie sending healing and love to him! What more could a guide ask for? Her long wavy hair the colour of warm autumn dropped over her shoulders like a flowing river, and her green eyes sparkled with the energy that was surging through her, yet he could still detect a flash of temper on fire behind them. "Maggie, I'll be fine…thank you—"

"White Eagle, thank God you're alright! You scared me half to death, so you did!" Her wide mouth and full pink lips erupted into a relieved smile. "Are you sure you're alright? Can you stand?"

He pressed his palm against her cheek. "A bit drained; nothing to worry about. I've been through worse…just give me a few minutes to clear the fog."

Evolus thundered. "Get used to the fog, White Eagle. It's your new home."

"Maggie, let's get out of here!" White Eagle jumped up, but his energy was so out of whack that he fell back down like a hopeless drunk. For a few seconds he had no clue where he was or what was happening.

"WHITE EAGLE!" She tried to pull him to his feet. "Get up! Get up!" But it was hopeless.

"Maggie," he whispered. "I'm going to send for a vortex so you can leave—"

"No! I'll not leave without you."

He widened his eyes. "You have to, remember?" He tried to stand, to get himself together.

Evolus struck again. He laughed as he fired a zap of red energy from his scaly finger, purposely missing White Eagle by inches. The red force left a huge, smoking hole in the mountainside.

On impulse, White Eagle grabbed Maggie and threw himself on top of her. "That's it! Maggie, you have to leave! When you see the vortex, run as fast as you can towards it—"

"No! Why can't you come as well? I don't understand!"

"I can, but I'll have to stay here and fight off Evolus while you get out first."

"But you won't be able to fight him. No! I'm not stupid! You're no match for Evolus like this. I'm going to hold him off until you recover."

His mouth set in a thin line and his nostrils flared. "Maggie, don't be so damn stubborn! I'm sending for the vortex and you'd better get your backside into it. I'm not asking you, I'm telling you! Evolus is showing us a small sample of his strength. What we've seen is nothing—a fraction of his capabilities!"

But Maggie's temper overruled her fear. She struggled free from White Eagle's grip, jumped up, and walked toward Evolus with a cold, hard, defiant glare in her eyes that didn't suit her. The distant shadows of Lady Marguerite surfaced from a place in her psyche. Oh, yes!—she had the courage to face him; she'd done it before. "Evolus, I've had enough of your poison."

Evolus laughed. "Call this poison? You've seen nothing yet!"

She could see the slanted red eyes of dark spirits all around her as they rose up on the sound of his laughter. Their wings sounded like the low hum from a million manic hornets disturbed from their nest, and their jeers were like a knife scraping along metal. Maggie pressed her hands to her ears. It was unbearable! They'd never get away, not now!

Evolus flapped his wings. The breeze sent her crashing to the floor. She instinctively wrapped her arms around her belly in an effort to protect her child. Without thinking, she screamed out, "I WON'T LET YOU HARM MY BA—" *NO!* The thought struck her again. *Don't talk! Don't even think about the child!* Terrified by her own words, she stopped talking abruptly and stared up at Evolus.

He turned her over with his foot, cocked his head to the side, and eyed her suspiciously. A low, menacing growl came from deep inside him, and small spurts of polluted air escaped his nostrils.

Desperate, White Eagle did his best to stand but could only flap about, helpless, like a small bug trying to turn itself over off its back. He knew they had to act now or Evolus would find out about the child. "MAGGIE! GET ADOLPHE TO HEAR YOU!" he shouted, in the hope of diverting Evolus's attention.

Maggie realised what was happening and sprang up to face Evolus. This time the fear inside her was positive. It came from a higher part of her—it spurred her on. The thought of the power between her and Evolus inside the baby terrified her. "Adolphe! Can you hear me? I forgive you!" she said, hurriedly. Nothing happened. She changed her tone, spoke in a quiet, gentle voice, and let the love pour out of her. "I love you, Adolphe. I do. I love you."

The love in her voice made Evolus scream in agony as Adolphe fought his way through him.

Adolphe looked wild, ravenous, like a fearsome savage about to rip her apart. Demonic transformation was complete but she could still see leftovers of how he used to look. He roared at her. "Well, Marguerite, revenge is mine at last!" He lunged forward, grabbed her by the throat, and pulled her to him. She could recognise that look anywhere—one of lust and rape. He ran his thumb over the lump in her throat. "For old times' sake." He pulled her head back, licked her neck. She felt his long, forked tongue stick to her skin.

She shrank back and shrivelled in fear like she always did in his presence, but then what she had to protect sent the fury inside her gushing through her veins like venom, and suddenly she felt frenzied, desperate to protect. The fear changed to survival; her instinct, to fight. She stared into his eyes. A frightening smile slowly crossed her face.

Her words were a low snarl. "How dare you! Let go of me or so help me God I'll see to it that you beg me for mercy!"

Adolphe stopped. There was something in her expression that he recognised. Puzzled, he retreated. Evolus surged through him, manic with rage at Maggie's orders. "DON'T MAKE THREATS YOU CAN'T CARRY OUT! YOU'RE IN MY WORLD—DON'T FORGET THAT!" he roared.

Maggie felt the fear but stood strong. "You've held on to me and Adolphe long enough, Evolus!" Her voice was weak with fear. It took every ounce of strength she had not to crumble before him but she couldn't give in. Not like all those years ago when Marguerite had backed down by choosing death. She didn't have a choice. Evolus wouldn't let her die. He'd infuse her with himself and the child—no! Nothing will touch this child. She knew in her heart that she could quite easily kill to protect him.

She clasped her hands together and took a few deep breaths. *God, help us.* Her soft, calm voice was like a melody infiltrating the underworld. "Adolphe, I forgive you. Come back, my love. Free yourself from the hell that you live in."

Green and purple veins bulged throughout Evolus's body as he strained to keep Adolphe under control. "You will pay for this! You and White Eagle!" he snarled. "How dare you challenge me!"

But he couldn't hold on to Adolphe's soul any longer. Adolphe surged out of him and freed himself from the monster he'd lived with for centuries. He found himself face to face with a woman whom he thought he knew from somewhere…but he wasn't sure…

"Hello, Adolphe." Maggie didn't smile. She didn't have time.

He felt dazed and confused. "Marguerite!" he said, shocked, as it suddenly hit him who she was. "What…what's happening? Where are we?"

She rushed over to him. "It will all come back to you."

And it did. Within seconds. He was horrified at the way he'd treated her and Caresse, and everyone else who had been unfortunate enough to cross his path in that lifetime. "Marguerite, I can't believe

I did those terrible things!" He was mortified. "Please…," he begged, "…please forgive—"

She put her fingers to his lips. "Shh…it's past," she said gently. "I made my choices." They embraced and clung to each other for a few seconds, thanked each other for everything they'd been through together. They realised that the experiences had provided valuable lessons to help them elevate consciousness. In that single moment they cleared years of karma by letting love move in and eradicate the hate from within their hearts.

Evolus spat the words out. "How touching—"

"You must go, Adolphe," Maggie urged. "There is little time left."

"But where do I go?" he asked, still in a state of shock and confusion. She looked around but couldn't see anyone waiting to take Adolphe to the spirit world.

Unknown to them, NeilA had already intervened and instructed one of G.U.N.'s special envoys to pick him up. The spirit world had emergency workers who specialised in lost soul retrieval. Their job was to help make the transition from the dark into the light easier for the souls that chose to free themselves from the demonic grip of the underworld.

"Come with me, Adolphe. I will escort you from here on." A kind man, the light glowing around him, smiled and held out his hand.

Adolphe didn't hesitate. He'd never known such peace, such freedom—and the love! He basked in it, revelled in it. He'd never stray from the love again. He looked at Maggie one last time. "Thank you," he said, "I love you." With that, his form changed into an orb of silver light and he was gone.

Evolus was livid. His anger caused mayhem throughout the underworld—even Earth felt his fury as freak storms broke out everywhere on the planet. Earthquakes and tornados ravaged the American continents, while Europe was hit with freak floods, the rain so heavy it was impossible to see through, and snowstorms raged with abnormal, freezing temperatures. Earthquakes and tsunamis hit Asia, while all over the African and Australian continents fires broke out as well as floods the size of some countries.

All around her Maggie could hear the tortured souls of demons that were trapped in the underworld scream out in terror.

White Eagle was inspired by Maggie's strength. Shakily he got to his feet and staggered over to where she stood. "We'd better get out of here fast! You were right when you said that Evolus had only played with us so far." But all around him he could hear the anguished cries of lost souls—Evolus would see to it that they didn't get the same idea as Adolphe. He knew that he couldn't leave without at least making an attempt to free them. "Surrender," he called out. "Free yourselves as Adolphe did. Go to the light. Evolus can't touch you there."

Maggie joined in. "Free yourselves. Feel the peace and the love in the light."

All around them, bright silver orbs began to rise just as Adolphe had done. Love was the only thing getting through to the demons, as more and more of them began to understand that their fear had no place in the light.

Roman and NeilA looked on as thousands of souls chose to return home. They hadn't bargained for this! Some of them had been lost in the underworld for aeons and so the only guides they had were the dark ones. They had to act quickly. It wouldn't be long before Evolus rounded up his legions and, disguised as G.U.N., they would build up at the borders between light and dark and try to suck the souls back in again. Oh, yes! Evolus and his terrorists would soon be out in full force, giving the word "temptation" a whole new meaning.

The souls trying to leave were already vulnerable. They were so starved of affection and kindness that Evolus and his army would be able to fool them into believing that a smile, a hug, or a simple slap on the back was proof enough of love. Of course, there would be no mistaking G.U.N. workers and their expression of love, which is why they had to amass them along the borders as soon as possible. The light-workers could penetrate the dark, like a light bulb being switched on, but the dark-ones were restricted from straying any farther than their own boundaries.

NeilA sent out a thought form of himself that materialised as a perfect replica throughout the spirit world's main stations. It was at those sites that all souls first stopped to rest and reflect on whatever experiences they'd been through. All other forms of communication instantly cut out and everyone immediately stopped what they were doing. When any of the elders made contact in this way, either something of great magnitude or something catastrophic was happening. "Open up the emergency white hole system immediately—an urgent situation is taking place. Many souls that have been trapped in the underworld are now choosing to return home."

The stations erupted in loud cheers and joy. NeilA lifted his hand and spoke over the excitement. "Shh…shh…please listen!" He spoke quickly. "We have little time. The souls are awakening in the dark and are in urgent need of assistance to get out of there. All envoys must assemble teams without delay and head into the underworld to help those who wish to leave." He paused. "There are millions—all councils get ready to accommodate the new arrivals and oversee their education and adjustment from there on."

Millions of souls were saved, drawing Earth even closer to ascension. It was a busy time as the migrants crossed the borders between Earth and the spirit world, but the rush of the surge didn't deter the celebrations of the souls coming together in peace at last.

⌇

White Eagle turned to Maggie. "Let's go!" All around them, silver orbs sprang up and vanished from sight. "Well, I'll be damned, Maggie!" he said, as the realisation of what was happening sank in. Up until then he'd been unaware of the process they'd set in motion.

"What?"

He whispered. "The souls! Millions of them leaving." Then he yelled, his tone more urgent. "Come on, we're running out of time!" He grabbed Maggie's shoulders. "Be brave! You're going to need all the courage you can muster. I've requested a vortex. We must make our way to it as fast as possible. Run! Give it your all! The vortex will take us back to the chateau. All we have to do is jump into it—but don't worry, once we get within a certain distance we'll be sucked in by the magnetic field around it. Once we reach that field, we've made it and we'll be out of this hovel once and for all! Got it?"

Maggie felt sick. "Won't it pull Evolus in with us?"

"No! Putting it simply, it's a light-vehicle. It's closed to dark energy but it will have been programmed to remain in the underworld for only a minimal amount of time. It's all to do with energy control. The light won't allow anything of theirs to be tarnished by the dark."

He grabbed her hand and they ran towards the spinning vortex that was made up from the energies of many spectacular colours, colours that Maggie couldn't even begin to describe, like none she'd ever seen on Earth. It put her in mind of an old spinning top she used to play with when she was a child, but on a much grander scale.

"Three minutes, Earth time, to board," a soft, ethereal voice said. The vortex strained as it tried to remain in the space it occupied long enough for them to embark.

"Why can't the vortex meet us?" Maggie asked, exasperated, as she ran alongside White Eagle.

Distracted, he answered, "The black hole that it's assigned to is unable to move out of the confines of the meridian it's been programmed to work with. We have to use one of Earth's meridians to transport you back, which means we have to work within the confines of time."

"Well, that makes everything about as clear as mud!" she said breathlessly.

He dragged her behind him. "For God's sake, stop beating your gums and get a move on! Any time now, Evolus will realise the vortex is waiting for us. Save your energy—you're going to need it!"

Sidetracked by the demons that were trying to leave, Evolus had given White Eagle and Maggie a head start but it didn't take long for him to realise what was happening. The scream he let out as he gave chase behind them made Maggie's soul rattle—*RUN! RUN!* It yelled at her.

"The vortex! He's seen it!" White Eagle looked back and saw

Evolus gaining on them. The mighty roar from his huge wings as he soared into the black and red sky sounded like a screaming aircraft engine. "Sorry, Maggie, we're going airborne. It's the only way we'll stand a chance against Evolus. Put your arms around my waist and hang on."

White Eagle shot up from the ground and soared upward at lightning speed. Maggie screamed, let go immediately, and rolled head over feet away from him. He shot down, grabbed her arms and pulled her to him. They were suspended in midair. His voice was anxious. "You've been through the worst! This is nothing! Do as I say and hang on. I should have taught you controlled out-of-the-body techniques sooner." He flung her onto his back, clamped her arms around his waist, and shot up into the air once again.

"OH-MY-GOOD-GOOOOD!" she wailed, clinging to him with her eyes closed. "It seems there are a lot of things you should have taught me sooner!"

He drew his knife from its holder and pointed it towards the vortex. Combined with their light, its pure silver blade would help to clear the psychic garbage in the atmosphere away from them. "We're nearly there!"

"One minute, twenty seconds, Earth time, to board."

Evolus flipped his hand toward them. The red strike of lightning he fired made White Eagle stumble in mid-flight—slightly. He dipped and turned with Maggie hanging onto him for dear life. *Oh God, oh God, oh God!* She was on top of him one minute and underneath him the next. She clamped her mouth shut and screwed her eyes up, too afraid to look. *I can't hold on much—*

White Eagle felt the pull from her doubt slow them down straightaway. "MAGGIE! NO ROOM FOR DOUBTS. WATCH YOUR THOUGHTS—CUP OF TEA, CUP OF TEA, REMEMBER!? WE'LL BE THERE IN JUST A FEW SECONDS—HOLD OUT!" It wasn't a request.

The vortex released a high-pitched siren that pierced the underworld. "Twenty-five seconds, Earth time, to board."

Evolus gave it his all! He lunged forward and grabbed Maggie's foot. Screaming, she let go of White Eagle and plummeted into the darkness. Evolus overpowered her, wrapped his huge, scaly arm around her waist, and tucked her into his side. "You will be my queen," he hissed excitedly into her ear. "Don't worry. I'll don an appearance that will have you begging me to keep you, remember?" He spoke the words softly into her cheek. He knew that if he could keep her for just a few more seconds the universe would be so much closer to being his. White Eagle wouldn't willingly abandon her but the vortex had only limited time.

"Ten Earth seconds to board." The voice from the vortex began counting down. "Nine, eight, seven…"

Horrified, Maggie screamed at her guide. "White Eagle, please… don't leave me!"

"Six, five..."

She thought she'd die of heart failure but then realised she'd rather die than spend another second in Evolus's company. White Eagle shot down after her, the vortex now way out of reach.

"Four..."

Roman and NeilA looked on. Roman stepped forward but NeilA held out his hand, gently signalling him to wait. "Give him a few seconds more to alarm us. We owe him that chance considering the undeniable courage he's shown so far."

"Three…"

White Eagle knew that he had to get Maggie back—now! "ROMAAAAN!" he cried out.

NeilA nodded at Roman. In an instant his figure transformed into a powerful golden energy and disappeared from NeilA's side.

White Eagle looked up to see a huge ball of light tearing through the underworld. He'd never felt so relieved. He sighed deeply… *Roman—*

"Two…"

Roman was surrounded by light—a mighty golden warrior. "White Eagle, why has it taken you this long to alert us of your whereabouts?"

"One—"

He fired a strike of forceful golden energy at the vortex and silenced it; he stopped time in its tracks. "You will have to explain your actions to the elders. You do realize that you might lose your position of spirit guide?" he said sadly.

White Eagle had proved his courage beyond measure, but he'd put himself, Maggie, and the child at incredible risk—a risk that needed the intervention of Galaxias. He slid his palms across his face. "Roman, I understand my actions are of concern. I'm sorry. I panicked. I needed to get Maggie back and forgot—"

"About the golden rule!" Roman interrupted.

"WHITE EAGLE!" Maggie was hysterical. "DON'T LEAVE ME HERE!"

"I'll let you know when the meeting with the elders is. I'll talk to them, do what I can, but for now it's not the most urgent matter at hand. The vortex will remain until you board it." A glint in his eye, he stood strong and proud, every bit the warrior. "Let's get Maggie back." He clanked his sword against White Eagle's knife to signal that the battle had begun. He looked at the knife, a standoffish expression and a scornful tone in his voice. He wanted to laugh out loud. "Call that a weapon? Here, have this!" He clanked White Eagle's knife with his sword again. It instantly changed into a huge rapier—a replica of the knife but huge and lethal. He smirked. "I can't have my warriors equipped with toys. Let's go get the job done!"

Demon after demon joined in the assault. Roman and White Eagle shot up and escaped their clutches. Gold and silver spurts of light flared from their weapons. They laughed and mocked as they ducked and darted like kites in a windstorm. The demons were furious but, blinded by the light, they couldn't get near the pair.

Roman turned to White Eagle. "Let's go and sort the big one out—these minions are no match for us." He'd never lost the taste for a good battle. They shot farther up into the sky toward Evolus and attacked him from both sides.

"ROMAAAAAAN!" Evolus was horrified. He dropped Maggie at once and shielded himself from Roman's radiance. He cried out in anguish as Roman's power overwhelmed him.

White Eagle instinctively shot after Maggie, cushioning her fall in the same moment that Evolus dropped her. He placed her on the ground gently and assured her he wouldn't be long. She watched him shoot off and soar into the sky at phenomenal speed to join what she would later describe as "a big, golden, angelic-looking cloud thing with some kind of intelligence about it—but at least it was on our side!" She watched as White Eagle and the cloud chased Evolus away, their combined light too powerful for him.

"Get Maggie out of here," Roman instructed. "I can handle Evolus on my own for now—we've worn his energy down for a while. I'll hold him long enough for the two of you to leave and hopefully long enough to stop him from alerting the rest of the dark hierarchy about the situation at the borders—at least until the souls who want to leave have escaped."

White Eagle shot back to Maggie. "Let's go! Evolus has met more than his match there."

"What is that?" She couldn't take her eyes off the angel-looking cloud as it chased Evolus.

White Eagle followed her gaze. "That is Roman, my friend and," he hesitated, "my guide." He winked. "No time to go into detail now—come on!"

She was drained. White Eagle clamped his arms behind her knees, threw her on his back gracelessly, and ran to the vortex. As soon as they entered its magnetic field the high-pitched siren rang out and the voice began repeating the word, "Board! Board! Board!"

The vortex sucked them in at phenomenal speed. White Eagle gently manoeuvred Maggie from his back. He looked down at her beautiful face and smiled. She hung, lifeless, like a rag doll in his arms. Due to the energy dynamics of the vortex, she'd blacked out and would remain that way until her spirit was transported back to her physical body.

7.

*A*ngelette's face could have been in a picture frame such was the shock on it! She sat motionless, with her mouth open, wondering if what she thought had happened had actually happened. She had literally been lifted off her feet and thrown across the room! *How could that be? Surely White Eagle…did he do that?* And then she remembered his words. *'Stay there, Angelette, until you calm down.'*

She looked across the large sitting room at Maggie. Her ravaged body lay listless in the corner of the couch. If it hadn't been for the slight rise and fall of her chest, Angelette would have sworn she was dead. She fought off an unbearable urge to run over and shake the life back into her. There was nothing she could do. *She's in the best possible hands. White Eagle is a powerful guide. He will do everything he can to get Maggie back.*

Tears rolled down her face as she relived the events. The fear, the smell, the anger. She swallowed hard. Her throat was so dry it felt like a stone had got stuck in it. *Calm down, calm down.* The uprising of terror ready to invade made her feel dizzy, surreal, as if her mind was leaving her body behind. She was tired of her work. She'd been working with the light since childhood and it had its downside. Dealing with the dark ones, hiding from them, duping them time and time again—the effort didn't get any easier with age. She felt weary and drained. All she wanted now was a peaceful life. It was time to give up and leave it to the younger ones.

She smiled cunningly, cocking her head to the side. *Ah-ha, where are you?* Something was slipping into her mind. She jumped up and shouted out, "BE GONE! BEFORE I SLICE YOU IN TWO!" She heard a pitter-patter sound across the room, shot her head around, and saw the black shadow of a small demon skulk underneath her writing bureau. She pointed her index and middle fingers at it like a gun. "I, SAID, BE, GONE!" she shouted, emphasizing each word.

She called out to her guide for help. Within seconds, Chandiran slowly rippled into focus, breaking the surface of Earth's atmosphere as if she'd been gently dropped in water. The light shone out of her. Her deep brown eyes and fine cheekbones accentuated her exotic looks. Her mass of silky, straight, blue-black hair fell over her shoulders like an oil slick to the bottom of her spine. She wore a long, white dress with a square neck and a gold sash that emphasised the high waistline. She looked at Angelette, then the demon, then Angelette, with an amused expression.

The demon howled and tried to run but didn't know which way to head. He hissed and spat through drooling yellow fangs. Angelette walked over to it, controlling it by focusing on the energy coming out of her fingers. It cringed in her presence. Its gargoyle features contorted with fear.

"How dare you come here with your filth! I won't allow any more crap from the dark to enter this house! GET OUT!" With a back-flip of her hand, the demon was fired across the room and landed at Chandiran's feet. Angelette walked over to a small gramophone and placed the needle on the already-waiting record to mute the demon's vicious growls from the rest of the chateau. Offenbach's "Infernal Galop" blasted out, antagonizing him even more.

Chandiran looked down, her amused expression now an annoyed one. "What to do with you," she said, tapping her arm with her long fingers. She wanted to finish his miserable existence for good, then she immediately scolded herself! She was supposed to be dragging these imbeciles up to her level, not allowing them to drag her down to theirs! Besides, she'd be in no end of trouble from the elders if she flattened it without a justifiable reason.

The demon curled his lips to reveal glistening teeth that could rip through anything in a fraction of a second. Claws out, he jumped up at Chandiran, ready to kill. But she was too fast for him. She seized him by the tail and, with a gleeful expression, grabbed his throat with her free hand. "You will go back to your master and tell him you can't win!" Her voice had a demeaning air to it. One-handed, she held him out and away from herself as she would any contaminated item.

She spied the portal he'd broken through elevated in the corner on the opposite side of the high-ceilinged room. She walked toward it and snapped her fingers to bring it into view. "Do you think you can hide your portals from us? I've been giving the dark too much credit. You're obviously more stupid than I thought!" The portal was quite beautiful, like a dazzling silver firework. "Request a vortex immediately, or I'll throw you in without one!"

But the demon had already demanded transport. He wasn't about to be flung into an empty portal! Who knows where he'd end up?! Infuriated at being the lesser strength, his skinny three-foot frame fought and snarled at the end of Chandiran's arm. A glue-like substance dribbled from his mouth. "You'll all suffer! You'll all die! Earth will fall to the Dark Lord! It won't be long until he rules all creation!"

The demon let out the most horrendous scream as Chandiran tightened her grip on his throat. Her hand glowed white with a touch of blue. The look on her face matched that of any hardened soldier. Offended, she spat air between her lips. "The Dark Lord, indeed! Feel that? That's my light you feel burning." Her eyes cut into him. "Just a trace of it. I dimmed it so as not to cause you unnecessary suffering… now! Don't threaten me or I'll show you what I'm really made of!" With her forearm, she side-swiped him into the portal then turned to Angelette as if nothing much had happened. "We must close that as soon as White Eagle and Maggie get back."

Angelette was tight-lipped, sweating, but in control at last. She walked over to Maggie and stroked the side of her face. "I can't bear to see you taken by him again." She placed a hand behind Maggie's neck. Her body temperature was quite cool. Concerned, she walked over to the fire and stoked it up. "The least I can do is keep you warm."

"Angelette, what took you so long to ask for my help?"

"I…I let my emotions—"

"Cause chaos!" Chandiran admonished. "My dear Angelette, remember that all dark energies feed on fear. When you find yourself in a negative situation, you become vulnerable to their influences. The fear you emanate adds to the problem. It weakens you and strengthens them." She smiled and raised her finger at Angelette. "Love! Is the only emotion that can help any situation get better. Any situation!" She frowned. "Your fear blocked all thoughts of me…and of Galaxias."

Galaxias—that word again!? There was something alarming about it. Angelette was still agitated. "Adolphe! He came here again!" She paused, rubbing the bridge of her nose. "It's, he, I…" Frustrated, she looked at Chandiran. "It is hard to explain. It was the undertone he brought with him—Evolus! I felt him, felt the terror he always put me through, and seeing Maggie like that…" She choked back the tears, looked at Chandiran, and let out a small laugh. "I can't seem to control my emotions."

Chandiran sat down on a sofa opposite where Maggie's lifeless body lay and signalled for Angelette to sit beside her. "Maggie wanted Adolphe as much as he wanted her. He couldn't have sucked her in without consent at some level."

Angelette walked across the room. "You didn't see the look of horror on her face. She had no clue what was happening. She didn't remember a thing about Adolphe!"

"She remembered him. She'd spoken of him in trance a short while before! She chose to deny him, bury him somewhere. It was Adolphe who couldn't rest. His soul was in torment over what he'd put her through. When Maggie arrived at the chateau, it was his soul that screamed at him to bring her in. It wasn't about to let her go again and have Adolphe's spirit stuck with Evolus for a moment longer—"

"But Maggie begged us to help her! Begged us to stop him."

Chandiran patted the cushion next to her. "Come, sit by me." She leant forward and spoke quietly. "Maggie begged you to stop him… but her soul begged her to face him. In the end, the soul will always get what it wants. It is the only way to progress. It might seem like years to those on Earth, but the soul is patient. It doesn't work within the confines of time." A casual air about her, Chandiran shrugged her shoulders. "I've told you all this on numerous occasions."

Angelette picked up a cushion, knocked it into shape, and sat down. "What is my role in all this? I know I can't progress until the spirit of Caresse is at rest."

Chandiran glanced at the cushion. "When Marguerite was commuting between her earthly life and the spirit world, Caresse offered to help her deal with Adolphe. As you know, Adolphe had murdered Caresse long before that fatal night when he attacked Marguerite. Caresse was one of the spirit counsellors who tried to help Marguerite with forgiveness. She knew that Marguerite had to release Adolphe from the curse that bound them together. What Caresse didn't realise was that guilt had got its smarmy talons into her, and you know guilt—once it gets a stranglehold in the mind it's hard to shake it. It whispered, taunted, nagged away at Caresse. Kept telling her that it was her fault that Marguerite had suffered such a brutal death. It wasn't so much a sense of duty Caresse held in her heart for Marguerite but a sense of guilt, and until she could release such emotion, she too would be stuck with the karma of that lifetime."

"But why would Caresse be affected by guilt in the spirit world? I thought we were free from such emotion there?"

Chandiran sighed, thinking for a moment. "Our emotional body copes much better in the spirit world, so in some ways we are free from the stronger feelings we may have collected in a certain lifetime, but once we return to the Earth's plane, any buried emotions that haven't been dealt with in a past life will find a way to manifest through into the new one. The whole experience of Caresse still lives in Angelette at soul level! The soul will not let matters that don't help to elevate consciousness go unattended. Only when the spirit of Caresse deals with her guilt will the soul of Caresse—now you, dear Angelette—stop prompting. Only then will the soul move over so that she can carry on with her journey."

Irritated, Angelette shook her head and blew an irritated gasp of air. "So not only do I have to deal with this life, but the soul makes me deal with an old one! That is not fair! Maybe it should try living on Earth if it thinks it's such a holiday!"

Chandiran hid her amusement. "The soul doesn't make you do anything…the spirit looks for peace. The soul shows the spirit how to find it. You don't have to listen…but the soul knows that your growth is impeded by old stuff. Why do you think that as guides we encourage people to let go of everything at death? The only emotion you need to carry over to the spirit world is love." She shot Angelette an adamant glance. "Nothing else will serve you. As for the soul living on Earth…it does! Through you! Every experience you have is a soul experience."

"I see."

Chandiran raised an eyebrow. "Do you, Angelette? Emotions have the ability to consume."

Angelette raised her arms in the air dramatically. "And I have already failed!" Irate, she turned to Chandiran, her eyes filled with anxiety and tears. "White Eagle had to throw me across the room before I made a bigger mess than I already had!"

"Angelette—"

"I'm doing it again, aren't I?"

"There is no such thing as failure. It is nothing more than a workout towards success, and would be better described as such."

"I never thought of it that way." She smiled. "You always have the ability to make me feel better." She frowned again. "So! Somehow I have to find the spirit of Caresse in my psyche and drive out the guilt she harbours?"

"Yes! She's stuck in your emotional body." Chandiran noted Angelette's exasperated look and smiled. "It's easier than it seems. In your role as Angelette your soul has brought forth many opportunities to enable you to get rid of the guilt that Caresse's spirit clings to. Don't worry about finding them. Let everything flow naturally. When a soul leap is made, you will feel it—it is impossible not to. Of course, this is not the only reason you play Angelette Bertrand…"

"What other reasons are there?"

"Many! The soul path is complex…besides, you know of your soul group. You have more idea than most."

Angelette leant forward. "Name one! I'm intrigued."

"The main one, you deny. When your role as Angelette comes to an end you will have worked it out. I'm not at liberty to tell you any more than that but I will tell you this: guilt is your main challenge yet again!"

Angelette was about to protest at being left hanging when Maggie let out a relieved sigh and roused herself slowly. She rolled her head sideways, too tired to lift it from the back of the sofa, and looked at Angelette and Chandiran with a foggy expression.

"What's happening? Where…" She felt heavy and sapped of energy. She smiled at the beautiful East Indian lady sitting a few feet away. "Are you a goddess?" she asked, awestruck.

Chandiran walked over and sat beside her. "No, Maggie, but I am one of the members of your soul group," she laughed. "Come, let me check you over." Like White Eagle, she had the ability to manipulate realms. In the physical realm, her makeup became physical. "I'm sure you've been through quite an ordeal." Chandiran placed one of her hands on the top of Maggie's head and the other on her solar plexus. "Hmmm, as I thought, energy levels depleted." She stood up, walked towards White Eagle, who'd appeared just behind where Maggie lolled. She smiled briefly and then her expression became intense. "I'd better zap you as well."

Angelette sucked in her breath, "Maggie!" Unable to contain herself any longer, she ran over, took Maggie's face in her hands, and planted kisses all over her. "How do you feel?" she asked, the words racing from her.

"Fine! Just a bit drained—"

"What happened? Did you meet up with Adolphe—and what about Evolus?"

"How do you know about—you too?"

"It happened to me a long time ago, about the same age as you are now…early twenties. Chandiran dragged me back before it was too late."

Dumbfounded, Maggie shook her head. "Of course…Adolphe murdered Caresse in that life as well…but what about your karma? Did you release it?"

"Caresse didn't carry the hatred you did. She was able to let it go through the counselling she received in the spirit world…but not the guilt."

Maggie was puzzled. "But how did you end up in the underworld in this life? You must have had a reason to go there?"

"Like I said, I was just a girl at the time and still honing my skills. I wanted to clear the chateau of the undertone that spoilt its otherwise faultless atmosphere so I called up some of its past residents. Adolphe smashed through the portal. Such was his force and the force of my fear, I was no match for him. He tried to drag my soul down with his. If it hadn't been for Chandiran…she rescued me before I'd crossed the boundary into the underworld." Angelette looked into Maggie's eyes. "Thank God I never made it to limbo like you did but I still saw—felt—Evolus through Adolphe. I'd never come across evil like it. Still haven't. Just as his force was about to snatch me, Chandiran and a few other guides yanked me back!" Her eyes drifted into empty space and she shrugged. "Anyway, that is the past. What about you? Did you lay Adolphe to rest?"

Maggie beamed. "Yes, yes, and Adolphe has found peace at last. He escaped from Evolus and returned to the spirit world. He was mortified at his behaviour. You have nothing to fear from him anymore."

"Yes, I can feel the difference in the atmosphere." Angelette looked edgy, and she took Maggie's hands. "Even so, we mustn't get complacent. I lost my fear of Adolphe a long time ago. When he showed up today, it was Evolus I felt." She sucked in her breath and a look of terror passed across her eyes. "I am no match for him, not alone!"

"Angelette!" Chandiran tilted her head. "Emotions…Evolus suffered a huge defeat today. He's not invincible!"

"Not yet! He gets stronger every time we face him—"

"Angelette!" A look of irritation flickered in Chandiran's eyes.

"You know what makes him stronger!"

"I know! But Maggie must be on guard."

"She doesn't need fear to guard her!"

Angelette turned back to Maggie. "Promise me that you will always be vigilant, Maggie. Evolus…he is devious, manipulative, and has a habit of turning up anywhere."

Maggie looked across at White Eagle and Chandiran and smiled. "But we have our protection." She turned to Angelette. "We mustn't let fear overtake us. It fuels Evolus..." She swallowed hard. "Angelette, I'd love a glass of water." She yawned, forgetting to cover her mouth.

Angelette picked up the small bell—

White Eagle and Chandiran both turned their heads and shouted in unison before trying to speak over each other. "NOT YET, ANGELETTE!"

Angelette and Maggie visibly jumped at the reaction of their guides.

White Eagle looked at Chandiran. He waved his hand, "After you."

Chandiran nodded at him then turned to Maggie and Angelette. "The room must be sealed. We have to close the portal otherwise it remains open to universal visitors. Some you'll like, some you won't."

"Yes, I'd forgotten about that!" Angelette turned to Maggie. "How about some cold coffee instead?"

"Please, I've a throat on me like the Sahara desert!" Maggie leant forward to pour herself a cup but Angelette told her to rest and insisted that she do it for her.

"Thanks." Maggie took the small china cup and saucer, and sipped its contents. "Ugh!" She flinched at the old, bitter taste. "That's woke me up!"

Chandiran looked at White Eagle. "Good to see you again, old friend, although not in the best of situations."

He smiled in an effort to hide his dejection. "Evolus has been quelled for a time. Not for long, as we all know. But at least Maggie is aware of the soul group she belongs to now; well, some of it. I just don't feel good about what she went through to find out."

A wise expression washed over Chandiran's dark, Eastern

features. "White Eagle, your emotional body is in tatters. Remember that Maggie exercised her free will and that lots of karma has been laid to rest. Today is a great day for our group. Let the dark feed on that!"

"You're right!" He shook his head. "I'm worn out. I need an energy boost. Would you do the honours?"

"Of course! Your energy is way down. After the fight you've had, I'm not surprised. Come!"

Taking charge, Chandiran asked the group to form a circle. They sat in front of the grand fireplace and joined hands. The fire crackled and threw off a comfortable warmth, as its flames curled around a large piece of wood.

Chandiran lifted her head to the ceiling and closed her eyes. Her dark hair dropped down her slender back even farther. "Let's feel the energy from source move in, through, and around us." Her voice was angelic, instantly calming, musical. "Ommmmmm," she chanted. "Ommmmmm…"

White Eagle and Angelette both joined her. "Ommmmmm, Ommmmmm." They let the "mmm…" last as long as possible, until their breath ran out, and then started the chant again in their own time.

Embarrassed, Maggie closed her eyes but refrained from joining in with the chant. Her down-to-earth persona didn't quite know what to make of it all. *What a rum carry on this is!*

"Ommmmmm," the group insisted. "Ommmm…"

All of a sudden, Maggie felt a slight breeze begin to circle her and gradually gain in strength—and a noise, quiet at first, got louder and louder as the group chanted. *What the hell!* Within minutes, she heard what sounded like a train rush by her at 150mph, faster, and the slight breeze had turned into a force-ten gale. Bewildered, she opened her eyes. Her dress was wrapped around her head! Mortified—*Did anyone see my knickers?!*—she pulled it down. *What on earth is going on?* The room was lit up by white light, and filled with millions of tiny stars that changed colours as they pulsed in and out. She couldn't take her eyes off them. *White light? Is this what God looks like?* she thought innocently.

The stars sparkled and spun at phenomenal speed as they moved in and out of countless multidimensional realities. They had a definite intelligence, and it was in this moment that Maggie realised she was witnessing the creative force that ran through the universe. This force was part of everything.

She watched as it consumed each member of the group. Terrified, she cried out, "DON'T COME NEAR ME!" But neither the stars nor the group heard her. "DON'T COME NEAR ME! I DON'T WANT YOU!" she yelled. The star things were poised all around her, waiting to pounce. She wanted to run but couldn't move. She was paralysed, held fast to the spot!

"OH MY GOD—"

"Shut up and enjoy the ride!" a quiet voice encouraged.

"Who said that?" She looked around nervously. But none of the group answered. They just sat there in pure bliss with their hair and clothes flapping violently around them.

"Me!" came the answer just as some kind of power shot through her.

She couldn't find adequate words to describe it. It felt like a potent form of electricity had sliced her open and closed her up again all in the same fraction of a moment. But it was only giving her a taste of what was to come. She brought her hand to her chest and gasped—oh, but the feeling that had gone through her! The stars hovered somewhere above her for a few seconds more before they formed what looked like a small galaxy and crashed through the top of her head. Accompanied by a whooshing sound, they ducked in, dived through, and circled her at lightning speed in the same way they had the others. In this instant, she realised that time and space didn't exist. Nothing was solid...everything was pure energy vibrating at different speeds; the slower the speeds, the more solid the manifestation.

She screamed out, but not in fear. She was filled with passion, ecstasy, bliss, and a sense of freedom—mental, emotional, spiritual, sexual. Oh, to feel this free all of the time! And the love! She felt it...felt it penetrate her! Penetrate everything! She'd never find the words to give it justice. It was a connection to everything. Nothing was separate.

The heat and sweat poured from her. Her hair and clothes stuck to her skin like they did in the middle of summer when she'd walk for miles around Dun Laoghaire just to sell a few wares or clean somebody's house. But the wet felt superb, not uncomfortable like it did then.

When the force, whatever it was, left her body, she felt incomplete. Disappointed. Addicted, ravenous, she wanted more. As if hearing her thoughts, it shot through her again. She screamed out in elation and surrendered to the power. Her breath was loud and jagged as it moved through her, slowly now, healing, filling every part of her. The sensation was intense. Bittersweet, pain and pleasure—then her mind and body climaxed into what she could only describe as a merging of everything, a spiritual awakening. Everything was made from the same stuff. Everything was one!

"Maggie, Maggie." White Eagle coaxed her back into conscious awareness. "Are you with us?"

"Do I have to be?" she said dreamily. She heard the rest of the group laugh somewhere in the distance. Resentfully, she opened her eyes and brought them into focus. Relaxed, she sat for a moment or two, and swallowed. "I'm so thirsty."

Angelette turned to Chandiran sleepily. "I take it the room is sealed?"

"Yes...time for me to leave." Chandiran bid her goodbyes and was gone.

"Me too," said White Eagle, trying to remain hopeful. "The elders are waiting. How do you feel, Maggie?"

"Just wonderful." She smiled at her guide. "I'll see you soon."

"Yes..." *I hope.*

≍

White Eagle wasn't looking forward to his meeting with the elders. He would be devastated if he could no longer work with Maggie on a regular basis. He'd remain with the group but her main contact would go to another leader. Worse still, he'd have to take a back seat in any decisions, the final say going to the new leader. This would be a challenge in itself because he knew better than anyone what Maggie was ready for. Surely the elders would take into account everything they'd been through together in this life and others? This situation would slow their growth considerably, but he wasn't concerned about himself. None of this was Maggie's fault. Why should her progression be impeded because of a mistake he'd made? No! He didn't care what the elders said! Even they were open to being questioned, and none of them knew Maggie like he did!

8.

*V*olonne stood still in time, happy to let the rest of the world pass it by.

The small, sleepy village set in the foothills of the French Alps sprouted out from a rocky ridge and was surrounded by hundreds of miles of peaceful, untouched countryside. The raw nature commanded an awe-striking atmosphere. Jagged hilltops, pines, vast orchards, and sky mirrored in clear lakes gave Volonne the ability to see everything from all sides.

Maggie soon decided that Volonne was a place where she could gladly spend the rest of her life. She spent hours staring into the blue-green waters of the Durance River as it snaked its way over rocks and dipped and dodged its way through deep ravines, valleys, and secretive forests. The sound of rushing water, the scent of olive trees, and the calming influence of the lavender which spread out forever was a natural sedative. It was all Maggie needed to feel at one with the world despite her situation.

Night-time brought a unique magic and she often enjoyed long walks on the grounds of the chateau under a moonlit sky. She felt as if she'd come upon a different world, a frozen world painted in midnight blue and carefully iced with silver shadows.

Volonne gave Maggie sanctuary. She was far away from the harshness of the life she'd endured in her native Ireland. Oh, she loved Dun Laoghaire, with its wild coastal paths, small country lanes, and unique architecture, but she'd never find the peace back home that Volonne had given her. Not with Patrick breathing down her neck.

Exasperated, David scolded her gently, worried that she might go into labour while out on her own. He made a point of asking her to join him as often as possible just to keep an eye on her, and they would take long, lazy walks down to the village. They looked like any other young couple. Since being in Volonne, David had refrained from wearing clerical attire so as not to draw attention to the fact that he was a priest. But this posed a problem he wasn't ready for.

In Volonne, he wasn't a priest. He was David, Maggie's husband, or that's what everyone assumed. And he didn't try to convince them otherwise. How could he? Newcomers to the village, staying at the chateau, her pregnant—obviously they were married.

A part of him believed she was his wife...should be his wife. Why couldn't she be? She was carrying his child. God, he loved her! Why couldn't he be with her, show the world how much she meant to him? He could leave the Church...alarm filled him. For God's sake! His mind tore into him, took over, as he relived time and time again every sin he felt he'd committed and every vow he felt he'd broken. But the thought of life without her was unbearable. And if it meant that he would rot at the gates of hell forever, she was worth it.

"Are you sure you're okay? The walk isn't too much for you, given your condition?" He always asked her the same question when they walked together.

She always gave him the same answer. "How many times d'you need telling? I'm pregnant, not ill! The exercise will do me good. Besides, I've never felt so healthy."

There was a distinctly medieval feel to the village. Its narrow streets and ancient houses with cathedral doors all had a story to tell. The Saint-Martin church and the chapel of Saint-Jean de Travaron added to the old-world atmosphere and brought a strong sense of mystery to the village. Maggie often got the feeling both buildings were following her with their eyes, and she'd stop and stare back at them indignantly.

But it was the *chemin de rondes* that never failed to attract her attention. She could see the soldiers still fighting their wars, oblivious to the fact that they were dead but aware that something wasn't quite right. Attracted to her energy, they would stop what they were doing and slowly make their way towards her with quizzical expressions on their faces. She kept promising herself that some day she would go in and help them to find the light, and for some reason, today, the urge to do so was undeniably strong.

"They're here," she whispered to David as the soldiers surrounded her.

"Who?" He steered her away from the old ramparts, knowing full well that she was talking about dead people.

"The soldiers. I have to help them leave," she answered, looking at the old ruins while trying to break free from David's grip. "David, give me ten minutes. I'll meet you in Café de Flore—"

He tightened his grip. "No! You know I don't like it when—"

She turned and glared up at him. "I talk to dead people! Yes! Spare me the lecture but I do. It's part of who I am. Respect that, David!" she snapped.

As always when he got irritated, the nerve on the side of his face started to pump up and down. "How many times do you need to be told? It's dangerous! You're playing with the Devil—and you're, you're putting the baby at risk," he fumed.

"Oh, for God's sake, get over the Devil thing! It was invented to put the fear of God up you! There's no such thing as the Devil. Such ideas are nothing more than an accumulation of like-minded thoughts and fears; negative energies that stick together en masse."

He pulled her into a shaded area out of sight and away from any curiosity. "You of all people have firsthand experience to prove his existence. You still have the battle scars to show for it." He grabbed her arm roughly and pointed at some of the faint scratch marks on her skin.

"That was my doing. I had to release myself from a negative situation to move on—"

"Look at what you've been through! How can you say the Devil doesn't exist? You have no idea of the power you're playing with."

She couldn't believe his smug attitude. "In light of me being the one who works with the power as opposed to being told about it by some old men from…from—" frustrated, she threw her hands in the air, "thousands of years ago! I'd say I'm more than aware of the power that exists…in me, in you, in all of us. That was the reason I went through what I did. And that's where the problem lies. Most of us have no idea of our power. Satan! It's just an accumulation of dark energy that is attracted to the lower vibrations, energy that most of us at one time or another have contributed to. If we're aware of the negative vibration at least we have the chance to steer clear of it and we all have the power inside us to do just that."

His eyes drilled into her, deep, dark, panic-struck. "Negative vibration, my backside! What kind of claptrap is that? You can use all the fancy words you want. The Devil is the Devil, and the sooner you realise it, the better!"

"David, listen." She touched his arm. "Let me explain—"

"No! I won't hear any more of this nonsense. Grow up, Maggie! You said yourself that you were possessed, out of your mind…that, that some force took you over in the hope that you would become like the thousands of other wretched spirits you encountered."

"Yes, I was possessed, possessed by my own thoughts, my own beliefs. Not by something outside of myself. Don't you see? It's all about what we create for ourselves. There are dark forces, but we don't have to be a part of them." She looked at him intensely. "It's all about what we believe. What do you believe, David?"

David sighed. "I don't understand…why would you create such an experience? By all accounts it wasn't exactly a walk in the sunshine," he said sarcastically.

Maggie struggled to explain herself. "There are many reasons why I chose to go through what I went through but I don't want to get into that now. To put it simply, what we put out is what we get back, and sometimes energy can follow us through different lifetimes."

"So you're saying that what we've done in a past life can affect us in subsequent lifetimes—give me a break! Haven't we got enough to put up with in this life without having to worry about what we've done in a past one? And what happened to that other little gem you always preach…what was it? Oh, yes. Living the moment! Bit of a contradiction in terms, wouldn't you say?"

"No! As far as the universe is concerned we're always living the moment, regardless of when that moment took place in Earthly terms. Living the moment means being aware…aware of your spirit, your self—spirit made flesh, in your words. And to answer your first question, even your present life has a past life. When we met all those years ago, we chose to have an affair, to get pregnant! Those things happened in our past but they're affecting us now, and we have to deal with them. It's the same thing, only in a different lifetime. Try not to see it as being something destructive. Look at it as knowledge… experience. A part of yourself that you can access at any time to help with your evolution."

"It all sounds like utter drivel to me! What books have you been reading? Where do you get such ludicrous thinking?"

"Not from any book!" she said hotly. "How about yourself?"

He rolled his eyes in disbelief and spoke on his out breath. "Well… the whole thing is preposterous! You're telling me that what we've done in the past will haunt us until we make it right. Only God has the power to forgive and He will have forgiven us long before that happens."

She could barely control her fury. He was such a bloody know-it-all! "God couldn't care less what we do! It's all about what we do for ourselves. Don't preach free will then take it away and give it back to God in the hope that he'll forgive us for using it!" She stopped for breath. Arguing was futile. "Look…we're getting off track. What I'm trying to say is this: If the spirit from a past life is dented, the energy from that particular lifetime will stay with you through other lifetimes and follow you into your present one. Your soul will look for ways to attract your attention towards that dent, giving you the opportunity to straighten it out. I'm not only talking about difficult energy. You will carry with you an accumulation of the good stuff as well, but it serves us to remember that when we succumb to any part of the…err, negative vibration, we will encounter like-minded thinkers and doers, here, and in spirit." Her voice went up a pitch and her expression was one of innocence, not malice. "I mean, how many miserable buggers do you encounter at church, David, who stick together? The happy ones stick together and avoid the miseries, don't they?"

"Maggie, please!" He wanted to laugh even though she annoyed the hell out of him.

"Look around at your congregation. You can learn a lot by reading the people that you attract into your life. Look at who sticks with whom, and compare their personalities. If you want to learn something about the type of person you are, take a good look at your friends."

"What about me and you?" he whispered.

"Some relationships have gone on through many lifetimes on Earth, and off it, and for many different reasons. We're part of a soul group that goes back a long way."

She remembered the first day that she'd cleaned for him and the profound conversation they'd had. He'd looked at her with a baffled expression. How could a girl so young, and uneducated at that, tie him in knots with her wisdom and intelligence? Even back then she'd known that David was unhappy, that he was questioning who he was with regard to the Church, his faith, his life. She'd known that one day he would walk away, give it all up. But until that day came he would remain unsettled and always be searching for the one thing he was missing—who he was! Not who he was told to be.

He opened the top button of his shirt. She was so damn stubborn yet the only person that could make him think, make him question himself, question his faith, and make him open his mind to other information and possibilities. Yet still he denied it. "Past life, soul groups, reincarnation—it's all trickery, put there for vulnerable people who don't know any better. It's Satan's way of collecting souls, Maggie. You'd better wise up, quick—"

Eyes bright, cheeks red, she retorted, "And you, and people like you, only know what they've been told. You have no idea of who you are, David." She turned to storm off in the direction of the old ramparts. "Now I have work to do!"

He softened and pulled her back. "I know that I love you more than anything else in my life." He tightened his hold, pinning her against him. Her face was set like granite. He used his lips to soften it. When he felt her tremble in his arms he brushed his lips lightly, teasingly, over her neck. Her scent was sweet, addictive. "I just don't want any harm to come to you, that's all." He traced her ear with his tongue. She tilted her head for more. Her heart beat small sounds of desire from her throat.

"David, I've never hidden anything from you. Communicating with the spirits…it's my life's work," she panted.

He stopped abruptly, tightening his hold. "You know how I feel about it. Why do you persist? What about the baby? I won't have it!"

Her passion turned to ice within seconds. "It's who I am! Accept that and stop trying to force your opinions on me. Now, please!" She fired a glance at the arms that trapped her. "I have to help the soldiers cross over."

He wanted to put his hands around her neck and throttle her. He freed her. His lips formed a thin line and the pulse on his temple beat hard and fast as he tried to control his temper. He turned his back on her, walked away, turned around, faced her, walked toward her again. "Why can't they cross over themselves? Why do they need you? The whole thing is absurd. Do you realise what you're saying, Maggie? Dead soldiers from God knows when, still engaged in battle with no apparent clue that they've been killed. It's ridiculous!"

The urge to laugh out loud welled up inside her. She pressed her lips together in an effort to stifle it. She understood how odd her claims sounded to people who had no idea of communication between human life and other existences—all of them open roads for the soul to travel."I'd better leave the aliens out of it, then," she said under her breath. *If he finds talking to spirits hard to fathom, the idea of alien nations will floor him!* Although this part of her gift she blocked. For some reason it scared the b'jeebers out of her. If, now and again, life other than the spirits got through to her, she'd tune them out immediately. It was as easy as turning the dial on a radio—she'd seen one of them in the underworld. It was on her side, and she had an incline that she might be one of them—it was this that terrified her more than anything.

"Pardon?" he said, irritated.

"Our beliefs follow us into the spirit world. If you believe Catholicism to be the ultimate truth then you will find like-minded thinkers—churches, congregations, the lot there—until you start to question it. So strong is your belief, nobody in spirit will deny it. Nobody has that right. But they will be there to plant seeds that pose questions, and they will be there to answer those questions when your mind is ready to receive other ideas and perspectives." She looked toward the old ramparts. "In the case of our soldiers here, it's anybody's guess. Some of them are from the Great War, but most of them are Spanish, from around the seventeenth century. So religion plays a part here, I'd say—"

"Would you really!"

"Yes," she answered, ignoring his sarcasm. "And then there is the question of violent death. Some people go very quickly. In the same instant they're alive they meet their death…living and dead at the same time. David…can you imagine?" she said, excited.

"I don't have a clue what you're on about!" he said vehemently.

She was taken aback by his manner. He spoke to her as if she were some kind of lesser being with a lower intelligence. Just as her own fiery temper was about to hurl obscenities at him, she realised that his attitude toward her was a reflection of how she was making him feel, and she calmed down. "In the same second the soldiers were alive and on the attack, they were blown to smithereens—their spirit took over their physical body and the soldiers carried on doing what they were doing as if nothing had happened. When people don't have a chance to prepare for death, a small part of them sometimes clings to the physical, to what they're used to. But the spirit will want to move on soon enough, and so the spirit world will provide a portal." She cocked her head to the side. "Or let's call it a kind of safe house that enables them to carry on as normal until intervention by a guide, or relative, can take place. Until that time comes, they will have no clue that their physical body has gone and their spirit has taken over." She read the questions on his face. "I know it all sounds confusing."

"But I thought you said that we all have guides and relations who are waiting to meet us at the time of death?"

"We do! And most of us will meet up with whoever it is that's come to get us. But for some, seeing Uncle Bill who's been dead for twenty years turn up as large as life can be a bit of a shock, especially if they've never believed in an afterlife. They can shut Bill out, refuse to see him. But this doesn't mean that he'll walk away and leave the unfortunate spirit to linger around forever. It is those same guides and relatives who have asked for my assistance in an effort to get the lost spirits to cross over. It's them who brought me here today, as they would have brought other mediums in the past. Hopefully the soldiers will listen to me but if they don't, then nobody will force them into moving forward. They have to be ready. For all I know, they might be waiting for God to come and pick 'em up. This won't make my job any easier because if their concept of God is what they've been told, they'll more than likely be waiting for a pair of ladders to drop out of the sky and lead them to the pearly gates above the clouds somewhere."

David laughed out loud at Maggie's way with words. "A pair of ladders falling from the sky.' Maggie, you're a born comedian, you are that—but just where are these spirits that you see? Are they on Earth, in a state of limbo, or what?"

He seemed to be calming down. She felt relieved. She'd always hated conflict but would argue her corner regardless. "Some schools of thought describe them as earthbound, but their physical body has gone so they're in spirit, of course, but... 'asleep' is the only way I can describe it. Their guides and relatives work with them in a kind of dreamscape until they wake up. Helping the earthbound to cross over to the other side is a specialised job in the spirit world. There are all kinds of techniques used to convince them to move on, but no spirit will be forced. It will always remain their choice."

"What about the soldiers?"

"What about them?"

"Aren't they confused? I mean Spanish from the seventeenth century, fighting alongside soldiers from the Great War? The World War lot must be wondering why the Spanish are dressed like they've come out of the Dark Ages, and what do the Spanish make of the dress and the weapons being used by the soldiers from the World War?"

"They're not aware of each other, not in the physical sense." She stopped talking and frowned, looking for words to explain it. "A photograph is the easiest way to describe it. Try to think of each being in a separate photo. Each photo concerned only with the time period that it is assigned to—" she didn't think the explanation fitted the question. She connected with White Eagle. *"Is there a clearer way to explain what's happening with the soldiers other than living in separate photographs?" she asked, telepathically.*

"Hologram is a good word for it Maggie!" He whispered in her ear. "But nobody really understands this word let alone the concept yet. They will in the future but for now, a living photo is good enough!"

David butted in on her thoughts. "… Like a photographic image that represents their lives? I think, isn't it He was thinking out loud.

She linked his arm and they walked a few feet toward a small wooden bench that was sheltered underneath an old oak tree; they sat down. "Yes, you could say that, only the photo I'm talking about is a living image. It's full of the energy of the life force that lives within it. It isn't a dead thing, or a static frame—it pulses with life. It is a living entity. We are at this time living in a present photographic image." She lifted her head and looked skyward, taking in the fresh air. The scent of the old oak mixed with honeysuckle was invigorating. She felt heady and light and alive.

The expression on David's face changed. Maggie knew that something inside him had clicked…"And God." He looked at her. It wasn't a question. His eyes had taken on a deeper sense of knowing. "Is everything," they both said together before laughing out loud.

"That's what being on the same wavelength is all about," she said. "When our thoughts meet up! Oh, and just to confuse you even more, there are future photos that we can choose from. This present image we live in can be changed at any time. There is a life being lived that involves you, me, and our child, and no adoptive parents."

"Then why can't we choose to live that life?"

"We can."

"But what of all the problems it will bring to us, and the child?" He rubbed the middle of his forehead with his index and middle fingers.

His third eye is twitching. He's beginning to see. "We create them. The image can be lived in any way we choose. It's up to us to create the life we want. Right now we can see only trouble with that choice. We see the Church, your congregation, Patrick, the views of society. This is all we see, so if we go down that road, this is all we'll create." An air of desperation entered her tone. "It doesn't have to be that way…I could keep the child and—"

He clasped her hands and smiled sadly. "Maggie, darling, stop right there!" he whispered.

She bit her lip. It was all true. They could create a life together, run away, never to be seen again. But trying to convince David of this seemed impossible. He didn't have the courage to give everything up to chance. Not yet…

They looked at each other in silence. Tears welled in her eyes. He took her hands, closed his eyes and pressed his lips to her palms. "Maggie, I'll pray for you while you're with the soldiers." He sighed. "But I'm worried. What if you end up in Hell again?"

"I won't! Not after the rollicking White Eagle got. There's no way we'll go there again, not unless we've got an army to back us up."

A mask of cynicism contorted his faultless features. "Oh, yes— White Eagle, your Indian brave. Why is it that an Irish woman has a North American chief as a guide? I can't remember how you explained it." He was being sarcastic; he wanted to pressure her.

Maggie knew he was lying but answered anyway, preferring to play his mood down. Her voice was flat. "Lots of mediums have Indians as guides. They've evolved spiritually. They're at a different level in consciousness." She shot him a challenging look. "Who better to guide?"

He stiffened, making his thoughts obvious. He wanted to blast her, tell her to stop being so bloody stupid. But he didn't. He should have had her locked up in a lunatic asylum years ago! *Talking to damn dead people, Indian braves, and now there's bloody soldiers from God knows when running around. Any psychiatrist would have a field day!* He looked down at her and held her captive with his glare. His face, even when dark, was extremely handsome with intense, angry black eyes. "Go! I'll wait at the café. You've got ten minutes before I come looking for you!"

She started to protest but thought better of it. She knew him too well. For a moment, the look on his face had sent a genuine shot of fear through her. One more word and she didn't doubt for a minute he'd drag her back to the chateau, and all the kicking and screaming in the world wouldn't stop him. She smiled, disguising her uneasiness. "I won't be long. I'd love a coffee—one of Emilie's specials."

9.

The heat didn't slow Maggie down on her way to the centre of the old ramparts. One arm up her sleeve, she retrieved a handkerchief and wiped the sweat from her neck and brow. *Okay, White Eagle, here goes. I'm going to help the soldiers cross over.* She raised her eyes upward and said out loud, "If they want to go, that is." She slipped the hanky back inside her sleeve.

The noonday sun was on fire. She sought shade in the dark shadows of the ruins and sat down against the remains of an ancient wall. All was peaceful. The healthy smell of grass and wildflowers lingered in the air. A few bumblebees busied themselves on the dandelions that grew between the moss and weathered foundations. She brushed the top of the small yellow heads just as a bee homed in on them. She felt it thump against her hand and quickly withdrew. The bee saved his sting, content that she'd taken the hint and moved over.

There was nobody about, not from her world at least, and she'd shut the soldiers off for the time being. Alone time had always been important to Maggie. She was at perfect ease in her own company. She sat for a few minutes more, listening to the birdsong and the continual hum of the bees until eventually they faded into the background.

She closed her eyes and inhaled deep, deep, breaths, waiting for the familiar shift in her consciousness. The deeper into trance she went, the less dense her energy became. Maggie likened the physical world and the spirit world to the electric fan in her bedroom at the chateau. The faster it spun, the lighter its propellers appeared, before they disappeared altogether. Her spirit body vibrated at a much faster rate than her physical body. When her vibrations reached a certain speed, her spirit would lift from her body and travel to other dimensions.

As a branch of her consciousness opened up to enable her to communicate with the soldiers, she felt as if she were literally going inside herself, as if she had taken a dive head first into the spinning vortex in the middle of her forehead—the third-eye chakra, or the mind's eye, as it was more commonly referred to. *White Eagle, are you around?* He was nowhere to be seen but she could sense his presence. She took a few more deep breaths and called out to the Spanish soldiers.

Within minutes her vibrations reached lightning speed, and her spirit body lifted and soared free of her physical body, which was left sitting up against the wall of the ancient ruins. Maggie crossed over from the physical plane into the lighter astral plane, and came face to face with the Spanish soldiers.

The soldiers eyed her suspiciously. *What is happening? Who is this woman? What is she doing here?* She looked different to them, more solid, not as translucent. Some of them ran away, shocked or frightened. *Is she a ghost or something?*

Maggie sensed that some of the soldiers were feeling uneasy so she concentrated on raising her vibrations even more. She needed to become lighter, more transparent, so that her energy would resemble theirs. This was the opposite of when spirits sought her out. It was then up to them to slow their vibrations down to a level that would meet hers.

At least twenty soldiers stood before her. Though dirty, the livery of their uniforms was still splendid. A mass of blue coats with gilt buttons and buckles, and edged with red cuffs and multi-coloured cockades, reached back into the distance. The men wore black hats ornamented with gold, which sat like semi-circles atop their heads.

The soldiers stared at her. Puzzled, anxious, none of them said a word. She clasped her hands, then clenched, then grasped one with the other, and then pressed her fingertips together.

Stop playing with your hands and get on with it! White Eagle telepathised.

She ignored him and addressed the soldiers. "Don't be afraid of me. I'm here to help you." Her voice sounded weak. She tried to carry on but found herself at a loss for words due to a sudden attack of nerves brought on by their deadly silent reception.

Some of the soldiers stood firm while others retreated slowly. Their auras were humanoid in shape and expanded at least six feet around them until they trailed off altogether. They were mostly grey and troubled, apart from tiny dots of light which glistened here and there inside them. Every now and again, when a thought influenced a soldier, one of the dots would spark and flash like a streak of lightning and echo within his spirit. Once he'd accepted the thought, the light would snap shut again and pulse like a small star.

Gives a whole new meaning to the phrase, 'The light bulb will come on eventually.'

"Please, there is no need to be afraid of me." Stuck solid to the spot, Maggie did her best to relax.

The Spanish captain moved in. He was scared and guarded, but he couldn't show fear in front of his men. He removed his hat. Its rim left a perfect imprint in his black, straight hair and revealed a tanned, worn-out face. His eyes looked like two black stones that had been trodden down and stamped way back inside his head. He fidgeted nervously. The skin on his scrawny neck spilled over the neckpiece of his uniform and shook as he spoke. "Who are you? What are you doing here?" *There is something angelic about her.* "Are you an angel?" It was more of a wish than a question.

Maggie's aura gleamed about her. To the Spanish captain and his men she looked like an angel from the Holy Bible. Some of them dropped to their knees, and made the sign of the cross.

"Oh, no—please! There's no need to kneel before me. Please stand up." She felt confused. "I'm not an ang—"

"Maggie, don't concern yourself with their beliefs." White Eagle interrupted. Using clairaudience, he whispered into her ear, but remained invisible. "Your job is to get the soldiers to cross over to the other side. We don't care how you do it. If they believe you to be an angel, they won't be as scared so it will be easier for them to walk through the white hole into spirit."

"The white hole?"

"Yes—the light, as many refer to it. Tell them to go into it."

She looked around for the white hole but it was nowhere to be seen. "Captain Perez, I'm here to help you and your men go into the light."

Perez narrowed his eyes. His right one developed a nervous twitch. "What light? What are you talking about?" He looked around. "I see no light."

She searched for words that wouldn't sound so absurd. Failing that, Maggie decided that the only way to tell someone that they were dead was to come right out and say it. "You and your men were all killed in the Holy Cross War!"

Perez was alarmed. "Killed! What do you mean? We are alive." His voice went up an octave with every word.

"Captain Perez—"

His dark eyebrows met in the middle. He spoke fast, fearfully. "How do you know my name? Is this a trick of the Devil?" He was getting more disturbed by the second.

White Eagle interrupted again. He remained out of sight and communicated telepathically. *Make the most of it, Maggie—pretend to be an angel or this lot will be stuck here until God knows when.*

She turned her back on the soldiers, walked briskly in the opposite direction, and whispered through clenched teeth. "I'm not passing myself off as an angel! God will have my guts for garters!"

White Eagle exploded into laughter. "God will have my guts for garters!' Where do you get such expressions? God doesn't care about white lies that work in the best interests of those concerned. It's intentions that count."

Maggie looked worried. "I don't know, White Eagle...I don't want to offend anyone—"

"Offend who? God? Stop worrying. God doesn't have the hang-ups humans have, and God certainly doesn't hang around, waiting to be offended."

"Are you sure?"

"Yes, take my word for it! I work in your best interests as well as my own so that we can evolve together. Okay, I'm not perfect, and I can get a bit carried away at times, but my intention is to act for the highest good of you, me, and creation on the whole. It is intention that the universe responds to, Maggie, the intention of the heart. And your intention is to help the soldiers, not lie to hurt them."

She felt more at ease. "So if he thinks I'm an angel I don't have to convince him otherwise?"

"No! We'll carry on with this discussion later. Right now we must crack on with persuading Perez and his men to cross over—look how quickly he's turned! He's already questioning whether you're from the Devil, when a moment ago he was ready to believe you were an angel. Besides, you are their angel for now. Anyone who can get them away from the misery of war is an angel in my book."

She still felt unnerved. The dark vibration of war was depleting her energy. She looked around for the light. "Where is the bloody light? How can I send them to the light if it isn't there?"

"That's our concern, not yours. Just do the job you've been asked to do before the captain here gets even more neurotic than he already is and loses it altogether."

She turned around and faced Captain Perez, did the sign of the cross, and smiled serenely.

The sound of White Eagle having a good laugh broke through her thoughts yet again. *I said play it, Maggie, not milk it!*

Irritated, she tilted her head back. Be quiet, White Eagle!

"Pardon." Captain Perez was getting more confused by the minute.

"Captain Perez—"

"How do you know my name?" he repeated. His eyes widened and beads of sweat streamed down his forehead. He wiped his brow with the soiled red sash that cut across his chest.

"I'm your angel."

The captain threw himself down at her feet immediately. "My

angel!" he called out dramatically. The rest of his men fell to their knees once again and bowed their heads, afraid to look at Maggie's face.

Oh no, not again! Embarrassed, Maggie walked over to Perez, lifted him gently by the arm, and asked him to stand. "Please, Captain, you don't have to kneel for me. Ask your men to stand."

He looked at her with a "But we should honour you" expression on his face.

She walked quickly into the throng of men, waving her arms in an upward motion. "Please! Stand up, stand up," she repeated, with a desperate edge to her voice. "Please…there is no need to kneel. Stand up. Stand up, all of you."

The captain stood up and gestured that his men do the same. As they did, the atmosphere changed from one of apprehension to one of complete peace and love. Maggie closed her eyes. She had felt this atmosphere before and could never get enough of it. Tears streamed down her cheeks. She knew the light had arrived.

The soldiers looked at the spinning tunnel of white-blue light a short distance away. Tears of joy spilled down their cheeks, and they cried out at the feeling of intense love and peace that surrounded them.

"Captain Perez, you must walk into the light. It's your passage to the afterlife. The peace and love you feel in this moment is nothing compared to what awaits you and your men there."

Captain Perez sobbed. The love atmosphere overwhelmed him, overwhelmed them all. "How can I thank you, my angel?" he said, clasping Maggie's hands.

She smiled. "By leading your men out of battle and into the light, Captain Perez."

"To the light," he ordered.

But his men, after suffering the misery of war for long enough, were already making their way toward it. They didn't give a hoot about the country that had sent them there! The time had come for peace. Enough of war and violence; they now felt only relief and liberation. There was no way they would let the light go without them. "To the light, the light, the light," they sang in their native Spanish as they marched towards it. They raised their rapiers high in the air and threw them like javelins as far away from where they were going as they could.

Maggie watched the great rejoicing and excitement as the soldiers met up with loved ones and friends on the other side. As soon as the men stepped into the entrance of the white hole it fired a rainbow of vibrant colours into them, and the grey, troubled cast of their auras slipped away, in much the same way as a snake sheds its skin.

Captain Perez was the last one to enter the light. He stepped into it, turned around, and smiled at Maggie. He looked up and stretched out his arms to soak up the atmosphere. "The love, the peace, the freedom; there are no words to describe," he said before he turned and disappeared. The white hole remained for a few seconds more and then snapped out of existence.

Remnants of peace hung in the air. Maggie smiled and whispered to herself. "Seems it's a little different for everyone when they cross, except for the love."

"TAKE COVER!" A man's voice screamed out, not too far away. She felt her heart leave her body! "TAKE COVER!"

Several soldiers dressed in WWI uniforms covered their heads and threw themselves into a muddy, three-foot-deep ditch behind a wall of sandbags. They shook with fear and shivered with cold as the rain hammered them inside their small foxhole.

The smell of burning flesh and death from the scorched bodies that littered the ground filled the air. It was a gruesome sight. Some were perfect, as if sleeping, while others had limbs blown apart or their insides out in the open.

Maggie felt weighed down by the tragedy and dark atmosphere that was spread all around her. Death and misery confronted her in every direction. She clutched her stomach and swallowed hard. She felt as if she couldn't go on much longer. She called out for assistance. "White Eagle, I don't think I can do it. I'll have to come back another time."

"Remember our conversations, Maggie. As Shakespeare once said, 'All the world's a stage, and all the men and women merely players.'"

She'd been well versed by White Eagle on life and death and why people opted for certain experiences. She thought back to her own death when, in the role of Marguerite, she'd been murdered by Adolphe. She remembered the love, the freedom, and the relief that had gushed through her when she'd finally conceded and given it all up for death. She reminded herself that the bodies strewn all around were no more than vehicles that had carried their owners through life—helpers that allowed them to live out experiences and evolve to the next level before being tossed away when it was all over. At least now some of the spirits that had abandoned them were at peace.

"TAKE COVER!" the man screamed again, just as the Zeppelin Z1 roared above her. The mighty war cry of its engine chanted as it peppered bullets into Maggie and everything else below it. The dead bodies jiggled about like jelly as even more bullets blew even more pieces out of them.

Maggie dove, and covered her head in fear. The plane was so close she thought it might land on top of her.

"Maggie, what are you doing?" The voice of White Eagle brought her back to her senses. "Why are you hiding? None of this can touch you!"

Maggie was shaken. "Oh, Jesus, Mary, and Joseph!" She sat up, put her arms out in front of her to inspect them for bullet holes, then wrapped them around her body and stroked and patted herself down in search of blood and injuries. "White Eagle, I'd forgotten where I was for a minute there," she said, relieved.

The soldiers looked on in utter amazement. Bombs were being dropped, and bullets were being fired all around this slip of a girl—and pregnant at that! But nothing seemed to touch her.

"What the hell?" a young private said, visibly shocked.

"Shh!" Officer Dunn pushed the boy to ground. "Get down, all of you! Keep quiet."

White Eagle spoke fast. "Maggie, the officer in charge, his name is Dunn. His whole battalion was damn near wiped out. We've had no trouble getting the rest of them over but these four, for some reason, prefer to hang around. Dunn has a…a kind of knowing that they're dead but ignores it. His ego made a foolish decision which got them all killed despite the warnings from lower ranks. He's having a hard time accepting that he was wrong, and a lousy time with the guilt that's eating away at him. He's fully aware that you're not from his world but he ignores the pricking from his conscience. He's in denial."

"So what the hell do you want me to do about it?" she said emotionally. After the experience with the Spanish and now this, her energy was drained, and the fact that bombs and bullets seemed to be going off in all four corners of her universe did nothing to ease her tension or her mood.

"Get them the hell away from this situation and back to where they belong!"

Maggie was bowled over by White Eagle's sharp response. He usually remained calm with her tantrums. "Alright, keep your wig on!" she said hotly.

White Eagle stifled laughter. "'Keep your wig on!'" He raised his voice slightly. "Stop taking things personally and get on with the job at hand."

"I'm not taking you personally, White Eagle. I just thought you were being sarcastic."

"I was! It was a reflection of your attitude towards me. You questioned me with sarcasm. I answered you with sarcasm. Need I remind you of one of the most basic laws of the universe? What you put out is what you get back—karma, Maggie, karma! Be nice!"

"Don't talk to me like—"

"Maggie, we have no time for this. Stop being so…oversensitive and get on with it!"

Raising her arms as well as her voice, Maggie stormed off in a huff, still arguing her case. "Don't give me orders!"

Officer Dunn and his men watched from the confines of the ditch they'd dug. "The woman's barking mad," Dunn said, rifle poised at nothing in particular.

"Who the hell is she talking to?" The Scottish sergeant took an old tin out of his jacket pocket. The paint on the front of the tin was scratched and worn, and gave the female that adorned it a wrinkled, rundown appearance. He poured a thin line of tobacco onto the small white paper in his palm, rolled it into a neat cigarette, and placed it in the corner of his mouth. Reaching into the same pocket, he took out a box of matches, struck one, and lit the cigarette. The flame on the end of it burned for several seconds before it was snuffed out.

Dunn grinned. "For god's sake, MacTavish! That thing's more dangerous than the fucking bombs being dropped on us," he said in an upper-class English accent.

The soldiers laughed quietly amongst themselves but remained low, all eyes on Maggie. They agreed with Dunn. The woman was walking about in a dangerous military area, arguing with herself. She was obviously a lunatic…probably lost her husband to the war.

"One of us should grab her before she ends up dead," MacTavish said, taking a long, hard drag on his cigarette.

Dunn let out an irritated sigh. "I need this like I need a fucking bullet in the brain. "What the hell am I supposed to do with a bloody woman out here? And by the looks of it, one ready to give birth at any time. What if she goes into labour?"

Miles, the young private, answered his officer. "What's the point of worrying about when she'll go into labour? Whatever happens we can't just leave her walking about on her own out here. Her being pregnant means we've got two of them to save."

"I've no intention of leaving her, Miles. I'm just thinking out loud. Cover me," he ordered. "I'll sneak up on her from behind." He put one hand on the sandbags and catapulted out of the ditch. "Pass my rifle."

Miles obliged, and then settled into position with the rest of the squad to cover his officer. Dunn lay still in the mud for a few seconds, never taking his eyes off Maggie. When he was satisfied that she had no clue he existed, he started to crawl towards her. Bodies floated on top of the thick black sludge and rubbed against him. Some were intact but sometimes only limbs remained. In the dark, covered in mud, he looked like a black panther about to pounce on its prey…skilled, silent, graceful. The only sound to be heard was the suck-suck of the bubbles as he forced himself on through the marsh.

His soldiers looked on, none of them saying a word. They couldn't figure out why Maggie was still alive. MacTavish spoke first. "What's with this woman? The rest of us would've been dead long ago. God knows how many damn bullets she's dodged."

"Look closer. She's not dodging them, sarge," Miles answered. "Look at how her dress blows from the force of the bullets." *She's got to be dead already—some kind of spirit or something.*

MacTavish eyed the boy next to him who was young enough to be his son. "But she must be dodging 'em." He looked back at Maggie.

"Them and the bombs that are exploding all around her, sarge. If I didn't see it with my own eyes, I'd say that her still being alive was impossible."

"It's a bleedin' miracle alright!" Cockney George piped in.

Lost in their own thoughts, the soldiers remained quiet. They were beginning to question, to think. They watched Dunn as he got closer and closer to Maggie, who still looked to be arguing with herself. They watched as the relentless barrage of bullets sprayed her time and time again. Yet she remained unharmed.

10.

"I'm going back! I'm not in the mood for this now. I'll come back tomorrow. It's your fault—"

"Grow up! But if it makes you feel better to lay the blame on me, fair enough! I can't believe how childishly you're behaving."

Maggie was furious. "Right, that's it—and why don't you, you, show up?! Why are you using clairaudience all the time? It's boring talking to thin air!" She quickened her pace.

White Eagle watched Dunn slither through the mud. He was well aware of the plan to capture her. "Maggie, where do you think you're going?" he asked, as he appeared right in front of her.

She jumped back and gave him a look that could have killed him if he weren't already dead! "I'm going to find a quiet spot to concentrate on getting back to my own life, and you lot can whistle!" She tried to dodge around him.

He kept walking in front of her. "A quiet spot, in the middle of the World War!" White Eagle kept watch on Dunn.

"There you go again, being sarcastic!"

"I wasn't! I was merely pointing out that you'd be hard pressed to find a quiet spot here."

"Get lost! Come back tomorrow when I'm not so wound up—"

"Listen! Officer Dunn is about to pounce on you."

Alarmed, Maggie turned abruptly. "What d'you mean?" Dunn stopped dead and lay still.

"They think you're a madwoman who's somehow got lost out here. They've started to question but are still a long way from accepting that they're dead! It would be a shame if you left now, Maggie. By tomorrow they might not be interested and we're back to square one." White Eagle was satisfied. Maggie was in a fighting mood; she needed to be to deal with Dunn, a stubborn bastard at the best of times!

"A madwoman, the cheeky beggars! I'll show them what mad is!" Her mouth racing on ahead of her, she marched towards Dunn. "Officer Dunn, get up out of the mud now!" She spoke to him as if he were a child. "The only reason I'm in this hellhole is to get you and your men out of it and I warn you, I'm not in the mood for soft-soaping, or listening to you pretend that you don't know you're dead!"

"Maggie! Use some diplomacy, for God's sake! You can't just tell people they're dead! Good grief, woman! Do I have to explain everything?"

"Look, White Eagle! I'm fed up. I want out of this place now! Don't start moaning at the way I do things! Using fancy words and explanations will only prolong the situation."

Dunn remained where he was. *What in the blazes?* He looked around slowly. *How does she know my name?* It was the only part of Maggie's thick Irish accent that he'd understood. Whenever she was angry, her softened dialect went straight back to old Dun Laoghaire.

Maggie marched towards him, red hair flying, dress flapping, and temper flaring! "Officer Dunn, stop pretending that you haven't heard me. Stand up, stand up now!" she ordered.

For god's sake! The fearless Dunn was scared to death. He slowly began to stand but refrained from reaching his full height. With one hand outstretched toward Maggie and a rifle in the other, he gestured that she should go with him. "Come with me before you get us both killed," he said hurriedly.

Maggie continued to walk toward him at a rapid pace. "Officer Dunn, look at me. The bullets: you can see them penetrate me, but they don't harm me. Why do you think that is?"

As she reached him, he stood to full height. His six foot, one inch frame looked down at the young, slightly built woman in front of him. He grasped some of what she was saying but for the most part struggled with her accent. "I…I…have no idea—"

"Look at yourself: the bullets go right through you in the same way they do me."

He knew she was telling the truth but still preferred to lie to himself. "Are you insane, woman? I'm giving you the chance to come with me willingly before I take you by force."

Hands on hips, Maggie shot daggers. "Put your hands anywhere near me and I won't be responsible for my actions, that I won't. And don't dare address me as 'woman' in that tone again! Where are your damn manners?"

Dunn's expression was a mixture of amusement and admiration. As if she could handle him! She barely reached his shoulder. He remained silent. He was tired. A part of him wanted to listen but the guilt he carried blocked his integrity.

Breathing hard, Maggie calmed her voice. "The bullets, the bombs. None of them makes the slightest bit of difference to you because— you know why, stop denying it!"

"I have no idea what you're talking about. Look, I'm tired. Stop making this more difficult than it already is."

"Spirits, Dunn, spirits! You know very well that you're in spirit form."

"Spirit form! What the hell is that supposed to mean?"

"It means that you're dead, Officer Dunn—"

"Maggie! Diplomacy, I said—damn it!" White Eagle pulled her back. The situation was getting risky. "I'm going to end this now if you don't calm down!"

She looked at him incredulously. "Why? What's the problem?"

"The problem is that if you scare him, it's another chance gone to waste. That's not fair on him or his men! And all because of an irate Maggie—!"

Dunn's stomach flipped over and over. "Dead? Yes, right…I'm sorry, Miss…err, Miss, Mrs.," he shook his head. "I haven't got time for this." He made a move towards her.

She jumped back and threw her arms out in front of her. "Don't touch me! You must listen. You have a responsibility toward those men!"

He stopped abruptly. "I don't need you to tell me what my responsibilities are!" They stared at each other in silence until Dunn decided to humour her. "How is it I can feel my heart banging inside my chest if I'm dead?"

Maggie's face softened. "What you feel is the etheric counterpart of your physical heart. The etheric body is identical to the physical body only it's a lighter, more transparent energy. Man has more than one body—at least seven, in fact, some believe twelve, thirteen even. I believe the number is infinite—all are energy in one form or another. As your vibrations speed up, the lighter you become. The physical body is the densest because its velocity is the slowest." She felt agitated. There was no time for explanations. "Look—we haven't got time to go into it now. You'll learn all about this stuff again once you go back to the spirit world where you belong!"

He barked at her more out of nerves than anything else. "Etheric what speeding up? What kind of tripe is that? I don't believe in life after death and all that claptrap."

"Because you fear it, Officer Dunn!"

"I fear nothing!"

"You deny everything! That's fear."

"How do you know me?"

Maggie didn't feel sympathy but she did feel the need to be firm. She went with her instincts. "My spirit guide gave me the lowdown on you. You led your men into battle despite the warnings from your sergeant that you'd get them all killed. Your ego wouldn't listen to him and you went ahead regardless. Now you blame yourself for their deaths." She raised an eyebrow. "Forgive yourself, Officer Dunn!"

Dunn froze. His square jaw dropped loose before it snapped shut again. He ran his tongue around his dry lips as if trying to seek out the right words, but none came. His dark good looks were now menacing, dangerous. "Huh!" he gasped. "What did you say?"

Maggie felt unnerved. There was something different about his eyes. So intense was his glare that it felt like a hundred cigarettes were being stubbed out on her skin. "I said my spirit guide told me that you ignored the warnings from your sergeant and can't forgive—"

He leapt at her and grabbed her shoulders. "Where did you get that information? You're a damn spy, aren't you? That's what all this is about!"

Maggie struggled but she didn't stand a chance. Dunn gripped hard and wasn't about to let her go.

White Eagle cut in. "Maggie, stay calm; don't let him see that you're scared. Just like the bullets, he can't harm you. It's your own fear that allows him to cling to you."

But Maggie was scared. "What do I do?" she fired back, still trying to pull free from Dunn.

Dunn thought she was talking to him. "You come with me!"

"Tell him that you'll take him to his dead body. I'll lead you there. He knows you're right but won't admit it. Maggie, stop struggling! Don't show fear. It breeds more fear, and he's already terrified."

"He's terrified!" she said out loud. "Dunn, stop being so bloody stupid! I'm not a spy." She tossed her head and looked at him as if he were pathetic! "A pregnant spy! Out here! By Jesus, I thought you had to have brains to pull rank in the British army!"

"There's no other explanation for you knowing my name and holding details that you should know nothing about."

"Take your damned hands off me! You have no right to—" She stopped struggling and stared him down. "Let me go!" Her tone was icy. He did as she ordered. "Thank you! I gave you the explanation, and in light of the overwhelming evidence how much proof do you need?" She beckoned him. "Come with me."

"To where?"

"To a trench behind that wall over there." She pointed toward his soldiers. "Behind your soldiers, more or less."

"My soldiers…how do you know—?"

Impatience registered on her face. "I'm not going to keep repeating myself. Follow me, Officer Dunn." She looked straight ahead and walked fast. "It's high time you and your men were on your way."

"I...I don't think..."

Something told her that the only way she would get Dunn to face himself was to use his troops as a weapon. She stopped and turned, offering her hand. "Come with me, Officer Dunn, if you want to lead your men to freedom—"

White Eagle cut in. "Maggie, warn him first. It will be too much of a shock if you let him come face to face with his own dead body, and the bodies of his men."

She answered telepathically, *I thought you said he knows he's dead?*

"I said he has a knowing. His subconscious sends him the information but he ignores it—his conscious awareness changes it to suit his programming. It's a kind of protection mechanism the mind uses. As soon as an individual sends out stress signals the mind reacts by blocking the source. In Dunn's case the source is about to hit him full on, as soon as he witnesses the bodies. If you don't warn him first, the fear will consume him and in all probability he'll head right back to the trench and tell his men to fire at you. If that happens, then they'll be stuck here until we can come up with something else. You're the fourth medium we've tried; most of them don't get past the horrors that surround them. One got as far as Dunn pouncing on him before he high-tailed it out of here." He paused. "You're doing alright, Maggie."

Her eyes darted quickly towards the trench and then at White Eagle before they rested on Dunn, one of the bravest men in the British army, yet he looked lost, ready to crumble at any moment. She kept hold of his hand. "I'm taking you to your dead body." She spoke gently. She knew her words would either fascinate him, or send him over the edge.

Visibly shaking. "My dead body?" He dropped Maggie's hand as if it were toxic, spun around, and headed quickly in the opposite direction. "I don't know what your game is but I do know that I've had enough of it!"

Maggie knew that if she let him go now he would remain here until someone, something, somehow could get the stubborn so-and-so to listen. "You really are a coward at heart, aren't you?"

He stopped abruptly, turned, and faced her. "A coward? Me?"

"You haven't got the guts to come with me. Go on, admit it! You may act like the big hero in your uniform, put on an outside show to impress others, but I see right through you. You're nothing but a bloody coward!"

"You know nothing about me. I'm a lot of things but a coward isn't one of them." He marched away.

Maggie grabbed hold of his arm and ran alongside him. Breathing heavily, her voice sounded desperate. "Then come with me, Officer Dunn. Do it for your men at least." He stopped. She looked up at him. "Don't jeopardise their chance of freedom again."

He could see the pleading in her eyes. "Alright, I'll follow you, but only if you agree to come back with me should the exercise prove futile."

"Thank God!" she said, relieved. She smiled at him. "I agree."

"Nothing to do with God; thank yourself!" Dunn retorted.

She put her arm through Dunn's. They walked toward the trench where his soldiers hid. "You don't believe in God?"

"I wouldn't say I don't believe. I just don't think it is as cut and dried as some say it is."

"Cut and dried?" she questioned.

Dunn looked thoughtful. "You know: some big cheese sits in an ivory tower looking down on his naughty children, condemning and judging. Surely if God exists he'd have something better to do."

"You would think so," she said, with a hearty laugh. "I know what my idea of God is, though I can't speak for anybody else."

The sound of Maggie's laughter warmed his heart. It had been such a long time since he'd heard laughter like that. Free from apprehension, not half-hearted, or laughter for the sake of it. He seemed to relax a bit. "Probably a woman! Women rule the world. You're proof of that: out here, giving me orders!"

"Oh, I'm a bossy one, that much we can agree on," she said, with a glint in her eye. "Yes, I'm strong and opinionated." She shrugged. "Big deal! It's funny how some of us are christened opinionated if we don't agree with other people's opinions! This is who I am whether people like it or not." An expression of innocence and questioning softened her face. "It's who I am, that's all! I don't understand why we put pressure on each other—you know, like we can only be accepted if we're one way or the other."

"I'd love to hear it." He stopped walking and looked at her. God was something he'd never really thought about, let alone talked about. But for some reason Maggie intrigued him.

"Hear what?"

"Your opinion on God."

"Oh…well, I wouldn't describe it as an opinion. More of an idea that accepts input as it goes along. But regardless of how much input goes into it, my basic idea of God will stay simple."

"Simple?"

"Yes…it's everything. God is everything. I'm God, you're God. The male, the female, the wildlife, the planets, the universes, all of creation, everything. God evolves with me at my pace. It seems ludicrous to me that God would hang about waiting to be found, and only turn up when I've suffered enough, or collected enough good points in God's opinion."

He looked at her, puzzled. "I've never really sat and thought about it. Maybe I should have."

"No! There's no rush. What's that old saying? Oh, yes: when the student is ready, the teacher will appear…in some cases, maybe. But what if it were the other way around? When the teacher is ready, the student will appear? I tend to think that we're all teachers as well as students." She slowed her pace, feeling Dunn's reluctance. As they approached the trench where his men hid, he was hesitant. Maggie turned to him. "Your men, they already sort of know…like you do."

"What shall I say to them? Shall I ask them to come with me or shall I go on ahead?"

She pointed. "It's up to you. See the wall behind your trench?"

He looked across. "Yes."

"That is the dividing line between here and the spirit world. The trench where your bodies are lying is parallel to the trench your men—their spirits—hide in. Once you and your men climb over the wall, there is no turning back. You will have made the choice to return home. In other words, you've allowed the light to come for you."

The rest of the soldiers climbed out of the trench one by one. With MacTavish leading the way they walked the short distance towards Maggie and Dunn.

"Miss," MacTavish nodded.

Dunn looked at Maggie. "This is...umm," then realised that he didn't know her name—

"Maggie," she said, shaking hands with the soldiers as they introduced themselves.

"Maggie has some, err, interesting news...she's here to tell us." Feeling embarrassed, he struggled to explain himself. He hunched his shoulders at Maggie, just as a bomb whistled overhead and exploded within inches of where they stood. The soldiers dived to ground but Maggie and Dunn remained calm.

Dunn looked down at his men. It was as if the bomb were a sign from the universe—he was about to drop one a lot more powerful in its aftermath! "The bombs, they can't harm us anymore. Maggie here, that's what she's come to tell us."

The young private got to his feet first. "We're already dead, aren't we?"

Feeling nervous, MacTavish sat up, reached inside his jacket pocket for his tobacco tin, and started to roll a cigarette. "Well, if I'm fucking dead—oh, pardon, Miss!" He looked up at Maggie. "It's been so long since we've had female company." He put the tin back in his pocket and continued, "If I'm dead, I may as well enjoy one last cigarette!"

Their laughter broke through the uneasy atmosphere. MacTavish was joking, yet he kind of believed it. It seemed ridiculous. He didn't feel any different but there was something not quite right...something he couldn't fathom.

When the laughter died down, all eyes were on Maggie. She looked at each of them as she spoke. "I know it sounds strange, but…," she looked at Miles, "…yes! In answer to your question, you're all dead, or 'in spirit.' It's your spirit that lives on. Death—it's just a transition, a move to a new home." She swallowed. They were all looking at her in silence. "It's beautiful on the other side," she said, in the hope of keeping them as calm as possible. She closed her eyes and remembered the love she'd experienced with the Spanish soldiers. She sighed, and opened her eyes again. "The love you feel, the freedom," she shook her head. "I can't describe it. But I can tell you this, there is nothing to be afraid of—"

"What about my cigarettes?"

Laughter, reluctant, filled the air once again. Maggie smiled at MacTavish, who puffed away on a cigarette as if it were his last. "What about them?"

"Can I take them to the other side?"

This time the men exploded into genuine, hearty laughter.

"Is that all you bleedin' think about?" Cockney George said, exasperated. "You've just been told you're dead, sarge, or weren't you listening?"

MacTavish got to his feet. "I know, I'm just joking with you—"

"Actually, you can take them!" Maggie cut in. "There's nothing you can do here that you can't do on the other side, so if you still feel the need to smoke, nobody will deny you."

"Really?" MacTavish looked astonished.

"Really." She was looking at Dunn, who was walking slowly towards the wall. "But eventually the need to remain attached to the physical and its habits will wear away," she said hurriedly. "Excuse me."

She caught up to Dunn. "Are you ready?"

He cocked his leg over the wall and sat with his legs dangling from either side of it. "I'm ready. Can I give you a hand over?"

Maggie noticed how rigid he sat, and how he refused to look at the side where the bodies lay. "No, you're on your own from now on. I can't cross the line. I could if I wanted to remain in spirit, but my time hasn't come yet. I still have lots to do on Earth."

He jumped off the wall as if he'd been zapped with electricity, and landed in a heap at Maggie's feet. Shocked, she stumbled backwards. "What's the matter? Are you okay?"

He got up quickly and brushed himself down. "You mean this is it? Once I land on the other side of that wall I can't change my mind?"

"Yes. I thought I'd made that clear earlier."

"You probably did. It…it's just all such a shock....I don't know if I'm ready."

Maggie walked over to the wall and rested her forearms on it. She leaned over and peered into the trench. They were all there: Dunn, MacTavish, Miles, and Cockney George. All lay in a heap on top of each other, shot to pieces. She felt the nausea and the overwhelming sadness rise up again. *All the world's a stage, and all the men and women merely players,* she reminded herself. She took a few moments to contain her emotions before stepping back to offer Dunn encouragement. "You don't have to go over the wall. But do you really want to remain in this, this…," she looked around, "…hovel for a moment longer?"

He didn't answer. Maggie noticed he was backing away again. "Dunn, I won't leave until your men have had a chance to speak for themselves. They have the right to make their own decisions." She glared at him. "If you don't give it them, I will."

He looked deep into her eyes, and saw her determination. He wanted to confirm what he knew was true, yet he just couldn't push himself to do it.

"You can see from here but it isn't pretty, not pretty at all." She offered her hand. "I know this isn't easy for you, but once the light comes, all traces of fear, of sadness, and loss…even the guilt, will leave you."

He was still hesitant. "I don't know…what if the bodies aren't behind that wall? What then?"

"Stop pretending! You know very well that they are! If you want to remain here that's all well and good—"

White Eagle broke in. He was visible to Maggie only. The men didn't need added confusion to deal with. "They're getting anxious on my side, Maggie. You're going to have to kick Dunn into touch. We'll come back for him another time. Give the others their chance."

She ignored his instructions. She'd get Dunn over no matter what! "Do you want me to ask MacTavish to ID them?"

"No! No, no, no. I should do it." He turned and looked over at the wall as if it was about to devour him. In one sense it was.

Maggie turned and looked up at him. "Take as much time as you want—"

White Eagle interrupted again. "On that side maybe, but some of the relatives on this side are limited as to how long they can hang around in Earth's atmosphere—"

"Wangle it, then!" she snapped.

"You don't understand. I can't just please myself! There are other factors—"

"I'm not interested! You can see how hard this is. What more can I do? Tell your factors that!"

White Eagle had had enough! "I'm not asking, I'm not arguing, I'm telling you! Now get on with it—"

"Who are you talking to?" Dunn cut in.

"Don't ask!" she answered, distractedly. "Look, Dunn, I don't want to rush you but I've been informed that we have to get a move on."

He was taken aback. "Why?"

"I don't know...I think it's something to do with energy and the different vibratory rates between Earth and the spirit world; that and a lot of other stuff. Anyway, I've not got time to find out and you've not got time to listen." She threw him a firm gaze. "Let's go!"

"Jesus, I'm scared." He was embarrassed to admit it.

"It's okay to be scared." She grabbed his arms and shook him gently. "You'll be fine. If you only knew what awaits you. You'll look back and wonder why you left it this long, why you were ever afraid."

He inhaled deeply, held onto the breath, and exhaled so hard that the hair on Maggie's forehead lifted. They looked at each other. "Well, here we go," he said. He closed his eyes, turned from Maggie, and walked to the wall.

"Open your eyes," she said, encouraging him. "I've done it, so you can."

He opened his eyes. He couldn't hide his nervousness but he knew there was no going back. He peered over the wall slowly. The sight floored him. "Jesus! Jesus!" He staggered backwards. It wasn't the gruesome scene that bothered him. He was well used to blood and guts by then. It was the shock of seeing himself and his men dead on one side of the wall, but alive on the other.

Maggie clung to him. "Calm down," she urged. "Your men, do it for them." She knew that the next few seconds were critical. "You must forgive yourself, Officer Dunn."

Tears stung his eyes. He turned to Maggie. "I killed them! It's my fault! Their families—MacTavish has young kids, and you ask me to forgive myself!" He took out a small canister from the inside pocket of his jacket, unscrewed the lid, and knocked back its contents. "I led them to death." He took in large gulps of air. "I'll never forgive myself for that." He took another swig, and swallowed hard.

"You didn't! Everything comes down to choice. There are forces at work here that you've no idea of. Now stop feeling sorry for yourself and lead them to life in the spirit world. Their loved ones are waiting and so are yours."

Maggie knew that he could rid himself of any karma by leading his men over the wall into spirit. She prayed he'd make that decision. But whether he led them or not, her job was to make sure they all got the chance. If he didn't give it to them she'd have to step in—

"Feeling sorry for myself!" He removed his helmet, roughed up his hair, and put it back on again. "You have no idea how I feel."

"Officer Dunn," she seethed. "Your men. They have the right to leave this futile non-existence they're in! Now do I do it, or do you?"

"Me…I should, but—"

She put her finger up. "No buts. 'But' is an in-between word for indecision. Your men—call them over. You can stay here if you want, but I've a feeling you'd be on your own."

MacTavish shouted over, wanting to know what was going on. Dunn shouted back. "Give us a few more minutes." He peered at the bodies for a second time, as if in need of confirmation. He downed the rest of the whiskey in his canister and let his eyes linger for a few seconds more. "You're right," he sighed, "I'll do it."

Maggie let out a relieved sigh. "Once you cross the line, Officer Dunn, you won't look back, I can promise you that."

"I'm scared." This time he didn't feel ashamed to admit it.

"You won't be. As soon as your feet touch the ground on the other side of the wall, you'll be filled with an indescribable feeling of peace and love. Trust me."

He didn't know her at all, yet something in his gut told him that he could trust her. He savored her face. It was a beautiful face. "Maggie, I won't forget you." He kissed the top of her hand. "And for what it's worth, my name is Victor."

She was surprised to find that the kiss felt like any other, even though he was technically dead! "Victor." *How appropriate,* she thought.

He leant against the wall, arms folded. "MacTavish, Miles, Cockney—get over here!"

The men walked over. They were already feeling calm. Though it wasn't visible, soft tendrils of the light had started to edge in and infiltrate the area. It took just a few moments for love to explode and blow the war zone to kingdom come. The gunfire, the aircraft, the bombs: they all got quieter, quieter, and faded out of existence as the light crept into everything.

"Listen," Cockney George said.

"To what?" Miles asked.

"Nothing…silence. It's so peaceful all of a sudden." He nudged MacTavish, and nodded over at Dunn.

"Are you alright, sir?" Cockney asked.

Dunn's mind was in turmoil. He could feel the excitement mixed with apprehension churning about in his belly. "I'm fine. Listen up.

What I'm about to say is going to sound very strange." He paused, trying to find the words. "Beyond this wall is another trench that lies parallel to the one we dug. When I give the order I want you all to take a look inside it." Miles moved forward. "When I give the order, Miles," Dunn barked at him. The two men eyed each other. Miles knew without a doubt what he was about to find on the other side of the wall.

Dunn continued. "There are four dead soldiers lying in the trench. It's going to be a bit of a shock to you." Damn! *What to say?* "Look, the bodies, they belong to us…they're ours. Take a look—we're all dead!"

Well! Talk about being diplomatic! Maggie thought to herself, forgetting the battle she'd had with White Eagle earlier.

The soldiers knew it, yet they didn't! Was Dunn losing it? What does he mean by "We're all dead?" Too scared to move, too dumbstruck to ask questions, they simply stared at their commanding officer, baffled.

"I know it sounds ridiculous. I wouldn't have believed it either but it's true—"

Miles made the first move. "I knew it!" But he didn't bother to look into the trench. He leapt over the wall before anyone could stop him.

Both Maggie and Dunn reached out to grab him but it was too late. "MILES, NO!" Dunn shouted. "YOU CAN"T GET BACK!"

As soon as his feet touched the ground on the other side of the wall, the light appeared. It looked different this time. It wasn't spinning like earlier when it had come for the Spanish soldiers. It weaved its way out of the spiritual dimension into theirs like silver strands of mist that had been electrically charged. Slowly it formed into a huge network of light made up of millions of vibrant colours. The spirit forms inside it busied about and were easily visible even though they blended into the colours of the grid. Maggie would later describe it as a huge gridded city bustling with life.

Eyes wide, jaws hanging loose, the soldiers stood awestruck as a kaleidoscope of colour moved across their faces. It was a miraculous sight. Trancelike, they couldn't take their eyes off the colours and the geometrical patterns that were contained within the light. It touched something inside them, something they'd felt separated from while staying on Earth. But now they were being given the chance to bond with it again, and the more they soaked up the light the more they realised that they'd never been separated from it in the first place.

Miles stopped dead! He felt so…different. Kind of lifted…bigger. He looked at his hands. He could see the glow from his aura reaching out to infinity. He looked at his mates. They could see the elation on his face. "I don't want to get back—MY GOD!" He sucked in his breath, clutched at his stomach, and bent double. "I've never felt anything like it." He turned and looked towards the light. "GRANDDAD!" he waved furiously. "GRANDMA!"

Two figures emerged from the light-craft and hurried over to him. The nearer they got to him, the denser they became until their forms changed from a humanoid mass of geometrical, coloured light, to the familiar grandparent likeness he was used to.

"Trevor, Trevor sweetheart. Here! Let me tune you in a bit." She bent down and placed her hand on his heart. "You'll be fine…there. Try and straighten up. Deep breaths, deep breaths."

In an instant, Miles adapted to the change. He looked at his grandma. "What is that?"

She was a chubby woman with short, curly hair and flushed cheeks, a typical mother hen type who'd be right at home baking and stitching quilts. "There's a few things that cause it—it's not easy to let go of the physical, even when it's already gone! It's one of the first things they try and get us used to over here—levitation!" She laughed. "There's a levitation class! You get a choice in what you're going to jump off, you know, like a mountain or a bridge. They even have replicas of things on Earth, like the Tower of London and the Statue of Liberty." She cocked her head back. "Bloody scary, your first jump! Anyway, less chatter—come here, let me kiss you." She cupped his face in her hands, kissed him like she'd never let go. The love and happiness she radiated could be felt by everybody.

"Come on, it's time to go. There'll be plenty of time for celebrations later." His granddad slapped him on the back. "I'd hug you if she'd let me get anywhere near you."

"Give me a moment, Granddad."

Private Miles walked over to the wall. The closer he got to the rest of the men, the more luminous he appeared. His aura sparkled, and like the grid it was a mixture of vibrant colours that blended together. He wanted to shake hands with the rest of the lads and encourage them to follow him. He threw his leg over the wall but was thrown backwards, as if he'd slammed, full pelt, into an invisible pane of glass. Shaken, he got himself together. "I guess this is about as far as I can go, so I'll say my goodbyes from here, lads." He turned to leave but stopped again, a thoughtful expression on his face. "I hope you decide to come home. This is where we belong…there's no fear, only love."

Miles walked into the waiting arms of his grandparents and together they walked towards the light. He was in awe as the closer he got to it, the more it took on the shape of a huge webbed ship of some kind, a spaceship of colour with a ramp made up of the same. When their feet touched the ramp their bodies took on the same density and colours of the ship. It was a grid of colour, but it was still easy to tell who was who on board.

Just as Miles and his grandparents were about to walk through the gateway onto the ship, they sidestepped out of the way for a small child who couldn't have been more than five years old. Oblivious to them, she ran screaming and laughing out of the light and down the ramp with a young woman chasing after her. The woman lunged forward, gripped hold of the girl's hand, crouched down to the same height, and stroked her black wavy hair. She spoke gently as if calming her down, and then pointed at MacTavish.

"Daddy! Daddy!" she screamed excitedly, running towards him.

"Jessie!" he whispered, disbelievingly. *It is her!* "JESSIE!"

Without thinking, MacTavish catapulted over the wall and was immediately hit with a sensation of intense love. Like Miles, he clutched his stomach and sucked in a large gulp of air as the love tore through him like an electrical tidal wave. It took him a few moments to compose himself.

"Daddy! Daddy!"

Hands on knees, breathing hard trying to adjust, he looked up. For a few seconds, he couldn't move from where he stood. He saw her. Running as fast as her little legs would carry her. A young woman paced behind—her spirit mother.

His arms outstretched, he sobbed, "Jessie, baby, I can't believe it!" He dropped to his knees. She all but disappeared in his arms. He'd lost his precious child to cancer just before the war started. He clung to her, buried his face in her hair, took in her smell, the softness of her skin, and the wonder of her baby chubbiness. "Jessie, look at you, you're beautiful!" Overwhelmed, he cried as hard as he had done on the day she'd died, the day he thought he'd never see her again. But this time he enjoyed the tears. He wanted to put them in a jar and keep them forever.

She wiped his tears away with her little hand and smiled at him, still missing a few teeth. "Daddy, don't cry. You shouldn't be sad." She looked concerned. "It's nice in the light, you'll like it."

"I'm no' sad, wean. I'm no' sad."

"Come on, we have to go." She took hold of his arm and tried to lift him to his feet.

He scooped her up in one arm, turned around, and waved at the three figures on the opposite side of the wall, too overwhelmed to say anything. He walked into the light with his daughter in his arms.

Maggie, Dunn, and Cockney cried openly. "Look at the state of us," Dunn laughed. "We'd never win a war in this state."

"On the contrary, Victor, love is the only way to win a war," Maggie said.

"Yes, I'm beginning to realise that." He looked at Cockney. "Well, Cockney, are you ready?"

"I don't know. Do I go alone or shall we go together? I don't have any relatives that I know of. I was brought up in an orphanage and I don't have many fond memories of that miserable hole, I can tell you that much." He thought about the years of physical and mental abuse he'd suffered. As soon as he was old enough he'd joined the army as an escape route from the despair he'd experienced throughout his childhood.

"There's somebody waiting for you, don't worry about that," Maggie said. "It's very rare for a spirit to have no relatives or friends. See that lovely lady there?" Maggie looked across at an elderly woman who hung back, waiting for the right time to approach. "Her name is Nell. She's your spirit guide."

Nell walked over to them. "Hello." She looked at Cockney and offered him her hand. "There are a lot of people waiting to meet you."

"Waiting to meet me? Like who?"

"Relatives that you never knew in this life: your birth mother and father, brothers, sisters. There's a lot for you to catch up on."

"I'm not interested!" he said aggressively. "They never wanted to know me when I was alive; why should I give a toss about 'em now?"

"Your interests and emotions will change once you join us on this side. You'll see the bigger picture—the reasons for your choices." Nell concentrated on sending healing and love to Cockney. "Come with me, George. I'll take you to places you never thought existed and show you beauty you never thought you'd see. You'll be free from the pain you've endured in this lifetime."

Cockney stared at her. She was familiar somehow…her words, her smile, the dark skin and black curly hair with slashes of grey here and there. And the huge bosom! He'd never forget how safe he'd felt as a kid when she'd nestled him to her. Then it struck him! "IT'S YOU!" he shouted out. "I've dreamt about you all my life." He recalled the dreams he'd had from as far back as he could remember. "The kind lady! You were the only kindness I knew…was ever shown. I wanted to sleep just so I could be with you."

Nell smiled. "That's right, only now you don't have to go to sleep to see me." She stood waiting, her arms outstretched. "Well? I'm not going to hang about forever. Are you coming or not?"

Cockney could feel her kindness penetrate him the way it did when he shared his dreams with her. He didn't need asking twice. He grinned. "I'll just say goodbye."

He leant over and kissed Maggie on both cheeks before turning to Dunn. The two men shook hands vigorously.

"Good luck, old chap!" Dunn said.

"You too, Officer Dunn."

"Victor," he corrected. "I'm sure there are no such formalities where we're going."

"See you, gov," he winked. "See you on the other side." Cockney jumped the wall. The love hit him full on, and he reacted in much the same way as the others had. Gasping for breath, he collapsed, clutching at his solar plexus.

Nell hurried across. She put one hand on his stomach, and the other on the top of his head. "Try to stay calm. You just need to adjust to the change in frequency." It didn't take long for the intense sensation that charged him to alter to his vibratory rate so that he could withstand it. It wasn't that the love sensation was painful. It just knocked the stuffing out of them.

Cockney clung to Nell as if he'd never let her go. The dreams they'd shared were the only experience of mother love he'd had while growing up.

"Come on, George, we'd better make a move." They walked into the light together, laughing and reminiscing at dreams he was able to pick out at random from his energy field.

"Wow! It's like looking at a set of living photos," he said, captivated.

"Dreams are real." Nell winked at him cannily. "They're a life unto themselves. If only we could get people to realise that while still on Earth."

Dunn and Maggie looked on in silence. The atmosphere had taken on a wistful air. "I guess that just leaves me, Maggie. I'm kind of looking forward to it now after witnessing the joy and celebrations." He looked pensive. "I'd never have believed it." His eyes were still on Cockney and Nell.

"Seeing is nothing—wait until you feel it." She turned to him. "I wish I could come with you."

He looked at her, puzzled, noticing a sadness in her but even a frown couldn't spoil her lovely face. "One day."

I could be with my child there. Something that isn't possible if I stay here—

"Penny for them?" Dunn shook her out of her melancholy.

"Oh…nothing really, I was just thinking how ironic life can be."

He laughed quietly. "Eh, it's that, alright!"

Maggie's attention was drawn to a short, stout, balding man in the distance. "Gerry is here. The two of you don't look alike."

"Gerry? Gerry who?"

Maggie looked puzzled. "Gerry Brambles—your brother, Gerry?"

"I don't have a brother. I have a sister but she's alive and kicking as far as I'm aware. Besides! His last name is different?"

"Strange! He's adamant he's your brother," she said, going off the information Gerry was relaying to her telepathically.

Gerry bustled over, red-faced and excitable. "Hello, I didn't get a chance to brief you properly, Maggie. Sorry about that." He looked at Dunn. "Hello, Victor." Once Gerry started to talk he didn't stop for a breath. "I'm sorry to put you on the spot like this, but under the circumstances I don't have much choice. Most of your close relatives, including your mother and father, are still alive, you see. I mean, I haven't been dead that long myself, which is why I'm so out of breath. I'm finding it hard to adjust to the air down here. You see, the thing is, when we first pass over our bodies take on a different…um, err, makeup. Yes, let's use the word 'makeup'—it'll be easier to understand—so we can more readily accept the air, which is alive by the way, something we don't realise on Earth." He cocked his head to the side as if in deep thought. "The air on Earth is full of all sorts of junk. It has to work extra hard at filtering itself out to enable it to give life to those that breath it in. Unfortunately, this makes it a lot less forceful…more heavy." He pulled his face. "Am I explaining myself?"

Dunn was lost. "Er…no!"

"The life-force in the air on Earth is buried under mounds of crap! And then of course, over here, we're on a bit of a higher level, not that this means we're better or superior, just a bit more evolved, which means that we from the higher levels can enter into the atmosphere of the lower levels, but if the lower levels try to get through to ours, they feel as if they can't breathe. They are automatically blocked from entering. The dark have been trying to come up with a way to break through this system for eons; they simply don't understand—"

"Gerry, stop talking and get on with it!" A spirit form from the light-craft waved impatiently.

Startled, Gerry looked back at the ship. "Sorry…yes, yes, of course!"

Maggie and Dunn simply stared at him with blank expressions. They could see how excited he was and had long since given up trying to get a word in edgeways.

"Anyway, Victor, when I was asked if I'd like to bring you over to spirit, I jumped at the chance." He pushed his black-rimmed spectacles up off the tip of his nose. "Absolutely,' I said to the official from the resettlement department. She's a very nice woman, what's her name now…?" he said, stroking his chin—

"Gerry, for God's sake, man! Get a bloody move on. You're holding up transition."

Gerry turned and fired back. "Alright, alright, Harper. Stop harping on!" Flustered, he turned to Maggie and Dunn. "God, he's got the right name…and always in such a bloody rush."

Maggie and Dunn glanced at each other, tongue in cheek. Gerry was oblivious to his own lack of restraint. *Gerry Brambles. Take away the first letter in his last name and what have you got?* Maggie smiled to herself. "How come the air isn't affecting us? We're in spirit form but we're not having the problems that you are with it."

"Well…your makeup hasn't changed. It won't until you're on this side of the wall." He pointed to the silver-blue cord that looked like a strand of thick electrical current attached to Maggie. "As you can see, Maggie, you still have the lifeline attached to your physical body—wherever you've left it. You're still getting your breath from the Earth…you're in a kind of dreamscape atmosphere, only you're aware of it. Being the gifted medium that you are, you have this ability."

He turned to Victor. "As for you, Victor, we know you're not one of Earth's because your lifeline has gone. You're no longer attached to your physical body. You just think you are."

Dunn turned and looked at Maggie. "What's attached to Maggie? I don't see anything…and I don't find it difficult to breathe here either."

"Because even though you've passed into spirit, you still choose to hang about in Earth's atmosphere. You still believe yourself to be a physical being, so you won't see Maggie's lifeline—her gift enables her to see it; and as far as the air on Earth is concerned, you won't have a problem with it until you've accepted that you are technically without a physical counterpart. In other words: brown bread, old chap. You haven't quite made the transition. Not until you jump the wall. It all comes down to thoughts and beliefs, and our creative powers. We see what we want to see, feel what we want to feel, and all that."

Dunn stroked his chin. "Sounds damn confusing to me…lifeline, vibrations, living air! What a load of hogwash—and you're my brother, you say. How can that be? I never had a brother."

"Our father, your namesake, the honourable Victor Dunn, had an affair with my mother when you were about three years old. Your mother, Florence, found out about it and told him that he was to have nothing to do with me or my mother, or she'd walk out with you and your sister and let the world know what a rotten bastard he was—"

Dunn went on the defensive. "Steady on! Dad and me have always been close. Best friends, in fact."

Gerry put his palm up in front of him. "Oh, him being a rotten bastard isn't my opinion," he said, flustered. "They were your mother's words, and Dad being Dad, he caved in to her threats. Well, apart from one. He promised her that he would have nothing to do with my mother, but there was no way he could ignore me. Florence protested but he called her bluff. He knew that she'd never leave him; she was too worried about what people would think. Anyway, to cut a long story short, I did have a lot of contact with him, and he made sure neither me nor Mum went short. He carried on seeing my mother, still sees her, though Florence refuses to acknowledge it."

He fished through his pockets and produced an old black and white photo of himself with his mother and father. "See?" But when he tried to pass it to Dunn, he encountered the same problem that Miles had experienced earlier. His hand seemed to hit an invisible pane of glass, whereas Dunn's hand went right through it, and seemingly through the hand of his brother. He put his hand to his forehead. "Oh, I'd forgotten about that…it's the force field. We can't go into the lower levels without being accompanied by a guide. It's a safety regulation. Sorry, Victor. You won't be able to hold it until you've made the transition to the other side of the wall, but you can see it, right?"

Dunn stretched his neck to get a closer look. "Well, I'll be damned! And I never had a clue about any of it until now. Yep, that's dear old Dad alright." He noted how happy his father and the woman in the picture looked. "He and Mum were always miserable together. As I got older I used to wonder why they'd stuck it out."

Gerry removed his glasses. "We've got a lot of catching up to do."

"Why do you need glasses over there?" Dunn asked, bemused. "I'd have thought any physical defects would have been buried with the body."

Gerry was impressed with Dunn's observation. "Not much gets past you. When we pass over we don't suddenly change into something we don't recognise. It would be too traumatic—"

Maggie cut in. "Plus it makes my job as a medium a lot easier. If spirits come to me with a message for a loved one, I have to be able to describe them to the person on this side. If he or she didn't retain their characteristics it would be very difficult for my sitters to recognise them."

"Two good reasons! There are a few others…habit, familiarity." Gerry chuckled. "I've not been dead that long. Sometimes I just forget that I don't need them." He burst into full-blown laughter. "We have a bloke with one leg who still hobbles around over there until we remind him—'Bertie,' we shout, 'grow your leg back, man!'" He noticed the baffled look on his brother's face. "It's an energy thing," he advised between laughs. "Sometimes the daft bugger is so startled he falls over and flays around on his back shouting for help. He gets no sympathy from the rest of us. We just stand there laughing until he realises he isn't legless anymore—"

"Gerry! Move your backside, or I'll personally see to it that you don't get to cross another living soul! You're holding the damn lot of us up!"

Gerry looked back hastily at the light-craft. Everyone had disappeared into it apart from Harper, who was having a dicky fit trying to wave them in. "Victor, I have to leave. They won't stay much longer." He stretched out his hand. "Will you come with me?" he asked, looking hopeful.

Maggie beamed. "What a lovely surprise, Victor: a brother you never knew you had."

He bent down and kissed her cheek. "Yes. Sad, really. We could have had so much fun growing up together."

"You'll be doing that anyway!"

Dunn hesitated, not understanding what she meant. "I guess this is it, Maggie. I hope our paths cross again someday."

"I'm sure they will," she said through a yawn. "Oh, excuse me; I'm so tired all of a sudden."

"How will you get back?" he asked curiously.

"The same way I came. It will take me too long to explain—now go! That...ship—whatever it is, is ready to leave."

Unable to resist, he wrapped her up in his arms, lifted her off her feet, and kissed her passionately full on her lovely plump lips. "Sorry! I know I'm taking liberties." Embarrassed, he backed off. "It's just that it's been so long since I've tasted a woman, and I've no idea how long it'll be before I get the chance again!"

It was the last thing Maggie expected. She simply stared at him, flabbergasted! *The cheeky...* It was the first time she'd had a passionate encounter with a dead person! She couldn't understand why it felt so, so, physical, until White Eagle cut into her thoughts. "If you could see your face," he chuckled. "No harm done, Maggie! A part of you wanted it, you know—"

"I did not!"

"Come on, Maggie. You're quite taken by the officer's good looks, and his uniform. A part of you was hoping he would wrestle you to the ground earlier—"

Mortified, she retorted, "Absolutely not! I'm spoken for!"

White Eagle loved to tease her. "By whom? The priest or your husband?"

"Very funny!" She smiled. "It was…er…nice. Very umm…"

"Physical?"

"Yes. Why is that?"

"Spirits tend to remain physical in their thinking for a while. You know that."

"Yes, but even so, I wouldn't have thought they would feel physical to me."

"Once he's jumped the wall and his vibrations have changed he won't. But right now, his main focus is still on Earth so his thinking will create that physical aspect of self that he's used to. What he gave you was a piece of his creative thinking and, of course, you gave him a piece of yours."

"I'm sorry, Maggie. I shouldn't have done that. Friends, I hope." Victor offered his hand.

She took it, and smiled warmly. "Friends."

"I hope he knows how lucky he is." Dunn looked at her bump and vaulted over the wall. Just like the others, he had no choice but to succumb to the love as it attacked him from all sides. Gerry held out his hand. Victor recovered as soon as they touched. The two brothers shook hands for the first time.

"We'd better run before they kill us!" Gerry laughed. "No pun intended."

Dunn was stunned at the overwhelming sensations that charged through him. "My God," he cried out. "Maggie, the love—"

"Let's go, let's go!" Gerry shouted frantically. "There's no time left!"

Harper jumped from the light-craft and raced full pelt towards them. "Move it! Board the ship now!" he shouted.

Maggie watched as Victor and Gerry sprinted in the direction of the light. When they made it, they jumped on board, swinging onto what looked like a drawbridge as it rose, Victor first, then Gerry, and finally Harper. As soon as the drawbridge closed, the craft shot off at terrific speed in a straight upward motion. It made no sound as it glided smoothly through millions of stars and galaxies, all sparkling and changing colour in an indigo sky.

Maggie stood alone. Mesmerized, she watched it fade into a memory.

11.

"Maggie…Maggie." She could hear White Eagle's voice. She turned around expecting to see him but was brought back down to Earth by the blazing midday sun. She turned her head away, squinted, and automatically put her hand up to shield her eyes. Still feeling a bit disorientated, she leant back against the wall. She wasn't sure where she was at first, but it was only a matter of seconds before she realised that she was back in the old ramparts.

She got to her feet slowly, stretched, and rolled her head from side to side. Her long ponytail swung behind her until the white lace holding it together slipped to the ground. The waves rolled down her back like a gust of autumn leaves. She shook her head, raking her fingers through her hair to untangle any knots. She picked up the lace and fixed another ponytail.

She made her way to the café with a happy feeling in her belly that was so strong it felt physical, like a hundred tadpoles wriggling about. *Was it safe to be happy?*

She stopped and sat down on the ancient bricks. They were warm from the sun. She took off her shoes and twiddled her bare feet about in the grass. It was cool and refreshing. She looked over at the hills in the distance. They looked alive, like great beings presiding over Earth and its inhabitants. Maybe they were? She sat and thought for a moment. Hers was a different world, a world of spirits and supernatural phenomena that didn't exist. A world she kept hidden from those who feared it but shared with those rare few who knew it.

The excited chatter of children caught her attention. She looked across at the wooden bench where she'd sat with David earlier. Two lines of children and a couple of teachers were making their way across the road to the old ramparts.

Just in time. Had they arrived a moment earlier she would have had to leave Dunn alone until another day. She stood up. She was looking forward to Emilie's coffee.

As she approached the café, the smell of soup and freshly baked bread and pastries made her mouth water. Café de Flore was their favourite. She and David had fallen in love with its charm and quaintness, and they even had a favourite seat nestled beneath the ivy. "Their love seat," the owners called it.

Hanging baskets filled with red and yellow begonias swayed to and fro at the side of the doorway, and the window boxes were filled with purple and gold pansies. The cocktail of colour mixed with the emerald green ivy provided good contrast against the whitewashed stone of the café.

The owners, Emilie and Henri Bedeau, always made a huge fuss over Maggie and David. Having no children of their own, over the months they'd come to regard the young couple as family. Though David spoke fluent French, the Bedeaus would do their best to speak English so that Maggie wouldn't feel left out. However, Maggie had made remarkable progress in learning the French language and Emilie and Henri thought it quite charming to hear the strong Irish dialect mixed with their mother tongue.

David was sitting outside, munching through some crusty bread. He was relieved to see Maggie back. He wiped his mouth with a serviette, stood up, and pulled out a chair. "Only five minutes late— I'll let you off with that. Another five and I'd have been dragging you back!" he smirked, then kissed both her cheeks.

She wanted to attack his lips, feel his love physically storm her, hot and hungry. Her eyes told him exactly what she was thinking and it took everything he had to stop himself taking her right then and there outside Café de Flore. The sexual magnetism between them hadn't cooled with pregnancy. If anything it had intensified.

"Don't," he said with a spark in his eye.

"Don't what?" she asked innocently.

He smirked. "You know! If we weren't in public, I'd—"

"I can't wait."

He poured coffee, sliced a hefty chunk of bread, and smothered it with butter and strawberry jam. "Here, get this inside you."

She took a bite. It was still warm.

"Ahh, Maggie, you are here. Bonjour." Emilie bustled over and patted Maggie's belly. "Not long." She frowned at the bread and jam. "Oh, but you should nourish. I bring soup—"

"Oh, there's no need, Emilie," Maggie protested. The last thing she wanted on a hot summer day was soup.

"No, no. Bread and jam no nourish," Emilie insisted. The small bell just above the door jangled as she rushed back inside the café, and again when she returned with a huge bowl of vegetable soup. "Now I leave you two lovebirds alone." She put the bowl down in front of Maggie.

David leant forward and whispered. "What happened to *my* soup?"

She tapped his cheeks playfully. "Poor baby! You must look nourished enough." They burst into laughter at Emilie's lack of concern for David's wellbeing.

"So how did it go? Did you put the battalions back in their rightful place?"

Maggie bubbled with excitement. "Oh, David! It's all so exciting. The soldiers, when they stepped into the light, the look on their faces. Even me, I could feel it, but not as intense as they did once they'd crossed over. Why we fear death I'll never know. It's the most beautiful thing in the world." David sat quietly and listened.

"I mean, that is our true home, the place we belong. You should see the love and joy when people meet up with each other again. One soldier, MacTavish—his little girl came for him. She had her spirit mother with her, of course, but she remained in the background. MacTavish was so overwhelmed he couldn't speak; even the two soldiers who stood with me were crying. David, once you get there, you never want to leave." She trailed off. "You're quiet. Is something wrong?" Her voice had gone from bright and bubbly to concerned and reflective.

He smiled gently. "No, I'm just enjoying your happiness." He could see how elated she was, and she was here, safe, with him. But this talking to the dead still put the fear of God in him. He looked at his watch. She'd been gone about fifteen minutes at the most.

"What time is it?" She swallowed a few mouthfuls of soup then gave up. She took a serviette and fanned herself with it. "I'll let that cool down! I'm sweating like a dog in the desert."

David grinned. "Sweating like a dog in the desert! I've never heard that one before."

Maggie thought about her grandmother and some of her infamous sayings, and chuckled. "It's one of my grandmother's; I think she made them up as she went along."

"It's just leaving 12:30."

Maggie looked at him, mystified. "12:30! You're kidding me."

"No...it's 12:30." He poured more coffee.

She remembered a conversation she'd had with White Eagle. *'There is no time as you know it.*

'Linear time is an idea that belongs to Earth. It helps humans put the universe into some kind of order suited to their perceptions. Everything happens at the same time. The past, the present, the future: they're all happening now, in this moment, in different dimensions, different probabilities. You can step into your past and access your future at any time, and so you can change it.'

'But how do I change it?' she had asked him. *'You make it sound so simple.'*

'It is that simple. When you catch yourself thinking, what do you listen to? What do you see? Do you visualise a happy future or a miserable future filled with problems? What do you believe? What do you feel? Feeling plus belief equals creation!'

"Well, I'll be!" she said out loud. "Now I get it!" She took a sip of her coffee. "How many cups of coffee did you drink before I got back?"

"I was just finishing up my first." He dropped his knife. "Why?" He bent down to pick it up.

"The concept of time…I think I get it at last. White Eagle has been trying to explain it to me for a while but I could never quite grasp it."

"Well, if you'd have been gone for more than fifteen minutes, I'd have come looking for you."

"David, I felt like I'd been gone all day. It's mind-blowing to think I'd been gone for only fifteen minutes." Magic flickered in her eyes. "It's the soul that does it!"

"Does what?"

"Directs everything. It has limitless aspects of itself all living out different lives, different expressions, all at the same time. There's a lot more to life here than meets the eye."

Emilie burst through the door of the café and started to clear a few tables. David put his hand up. "Emilie, large scotch on the rocks when you're ready, please—you've lost me, Maggie. You're driving me to drink," he joked.

"I need a pen and a piece of paper."

He scanned the pages of the newspaper until he found a small area with relatively little print on it. He ripped it out and slid it over to her, passing her a pen from his shirt pocket at the same time. "Here." The flimsy paper flew off the table and fluttered gently from side to side like a feather on the breeze until it reached the ground. They both bent to get it, but David insisted, "I'll get it. I've got dropsy today."

"Would you like paper?" Emilie asked Maggie as she set David's drink down in front of him.

"No, thanks. This is good enough, Emilie."

Emilie busied about, humming nothing in particular. Maggie drew a circle on the paper and wrote the word "soul" in the centre. She then drew a number of lines branching out from it. On one line she wrote her name.

"This is my soul." She pointed to the circle. "And here it is living out an experience, which is me, the spirit of Maggie. But over here, maybe my soul is living out an experience as a Middle-Eastern man." She wrote "Arab" on one line and proceeded to fill in the rest as she spoke. "And here my soul might be a…politician. Here, maybe a soldier or a rebel. Here a nun." She pointed to the different lines. "These lives are multidimensional aspects of the same soul."

"Aspects...what do you mean? I don't understand."

She thought for a minute. "Spirits! Call them spirits. It will keep things simple."

"Really!"

"The soul has many spirits, all living out a soul experience." She put her hands on her chest. "I'm the spirit of Maggie, for example, and in one of my past lives I was the spirit of Marguerite. I told you about her. But it isn't limited to my individual spirit. The soul can direct the countless experiences of other spirits as well as mine, all at the same time! All these different spirits belong to the same soul...like me and you." She tapped the paper with her pen, looking pensive. "Isn't that fantastic, David?"

He sat back in his chair and put his hands behind his head. "Definitely not a nun, not you!"

"And then we have our past, present, and future lives."

"Oh, God, as if we haven't got enough to contend with." He took a swig of his whiskey. "Where do you dig this stuff up from?"

"Imagine if we could access our past to help us with our present, or even our future—"

"No, thanks!" he said, at a loss.

"Why not? Where's your sense of adventure?"

"I have enough problems dealing with David. The last thing I need is hundreds of me running about!"

"David! Be serious." She slapped his shoulder.

"I am!"

"Right, if you're having a problem getting your head around the concept of no time, think about it this way. My soul is presently the managing director of all these living photographs." She pointed to Maggie, the Arab man, the soldier, the rebel, the politician, and the nun. "And over here, my soul manages some past photographs." She drew more lines, branched them off from the circle, and wrote "Marguerite," "little Johnny," and "Anne Boleyn."

"Anne Boleyn!" David exclaimed, chewing on a mouthful of bread and jam.

She stopped writing and gave him a huffy look "Well, you never know! I'm sure we've all been, or will be, royalty at some time or another. Over here, my soul manages some future photographs." She drew more lines from the circle and wrote: "orange alien," "blue alien," "beautiful angel." "It manages all these experiences, all at the same time! Isn't that bewildering?" She nodded emphatically.

"Hold up for a minute. Are you saying that Maggie is the same spirit as the politician, the Arab, the nun, and whatnot?"

"No…although I bet you've hit on something there…hmm…I think White Eagle would describe that as probable realities. You know, whatever thoughts we think have a frequency so they go off and create other realities for us to live in—get it?"

"In a word, no!"

"Oh, never mind! We can discuss that another time."

"Can't wait!" he answered, deadpan.

She ignored him. "What I'm saying is, Maggie and the rest of them all belong to the same soul. We're part of the same soul group. Maggie's spirit is but one aspect of that soul, and her experiences will enrich it, just like the nun and the others, yet we remain independent from each other whether in the past, present, or future. I think we can probably access each other as well," she said, thinking out loud. "Well, the soul part of us, that is. Maybe the Arab explains why I have such an avid interest in all things Arabic, and why I feel drawn to that particular part of the world. And then of course there's the past-life thing."

He nodded his head. "Of course."

"Maybe I was an Arab man in a past life, if you want to look at past as past, that is."

"An Arab man! Maggie, some of the stuff you come out with… it's just too ridi—"

She put her finger up, and her dialect raced back into thick Irish. "David, always be open-minded, otherwise you can learn nothing and you'll be stuck in the same place until…until someone shoves a stick of dynamite up your ars—"

"Yes, yes. I get the picture, thank you very much. So what you're saying is that in past lives we may have been male or female." He threw his hands up in exasperation. "We may have been a king, queen, beggar?! It all sounds very strange to me. Do you want anything else to eat?" The subject was giving him a headache.

"No, thanks. And don't forget the future. In spirit, we might decide to come back to Earth and experience a particular culture, and so we will be born into a family who will better fit the experiences we're looking for—"

David leant forward. "So now you're saying that we hand-pick our parents?"

"Yes, but not just our parents—everything! All our experiences are choices at the spiritual level, and it is those choices and our reactions to them that enable us to grow at soul level."

"I wonder why our little mite here chose us?"

"Us and the adoptive parents." Her eyes filled up. She could sense David's sadness. "There could be a million reasons for any one choice. Maybe he's stepping into the past to change the future."

"Stepping into the past..." He shook his head. "This is all very intriguing, but very easy to get lost in." He lifted his glass. "Emilie, another Scotch, please."

"When we reach the spirit realms, we might choose to step back into any past life…or future one, for that matter. Let's replace the words past life' and future,' with living photos' to save confusion—"

His tone was flat. "Save confusion!"

"Yes." She pointed to the drawing on the paper. "Keep going back to the soul being the managing director of all these different branches, all at the same time. Our baby could be a very old soul. He might be here to change the past, or it could be that he's here to stop something catastrophic from happening in the future. Who knows?"

"Or maybe it's something simpler, like the experience of being adopted."

"Maybe." But she knew this wasn't the case. After her experience in the underworld, she knew that there was much more to the pregnancy. The child she carried had a job to do and so did they. If only she could find out what it was. It might help ease the pain of giving him away. "And there's not only the human way of life to choose from. The choices we have—it's infinite."

David looked thoughtful. "Yes, well, I'll certainly choose to come back as dog next time if that's an option: fed, roof over my head, walked and patted just for wagging my tail."

"David!" she exclaimed. "I thought you were going to say something serious."

He smirked. "Why do you keep thinking I'm not being serious?"

She looked pensive. He was teasing her again. She giggled. "All right, Mr. Serious, listen to this. Some belief systems do maintain that the choice of being an animal or even something inanimate is a possibility. Some even believe that an old soul might take up residence as a tree or a mountain, just to rest for a while. In other words, the soul can manifest and experience everything—UFOs, aliens, the lot, can come into the equation!"

David roared with laughter at the serious look on Maggie's face. "I don't know how you keep your face straight, I really don't."

She slapped the table lightly. "I'm not joking, David. Be—open—to—everything! This table, it's made up of the same stuff as us. It vibrates at a different rate, so it's denser than we are." She saw the look of confusion in his eyes and stopped short.

"Aliens, people having a rest disguised as a tree." He reached into his pocket, took out his pipe, and filled it with tobacco.

"Not people, David. Souls! There is more to the universe than just people."

He sucked on his pipe to get it going. "Maggie, be careful who you say this to. Patrick would have you locked up for a lot less!"

"Patrick is an arse-hole."

He raised an eyebrow and continued to suck on his pipe. "I know what he is, but let's keep the faith—and I don't like your language!."

The atmosphere went decidedly cold at the mere mention of

Patrick's name. Maggie visibly shuddered. "See how the negative vibration works? Just the mention of his name puts a damper on the day. And I was having such a wonderful time."

"Then don't let it! Protect yourself, Maggie. Isn't that what you always tell me to do? Are you not living with Patrick by choice? What is the relationship giving the pair of you? Can't you change your future with him? See what I mean? It's all so easy to talk about, but to walk the talk is a different story altogether."

Gloom seeped into her pores. Her face took on a desolate look, just like a light had been snuffed out. "I know." *But I will change it. I don't know how, but I'll do it. I'll be damned if I put up with Patrick all my life.* She smiled. The smallest thought of getting rid of Patrick for good lifted her spirits instantly.

"By the look on your face I'd say that you're back in the good vibration." He set his pipe down and sliced off some more bread. "Would you like another piece?"

"No, thanks! Where on earth do you put it all? Aren't you full?" She shook her head in disbelief. "Anyway, getting back to aliens. You can't possibly believe that human existence is the only option the soul has? You limit yourself, David."

"For now I'll choose to stay limited. The whole idea of little green men flying around in spaceships goes against everything I've been taught."

"My point exactly! What you've been taught. Teach yourself. Put all your teachings aside and think for yourself. The idea of human existence being the only choice in the universe is as unrealistic to me as it is limiting…and what if there are countless other universes? David, it is so important to think, and be open!"

David groaned. "You've given me enough to think about for one day. Let's go for a walk by the river, talk about the weather, and commune with nature." He stood up.

"I'd love to walk by the river. D'you think we should take a cold drink? It's still quite hot."

"Sure, and we'd better pay the bill while we're at it." He held the door to the café open for her.

Henri was busy serving wine behind the counter. "Bonjour, Maggee, Daveed. One minute, *s'il vous plaît*."

Emilie raced out of the kitchen. "You leave?" She waved her hand from side to side. "No bill today—"

David slapped some paper on the counter. "Oh, we can't do that, Emilie. You're very kind but—"

Emilie picked up the money and grasped David's hand. "A gift for you," she smiled.

"You're too kind." He kissed her cheeks. "I'll pay you back."

"Your kiss is my payback, and your presence in my home." She turned to Maggie. "And my lovely Maggie."

Henri walked over. "You leave? I see you tomorrow?"

"More than likely, Henri. But only if your wife lets us pay the bill," David teased.

Henri took Maggie and David to one side while Emilie got some water and picked out some fruit for their walk. "Did you see the strange happenings in the sky in the early hours of this morning?"

"What strange happenings?" David asked, taken aback.

"I don't know what it was, but lots of lights and—"

"Military activity perhaps—"

"No, no, too fast and smooth, no noise, and shaped like little coloured balls. Nothing like I've ever seen."

"UFOs, Henri?" Maggie suggested.

"I think, perhaps, and am open, Maggie." He more or less used the same words that Maggie had said to David just moments earlier.

David's face was ashen. They left the café in silence but Maggie stopped just outside the door. "I think and am open, Maggie." She looked at David. "Did I not say that to you moments ago? And given the conversation we've just had? Henri couldn't have heard it. He never showed his face the whole time we were outside."

"Coincidence, Maggie, pure coincidence."

"I agree. But be aware of coincidences, David. They happen for a reason. I call them messages from the universe."

12.

*M*aggie awoke in the early hours of the morning with a strange feeling. She sat bolt upright and looked around. Her breathing was fast and sharp and her heart skipped around unevenly. There was something in the room! She turned over quickly and found the lamp on the bedside table. Its light filled the room with a warm, orange glow and filled her with a sensation of instant relief. She stared at the black shadows of objects that the lamplight accentuated. Doubled in size, they loomed over her: a few plants, the dresser with her brush and toiletries placed neatly in the centre, and the clock on top of the marble mantelpiece. Its large, spear-shaped hands pointed to 3:15. She watched the pendulum swing for a few seconds. Just as she turned away, it stopped. *Strange!* Then it started again. *Stop it, Maggie!* she scolded herself. *You're letting your mind run away with you, so you are!*

She threw back the blankets, swung her legs over the edge of the bed, and sat with both hands flat on her belly as if making sure the baby was still there. The weather was unusually warm for the time of year. She felt sticky and uncomfortable. She picked up the jug on her bedside table, poured a glass of water, and drank heartily. She felt its coolness slide down her esophagus . It tasted good and brought instant comfort to her dry mouth and throat.

Everything was set for Aedan's arrival. Towels, fresh linen, cotton nappies, even the adoptive parents, who'd requested that the baby be handed over as soon as possible. It was for the best, they'd arranged

145

with David. "It will lessen the bond between Mother and child." *As if!* she thought to herself. After the initial shock, she'd bonded with the baby as soon as the doctor had given her the news that he was growing inside her. But she understood their way of thinking and had agreed to let Aedan be taken as soon as possible so that she could get on with her heartache. Besides, she knew that if she held him in her arms she'd never let him go, and so Angelette, at Maggie's request, had agreed to take the baby immediately—something she wasn't looking forward to doing.

She felt the need for some fresh air. She stood up, then looked down at her bump. *Any time now.* Anxiety rolled around in the pit of her stomach. She was already two weeks past her due date and beginning to wonder if Aedan was ever going to put in an appearance. She didn't want to go into hospital but if he didn't get a move on soon, she would have to be induced. David had insisted that if there was the slightest sign of complications setting in there would be no home birth. The fact that Angelette had seen to it that Maggie would get the best possible care available had so far failed to sway his opinion.

She walked over to the patio doors and drew back the curtains. She couldn't see a thing. It was like being on the top deck of a ship at night, surrounded by black. Wide awake, she decided to sit outside for a while and enjoy the dark silence. She had always found the nighttime so peaceful. She walked back to the bedside cabinet, switched off the lamp, slid into her slippers, and wrapped herself up in a thick candlewick nightgown. Even though the weather was warm, there would still be a nip in the air outside.

She opened the patio doors wide. The night air charged in like an angry schoolteacher and quickly removed the thick stuffiness of the room. She stood on the balcony for a few minutes, breathing in the cool breath of the night. The soft hoot of an owl in the distance added to the tranquility. It was so peaceful. She sat down and rocked to and fro on the squeaky old rocker that didn't fit with the rest of the furnishings at the chateau.

It was a beautiful night, no doubt about that. But it was iced with a tinge of uneasiness…something peculiar that she couldn't put her finger on. She put her hands on her belly. "When are you going to come? Wouldn't you prefer to be born here at the chateau instead of in a hospital? It's a beautiful place to make your grand entrance, so it is, and at least we'll have some privacy before I…" The heartache, the longing surged within her. "I would give anything to keep…" Tears fell. She sucked in her breath. "Know that I love you…I'm not giving you away because I don't want you, and your dad, he's a good man. Oh, he has his flaws like the rest of us. He worries too much about what other people think, for one, but then again, so do I at times."

The baby kicked hard inside her. She knew he was an old soul and that he could understand what was going on. She salvaged some happiness from the moment and reminded herself that the baby had also made choices. "If you don't give me some sign that you're on your way by tomorrow, your dad will whip us off to hospital and—"

All of a sudden, a sharp breeze that had no place being there whipped through her hair and underneath her gown, lifting it to her knees. She caught its hem and held it down around her ankles. A few leaves swirled around in the corner of the balcony, trapped by a small whirlwind. Then, as fast as it had started, it stopped again like nothing had happened.

She shuddered. Not with cold. She looked at the leaves, then up at the sky. All was still, but her instincts along with the uneasiness in the air had intensified and told her that something was about to happen. She wasn't alone. She could have sworn she saw what looked like a tadpole—a small red light with a tail—wiggle through the sky for a few seconds…or did she? She looked back at the leaves. Had they moved? Maybe she'd imagined it?

Eyes fixed on the sky, she stood up. The chair rocked and squeaked behind her. She walked to the edge of the balcony. All of a sudden, the tadpole thing shot from out of a cloud, then in, then out again. On closer inspection it looked like a red, sphere-shaped light. It bobbed about high in the distance then stopped abruptly. Suspended. Waiting. "What in God's name?"

In a flash, it was joined by a green light, then a purple one, a white one, a yellow one, orange, blue, until there were at least fifty of them grouped together, bobbing about side by side. Suddenly, two of the lights broke away from the others and started to somersault over each other, as if putting on a show for Maggie.

"They see me!" Her heart hit her chest so hard she thought the impact might stop it altogether. She darted for the safety of her room but the French doors slammed shut before she got to them. "Jesus Christ!" She pounded the doors, shook the handles, but couldn't budge them. She screamed out in the night, terrified. "David! Angelette! Help me!"

The lights were getting closer. The whole south side of the chateau, along with Maggie, was lit up in a multitude of colours.

Realising that the doors were not going to open, she stopped thumping and rested her head on the glass. She didn't dare turn around, didn't dare breathe. She'd communicated with spirits from being a child, and had shared numerous discussions with White Eagle regarding other intelligent life that existed in the universe, especially the Galactic United Nations—and Galaxias. He was always going on about them. Nevertheless, she'd always blocked communication with realms other than the spirit world, refusing to admit that the idea of extraterrestrial life filled her with dread for some reason.

"WHITE EAGLE, WHERE ARE YOU?" she cried out. No response. "WHITE EAGLE!" Sweat ran down her back and face. She'd been scared before but not like this. Scared when she'd got into trouble at school from the teacher, scared when Patrick had beaten her senseless on more than one occasion, even hospitalised her, scared when the doctor had told her she was pregnant, and scared of the situation that her life experiences had got her into so far. But nothing compared to the fear that encircled her in this moment for something she had no perception of.

"GO AWAY!" she screamed. "I'M NOT READY TO MEET YOU...WHITE EAGLE, WHERE THE HELL ARE YOU?" She heard a voice. It was a beautiful voice, kind and mellow.

"Maggie, turn around. Turn and face us."

She closed her eyes and didn't answer.

"We're not here to harm you." It was NeilA who spoke.

She swallowed hard. "Who are you?" She still wouldn't turn around or open her eyes.

"We're part of your soul group, that's all! We just live in, let's say, a different universe."

His tone filled her, echoed through her soul. She felt her whole body vibrate with its resonance. There was no separation. She was a part of it; a part of the voice, like a piece of her had gone into it.

Her breathing slowed. She opened her eyes but remained fixed to the spot. She looked down at the balcony floor, then at her feet and arms. Everything was drenched in the most vital, effervescent colours, yet she could see right into them. It was like looking into the sun without pain. She spoke into the French doors. "I won't talk to you without White Eagle," she said hurriedly, hand still on the door handle. Despite her fear and the lack of response from White Eagle so far, the trust that she held for her friend was unshakable.

"Good girl, Maggie! That's what I like to hear." White Eagle turned to Roman and NeilA. "See? I've done some things right," he beamed.

NeilA smiled. "You've done a lot right, proved by your position within G.U.N. Like we said at the meeting, the trust between the two of you and the courage that you've shown is to be commended, which is why you kept your place as Maggie's chief advisor. However, the golden rule is paramount and will remain so. We trust you won't make the same choice again—"

"White Eagle, what's going on here?" The relief at the sound of his voice raced through Maggie.

"Maggie, look through the doors into your room."

"Why?"

He raised his eyes and sighed. "Just do it!" *She always had to question!*

Her breath had caused a cloud of condensation to appear on the small glass pane of the door. She wiped it clear with the sleeve of her nightgown and peered through. "Holy!" Startled, she jumped. White Eagle and two beings stared back at her.

The two beings were lit up as if they had light bulbs stuffed underneath their gowns. White Eagle looked small in comparison. They were at least seven to eight feet tall, and wore long, golden robes with high collars, patterned throughout with a silver network effect, like an elaborate light system.

Her instincts were on full alert and though she was frightened, something told her that she was face to face with two very evolved beings. Their heads were hairless and larger than that of humans. Their skin radiated an orange glow that shimmered around them, but it was their eyes that captivated her. Huge and soft, like calm pools of love, they sparkled all the time as if full of tears, and though gentle, they pierced her, sliced her open, read her soul. On closer inspection she noticed how their skin, their eyes, every part of them, constantly changed colour with their surroundings, the air, the atmosphere, even her mood! The beings were taking everything in. They weren't merely a part of creation, they were creation in the making...and aware of it.

She gasped, her heart pounding a fast, uneven rhythm. She stumbled backwards and grabbed the small patio table to steady herself. White Eagle turned and said something to his companions and they immediately changed their appearance.

Maggie rubbed her eyes and wondered if what she'd just witnessed was a combination of darkness, imagination, and tired eyes. The two beings disappeared and were replaced by two human-looking individuals. One of them had long white hair and a matching moustache that grew into a beard. He reminded her of a fairy tale wizard but without the usual flamboyant gowns.

The other had short, dark hair, was clean-shaven, and looked more Egyptian. His eyes looked as if they had a thin layer of eyeliner underneath, and his hair was as black as the night outside. They both wore very mundane clothes, not camouflage gear, but a kind of khaki clothing with high, dark brown boots that resembled an odd kind of soft leather, and waistcoats made out of the same material—certainly not what she'd have expected to see on aliens! Then again, White Eagle always maintained that when aliens visited Earth, they often dressed down a bit!

"Maggie, I'd like to introduce you to Roman, my advisor—you've seen him before, remember?" He pointed to the white beard. "And NeilA. Both big cheeses with G.U.N.—and Galaxias, but we won't go into that."

"What in the blazes!" She turned around and looked up into the night sky. The balls of colour remained motionless, suspended in midair. Their colours sparkled over the tops of the trees, the chateau, her, everything. She couldn't understand why the others didn't wake up. The colours were so intense it was impossible not to notice them. She looked down at the grass below the balcony. It looked like a carpet of rainbows. Everything seemed to twinkle and vibrate. The scene was daunting, awe-inspiring, hard to describe—

"MAGGIE!" Angelette called to her.

Maggie looked across at the balcony adjacent to hers. Angelette had moved into the room next door in case she went into labour during the night.

"What is happening?" She was bewildered.

Maggie turned and looked through the glass doors into her room. White Eagle and the two beings had gone. She turned the doorknob, releasing the lock with no effort this time, and stepped inside the room. It felt different, healed somehow…calmed, light. She turned around and ran back outside to the edge of the balcony. The lights remained. "WHITE EAGLE!" she yelled out.

A purple sphere broke away from the rest. "I'm still here."

"Are you the light?" she asked, stunned.

"Of course. So are you! So are we all," he teased.

"No, not that light, the light in the sky," she said, frustrated.

"It's one and the same, Maggie. Light is light."

"You know what I mean! The purple sphere-shaped thing that is talking to me!" She was getting impatient.

"Oh, am I purple today? It must have been something I ate earlier!" Roman, NeilA, and the rest of the crew laughed quietly.

"Stop that or I'm going inside!"

"Patience, Maggie, patience. Yes—I—am—the—purple—one," he joked, in a most commanding voice. What Maggie was seeing were the colours of the individual beings on board the ship. The ship itself was concealed.

"What's goin' on? Have you brought these beings here just to prove their existence?"

"To prove their exist—good heavens, no! They've more pressing things to think about. Actually, they brought me here. We've decided it's time for you to meet them."

"Me! Why? What can such, such…divine ones want with me?"

"Maggie, remember you, too, are divine. Why wouldn't they want to meet you?"

"Because I'm just an ordinary woman who makes mistakes—"

"As I've said on more than one occasion, there are no mistakes, only experiences. Creativity takes on many guises. Some of Earth's best inventions, at the time of their inception, were first deemed to be mistakes. As for ordinary people! The human is extraordinary. Such are the complexities of the energy system: the DNA coding, the subtle bodies, the internal blueprint. Why, even the chakra system alone defies—"

"Um, um!" Roman cut in. "White Eagle, we must press on. Perhaps you could continue this conversation some other time."

"Oh, of course. I'm sorry, I get a bit carried away. Maggie, how many times have we discussed the uniqueness of the human and the potential of all individuals? Don't fence yourself in."

"Yes, I know, but…well, I haven't, you know!" She got more and more flustered. "I don't behave in a way that's…appropriate—"

"Meaning what, exactly?"

"You know! Having…being preg—"

White Eagle smirked. "Having sex with a priest—"

Horrified, her body stiffened. "Don't shout it out!"

"Maggie, our friends have already explained to you that they are from the same soul group. They know all about the baby. There are a lot of complexities involved that you're not aware of, not at Maggie level, that is. The soul is a different matter, of course."

"Meaning?"

"Meaning they couldn't care less about trivial matters such as whom you choose to have sex with, as long as it was a light-worker who impregnated you. You're letting old teachings get in the way of your inner reasoning. Besides, the time will come when priests will marry. Religion needs to realise that to deny a priest sex is to deny him spiritual intensity in one of its highest expressions—"

NeilA put his hand on White Eagle's shoulder. "Speed up! The military are on the way," he said quickly.

Maggie didn't hear NeilA, but she noticed that the lights had become somewhat jumpy A low, humming noise in the background was getting louder and louder, until it suddenly became so unbearable it hurt her ears. Maggie's heart clouted her ribs. She instinctively put her arms on top of her head and dipped her shoulders as two Breguet 19 fighters zoomed out of nowhere and began firing at the lights in the sky.

Overwhelmed, she shouted out, "No! Don't hurt them!" She couldn't believe how protective she felt towards the things in the sky. It was as if she were watching her family being shot at. "Don't shoot! Stop it! Don't shoot!" she yelled, as if the pilots could hear her.

She looked over the balcony to see if there was any way she could get down into the garden below but there wasn't. The tomboy in her would have scrambled the ten-foot drop quickly enough if she hadn't been pregnant.

She ran inside and managed to stop herself from flying over the edge of the bed. With her arms positioned underneath her belly to stop the baby from bouncing, she ran as fast as she could out of her bedroom and down the long corridor towards the flight of stairs that led to the garden. She looked back; there was nobody about. *Unbelievable! How the hell can they sleep through this lot?!* She flounced down the stairs to the thick cathedral door that led outside. She grabbed the rusty old handle, pulled hard, but it wouldn't shift. The door was locked. "Damn!" She looked around and searched frantically for the key before realising it was still in the lock.

"You idiot, Maggie," she said to herself, as she fought with the lock. Her nerves got the better of her. "Oh my God! Oh my God!" It seemed the faster she tried to go, the slower she went. Hands shaking, she fumbled with the handle and shook the old door. "Open up, open up, you old bastard!" But the door remained locked solid. "Please open, I have to get outside," she babbled to herself. At last, the door opened, creaking and groaning in protest. "Be quiet, will you?" she whispered, squashing through as small a gap as her belly would allow.

All hell was going on outside. Everything was still lit up in colour, including the two jet fighters. Maggie ran through the garden like a madwoman, waving and shouting hysterically, never taking her eyes off the action in the sky. "Stop firing, they're peaceful!"

The fighters showed no mercy. They flew at the lights again and again, spraying them with thousands of bullets.

On board the ship, NeilA had everything under control. His only concern was Maggie. "She's very distressed. I'm worried about conception—not earth's general idea of conception of course!" he said to White Eagle and Roman Before turning to the rest of the crewmembers. "Disarm the aircraft. Cut their power but maintain the safety of the pilots. I need to think—"

"Better be quick," Roman cut in. "The white hole is ready to go."

NeilA looked across at the white hole in question. Its energy was losing vigour. The vibrations were slowing, which meant that a portion of its energy was already outside Earth's atmosphere. "If we can't use that one, we'll just have to hang around Earth until it's been replenished or another one is opened up. Our mission is all that matters. It will be successful. Maggie isn't ready so it's taking longer than anticipated." He glanced out at the two jets.

Without warning, all went quiet. The engines, the bullets, everything stopped. Maggie stopped dead. Breathing heavily, she stared upward. The planes, like the lights, hung suspended in mid air.

Agitated, the French pilots tried to contact each other and home base, but nothing! No response. The radios, electronics, engines— everything was dead! Yet they remained stock-still in mid air, and there was not a thing they could do about it. The strange lights were everywhere: in front, at the side, the back, on top, and underneath the aircrafts. They seemed to be curious about the machinery. The pilots knew intuitively that the lights were responsible for the loss of their engines, yet for some strange reason, the longer they sat there the more at ease they felt. Whatever these lights were, they were using some kind of communication technique to relay to the pilots that they were peaceful.

White Eagle, Roman, and NeilA walked to the opposite side of the ship to get out of the general hustle and bustle of the other crewmembers, and sat down. They watched Maggie closely on the grounds below by means of a small hologram that played out like a live theatre show before them. NeilA turned to White Eagle. "Let Maggie know that she must bond with the child. It is imperative that she doesn't allow her friends to take him right after the birth."

"Why?" White Eagle asked, troubled. "Maggie is already distressed at having to give the child up for adoption. It seems unjustifiably cruel to let her form a stronger bond with him than she already has."

"We know this, White Eagle, but choices have been made. I don't need to remind you of that fact—"

"Even so, Maggie's welfare must be—"

"White Eagle," NeilA said quietly, "I understand your concern for Maggie, but do you not think that her welfare is paramount in our thoughts?"

"Yes, yes, of course, but—"

"Then please let me finish." NeilA remained calm. He had always admired White Eagle's courage, and his ability to question. "As you know, Maggie's emotions are blowing in many directions. One minute she wants to keep the child and feels that he will be better off with her, as his birth mother, not to mention her concerns about who the adoptive parents are, but in the next minute she believes that he would have a better life if she gives him up. He will have wealthy parents, an education—things she deems that on her own she could never give him.

"Of course, she knows that should she keep the child, she will be on her own, because her husband is not the kind of man that anyone can reason with. Indeed, Patrick is influenced more often than not by the negative vibration—jealousy, possessiveness, tendency to drink. He's an out-and-out bully. At his hands, Maggie's life has been harsh and miserable, yet she's remained light-hearted nonetheless." His voice slowed and took on an intense tone. "However, there is not a chance in her world—or ours, for that matter—that should she choose to keep the child, she could ever risk Patrick finding out about him, so she has only one option, which is to leave him. We must never underestimate somebody like Patrick. Maggie knows that."

"NeilA, Roman, the white hole!" Remul, one of the crewmembers, rushed over. "There's seven Earth minutes left to access it, at the most."

NeilA and Roman looked at White Eagle. "Excuse us," they said and raced over to evaluate the situation with the white hole. White Eagle—being, in his words, "naturally inquisitive," but in Maggie's, "naturally nosey"—chased after them.

Roman looked at the white hole on the small screen being monitored by Remul. "Bring it in, please; we need to get a closer look at it."

Remul looked taken aback. "I can't, Roman. The technology governing the release of the hologram is sensitive to the frequency of only your soul note and NeilA's. It won't accept any other."

Roman shook his head. "Of course, of course, I know that.". When we get back remind me to see to it that while travelling the technology is tuned to your frequency as well as ours."

"How come only certain soul notes?" White Eagle was intrigued.

Remul nodded at Roman as he answered the question. "We can't let the dark interfere with our whereabouts. The white holes in question are tuned to accept frequencies that travel along a specific wavelength. Security is further enhanced by tweaking the frequencies to accept only the unique soul notes of selected individuals."

Roman let out a long, shrill noise that echoed around the ship. The sound moved in and out of his mouth like a creature with a life of its own. Its echo sounded like a fusion between a whale and a dolphin. White Eagle's telepathic skills informed him that Roman had requested access to the white hole travelling along Meridian Gavarnie, in the Hautes Pyrénées area of France, Earth's atmosphere.

Roman turned to White Eagle. "The note is the sound made by an organism. On Earth, it would be the voice of a person, the cry of an animal, the chirp of a bird—all species have an individual note even though they may sound the same."

A mini replica of the white hole, about nine meters in diameter, flashed in front of them. Roman, NeilA, and Remul discussed its condition and whether or not it could withstand their journey to Galaxias.

Roman scratched his head and looked at White Eagle. "It might get us to the spirit—astral—world, whatever you want to call it!" He turned to NeilA. "What do you think? Will it get us to astral if we push it?" He didn't wait for an answer. He pursed his lips and looked at Remul. "Contact them and let them know we're on our way." He paused for a few seconds. "Forget it! Contact Galaxias instead. Tell them to open up another white hole at their end. Have our crew work on opening it up at this end. It will take a while but it's quicker than waiting until this one is replenished." A look of concern crossed his face as he eyed NeilA. *We'll have to get him home as soon as possible after conception between he and Maggie is finalized.* He turned to NeilA. "Or do you have any other ideas?"

"No. I think your decision is the right one." NeilA walked toward two of the crewmembers who had both feminine and masculine traits, like some kind of combinant beings. "Lumi, Atla, keep the ship disguised as a cloud until we're ready to leave Earth. Otherwise the world's military will swamp Volonne like a plague. We don't wish to cause unnecessary panic by letting Earth's governments know that we can disarm them whenever we see fit."

13.

White Eagle studied the white hole with a quizzical expression. It spun wildly, but every now and again it would lose velocity and a small part of it would flicker out of Earth's atmosphere. "Roman, how come you can't recuperate in the spirit realms for a while? The astrals are always happy to see you."

"I'm still mulling over the possibility."

He turned to Roman. "Well then, what's the hold-up? The white hole will have no problem getting you there. Why not come after conception between NeilA and Maggie is complete instead of loafing around Earth longer than necessary?"

Roman cocked his head to one side and looked over at NeilA as if studying him. "After conception, NeilA will need expert energy manipulation to rebalance, so it's vital we get him back into the vibrations he's attuned to as quickly as possible. The spirit—do they prefer "astral" or "spirit"? I always forget."

White Eagle shrugged, "They don't care."

Roman continued, "Anyway, the spirit world is a high vibration but not high enough to sustain NeilA's intricacies. It wouldn't be such a problem if we were alone but with the rest of the crew to consider," he paused as he looked out at the two aircrafts before continuing, "we'll all be in need of replenishment." He sighed. "It takes a lot out of us when we visit—pardon my phraseology—the lower levels. They're like vampires to the higher energies; they cling to us, sap the force out of us. You know that."

"You can't protect yourself?"

He turned to White Eagle. "Of course! But after conception our energy will be minimal. Not enough to cause any problems so long as we can get back right away. The problem with protection at our level is that we don't have any control over it. It's inbuilt. If we were to stop over and our energy became critical, it would turn in on itself. In other words, a battle of higher and lower energy systems would commence and, unfortunately, the astrals wouldn't stand a chance against us. We'd swallow them up—they'd cease to exist. You'd be okay, what with your Galaxian blueprint, but the rest would be annihilated."

"But I thought energy could never be destroyed?"

"They wouldn't be destroyed, they'd be sapped into us—they'd sustain us, be a part of us. Lose their individuality."

"I see."

"Such a scenario would have devastating results, and not only for the spirit world. They're the gatekeepers, the galactic lookouts for Earth." Roman lowered his voice. "She'd have no protection, at least long enough for the dark forces to move in and take over. They'd accumulate a lot of power. We can't let that happen. As you know, Earth is a major player in this galaxy. She holds a prime position and provides a network for many species. Without Earth, all creation is under threat."

The rest of the crew turned and looked across at them. They could sense Roman's primal instinct to protect. It flooded the ship and reinforced a sense of valour in all of them. They never took their positions for granted but it was good to be reminded now and again.

"If energy can't be destroyed, why don't you just put us back when you've finished with us?"

Roman threw back his head and laughed. "Throw up after stuffing ourselves, you mean?" He shrugged his shoulders. "We can. We would. But by this time the damage would be done. We'd be at war, White Eagle. The dark have been trying to cause such a scenario since first seed. They know that if they get their way, creation would be ruled fifty-fifty, so to speak. Galaxias for the first time would no longer be the dominant force." He grimaced. "It doesn't bear thinking about—the sooner the soul split is synchronised, the better."

"Synchronised," White Eagle repeated.

"That's right. For a few moments after conception it will take a lot of NeilA's energy to attune the new soul to the exact wavelength that his soul—NeilA's—vibrates with. No easy task at such a high level and we cannot risk failure, not with this kind of power. Should he fail, and the child be endowed with a portion of NeilA's energy yet out of sync with his wavelength, the exercise is finished. We couldn't allow the child to remain on Earth. Maggie would lose the baby, and his spirit would be taken by you to be nurtured in the astral regions.

White Eagle rubbed his chin. "I see that…his power influenced by the dark—"

"Such a scenario at NeilA's level is impossible. As you well know, the dark are helpless against the higher powers."

"I was referring to the child—"

"The child is a split-off from NeilA but will be powerful in his own right, that much is true. That's why we must ensure that he remains on the same wavelength as NeilA and the rest of us. He will be under the constant nurturing of G.U.N. and Galaxias, but he'll be responsible for his choices just like the rest of us. Of course, at times while living on Earth, he will be tempted by the lower forces. How he reacts to such stimuli is up to him, but let's not forget who seeded his soul. A power such as NeilA will always prevail. But if the child wasn't on our wavelength it would be much harder to keep track of him, keep him in line with our ways—something we can't risk when dealing with this kind of strength."

"But what if the dark somehow get wind of the child?"

"Every precaution has and will continue to be taken to ensure he remains hidden. Why do you think Maggie didn't get pregnant by her husband?"

"Ah ha…," White Eagle nodded slowly. "He's the dark one."

"Exactly! History repeating itself? The dark have tried to impregnate a Galaxian since Earth began. What they don't know is that we're well aware of their moves. We keep the dark and their antics close. One of

Maggie's jobs, amongst others, was to get pregnant but not by Patrick—though she had to keep him in her midst—but to another light-worker, a Galaxian, and at the same time it had to be someone that the dark would never suspect. Hence David's role as a priest."

White Eagle looked puzzled. "So in Maggie's past life as Marguerite she had no choice but to die, or risk bringing a child into the universe that held the power of the light but tinged by the dark in his soul? What happened to free will?"

"She had a choice and made what she felt was the right decision."

"What if Marguerite had decided to keep the baby and not die at the hands of Adolphe? How would Galaxias have reacted?"

Roman's tone was nonchalant but sure. "Galaxias will never infringe upon free will. One of the most basic laws of the universe restricts us from doing so. We intervene only at the originator's discretion. I explained that to you years ago while you were still living on Earth."

"Sometimes it's good to be reminded of what we already know at a deeper level—another one of your teachings. But I'm still curious as to what would have happened had the baby and Marguerite taken matters into their own hands by going against Galaxias?"

Roman looked pensive. He chose his words carefully. "Then there would have been an all-out battle for the child between G.U.N. and the underworld. This doesn't involve only Galaxias. We're all in it together." His voice was quiet but there was no mistaking the power in his words.

Roman's soul note played right through White Eagle, as if he'd literally struck a cord inside him. Not only him: once again the rest of the crew, including NeilA, momentarily stopped what they were doing and looked over at them.

Roman smiled back. "Carry on." It was always reassuring to know they were all on the same wavelength. Oneness was comforting, indeed.

White Eagle looked awkward. "Roman, I'm sorry that I even mentioned the dark—"

Roman put his hand up. "Don't be! I'm here to answer questions.

Besides, we have no fear of the dark. They wouldn't last a heartbeat at our level but the mere mention of them does bring in a sort of nasty air." He stopped, trying to find words that would describe how even the smallest thought of the dark could soil his world if he let it.

White Eagle nodded assertively. He had no problem describing what Roman was thinking. "Like stepping in a great big dollop of dog sh—"

"Yes, yes. Thank you, White Eagle! That is a very apt description indeed." The expression on Roman's face prompted roars of laughter to fill the ship.

NeilA smirked and held up his hand. "Okay, okay, let's get back to work; we're behind as it is." He nodded toward Roman. "I'll be right over."

White Eagle was puzzled. "What's so funny?"

Roman turned and looked at Maggie's hologram on the adjacent side of the ship. "You are!" he said, as he walked toward the image. "It's a wonderful thing, a sense of humour, especially when it's natural like that. Now! Getting back to Maggie."

"Does conception take long?" White Eagle followed Roman to the hologram.

Roman frowned. You never can tell. So much has to be taken into account. Conception, or soul splits as they're often referred to are very rare as you know. Conception on Earth is complex enough but the intricacies when dealing with a being like NeilA are intense!— Look at some of the great masters that have been born on Earth to human beings…their lineage is cosmic White Eagle!— Jesus! Buddha! The scriptures have barely touched the surface!" Roman stared at White Eagle, his expression piercing before whispering, "A soul split will take place only under perfect circumstances. If there is the slightest doubt, it will not happen. They cannot be rushed!" He walked into the hologram and stood at Maggie's side. "Give me a moment." He disappeared inside Maggie's holographic image, which was identical to her physical one. Within seconds, he'd attuned to her energy, checked out every aspect of her being, reappeared, and walked back to White Eagle. The physical Maggie remained in the garden below, oblivious to him. He looked at White Eagle and tipped his hand from side to side. "Hmm, still a little edgy. Now…where was I? Oh, yes. As you know, we cannot risk the dark interfering with the soul of the child. His power will be phenomenal even at a young age—his parents are Galaxian workers. They've earned considerable power in their own right, which will be combined with NeilA." He cocked his head to the side, raising his eyebrows. "You can imagine. Even the slightest contamination from the dark could cause a lot of unnecessary suffering on Earth."

"Marguerite got pregnant! The dark beat the odds!"

"Let's not forget how powerful the human ego is, especially when the creative juices are flowing. Our light-worker, in her human role as Marguerite, was desperate for a child. She'd always seen herself as a mother someday. Unconsciously, Marguerite craved to become pregnant, a craving that proved too strong for her to overcome at the conscious level even though she knew that the child would be heavily influenced by Adolphe from the day he was born. She dreamt about being a mother, visualised a child in her arms suckling her breast, and told herself that she wouldn't let Adolphe's energy anywhere near him. In the end, this was the decision she made. She got exactly what she focused on. She brought the child up in the spirit world, held him, nurtured him, and has since introduced him to Adolphe, who, as you know, recently returned home."

"But what about Caresse, the servant girl, pregnant by Adolphe—Evolus! A light-worker, and the dark, the dark got through—"

"No, they didn't. Caresse was pregnant by the stable hand. Such was Adolphe's ego that he didn't believe for a moment that Caresse would dare be unfaithful to him. He really believed the child was his. Even so, we had to keep the child away from him. The stablehand was another light-worker. It was he who disturbed Adolphe and stopped him from murdering the child on the day Caresse died."

"Ha! Galaxias really are in places that one would never suspect."

"Of course! But a lot of people on Earth fail to recognise it. Instead they use money, power, and intellect as a kind of class system, and underestimate the bum on the street."

"How is Maggie doing? Do you think she's ready?" NeilA joined them. "Excuse me, I don't mean to barge in but conception will commence any time!"

"Still a bit edgy," Roman answered. They stood in front of the hologram, all eyes on Maggie.

NeilA leant forward. "She seems to have calmed down a bit since the military stopped firing at us. I see no reason to wait any longer. Let's go."

"Which room?" Roman asked, chasing NeilA.

NeilA stopped, looked thoughtful, then paced on through a maze of passageways. "Orange, I think. It doesn't matter because every colour will be incorporated into his energy system—"

"Which system?" White Eagle wanted to make sure that the energy system they were talking about was the chakra system—spinning energy centres that were aligned to a certain colour and responsible for all aspects of physical, creative, emotional, mental, intuition, and spiritual life while living on Earth.

"The chakras," NeilA answered. "They have a tough job on Earth. Sometimes they get so clogged that the creative force can barely move through them. When that happens the magnetic field that surrounds the human becomes damaged, and all kinds of physical and emotional problems set in. Hmmm." NeilA seemed to be paying attention to an unseen force. He nodded as if in agreement. "Yes, as I thought. While this child is living on Earth, his creative energy will be repressed more than any other, so let's give his orange chakra a booster from the start."

They walked through a multicoloured, geometric opening shaped like a snail's shell. For a brief moment, it gave White Eagle a strange sensation, knocking him sideways. His head spun, as if he'd been rushed by a choir with a million voices, and he felt like he'd been stretched by an old-fashioned torture device but without the pain. He stumbled through to the other side of the opening but managed to stay on his feet.

NeilA looked him up and down. "Are you alright?"

"No...I, I feel really weird...heavy and slow, sort of." He felt like a gramophone playing in slow motion.

NeilA spoke to Roman with a questioning look in his eyes. "Oh! We mustn't have changed the velocity. Only certain workers are allowed into these chambers unless we lower the standards," he joked.

Roman stopped abruptly and turned to White Eagle. "Sorry, that was my fault. I didn't alter the frequency enough." Using his fingers, he drew a rectangle shape in midair. A screen appeared and he pressed a number of buttons on its keyboard. The ambiance in the room changed immediately and White Eagle was able to move around unrestricted. Roman waved his hand across the screen. It disappeared instantly.

They proceeded to make their way down a long hallway lined with separate entrances, each with its own unique colour. The entrances were vortexes that pulsed and swirled, and shot out tiny sparks of energy at random. It was impossible to see through their colours into the space they guarded.

Once at the orange entrance, NeilA ran his hands over its surface until it accepted him. His hands, then his arms submerged into it. "Access authorised." There was no opening. He simply walked through it. Roman followed with White Eagle behind. The energy in the room was overwhelming for White Eagle. Although evolved in his own right, he wasn't used to such high frequencies and found himself collapsing into them.

"Damn!" Roman was irritated at his own carelessness. "I could have sworn I'd lowered the frequencies sufficiently for your comfort... give me a moment."

White Eagle panicked. "Roman, I can't breathe!" His face started to twitch, as though he were having a nightmare while wide awake; his body felt like it was on fire.

Roman and NeilA glanced at each other. "Of all the times!" Roman was exasperated. "It's not our frequencies, it's his! Just when we're stuck in Earth's time system! This is all we need!"

"It doesn't matter." NeilA nodded his head. "Get hold of him.

It looks like we'll be staying around Earth until the white hole is replenished anyhow. It will be safer that way, so now is as good a time as any."

They grabbed White Eagle on either side. "Do you think he needs the chamber?" Roman asked.

"Good idea. It will help him adjust quicker."

Roman snapped his fingers. An image of himself appeared to the crew outside. "Chamber, please—orange!"

Atla ran seven tentacle-like fingers over a crystal switchboard until the fourth one stuck fast onto a small piece of quartz. The seventh finger grew at lightning speed and attached itself to the middle of Atla's forehead. An advanced form of communication between Atla and the crystal began. "On the way, Roman."

In the orange room a huge piece of quartz crystal, at least four metres long and three metres wide, started to manifest slowly from a beam of light that poured in through the ceiling. Within seconds, the crystal blended with the energy of the room and radiated a magnificent iridescent shade of orange.

White Eagle clutched his chest just as his legs crumpled beneath him. "I'M GOING TO BURST!" He felt as if he were expanding from the inside out.

Roman was unperturbed. "Stay with us. Try to remain calm while your energy blends with the atmosphere of the room."

White Eagle was anything but calm, and his voice wasn't helping matters. It had taken on a high-pitched tone that he didn't recognise. "WHAT'S HAPPENING TO ME? MY VOICE!—"

Roman remained composed. "Calm down, calm down." He wanted to laugh! White Eagle's expression at the sound of his own voice was priceless. "Your energy is being raised up a bit—nothing to panic about."

White Eagle felt as if his breath, on the inside, was blowing him up like a balloon. The feeling was so strange, so alarming. He felt as if he were literally going to explode into nothing. "I don't want to be raised, I'm happy as I am! Roman, make it stop!" he demanded.

"I can't! I don't have the authority. In a nutshell, you've elevated your consciousness to the next level. Congratulations! It will be over in no time." Roman and NeilA hurried him over to the crystal, and unceremoniously threw him at it.

There was no door, no opening. White Eagle felt as if he'd passed through a strange liquid which was filled with tiny particles resembling snowflakes. Nothing was solid. "AHHHH!" he screamed again and again as he floated about inside the crystal. It was the weirdest feeling. The crystal looked solid but was liquefied. Not liquid in terms of water, more in terms of energy. He wasn't in pain, but the terrific speed of the energy as it rushed him was terrifying. He felt his subtle bodies, especially the spiritual and cosmic bodies, grow in a series of short, sharp spurts, and his chakra system spun out of control. "I don't want my consciousness elevated! I never asked for this! Why did you do this to me?"

"I didn't do it to you!" Roman's reply was a mixture of laughter and exasperation. "Only you have the ability to elevate your consciousness, and so the Originator has seen fit to promote you—to raise your vibrations up a bit. You know, open you up to new stuff." He sighed. White Eagle didn't have a clue what he was talking about. "Don't worry. Most of us react in the same way until we get used to it. It's our light that scares us. We're more afraid of our light than we are of our dark. It's the power you see. There's nothing we can compare it to—relax!"

White Eagle looked all around the crystal, gawping at the orange particles. He made a grab for them but they moved through his fingers like fresh air. He closed his eyes. He could hold them with his mind—feel them even, but they didn't respond to the physical part of him. Even though he was a spirit, every now and again he liked to use his physical aspect, but the particles were there to remind him that nothing is solid. He floated as if in water, letting the particles soak him up. Once he realised he was a part of them he started to adjust much quicker. He felt lighter, expanded, almost as if he were the same size as the universe itself. He looked at his body. His form had changed into an elaborate expression of life. Thousands of golden threads shimmered with a blue current inside them that could be seen rushing through silver channels.

Roman studied White Eagle. "Is it getting easier?" He cocked his head toward NeilA.

"I'll leave you to it. I want to sense out Maggie." NeilA walked over to a silver, disc-shaped object about a metre in diameter. He leant on it briefly. He started to draw a rectangular shape but changed his mind and voiced his request instead. "Requesting hologram in the present, Maggie O'Connell, Chateau Saint Esteve, Volonne, France, Planet Earth." The living image blinked into existence immediately.

Roman repeated his question to White Eagle.

"I think I'm…," he hesitated, "…I feel fine."

"Are you ready to come out of the chamber?"

"You tell me! Will I look like this?" He scanned his new appearance. "My charges won't recognise me."

Roman smiled. "It's up to you. You'll still be able to change form whenever you feel like it. Promotion doesn't mean that you'll lose your old abilities."

"I think I'll be okay to leave. I'm feeling better…calmer, at least." He walked out of the chamber looking like his old self. "I still feel a bit light-headed, though."

Roman was distracted. "Light-headed…that's a good sign. Come, we didn't expect conception to take this long." They walked over to where NeilA stood watching Maggie. "Disc, White Eagle?"

"Err…sure, I suppose. Thanks."

Another two of the strange silver discs manifested out of the empty space that was referred to as "nothing" on Earth. They hung motionless in the air about six feet away from them. Roman flipped his hand towards himself impatiently. The disc shot forward at terrific speed. He flipped his wrist, caught it, and commanded, "Rest, please." The disc formed into a clear gel-looking substance which shaped itself to his body. He relaxed into it.

The disc was new to White Eagle. Not being used to it, he fought with it. Every time it tried to mould to him, he tore it away and threw it as hard as he could in the hope that it would go back to wherever it came from. But steadfast, the disc returned, and positioned itself a few inches away from his face. "What the hell? Get away from me!"

Roman and NeilA shot each other amused glances. "What are you doing? Just sit on it!" Roman reached out. Like Atla, one of his fingers grew. The suction pad on the end of it attached itself to the disc. "Here, sit on it! It won't bite."

"It feels weird!"

"Give it a chance."

White Eagle grabbed the disc on either side and positioned it beneath him, but as soon as it started to mould to him he jumped off and tossed it away hard, in the hope that it wouldn't come back.

NeilA stopped leaning on his and picked it up. "Like this,." he said, before sitting on it.

Roman shook his finger. "What are you scared of?"

"I'm not scared!"

"Then just sit on the thing instead of jumping about like a damn fairy!"

"I'm no fairy!"

"Then stop acting like one!"

Slightly affronted at being compared to a mere fairy, White Eagle clung to the disc and was amazed at its ability to change form. It didn't take him long to get used to it. "Wow! There's nothing like comfort."

All three of them floated about, weightless. Using the power of their minds, they could direct the discs to move to any part of the ship they wanted.

They studied Maggie's hologram. White Eagle didn't appreciate her anxiety. "She's calmed down a bit, but she's still on edge."

NeilA gave him a reassuring smile. "She'll be fine. Remember, she's been through much worse."

White Eagle frowned. "Isn't it an infringement of privacy the way you can pull up these holograms?"

Roman continued to watch Maggie. "What do you think? You've

used the system on many occasions."

"Only when necessary and the contracts were sealed between me and my charges. I've had their permission."

"Same thing. In Maggie's case, at a deeper level, when she agreed to carry the child she set herself up to remain under our protection. We have the permission of all our workers, you included, to remain with them should they slide, or find themselves in a, let's say, overwhelming position...as you did, in the underworld."

"Couldn't the dark pull up a hologram? What if they get a hold of what's going on here?"

"They can pull the holograms for their own workers. But just like the white hole you saw earlier, our holograms are protected by individual soul notes. We can pull you, Maggie, and others, because we've had your permission even though you may not remember the sanctification between us; even so, there are times when we will intervene regardless. We're sensitive to the emotions of our workers while they're on Earth. If they get too overwhelmed we'll step in. Of course, the Originator has the final say and may tell us to butt out, so to speak."

"And the dark...can you pull up their holograms?"

"Oh, yes—we can. This is only because they are constantly trying to break into ours and in doing so inadvertently give us permission to break into theirs—what you put out you get back. The difference being that we've mastered the art, and they haven't. Of course, we have to be aware of what they're up to in the first place so that we know where to look, but sometimes their secrets are well guarded and the Originator might warn us of an up and coming disaster so that we can help lessen the blow. Now...!" Roman put a hand on White Eagle's shoulder. "We'd better get on with conception."

White Eagle looked pensive. "Indeed...so many questions."

NeilA gave them a sideways glance without really taking his eyes off Maggie's hologram. "It's good to ask questions but don't let them swamp you; otherwise, things never get done. Sometimes you just have to rush into things...go with the flow, the flow of the universe."

He punched the air with his fist, his full attention now on White Eagle. "The magic, White Eagle." He was full of enthusiasm. "You know; that simple, comfortable feeling that says you're doing the right thing even though the odds are stacked against you."

"Yes, but Maggie is…I feel responsible for her."

"Good! The position of spirit guide shouldn't be taken any other way."

White Eagle was insistent. "I know we need to crack on, but I still have questions that I'd like answered before we do." NeilA looked at Roman and nodded. They turned to White Eagle expectantly. "How much do Maggie and David know about the child they're responsible for? Do they realise that he is a split-off from a supreme power? Do they know that they're Galaxian workers?"

Roman spoke. "At soul level, yes. At human level, no…although there's a constant bleed-through from the soul but the ego usually overrides the information. Over the years it is your job to explain it to Maggie and, in turn, she'll explain it to David. Of course, one day he's going to be roped in, so to speak, but for now we'll go easy on him. She has already accepted that we are a part of her soul group, and she knows something of her role with Galaxias, having viewed one of her past lives. Maggie is much more open to receiving information than is David. Even so, she has no idea of the status we are talking here and she's happy to keep it that way. Unfortunately, like most people on Earth, she sees aliens not as another one of the countless paths for the soul to experience, and a way to elevate consciousness that is open to all souls."

He shrugged. "She has no fear of the spirit world because having dealt with it since as far back as she can remember, she's used to it, but anything beyond that fills her with dread. She's just not ready for us." His eyes narrowed. "Not ready for herself would be a more apt description. Now that your consciousness had been opened up to the next level, you may find yourself in a similar position at times. There'll be things you have no concept of."

"And the child…she has no idea that he is…different, the power?"

"Only at soul level. At Maggie level, all she wants is a normal baby, not a divine being, as is the terminology on Earth. Of course, they fail to realise that everyone is a divine be—" he stopped abruptly and shot NeilA a knowing glance.

NeilA looked edgy. "We'd better move along. White Eagle, can you advise Maggie to bond with the child?"

"But why? She's already attached…and I know Maggie. Once she holds this child in her arms, she won't give him up. That will make her life even more complicated than it already is. A single woman with a baby…she'll be dragged through the mill—"

"There are ways to get around things. There's no point dwelling on a scenario unless it's the one you have, let's say, shares in. Despite how it looks, this child is off to a good start. Right now we're not concerned with her decision, only with the immediate future. It's important for Maggie and the child to form a strong bond immediately after the birth. This is mother love; without it a child is never complete. His nurturing, his power, everything, will be affected if this love isn't transferred to him as soon as possible. Even a child such as ours needs this basic start in life when on Earth. Believe me, White Eagle, we wouldn't put Maggie through unnecessary heartache."

"Can't he get it from his adoptive mother?"

"It depends on what level she's at with her thinking. She can if she realises that the biological process plays a very small part in the overall parenting, but even so, his power would be affected. It was always the three: Maggie, David, and the child. His adoptive mother can give him everything Maggie can, except a piece of Maggie's power."

"I see." White Eagle looked troubled.

"Any more questions?" NeilA stood up. "Conception has started."

"If Maggie decides to keep the child, do you know the outcome?"

He shrugged. "The future is subjective. It can change in any given moment. While on Earth, the child will make choices, change his mind, emotions will get in his way. We will be there, of course, but cannot interfere other than to prick his conscience and remind him of the job he has to do—unless something drastic happens and we are instructed to intervene. Remember that he is still a child on Earth. He will need a lot of help handling his power."

"Are you going to guide him, NeilA?"

Roman and NeilA eyed each other. White Eagle noticed the awkward silence. Roman spoke. "Naturally, Galaxias and G.U.N. will have a role to play, but at the last meeting the elders decided that you will be his coach while he is on the Earth plane—"

"ME!"

"Is there a problem?"

"I…I'm not ready for such a position."

Roman moved forward with a twinkle in his eye. "White Eagle, you've turned white!" Both he and NeilA burst into laughter but stopped when they sensed White Eagle's uneasiness. "Why do you doubt your capabilities?"

"I don't know…I…it's the responsibility. I haven't had the, the, experience—"

"Fear, White Eagle. Don't let it go any further." His voice was soft.

White Eagle opened his mouth to speak but forgot what he wanted to say. Head bent, he toyed with an arrowhead that was attached to a piece of cord around his neck.

"White Eagle, it is a great opportunity to walk with a child such as this."

"I'm grateful to you all and the trust you have in me, but I just don't think I'm up to the position." He looked up into Roman's eyes. "What if I let you down? The child…?"

Roman brushed him off. "How many times have you advised Maggie when she's been afraid to go further? 'Walk your talk,' you say to her. Besides, you are chief advisor to his mother. It makes perfect sense that you look after them both. The bond is already there."

White Eagle was hesitant. "I don't know…"

Roman persisted. "Think of the child as a nice surprise, an addition to your family. Besides, you're not on your own. I'll be around." He smiled kindly. "If you don't wish to take the position we have Sidney lined up as your second."

"Sidney! You think he's ready?"

"When we drew up a list for potential guides, only those we felt up to the task were considered. It was your close bond with Maggie that swayed us in your favour. Might I add, Sidney showed no such apprehension. He accepted position of second, with grace."

"Any others?"

"A whole team. Most of them will stay in the background. Then there's NeilA and myself."

He relaxed a bit. "Okay then, like you said, I'm not alone—"

"We can't wait any longer!" NeilA interrupted. "It is time! No more questions!"

NeilA sent a thought form replica of himself to Remul and the rest of the crew. "Return the aircraft safely to their base. Conception has started. You will not hear from us now until we're ready to initiate it." The thought form blinked out of existence.

14.

Awestruck, Maggie watched a huge cloud swallow up the lights. It was a striking sight. Its centre burned like the sun and gave off pale, yellow beams that faded into electric blue and lit up the dark sky behind it. It had a funny shape, more like a disc than a cloud. The two aircraft dangled underneath it like toys on an invisible piece of string. She caught her breath—worried they were about to drop out of the sky as they turned suddenly—but relaxed when they headed back in the direction they'd come from. Their engines silent, they flew through the sky smoothly, as if being glided by an invisible pair of hands.

Inside the planes the pilots were calm. Their instincts told them they had nothing to fear. They knew that the aliens—whatever they were—were taking them back to base. All doubt in their minds as to whether humans were the only intelligent life in the universe was removed!

Maggie watched the aircraft disappear from view. A weak smile crossed her face. She headed back to the chateau. She felt uneasy but not as scared as she'd have anticipated, given the situation.

"Call to her, White Eagle," NeilA urged.

White Eagle appeared at Maggie's side. "Maggie, I need to speak with you."

Alarmed, she jumped back. "Blazes Kate! You could have warned me you were coming!"

"Sorry, no time. We must hurry."

She looked puzzled. "Hurry what? What are you talking about?" She carried on walking toward the chateau.

"Conception. The baby, the soul must initiate—"

"White Eagle, you're about nine months too late!" she joked.

"No, no, let me explain. The spirit of the child has been growing inside you but conception hasn't taken place yet. The soul is now ready to initiate his growth, his purpose." White Eagle struggled to find a way to explain it.

"What are you babbling on about? I've felt him kick inside me." Her eyes sparkled. "Felt his heartbeat, his life run through me, parallel to mine. He's already got a soul!"

He took her arm. "Stop for a moment; listen to me." She slowed down and looked up at him.

"Remember the soul/spirit conversation you had with David?" She nodded. She felt apprehensive. Something was going on! "It's the same thing, only this child is an advanced soul—old, even ancient, in Earth's terms. The spirit is growing inside you, and it can come and go at will, don't forget, but the soul connection won't happen until he's ready to be born." He paused, reading her face. His expression was intense, serious. It was time for her to realise, to see. "You have chosen to give birth to a soul with knowledge and wisdom beyond the comprehension of the human brain, Maggie."

She eyed him suspiciously. "What do you mean? Why? Why does his soul connect so late in the day?" she asked tightly.

"As a rule, they don't. It's just that some souls have more complex issues attached to them, and many reasons that might justify a new perspective. You or the child, his spirit, even the soul, may decide to alter course. Things change, circumstances, etc."

"Are you saying the spirit can be born without a soul connection?"

He shook his head. "No. But the spirit may decide to ignore the connection, do its own thing, go its own way. This is why so many people on Earth seem to be lost. They need to reconnect with their source."

"But what's so special, so, so different about this soul? We're all special, aren't we?" She felt scared but tried to make light of it.

White Eagle rubbed his brow with his fingertips and looked down at the grass, searching for an explanation. "Okay, you've heard of the expression 'soul mate'?"

She looked at him as if he were stupid. "A term used by lovesick teenagers!"

He gave her a bemused look. "You're only just out of nappies yourself! Anyway, I don't want to get off track," he continued. "This soul and the baby you carry are soul mates in the true sense of the word. This baby is a…a, split-off from another soul, a powerful—no! I don't want to frighten you—an evolved soul. Unbelievingly evolved, as I said earlier, like nothing the human brain can comprehend."

"Like a twin, you mean?"

"Yes, yes," he said excitedly. "As the egg splits in half to form twins…" He looked thoughtful, and traced his top lip with his index finger. "But this soul can split many times into many things, and it has been given permission from the Originator to form many new souls from itself if it so desires."

Baffled, Maggie stared at White Eagle. "Are you saying that this soul is so powerful that the Creator has allowed it to break free and produce souls that are not attached to the Creator at all?" Horrified, she gasped, turned quickly, and headed for the chateau. "I don't like it! I will pray to God tonight and ask for intervention in this. I know that you think this…this being is evolved, but I don't want anything to do with a soul that doesn't come from the same place you and I come from!"

White Eagle chased after her. "Maggie, wait! You don't understand—"

She stopped abruptly and searched his face for an explanation. Deep down she knew that he wouldn't involve her in something that would cause her harm. "Then help me to."

"Please, just hear me out. You know I wouldn't endanger you in any way," he said, as if reading her thoughts. "Not intentionally. You have to trust me on this. I'm having a problem explaining it, that's all." She waited patiently. "Okay, okay," he whispered to himself. "It's not that this being…this soul—" He stopped. "Let's give him his name."

"You know it!" she stated, incredulously.

He tried to lighten the mood. "Of course! I wouldn't allow any Tom, Dick, or Harry to impregnate you!" She laughed nervously. He took her hand. "This may come as a shock."

There was silence. Maggie broke it. "Oh, God!" She looked away, then back at him. "I'm going! I don't like it!" She tried to pull away. He pulled her back gently. "It's NeilA."

The colour drained from her face. "NeilA, NeilA," she whispered, waiting for it to register but fear blocked her. "I don't know any bloody NeilA! What kind of a name is that?"

NeilA cut in telepathically to White Eagle. "We're almost ready. Forget the explanations."

White Eagle looked up at the cloud. "I can't!" he snapped.

"Can't what?" Maggie asked.

He shook his head in frustration. "I'm talking to myself. Look, Maggie. There are a few souls in certain universes that are so powerful, so evolved, that their essence is pure. So pure, that it matches that of the Originator, the Creator. This is why the Creator grants them certain, let's say, privileges, but even so, they still work with the Creator. They are not separate. You've misinterpreted. They are on a par, yes, on a par is a good way to describe it; their energy is intricate…balanced. It has blended with the Creator's. They are one…one soul with individual aspects. It is the same with all of us but NeilA is at a different level." He noted the look of absolute confusion on her face, and shook his head. "Look! I don't want to get too deep—"

She raised her eyebrows and opened her mouth—

Time was short. He interrupted before she could say anything. "They've cleared all garbage from their energy fields, whereas the rest of us are still working on it." He paused. "The child is an old soul in one respect, but a new one in another. Do you understand…am I making myself clear?"

"Yes, yes," she whispered, trying to digest it. "Why me? Why have I been chosen to carry such a child? And that makes my decision to give him up even harder. What if I give him to the wrong people? I don't know the adoptive parents—"

"Maggie, you've made choices; you just don't remember making them. The child has made choices. We all have, everybody involved.

Granted, choices can change but the soul purpose will always remain the same."

"I'm frightened. I don't understand why I have to do this. You said things change. I'm changing my mind. I want to give birth to a normal child, not one from a powerful being or whatever you want to call it."

Roman and NeilA looked on, glued to the hologram. "It's too late to change now," NeilA whispered. White Eagle got the message.

Maggie stormed toward the chateau. "This isn't fair! How can you tell me this now? Why didn't you mention it before?"

White Eagle was frantic. "Because that was the deal, the divine agreement—"

"Stop prattling on about divine agreements. I remember no such thing."

White Eagle took hold of Maggie's shoulders roughly. "Think about your dreams, your meditations, the old man you sit with in your dreams—"

She looked baffled. "The wise old man?"

"Yes. He's a symbol. Try to remember the conversations you've had with him. He's the agreement. In the waking state, you remember very little. Even in the dream state, if your fear is powerful enough. Marguerite is a good example. It was only recently on your trip to the underworld that you came upon her, yet so soon after the experience you remember very little. It is the same with your divine agreement. It was made at a different level of consciousness, one that is buried underneath your physical layers, even your astral layers—the same state that you are in now."

"Now? I'm real! I'm here!" She rubbed her arms to make sure. She looked at him confused,. "I'm real! This is real!" She looked around at her surroundings.

He stared intensely into her eyes, his voice evocative. "Yes, it's very real, Maggie. I hope you'll remember this conversation." They stared at each other in silence.

NeilA turned to Roman. "It's time." He stared at Maggie through the hologram, and inhaled deeply.

"Huh!" Maggie gasped, and clutched her stomach. But her eyes remained locked with White Eagle's.

NeilA inhaled again and again. Maggie couldn't speak, couldn't move. The only thing she could do was breathe in unison with NeilA, unaware that she was consumed by his force.

"Lay her down, White Eagle," Roman instructed.

White Eagle gently laid Maggie down on the grass, which still resembled a carpet of rainbows. The colours penetrated them until they were completely submerged. They looked like moving colour parts.

Other than deep, deep, breathing, Maggie still couldn't function. It was as if everything was being renewed inside her. She wanted to hold her belly, feel her child kick, know he was safe. She tried to bring her arms up but they lay heavy, motionless, by her side. She knew that all she had to do was get through the fear and believe. She decided that if it was time to die, she'd go holding her baby. She forced her arms, willed them up, until they moved slowly and enveloped her belly.

NeilA carried on inhaling in sync with Maggie, never taking his eyes off her. She looked at White Eagle wide-eyed, horrified. She couldn't think. She tried to speak. No words came out. She wanted to know what was happening to her. What was wrong with her breathing?

White Eagle spoke softly. He knew she was terrified. "Shh, it won't take long."

NeilA appeared in front of them with Roman at his side but this time they had thrown off their camouflage. Maggie had to see, had to know who they were—had to know who she was. Satisfied with the air she was inhaling, he regulated his breath, so that she could breathe normally. Conception could only take place in pure air. There could be no chemical or psychic toxins.

Stark terror filled her. *Oh my God! The child I carry—it's one of them!* She bolted upright, fighting with every ounce of her being. She turned to White Eagle and slapped him hard across his face, then again, and again. "How could you?" she screamed at him. "I'm not doing this! I won't have one of them. I can't! It's not normal! I just want a normal baby!"

It took White Eagle a few pauses to get over the shock of Maggie's slaps. "Shh, shh, Maggie, try to be calm." He grabbed her arms before she landed him another clout. "You are having a normal baby, whatever that is. Your child isn't going to look like them. He'll look like any other human."

"It's not the looks," she sobbed hysterically. "It's what it is—an alien!" She was horror-struck. "I can't do it! I won't!"

NeilA intervened. "We're all aliens." He walked toward her slowly. "An alien is just another way for the soul to express itself... a natural expression. There is an aspect of your soul in my world, Maggie, you know that—"

"Stay away from me," she snarled. "I mean it! Don't you touch me—what's that? What are you doing?"

A stream of orange energy with a spiral pattern cascaded from NeilA's middle. He looked for a simple explanation. "Creative energy."

Maggie knew instinctively that once this energy stuff got to her there would be no going back. She started to scramble backwards on her elbows. "Please don't touch me. Please, I don't want to do it," she sobbed. But NeilA carried on walking toward her slowly, menacingly.

White Eagle tried to hold her and calm her down but she threw him off. "Don't you touch me! Don't touch me! I trusted you. I'll never forgive you for this, never!"

All of a sudden, White Eagle jumped up and stood between Maggie and NeilA. "I can't allow it to go any further...she's too upset." He was terrified. He knew he was no match for NeilA, but even so, he couldn't stand by and watch Maggie in so much distress.

Roman smiled.

NeilA stopped abruptly. His colours had taken on White Eagle's mood, which was mostly grey with the odd bit of red dotted here and there. He smiled. "Well done, White Eagle! I feel your fear, yet you battle regardless! You are definitely the one."

White Eagle didn't know what to make of it. He'd expected a reaction but this was a far cry from the one he thought he'd get. "The one?"

"Yes, the main influence in the child's development on Earth. A few of the elders had their doubts but I'm sure they've just had them demolished. Thank you for that."

"I'm sorry to let you down but they were right. I can't allow the soul split to take place. I've never seen Maggie so upset—"

Breathless, Maggie stopped trying to get away and looked on.

Using his hand, NeilA gestured White Eagle to be quiet. "I'm sorry, White Eagle, I don't wish to pull rank on you, but I am! There's no going back."

Shocked, White Eagle responded, "Pull rank on me!"

"Call it divine intervention—it sounds better. Things are now in place for the child's arrival. Conception will proceed." NeilA closed his eyes as if listening to something.

The atmosphere took on a sudden calmness, a lightness that White Eagle had never before experienced. An all-consuming, loving sensation saturated him. He'd felt love before, but not like this. It was overpowering, omnipotent, an unconditional love. In this moment he knew that everything was as it should be. This was a momentous event for him...divine intervention. The Originator was in the process of intervening right in front of him. He was sure that it had happened many times before but he'd never been aware of it. All fear removed, he surrendered to the moment and stood aside to allow NeilA to spread his seed.

"NOOOOOOOO!" Maggie's pitiful screams faded out into the night. Unlike White Eagle, she'd missed the moment. Still consumed by fear, she'd allowed it to pass her by without giving it a first thought, let alone a second one. "NOOOO!" She arched her back and scrambled backwards on her elbows once again in an effort to get to the chateau.

NeilA looked down at her. The orange energy pumped from his middle, filling the air with an omnipotent force that obliterated all pollutants.

Helpless, she stopped, and looked into his eyes. "Please don't," she gasped. "I don't want a baby with you!"

NeilA smiled and knelt down to her level. "Maggie, I won't harm you…I love you."

His voice, so soft, floated right through her like a wind chime. She felt as if she were under hypnosis—aware, yet not there.

"Be calm," he whispered. "Let the energy take you, let it penetrate…love you…shhhhh…" He stroked her brow, her face and arms, then her stomach. She clutched it protectively. "It's okay," he reassured her. He slid his fingers down her neck and shoulder, caressed her arm, circled her fingertips with his.

She felt calmer. His touch, like his voice, travelled to her core. A slow ripple of heat started to throb in her feet and move up through the rest of her. His touch was pure energy. She started to simmer slowly. With every stroke, she got hotter and hotter until she felt him sear through her. She moaned quietly. "My God! What's happening to me?" His energy stroked every part of her body, inside, outside; she felt it caress and heal her. Despite herself, she moaned again only louder, as if she had no control over the sounds escaping from her throat. "Oh, my God!" His energy rushed her; the tenseness, the fear, the heartache, poured out. She gasped, "Sweet Jesus!" The ripples of energy moved from her toes to her brain, filling her mind.

NeilA stood. She gazed up at him. She knew he wasn't finished but she didn't care; the tables had turned. She wanted more of him. The silhouette of her outstretched arms against the dark blue sky reached out to him like branches clutching at the wind. "Don't go, don't leave me," she whispered.

He looked up at the huge cloud and called to his crew using the same kind of sound Roman had used to bring in the white hole for assessment. He looked down at Maggie's baffled expression. "I asked them to let the love in their hearts flood out."

The coloured lights emerged from the cloud like snowflakes: beautiful, every one of them a unique pattern. They floated to the ground and joined Roman and White Eagle to form a circle around NeilA and Maggie. Their individual colours blended together and snaked around everything in sight. The effect on the chateau and its grounds was dramatic. It looked like a surreal piece of art, or some kind of strange new world found in a fantasy book. The colours were vivid, alive. They had an intelligence of their own. They pulsed and glowed and blew life into everything…into her.

Mesmerised, Maggie looked on. She'd never seen anything so different, yet so magnificent. The lights had changed form. No longer glowing orbs, they resembled NeilA and Roman. You could see the uniqueness of every one of them, but it was obvious they'd come from the same race of beings.

NeilA carried on making the strange sound—let the love in your hearts flood out. The energy was intense. It was as if Earth had suddenly shrunk into one small moment. Just as she thought the energy couldn't get any stronger, it did. It doubled, tripled, more—Maggie felt the universe birth inside her. She screamed out in ecstasy. "NOWWWWW!"

The beings called out in unison on her scream, and could be heard above it. It sounded like something that could be found underneath the ocean. The grounds of the chateau erupted into a crescendo of sound and light.

NeilA turned, stood over her, and looked deep into her eyes. "Are you ready?"

"Yes! Yes!" she panted.

He knelt down beside her and laid his hand flat on her belly. This time her arms remained by her side. Fear was gone. Only trust remained—this was what they meant by "conditions for conception had to be perfect." She knew that NeilA would never hurt her or her child.

"Are you ready?" he asked again.

She looked up at the sky, bathed for a moment in the silver light of the moon before it hid behind a cloud. "I'm ready."

His energy condensed behind her back, lifting her up. He straddled her. She felt no weight. He looked into her soul. "Are you ready?" he repeated for the third time.

"I'm ready." She looked deep into his eyes and saw who he was. "My God, I don't know why I feared—"

"Don't think about fear. Stay with love." The orange energy

flowed from his middle into hers.

The sensations running through her drove her wild. She arched backwards in a frenzy. NeilA put his arm out, caught her, and pulled her to him. Relentlessly his energy pumped into her. She felt it enter every pore, replacing her lifeblood. He stopped to allow her to rest. She looked at him and cradled his beautiful face in her hands, "I love you, I love you," she said breathlessly.

All around them a low hum resonated beneath the cry of the beings. They chanted in tones and notes that she didn't recognise but it didn't matter. She moved with the music, the pulse, the energy—and even though she was aware of them, it was as if time belonged to her and NeilA alone, as if they were the only two present.

His energy was ruthless; he took her again and again. The pulse in her head pumped in time to the blood rushing through her veins—to NeilA's pulse. He tipped her back and lay weightless on top of her. She spread herself wide, not wanting it to end. "Almost done," he crooned.

"No, don't stop, don't let it be done," she gasped.

His lips brushed hers, soft, gentle, pure energy, no physical touching. But hers were hungry. She wanted to devour him, savour him. The sweat poured from her. Her long red hair stuck to her. "Take all of me!" she demanded. She wanted to feel his soul join hers. "Do it! Do it!" She took his hand, laid it inside her nightdress, raised her breast to him. "Let me feel your soul inside me."

A wave of heat seared through her, jolted her body. Brutal, gentle, a bittersweet sensation she couldn't stand yet couldn't live without. It started in her feet and moved like a tiger through her body. Her throat chanted out small sounds of pleasure that got louder, louder, with every thrust. Impatient now, she pushed NeilA away, ripped off her nightdress, and straddled him. Thrusting, panting, clawing, hungry— like a predator going in for the kill, she screamed out. Inhibitions gone. She was in control. She felt liberated, satiated; she felt her power. She wanted it all, David, the baby, NeilA—and she'd get them!

Beads of sweat dripped down her naked body. She sat upright on top of NeilA, circling and thrusting in time to the chants while the rest of the beings looked on. She lifted her arms up to the sky, raised her head to the universe, and surrendered. She cried out, "Here is my heart, it's yours!" She looked down at NeilA, took his hands, held them to her breasts. The moment was beautiful, loving, free. She stopped thrusting for a few seconds, looked down at him, then started again slowly, gently. She moaned, then screamed in pleasure as her hunger, along with her thrusts, became more urgent. The pulse in her head beat faster, faster. She cried out his name as his energy flooded her again and again. Dizzy, she reeled with ecstasy. She felt his soul enter her. "NEILAAA!" she screamed, "NEILAAAAAAA...!"

The moon shot from behind a cloud for the briefest moment, bathing them in its light. The beings stopped chanting; their silhouettes were black against moonlit blue. All was still. Not a sound could be heard until the cry of a wolf in the distance howled for at least ten seconds, and then once again, until the whole pack joined in.

15.

"AEDAN...NEILA...NEIL...!" Maggie woke up shouting out some kind of strange name she'd never heard before.

She rolled over, tried to get comfortable, and then realised she was soaking wet. Her nightdress, hair, even the sheets were stuck to her. She sat bolt upright, turned on the bedside lamp, and looked at the clock on the mantelpiece. 3:15 a.m. *I thought...didn't this just happen?* "I must have been dreaming," she whispered.

Confused and still half asleep, she looked around the room. Everything was the same, the shadows, the time. She threw off the covers. She had a strong urge to go to the bathroom. A pleasant sensation of wet warmth trickled down her legs. "My God! My waters!" She grabbed a few towels from the small wooden crib by her bed, and shoved them underneath herself just in time to catch the waterfall that was cascading between her legs.

She felt no panic, just a feeling of excitement mixed with a tinge of apprehension.

"I should wake Angelette." But the need to be alone with her child coursed through her, strong and defiant. She carried on talking to herself, looking at her belly. "No! It's me and you. I'm having you to myself for a few hours at least."

She couldn't believe how much at peace she felt. She knew that everything was as it should be, and that she and the baby would be fine. It was as if some unseen...thing, power, being—she didn't have a clue what—was helping her.

She reached over, pulled some more fresh towels from the side of the crib, and put them underneath herself. Her instincts told her Aedan was about to make his entrance. She started to pant fast and hard like a dog after a good run.

The contractions came one after the other. It felt like an elastic band was being stretched inside her lower back Funny, everything she'd heard on the subject of giving birth was about how painful it was. But the only pain she felt was from the mental torture, happy to remind her that she had to give up her baby within hours of his birth.

The urge to push came back fast and furious and lasted for about thirty seconds…but nothing. She tried to relax, to catch her breath, but within no time she felt the slight tightening in her lower back, and the urge to push return stronger than before. She pushed harder, longer. "Come on Aedan…the quicker you arrive, the more time we'll have together."

But he wasn't ready. She felt impatient. She wanted him in her arms. She sat upright in a squatting position, and aligned her back against the dark, wooden headboard. The strong mahogany was solid. It gave her a sense of security.

She panted for what felt like an eternity; she strained and pushed down into her bottom with every bit of strength she could muster. "Aedan, come on. I want to hold you, get to know you a little bit before—one more push!" But still Aedan refused to make his grand entrance.

She put her hand between her legs. She could feel his head. It was wet and sticky and peculiar! A little person was coming out of her!? She gasped and laughed at the same time. "One more push, Aedan, one more."

She pushed again, this time determined it would be the last. She was right. Both hands were between her legs, ready to catch him—and catch him she did! Aedan shot out of her! Head, shoulders, legs, feet. He chased away any delusions she'd had about him entering the world slowly, and in a dignified manner! He screamed out his indignation.

Tears of joy streamed down her face. She pulled him from her, lifted him in the air dripping and bloody. "AEDANNNNNNNN!" She howled his name in unison with a pack of wolves somewhere on the grounds of the chateau. She held him high above her for a minute or two more. His small arms and legs thrashed about in temper, and he never let up screaming. "Aedan, Aedan," she sobbed. She laid him on her breast. "Look at you; you're perfect, just perfect." She looked at the clock. 3:33 a.m.

He grunted impatiently and thumped his small head against her chest in the hunt for food and comfort until he found her nipple and fixed on. "Shh," she soothed. "We don't want to wake anybody."

She reached over to the crib, took another towel, and poured a small amount of water onto it. She wiped Aedan gently, making sure she got into every nook and cranny of his soft, dimpled skin.

Besotted, she took in every part of him. Every finger, every toe. He was strong and solid. Something about White Eagle kept popping into her head. *He will be normal,'* she kept hearing him say. *It's very real…remember this conversation, Maggie.'*

"What conversation?" She looked over at the patio doors. Coloured lights and military aircraft flashed before her eyes, and then some strange-looking beings. She shrugged it off. *Dreams.* She wiped Aedan's mass of spiky black hair with the damp towel. Through his red and wrinkly skin, she could see that he was the image of David. The broad nose, the strong jaw line were already evident.

"Oh my God, you're beautiful, just beautiful," she crooned. "You've got your daddy's looks; by God, you have that! You're the spit of him!"

'What if the child is the image of me?' Remnants of a past conversation with David whispered to her. She laughed quietly to herself. "There's no denying who your daddy is, that's for sure." Eyes closed, he relaxed his mouth, stopped suckling, and listened. "You know I love you, don't you?" She massaged his face; she couldn't leave him alone.

He opened his beautiful eyes and looked straight at her. They were David's eyes: deep, soulful brown, almost black, with the longest lashes. They stared at each other for the longest moment. She smiled. He continued to look into her eyes…look into her. He knew who she was. Her tears fell onto his tiny chest. She wiped them clean. All the while she cried quietly. He felt her pain and started to cry softly, a warning that he was getting ready to bawl. "Shh, shh, I'm sorry, I'm sorry. I'm not going to let anything spoil this moment…shh, shh." Her nipple remained in his mouth but he refused to feed. He coughed out small, distressed grunts, like a car getting ready to rev.

Their eyes remained locked. He was the most beautiful, precious thing life had ever given to her, and she knew, absolutely, there was no way on Earth she'd ever give him up. She felt his tiny body stiffen in her arms, watched his face turn red and his small hands clench into fists. "It's alright, Aedan. Shh, darling, shh. I'll never give you up. Never!" Her voice was protective, aggressive. "Never!"

She sang quietly one of her favourite Irish folksongs: "My love said to me, me mother won't mind…and me father won't slight you for your lack of kind…" At the sound of his mother's voice, wrapped up in her love, it took just a few seconds for him to stop struggling and close his eyes. Maggie carried on singing: "And then she turned homeward with one star awake, like the swan in the evening moves over the lake…"

She closed her mind and stopped the constant questions about keeping him, how would they survive, what will people—David—say? She didn't care. Aedan was her life. She closed her eyes. "It will not be long, love, 'til our wedding day…"

Mother and child fell asleep together.

16.

Angelette was between worlds—half in, half out of sleep. She could have sworn she heard the cry of a newborn. She tried to move, go to Maggie, but sleep paralysis pinned her down. She lay there patiently, aware that sleep paralysis was nothing more than her spirit trying to get back into her body after its sleep-time travels. Once it made it, the paralysis would be over.

It lasted a few seconds but felt like forever. She jumped out of bed and ran to the patio doors, flung them open, and ran out onto the balcony. Everything was peaceful. A slight breeze rustled the trees and tiny drops of rain cooled her face. She looked up at the indigo sky and smiled. The stars were out in force. Some of them were blocked by a huge blue cloud, but she could still make out Orion's Belt.

"Orion's Belt. Orion, the Hunter," a voice swam through her head. "What! Why are you? What does it mean?" she whispered. She glanced across at Maggie's balcony. *Did it happen…Was I dreaming? The colours…*

She saw Maggie running through the garden in her nightdress. "MAGGIE!" she cried out. But when she looked again, Maggie wasn't there. Angelette rushed back inside. It had all seemed so real. She looked at the clock. It was a few minutes away from 4 a.m. She felt the urge to check on her friend and hurriedly put on her nightgown. She closed the bedroom door quietly and padded down the hallway to Maggie's room. She knocked gently and put her ear to the door. No answer. She hesitated, not wanting to disturb her, but something nagged and told her that she must. She knocked again. No response.

Despite herself, she opened the door and crept in. As she got to the end of Maggie's bed she stopped dead in her tracks and gasped out loud. They looked like the Madonna and Child. Peaceful. Content. Their auras glistened around them like halos. The bond between Maggie and her son held Angelette in a vise-like grip.

Why hadn't Maggie called her? *This will only make things more difficult.* She sighed and stood for a while longer with tears in her eyes. She wanted to go over, hold the baby, embrace Maggie and congratulate her, yet she didn't want to disturb the rare moment mother and son would cherish together.

Maggie yawned and stretched slightly; she had a feeling someone was watching her. She opened her eyes, smiled at Angelette, then looked at Aedan as if to say, Look what I've done! The happiness she felt inside radiated from her. The two women stared at each other. Neither of them spoke. In that moment Angelette knew that Maggie would never give the child away and she vowed to herself that she would do everything in her power to help them stay together. She walked over slowly, sat down on the side of the bed, and kissed her friend's cheeks. "Maggie, he is beautiful. I am so proud of you both," she whispered. "I want to hold him, but I wait until he wakes."

Both women laughed and cried together. Angelette walked over to Maggie's dresser and pulled out a couple of linen handkerchiefs from the top drawer before sitting down at the side of the bed again. Careful not to wake Aedan, she leant forward and dabbed Maggie's cheeks. "Look at the pair of us," she sobbed.

Aedan's tiny legs and body went rigid in Maggie's arms. With his head rolling from side to side, he parted with trapped wind, and what sounded like a full nappy—very loudly for such a tiny person!

"Well, Aedan!" Maggie exclaimed with a look of surprise. "That's what you think of it so far!" The women collapsed into laughter.

"Oh, Maggie, please let me change him." Angelette leant over and took Aedan from her. "Come to me, little one. Let's get you cleaned up." Angelette nuzzled Aedan's hair. "Ahh, the baby smell, there is nothing like it."

"You can say that again!" Maggie joked.

Angelette laughed out loud and laid Aedan on his back. "I wasn't meaning *that* smell!"

"I know what you meant."

Angelette held both Aedan's feet in one hand and removed his nappy with the other. Folding it over a few times, she cleaned the treacle-looking substance from his bottom. "There you are. Let's get rid of this sticky stuff." Maggie passed Angelette a damp flannel. When she'd done, she sprinkled him with talcum powder and wrapped a clean nappy around him. "All done," she crooned, rocking him to and fro. "Can I hold you for a few more minutes? I don't want to give you back to your mamma." She looked at Maggie. "Why didn't you call me? Weren't you frightened on your own?"

"I don't know. I just had a feeling we should be alone. I thought I'd be scared but I wasn't, not at all. It was so easy, no pain, nothing."

"You're not going to give him up, are you?"

Maggie's heart turned into a fist and knuckled the inside of her chest. "No! I can't! Just the thought of it makes my heart explode."

"What will you do?" Angelette ignored the small, level-headed voice in the back of her mind.

Maggie looked at Angelette helplessly. "I don't know. I realise it won't be easy on my own. No money, no husband. If Patrick found out, I can't imagine—" she broke off.

Angelette touched her hand. "Don't think about him. It spoils the moment."

Maggie was determined. "All I know is that Aedan should be with me, and that's what I'll focus on."

Angelette raised one eyebrow. "And David?"

"I hope that when he sees him…I don't know. I love David." She threw her head back, shot Angelette an icy glare. "I would do anything for him, except give up our son."

"Would you let him go?"

Maggie thought hard before answering. "Yes…yes," her voice barely a whisper. "I realise the position he's in but I don't care. My sole focus is to keep Aedan."

Angelette looked at her young friend and sighed. Over the past months she'd come to love Maggie as her own daughter. "Well, then, we just have to wait and see what turns up, but right now we should think about calling the nurse to sort out the umbilical cord…and then there's David?"

"No, not David!" Maggie urged. "Not yet."

"Why? He has to know his son has arrived—"

"I know, but that time isn't now. It'll do tomorrow sometime… when the nurse has gone. I'm tired…too tired for a heavy meeting." She smiled. "I'd kill for a cup of tea!"

"A cup of tea! You British and your tea," Angelette scoffed.

"I'm gasping," Maggie laughed. "Besides, a good cuppa' is the answer to any problem."

"Well, then, I will do that right now." Angelette handed Aedan back and stood up.

"Angelette."

"Yes?"

"Could you bring the tea? I don't want anybody knowing about Aedan until I've…well, you know, until I've…until David has seen him."

"Of course! Besides, I wouldn't disturb the servants at this hour."

"Could you see to it that the nurse enters and leaves without alerting anyone?"

"Stop worrying! I'll see to it. Now, we must get you cleaned up, and that tea."

17.

David walked into the conservatory expecting, as usual, to find Maggie sitting there struggling through the French daily newspaper while she sipped her early morning coffee. "She must be sleeping in," he said, unaware that he was talking to himself. "Huh, unusual."

He walked toward the window, put his hands in his pockets, and looked out at the typical autumn day. The gnarled trees, strangely beautiful in their twisted emptiness, hurled their old leaves onto the grass below. Green faded into yellow, red faded into brown; dried-up remnants of what used to be scuttling around on the tired wind in search of a place inside the earth to hide forever.

"The old must go," a voice whispered to him. "Things have changed." He looked around expectantly, but there was nobody there. He shrugged it off as his mind playing tricks, and looked across at one of the chateau's ornamental lakes. "Christmas will be here before we know it," he said, just as a flock of birds erupted from a large silver birch that had stood over the lake for hundreds of years.

He hummed along to Vivaldi's "Autumn" which played quietly in the background on a small gramophone. Angelette loved music and filled the main rooms with it. She had a huge selection of records: classical, French, jazz, blues. He'd always loved classical but he'd never really listened to jazz or the blues until he came to the chateau, and he'd developed quite a taste for them.

In his imagination Maggie walked toward him, the leaves crunching beneath her feet. She looked up, waved, and turned to Aedan, who was about eight years old and running and playing excitedly with a dog.

"There's Daddy," she said to him. He stopped suddenly, beamed up at David. "Daddy...Daddy!" he screamed, running, arms outstretched. David lifted him high into the sky and spun him around. His childish laughter filled the air...filled David.

"Is anything worth giving them up for?" The voice jolted him out of the picture in his head, and out of the life he wanted to live, a life that was buried in layers so deep that he could pretend it didn't exist. He turned; there was nobody there. *I'm going bloody mad.* He looked at his watch. 8:32 a.m. He stood a while longer in the hope that Maggie would arrive soon and they could breakfast together.

He could live happily ever after at the chateau. The magnificent nine hundred and seventeen acres had been home to wildlife for hundreds of years. Deer, foxes, squirrels, wolves, owls, and even a rarely-glimpsed golden eagle graced its grounds.

David often prayed in the ruins of a small Celtic temple that was hidden amongst the oak trees and undergrowth behind the stables in the south part of the grounds. The temple was evidence of the Roman invasion. The Celts had no use for such limitations but had been forced into building the structures. Nature was their temple. The divine was in all things: the rivers, lakes, mountains, and trees. It couldn't be confined to a man-made structure, something David agreed with subconsciously.

"Breakfast, Monsieur." Yvette, one of the housekeepers, bustled towards him.

He turned from the window, walked over, and took the tray from her. "Oui. Merci, Yvette."

He poured himself a piping-hot cup of coffee and added an ample helping of cream and sugar. The steam was still coming off the freshly-baked bread. His mouth watered as he cut into it. He sliced a hefty chunk, smeared it thick with butter and jam, and bit into it, leaving an imprint of his teeth sculpted along the edge.

He looked at his watch, picked up the newspaper, and decided that if Maggie didn't put in an appearance soon, he would walk over to the small temple and have a word with God before they left for the hospital. He knew that Maggie wanted a home birth, but given that she was two weeks late, he was adamant that hospital would be a lot safer. With her first child anything could happen. Something wasn't right, though. The day had a strange feel to it. Something had been nagging at his insides ever since waking up at 3:33 in the early hours.

⋈

Angelette stood in the small room just outside the entrance to the conservatory. She wasn't looking forward to telling David that his son had arrived in the early hours of the morning and nobody had bothered to let him know until now. Then again, as far as she'd been led to believe, the child was the result of Maggie's folly due to an unhappy marriage, and nothing to do with David. He was merely acting as her companion, the caring village priest who'd taken it upon himself to look after her welfare. When the archdiocese of Dublin had contacted her, they'd requested that David's priesthood be kept quiet unless David instructed otherwise.

Regardless of what she'd been told, and Angelette being Angelette, she'd known the child was David's within minutes of being introduced to him. She braced herself, smoothed down her dress, and inhaled. Her heart banged. She wanted to get it over with. She paced into the conservatory sounding as bright and bubbly as she could muster. "David, good morning…and good news."

He immediately got to his feet. "*Bonjour.*" He pulled out a chair. "Coffee?"

"*Oui, merci.*"

He poured the coffee. "Beautiful day…bit chilly by the looks of things but if you're wrapped up these are the best days to enjoy a good hike."

Angelette sipped her coffee. She knew that he'd heard her words so why did he pretend he hadn't? *He's in denial.* Her eyes penetrated his. "David." Her tone was firm but gentle. "I have good news."

He waited, not daring to ask. He already knew what she was about to tell him. The one thing he'd prayed wouldn't happen, had. Maggie had given birth and bonded with the child. As his nerves got the better of him, he suddenly felt as if he were fading out of one existence into another, that Angelette was merely a figment of his imagination. He sucked in his breath, realising how easy it was to lose the mind, and he cautioned his to stay with him.

Angelette saw him go rigid. The emotions flipped across his strong face like a slideshow. There was no surprise, just something…a look that she couldn't fathom. Concern, anguish, love, all mixed up together. "You're so…the baby, he's beautiful…perfect—"

Both hands on the table, he jumped up, sending the chair crashing to the floor. The veins in his neck bulged as he tried to get words out that weren't controlled by anger. His face changed colour with every second that passed—blue, red, then white. "And nobody bothered to let me know?" he spat.

Angelette's stomach turned over. Anger was ugly. It terrified her. She stood and grabbed his wrists, an automatic response to his fury. "I'm telling you now, Monsieur!" She glared at him. Her expression challenged his reaction: Why should I give you preferential treatment?

It worked. He picked up the chair and sat down. This wasn't his child. He was merely taking care of Maggie. He didn't know what to think. He wanted to race to Maggie, hold her and his son in his arms like any normal new father would do. He slid his hand through his hair. "Why didn't you take the child? They weren't supposed to bond." Frustrated, he flipped his hand in the air as if trying to brush everything away. "Now it's only going to be more heartbreaking for Maggie to let him go."

"She didn't alert me—"

"Didn't alert you!?" Shock ripped through him. "She gave birth alone?" He was horrified. "Are they alright? Has the nurse—"

"*Oui, oui*, they are both fine."

He jumped up again. "I must see them." He swigged the rest of his coffee, slammed the cup back on the saucer and didn't notice that it split clean in two. His words rushed out. "I must go I have to go is it alright if I go now?" Nerves fired every part of him. "Are they awake? I won't disturb them, will I?"

Angelette nodded. "Maggie and Aedan are expecting you."

He shook his head, squeezed his lips together as he fought back the tears. "What a mess," he said quietly.

Angelette stood up and put her hands on his shoulders. "David, you're a good man. Don't torture yourself."

"A good man. You have no idea—"

"I do. We all make choices. There are deeper reasons being played out in the background for our experiences. It is our reactions that count…the way we handle our choices."

"Our reactions…" A single tear rolled down his cheek.

Angelette wiped the tear away with her thumb. "Live the moment," she urged him.

"Live the moment," he repeated. "One of Maggie's sayings…I don't understand."

"Don't worry about Maggie and Aedan bonding; there is nothing you can do about that now. It has happened. When you see them, it is a new moment. Live that one without concern for the old one. You can do nothing about it. They have bonded, and that is that." She shrugged nonchalantly. "Besides, mother and child had bonded long before the birth."

18.

A flood of emotions raced David up the stairs three at a time. The butterflies in his stomach were not happy ones. They fluttered about in a frenzy, trying to escape from the torrent of thoughts that invaded his mind. *I'm going to have to take the child from her as soon as possible, contact the adoptive parents, arrange to hand him over. It won't be easy. She'll never forgive me…who can blame her? What a despicable creature I am! I'm not worthy of anything, Maggie, Aedan, the Church…*

When he reached the top of the stairs he looked up at the ceiling. *God help us. She'll be heartbroken, probably never get over it.* He put his hands behind his neck and stretched it backwards. *What have I done?*

He made no attempt to be quiet as he ran along the passageway towards the bedroom. "Maggie!" He burst through the door. His voice went on ahead of him. "What are you playing at? Why didn't you let Angelette know that you were in labour so she could take the baby? You've only caused more heartache for yourself—"

He stopped dead! The sight of them crashed into him like the iron ball he'd seen the navvies use to demolish old buildings. Maggie held the contented bundle to her breast. He had never seen anything so beautiful. She looked up at him. Her soft smile erupted into a full-blown beam. Motherhood suited her. Maggie had always been beautiful but motherhood seemed to have brought out an innate glow, something he'd never seen in her before. Time stood still in this new moment.

She looked at Aedan as he suckled her breast; she pulled him closer. "Here's Daddy," she said. "Here's Daddy come to see you.

Now be on your best behaviour."

David walked over and stood at the side of them, at a loss for words. He watched Aedan's small lips pump contentedly on Maggie's breast without a care in the world.

Maggie patted the bed. "Sit down."

Aedan stopped feeding, stretched his body rigid, and started to grunt. "Oh, oh, that nasty wind." She tipped him forward and patted his back.

Speechless, David couldn't take his eyes off his son. To think that he and Maggie had made…this, this little miracle, a true miracle if ever he saw one. He felt weak; he wanted to drop to his knees. It was the strangest feeling, as if his life had burst out of him and into Aedan.

Maggie realised he was overwhelmed. "Do you want to hold him?"

"I…I won't hurt him?" he asked, still gazing at Aedan.

"Of course you won't hurt him; babies are tougher than you think." She passed Aedan to him.

"It's just…he's so tiny." He took Aedan carefully, slipping his arms awkwardly underneath hers.

"Be careful to support his head. Don't let it flop about."

He cradled his son to his chest. "He's barely bigger than my hand." He put his little finger inside Aedan's palm. The baby immediately curled his tiny fist around it. "He's so strong…" He broke off, not able to contain his emotions any longer. "Heavens, Maggie!" he sobbed. "I can't tell you how I feel…he's…I've never…he's a miracle, a tiny miracle, so he is."

He looked at her. She was smiling through her heartache. The sadness in her was so strong. If he'd have reached out, he would have been able to pull a piece of it from her.

He looked down at his son, who had fallen asleep in his arms. He nuzzled his hair, took in his smell. His primal instincts kicked in and he knew that he would do everything in his power to protect him, protect Maggie, the two most precious things in his life. This was the new moment Angelette spoke of, the one that told him that he couldn't give them up, wouldn't give them up! The scandal, people's opinions—he could live with the lot of it, but he knew as he cradled his son in his arms that life would be nothing without him and his mother.

He reached out. His huge hand caressed the side of Maggie's head. He played with her hair, twisting, stroking, kneading it through his fingers. He caressed her face, traced his middle finger over her nose, around her lips, brushed the back of his hand up her jaw line. She laid her head into it, enjoying his tenderness.

"I never did say it, did I?"

"What?" Her tears ran down his hand.

"Thank you. Thank you for the miracle I hold in my arms." The energy among the three of them was profound. "I never did thank you. I was too concerned about the opinions of others. What a selfish—"

"It's alright," she answered, breathlessly. *Is he changing his mind?*

She felt the small piece of hope start to smolder way down inside her, the piece that had never left. The same piece that had her imagining them together as a family, had David playing football with his son, picking him up from school, tucking him in, and reading to him before he went to sleep.

Aedan's tummy rumbled loudly. David looked down at him. "Just like your mother!"

"Here," Maggie laughed. "You'd better get used!" She stopped abruptly. "He's due for a nappy change."

"I don't know how to change his nappy! We never touched on it in seminary."

But Maggie would have none of it. "Here!" She passed him the white terry cotton. "There's a first time for everything."

David laid Aedan down tenderly, scared he might break. He undid the huge safety pins with blue heads that were fastened on either side of his nappy.

"Rule number one," Maggie instructed. "As soon as you take the old nappy away put the new one underneath him, that way if he decides to pee or pooh while you're in the middle of changing him, it won't go all over the place."

"I see." David took the fresh nappy and laid it underneath the tiny infant who seemed to have got lost in the thick eiderdown. "Now what?"

Maggie handed him a damp cloth. "Freshen him up with this. Make sure you get in his creases."

"His creases?"

"Yes, the little hidey-holes underneath his fat." She lifted one of Aedan's legs and stretched out the crease. "And it's very important to clean his little willy properly, underneath here." She lifted it gently. "And around these—"

"Maggie, I think I know how to clean his willy, thank you very much!"

Startled, Maggie said, "Course you do! What was I thinking?"

Her heart felt as if it were being compressed between two stone slabs as she watched father and son bond. How many times would he do this? Would she ever see David again once she'd told him that she wouldn't give Aedan up? She handed him the talcum powder. "You're already an expert," she teased.

Deep in concentration, David's face was very close to his son's shiny red bottom as he finished up with some talcum powder. It was a very intricate operation! "Not quite," he said, just as Aedan decided to pee all over him. Shocked, he looked down at his son and watched the small glistening fountain get smaller and smaller before it disappeared altogether.

Maggie screamed with laughter at the look of sheer disbelief on David's face, and handed him a towel. "Here!"

"Well! I wasn't ready for that!" he said, laughing with her and drying himself off.

"He's just christened you."

As soon as she said it they stopped laughing and looked at each other in silence, realising the symbolic significance of the moment. Aedan's tiny legs were kicking away. He turned his head one way then the other, his eyes wide, checking out the room before he finally rested them on his parents. They looked down at him. The casual remark made by Maggie was complex in its aftermath. No words passed between them. The thoughts that went unsaid were the magicians.

David cleaned Aedan again, picked him up, and lulled him off to sleep. "There, there, beautiful boy."

"Lay him in his cot."

"No, I'm happy to hold him, for as long as I can."

Her heart sank. She'd got it wrong. He was obviously still under the delusion that she was going to let him take Aedan from her and give him to somebody else. Just the thought of it made her feel sick. Her stomach tangoed with anxiety. For the first time in as far back as she could remember she was at a loss for words. She felt decidedly shy with David. She leant past him and poured herself a glass of water. *I have to tell him. Do it now. Get it over with.*

"Water?"

"No, thanks." His eyes were fixed on Aedan.

The scenarios had played out in her mind over and over. The scenes, the fights, the tears; Aedan crying at their words; her nursing him back to sleep, reassuring him. She'd thought about nothing else. *How will you look after him?* David had asked her a million times in her head. She never replied. She didn't know the answer. It didn't matter. Whatever happened, she would take care of her son until her dying day, and after that. Yet deep inside she never gave up hope, never stopped reversing the situation in her mind. Changing the scenario time and time again, she'd imagine the three of them together: Aedan in his pram, David pushing as they strolled around a park somewhere, not a care in the world.

"Penny for them?"

Distracted, she shook her head. "No, no. They're worth a lot more." She avoided his eyes. He'd always been able to read her. *Tell him!* She tried to psych herself up. *Leave it a few minutes. Surely if he's with Aedan long enough, he won't be able to let him go.*

David looked at her. He pulled the small Celtic cross from his trouser pocket. "Remember this?"

"My cross!" She held out her hand.

He bypassed her and placed it around his son's neck. It reached his toes. "He's the third piece," he said quietly. Her words echoed in his head. He looked at her. "Remember?"

"David," her tears fell, she sucked in her breath. She looked at her son asleep in his daddy's arms, took his teeny hand, and stroked it gently. "I can't give him up." She tightened her lips. "I can't do it." She looked up at David. "I love you more than anything...you and Aedan. I don't expect you to leave the Church and everything you know and love for us." She looked back at her son and shook her head gently. "But the thought of giving him away, never knowing who he is, who his parents are, if he is loved." A dangerous tone entered her voice. She glared at David. "I can't do it. I won't do it—"

He butted in. "Maggie, I—"

"Let me finish! You can see Aedan whenever you want, but I'll tell you now: I don't plan on returning to Ireland. I won't risk Patrick ever finding out about him." Her voice faltered. "He'd kill him, you see, and me."

The terror that smoldered in her eyes ignited his anger. His voice was lethal. "I'd kill him before he got within walking distance of either of you."

Dazed, she simply stared at him. It was an odd statement considering he wouldn't be around. She brushed it off. "It will be hard, not having you around, almost unbearable. You're the only man I've ever loved, but now there is another man in my life. He needs me more than you do—"

"Does he?"

She avoided his glare. "Yes! You can take care of yourself, but Aedan, he still needs me." She broke off in an effort to hold back her tears. "I know it won't be easy for us, but we'll get by somehow." He passed her a handkerchief. Her hands trembled as she took it. "Thank you." She wiped her nose and cheeks. "Without you in my life, a part, a part of me will...will, be gone..." Her body convulsed. Wracked with pain, she sucked in large gulps of air, too distraught to talk.

Aedan stiffened and clenched his fists. His small arms started to flay, and his face turned a deep shade of purple. David nestled him into his shoulder. Rocking him gently, he pressed his cheek into his son's.

"Shh," he crooned, "everything will be alright." Feeling secure in his daddy's arms, Aedan calmed down instantly.

Maggie looked on; her anger bubbled inside. *Why can't a man devote himself to God as well as to his wife and child? It's so unfair.* "You're a natural. Seems you were meant to be a father, Father." She glowered at him. Her eyes glazed over and set like two frozen ponds.

Her stab of sarcasm didn't go unnoticed; neither did the icy atmosphere. "Yes, I was...or we wouldn't be here," he answered softly. "Maggie—"

Her temper seethed but so far she had managed to contain it. "Don't even think about it!"

"What?"

"Asking me to let Aedan go. I find it offensive," she hissed. "I can't believe how selfish, how, how, hardhearted." She leant forward, stuck her chest out. "And the fact that you can just pass him off like something you'd hand over to a, to a...," she struggled for words, "...to a secondhand store! It's beyond me. How can you do it, let him go? No matter what happens in my life there's not a cat in hell's chance that my son won't be a part of it—"

"Maggie, listen—"

Her temper exploded. She put her hand up. "No, you listen for a change! You've called all the shots, made all the arrangements without a single thought for my—" She looked at Aedan. "Our feelings. It was all about you, the Church, what people think. Well, I don't give a damn what they think, David." She lost it. "They all piss in the same pot—"

Furious, David gritted his teeth. "Don't use language like that around my son!" He stood up. Aedan started to scream. She paused, looked at David, and opened her mouth. His face turned dark and hardened into that look that told her she'd crossed a line. "Don't! I'm warning you."

He walked around the room with his son in his arms. "Shh, shh, shh, we don't mean it, go back to sleep, shh, shh..."

Angry, she waved her hand in the air and beckoned to him. "Give him to me! He's ready for another feed." She held her arms out. "Give him to me!" she ordered.

Aedan had stopped crying. David made no effort to hand him over. He merely stood and stared her down. The chill he gave off made her shudder. "He needs feeding," she repeated, backing down.

His eyes cut into her. "I don't think so. He looks contented enough to me. I think you owe him an apology. What were you thinking using language like that around him? I don't care where you use it, Maggie, I really don't—the sewers, the gutter—but you don't use it around him."

"You're right!" His words hit home. "I shouldn't have come out with…I lost my temper. Give him to me." She waved her fingers towards herself impatiently. He walked over, sat on the bed, and passed Aedan to her. "Come here. I'm sorry…I'm so ashamed of myself." Aedan sought out her breast. She stroked his head gently. "Forgive Mamma. I lost my temper. I can't promise you that it won't happen again, but I'll try not to let it happen in front of you. I'm under a lot of stress, but that's no excuse." She looked at David. "Why can't it be a happy occasion…a new baby, new parents? Why can't we be like everyone else—simple?"

David buried his face in his hands, stretching the skin across his cheekbones with his middle fingers. "Maggie, what are we going to do? We have a lot to talk about."

Her expression hardened. "You know how I feel. I won't change my mind."

"I'm not trying to convince—" There was a knock at the door. "Damn!" he said, frustrated.

"Language," she berated.

He glanced at her sarcastically, paused, and stood up. It seemed he wasn't meant to give her his side of the story. He opened the door. Angelette stood there, tray at her chest. "Tea break," she said sternly.

He stood aside and let her pass. "You're an angel."

"You've only just realised!" She floated by him and smiled at Maggie. "I had the feeling the pair of you needed relaxation time."

"Your feeling was right." Maggie answered.

Angelette set the tray down on Maggie's dresser. "Here, let me have him for a few minutes and then I'll leave the three of you alone."

Maggie passed Aedan to her. "He doesn't seem to be hungry today. Keeps trying, then stops."

"Come here, little cherub. David, pour the tea, please." Angelette showered Aedan with kisses. The interruption gave Maggie and David time to clear their minds and calm down a bit.

Maggie twisted the top button on her nightdress. She had a wistful look on her face. "I'd love some fresh air."

"A bit soon, sweetheart. They say two weeks bed rest."

"I don't think that's necessary—it's much too long. Surely the fresh air will do me good, and Aedan."

"Maggie, listen for once in your life!" David butted in.

Wide-eyed, Maggie protested, "I'm just saying that it seems too—"

"Let's compromise," Angelette said, diffusing the tension. "A week should be good enough."

"A week indoors!" Maggie was dismayed. She'd always loved the outdoors. "I won't be able to bear it."

"Well, then, why don't you have breakfast in the conservatory tomorrow? Not quite the same, but at least it will get you out of this room—and you can show Aedan off to the staff. They are dying to see him."

"Isn't it a bit soon?" David cut in.

"David, having a baby doesn't mean I'm helpless and have to be mollycoddled forever! I'm not supposed to do anything strenuous for a while but I can manage a walk down a flight of stairs."

"Maggie is right, David. She'll be fine," Angelette reassured him.

David poured the tea. "Add your own milk and sugar. I'm off for a breath of fresh—" The two women stared at him accusingly. "Err, I'm not the one who's just given birth," he said defensively.

"And a breath of fresh air doesn't mean filling your lungs with pipe smoke!" Maggie cut in.

He bent down and kissed her cheek. "I won't be long." A moment of silence passed between him and Angelette. He nodded and left the room.

19.

Angelette stared at Maggie.

"What?"

"You know!"

"Know what?"

"Stop pretending. Have you told him that you are keeping Aedan?"

"Yes."

"And?"

"I don't know," she said through a yawn. "Excuse me, I feel really tired. He hasn't…we had a bit of a falling out."

"Yes, I could feel the tension between the two of you."

"I told him that I don't give a damn what he thinks, and that there isn't a cat in hell's chance of me giving Aedan up."

Angelette raised her eyebrows, "Well, that is one way of telling him! And he made no comment?"

"No. He was more concerned about my language in front of Aedan. Jumped straight down my throat and I don't blame him. I feel terrible. My temper got the better of me."

"Let go of your guilt; it can cause more problems than a few choice words ever could." She shrugged and kissed Aedan who was wide awake in her arms. "Besides, bad language can be a positive way of releasing pent-up emotions. Isn't that right, little one?" She stood up and walked over to the patio doors. "Let's show you the great outdoors." She turned to Maggie. "I think it is a good sign that David was upset by it."

Maggie picked up her tea. "Really? Why?"

"He felt the need to jump in and protect his son." Angelette stared out at her acres. "It doesn't seem like the behaviour of a father who is ready to give his child away."

Maggie perked up. "Do you think so? But in one minute he says things that build my hopes up, and then in the next one he demolishes them."

"How so?"

"When he held Aedan for the first time, he broke down." Maggie's eyes filled with tears. "Said thank you for the miracle. I can't tell you how that made me feel." She started to blubber again. "God, I've never stopped bloody scricking."

"Pardon…what is scricking? I've not heard this word before."

Maggie laughed. "Oh, you won't find it in any dictionary. It's slang for, crying…crying, you know, blubbering and the like. But then, a few minutes later, I told him to put Aedan in his cot but he refused and said he wanted to hold him for as long as he could, like he had to grab as many opportunities as possible to be with him." She made a subconscious note, reminding herself that she really should try to speak the queen's English in front of Angelette.

"Oh, I don't think that means he wants to give him up!" Angelette scoffed. "He is a new papa; of course he wants to hold his son. Look at me, I am doing the same." She walked around the bedroom explaining what everything was to Aedan, in French. "*Horloge, plante, manteau de cheminée, brosse…bon garçon.*" She giggled at Maggie. "We have him speaking fluent French by the time he is six months old." She hugged him to her. "I feel just like David. I'm going to grab Aedan at every opportunity I can. You're so beautiful, aren't you?" She slapped noisy kisses all over him. "Grand-mère loves you." She looked at Maggie. "And what about the kiss?"

"What kiss?"

"David kissed you before he left the room, just like any man kisses his wife. In that moment he'd forgotten all about me, yet as far as he is concerned I'm not supposed to know that Aedan belongs to him. He is supposedly just doing his duty as your priest."

"So he did!"

"See how the human mind works, Maggie? You didn't give the kiss a second thought. You are so busy focusing on what David isn't doing that when he does do something positive, you fail to see it!" She sat down on the bed.

"Oh, that's not fair!" Maggie protested.

"Oui! This is how I see it."

"He has no understanding of my feelings."

"I disagree with you. Cut him a…give him some—"

"Give him a break, cut him some slack!" Maggie interrupted irritably.

"Yes, that! Look at the position he is in: a priest who has fathered a child with another man's wife—"

"Oh, poor David!" Maggie said, sarcastically. "He should have thought about that when we were in bed together."

"I'm sure he did. His guilt would have been in bed with you also…and let us not forget the part you played. You chose to have an affair…to love David. You can't blame him for the situation you are in. You must accept some of the responsibility."

Maggie felt aggravated. Angelette was taking sides! "I do! That's why I'm keeping Aedan." *Is that not obvious?* she wanted to scream at her.

"Yes, where Aedan is concerned, but you still resent David for not having the guts to walk out on the Church, his congregation, and society in general! You think that because he got you pregnant he should do the right thing, which in your mind is to walk away from everything he knows and has worked for, to be with you and Aedan—"

"That's not true, Angelette! I know that David loves me more than the Church, I know it! He would be so much happier with us, if he could only stop worrying about what other people think."

Angelette softened her voice. "Then stop worrying about what decision he is going to make." She stroked Maggie's hair. "Darling, you can't make someone do something until they are ready. David is scared. He sees life in a different light than you. He feels that he has let you down, now Aedan, as well as the Church—not to mention God!

He thinks his sins will follow him for the rest of his life and after that. His love for you pours out of him, anyone can see that. I'm amazed there are no rumours flying around your village in Ireland."

"It's like you said earlier: people see what they want to see. Even if the thought has crossed their minds, it would be unthinkable! So they bury it somewhere in the hope that it won't resurface again."

Angelette stared blankly. "Yes, but things never go away until you face them," she whispered, looking at Aedan. "I wonder what is in store for this little one?"

Maggie watched Angelette curiously. "Why did you never have children? You seem to be a natural mother," she said bluntly.

Angelette winced. "Err, I…" She was visibly shaken. I did carry to term but the baby died not long after I gave birth, a little boy."

Maggie felt her face burn with embarrassment. "Oh, I'm so sorry, Angelette. I didn't mean to drag up painful memories. I'm too nosey for my own good."

The blank look still on her face, Angelette's voice was barely a whisper. "It's okay. Stillborn, the doctor called him. I named him René, which means reborn. It broke my heart at the time. It's strange: some days I can talk about him and feel fine—no tears or sadness—then another day, I fight to hold them back even though I know more than most that he is alive somewhere. I've seen him grow up, been a part of his life in my dreams, but then when I awake it feels so empty without him, and I forget most of the dream. I can't tell you how many times I've wished he was here over the years. That I could take him to school, hug him, go on holidays, build sandcastles, see his face on Christmas morning." She frowned. "Just the simple things that we missed out on, you know—"

"I'm sure that you have done a lot of those things in the spirit world together," Maggie cut in.

"Yes, that is what Chandiran tells me, but I just don't remember. For years she has been telling me to meditate on my dreams and it will all come back to me…but first I have to remove the blocks that my mind set up to protect me from my own pain." She shrugged.

"Thinking it is doing me a favour, I suppose."

Maggie was puzzled. "How come you can't see him other than in your dreams? You communicate with the spirit world as easily as you communicate with the physical one."

"Well, it's a bit different with children. They have to come at the discretion of their spirit parents, at least until they reach a certain level of understanding, and when they do reach it there can be many reasons why the child might shy away from making contact…feeling afraid, not being used to communication between our worlds, that sort of thing. When I am in dreamscape I am in their world, the spirit world. They are in familiar territory so their spirit remains light, but in our world they feel different, bogged down, heavy. For spirit children this can be very disturbing until they get used to it, and even when they are used to it the spirit parent will accompany them." She smiled. "Maybe it's like going on a day trip! They come when their parents have time and it has been planned. Then there's my own blocks, of course."

Maggie contemplated for a moment and tucked her hair behind her ears. She could feel the sadness in Angelette. "I know you can never replace one child with another but perhaps it would have helped lesson the pain if you and your husband had tried." She stopped. "I'm sorry Angelette, it really is none of my business. Tell me to shut up."

"No, really! I feel that it is your business." She paused but kept eye contact with Maggie. Her expression was thoughtful, as if sizing her up. "I never was married in the traditional sense, more social. But I did love him. Jacques was a dear friend, but on the rare occasions I tried to show it physically, it was a disaster."

"I see. You loved him so much, you couldn't find anyone to fill his boots!"

Angelette laughed. "You have some funny sayings. Um, err, not exactly, but yes, it would have been hard to find someone to fill his boots. Not many people accept you for who you are."

"Oh, oh! You have that look on your face," Maggie laughed.

"I have had my share of lovers—"

"But none who could come close to Jacques. Oh, how romantic!

You should write a book. Lady of the chateau loses the love of her life and pines forevermore—"

"I like women, Maggie!" Angelette said flatly. "All of my lovers have been women."

Maggie sucked in her breath. Mouth wide open, she was stunned.

Angelette stifled laughter at the look of out-and-out shock on Maggie's face. "We see only what we are conditioned to see. You are shocked, no?"

"Err, a little!"

"I hope it doesn't change our relationship, Maggie. I love you as I would a daughter. Being a lesbian doesn't mean that I want to have an affair with every woman I meet. That is a very ignorant way of looking at my sexuality."

"I'm sure."

"Well, this is a rare occasion."

"Why?" Maggie was still wide-eyed.

"Maggie O'Connell, lost for words."

Maggie continued to stare blankly at the woman she had come to love over the past few months. A woman who she had formed a deep and lasting relationship with. She laughed quietly. "I'm sorry, Angelette. It's just so…unexpected. I never thought for one minute…I mean it just never crossed my mind."

"Why would it? You simply assumed I was a widow, childless through medical reasons; after all, it is expected that married couples have children otherwise, no?"

Maggie thought about her own naïveté. "I must admit, I had thought that it might be medical! You never fail to amaze me, Madame Bertrand."

"It's not très psychic, just a good understanding of how the human mind works through years of experience." She winked at Maggie and looked down at Aedan. "Ahh, his eyes are wide open. You understand everything we say don't you, little one? Come to Grand-mère." She lifted him to face level and showered him with noisy kisses all over his face and head again. "Oh, you're so beautiful. I love you! I love you! I love you! But I have to give you back to Mamma because I have things to do in the village, yes I do," she said, exaggerating her head movements. "Oh, yes, I do." She passed Aedan to Maggie. "Is there anything you need from the village?"

"I don't think so...although I have been craving chocolate." Her mouth watered at the thought.

"What!? You have no chocolat?" Her French accent strong, Angelette feigned shock. "My God! All new mammas must have *chocolat*."

"And new grand-mères."

The two women stared at each other in silence. Tears welled up in Angelette. "Now I am scricking," she said. She bent down and kissed Aedan one more time before kissing Maggie on both cheeks. "Chocolat it is."

She turned to leave but suddenly stopped and looked back as she remembered a thought in her head. "Ahh, yes, that was what I wanted to tell you. Last night, I had a very vivid dream. I saw you on the balcony surrounded by coloured lights that came from the sky. I thought I'd mention it because dreams have significance and this is a good dream—lights, colour. You looked frightened but my overall feeling about the dream is positive. I could have sworn it was happening; I even woke up, ran outside, and thought I saw you running through the grounds in your nightclothes—What is the matter? Are you alright?"

Maggie felt her blood run cold, then hot, then cold again. All colour drained from her face. "By Jesus! The lights...I...I saw them too! How can that be? Were we sharing a dream?" she asked, hoping this was the case and that it was just a dream. But something in the recesses of her mind...

"It's a possibility." Angelette looked troubled. "Our truest life is when we are in dreams awake," she said, quoting Thoreau. "Maggie, can you remember anything else?"

Maggie thought hard. A flash of something...strange beings, White Eagle...she shook her head. "No, I don't think...but then again." Small fragments started to play back. "White Eagle, weird-looking beings, se—!" She stopped abruptly, as her mind conjured up a graphic image of her enjoying wild, unabashed sex!

"Holy mother!"

"What?"

"Did you have sex in the dream?" Maggie asked shyly. Her face and neck flushed with colour.

"I wish!" Angelette joked, in an effort to reassure her. "Did you?"

"I don't know…kind of, I mean not like the sex I have with David. I was penetrated but in a different way."

"What kind of way?"

"It's hard to explain…energy, would be the easiest way to describe it. It's kind of like being penetrated by the universe…through the spirit…everything, until even the soul is entered." She looked at Angelette innocently and lowered her voice. "The sensations weren't only physical, but spiritual. No fear, no guilt—a psycho-spiritual, sexual, ethereal experience! It was definitely out of this world, wonderful!" She stopped, not wanting to admit that it was the best sex she'd ever had even though it wasn't like sex at all!?

Oh, dear God… "Who with?" Angelette urged. Something in the back of her mind nagged her. "Can you remember?"

Maggie's heart thumped hard in her chest. "No…I don't think I want to!"

Angelette's jaw dropped. Her face white, her suspicions correct, she murmured, "A soul split."

Her words sent chills through Maggie. Somewhere inside she knew exactly what Angelette was talking about. "B'Jeysus!" she whispered in native Irish slang.

Angelette felt as if her legs were about to give way. "B' Jeysus is right," she whispered shakily.

Maggie felt hot, sick. Nausea started to rise as she caved into the staggering feeling coursing through her—a feeling of dread. She picked up her book, *The Undying Fire* by H. G. Wells, and began fanning herself with it. "Angelette, don't! I'm scared—"

"Don't be scared, sweetheart." Hearing the panic in Maggie's voice helped Angelette quash her own fears. She rushed to Maggie's side and hugged her. "A soul-split on Earth is like a rare and precious gem. It will be kept in a case. Only those who wish to look upon its beauty will see it, but it will remain protected from those who wish to steal it for their own agendas." Angelette stood up. "Now—we have more important things to do than talk about soul-splits," she said, playing it down. "I'll come and see you both later." She got up and walked toward the door—

"Nay...the name 'Nay keeps coming to mind. I don't know any Nay, do you? Was there a Nay in your dream?" Maggie's nerves made her repeat herself.

Angelette's heart stopped with her motion. She looked like an ice sculpture but didn't flinch. She swallowed in an effort to moisten her dry mouth. Her voice cracked but she regained her composure when she saw the glimmer of fear in Maggie's eyes. "Perhaps he is the handsome lover in your dream," she answered nonchalantly. "Why would he want to bother with an old woman like me, when he can have you?"

"A very beautiful older woman," Maggie answered, feeling more relaxed. Aedan let out a sudden yell as if in agreement. Maggie shook her head. "Dear me! You've a right pair of lungs on you."

"I'll see you this evening." Angelette breezed out of the room. She closed the door, pressed her back against it, and gripped the handle in an effort to steady herself. Cold sweat ran from the back of her neck down her torso. She wiped her neck with her hand. She felt excited, awestruck, scared—*Keep the fear away!* "Oh God, Oh God," she whispered to herself. "NeilA!" Her stomach twisted. She closed her eyes, and prayed in silent gratitude for the gift of Maggie, David, and their son, and at the same time asked for protection as well as help with the responsibility, for all those involved. She was under no illusion about the power that was contained in the small infant who was at this moment yelling for his mother's breast just like any other newborn.

She raced down the wide staircase into the kitchen, walked over to a small cubbyhole, and dragged a heavy camelhair coat from the hook on the back of the door. Struggling to find one of the sleeves, she pulled it off again impatiently, leaving one sleeve inside-out. "Merde!" she cursed.

Yvette stopped chopping carrots, wiped her hands on her apron, and took the coat from Angelette, saying, "*Ici!*" as she helped her into it.

"Merci." Angelette kissed her tenderly on the lips. They held it for a few seconds. Over the years their relationship had mellowed yet grown stronger. No secrets, no pretence. With an openness that enjoyed conversation as well as silence, it had soared to new heights and intimacy, like the Monarch when it breaks free from its cocoon. They were older but felt younger, and had grown beautiful together.

Before Yvette could ask any questions, Angelette was out the door winding a thick, brown wool scarf around her neck. Shopping bag over her shoulder, she raced down the driveway. She stopped at one of the cars, but decided to walk into the village instead. It was a beautiful day, chilly, but she was wrapped up well enough and needed the fresh air and extra time alone.

She looked up at the sky. The weird solitary cloud still hung over the chateau and could be seen for miles around. She'd never seen a cloud like it before; it was huge, and the strangest shape, like some kind of giant disc. The only thing that hadn't changed since the previous night was the cloud's colour, metallic blue with a white-gold centre. It seemed to follow her down the country lanes. She stopped for a few moments, mystified, wondering why it seemed to be the only one in a cloudless sky. Her breath formed clouds of its own in the chilled autumn air and her nose and cheeks took on a healthy glow. The country lanes were so peaceful. The only sounds she could hear were from the river going about its business, and the birds flying from branch to branch, puzzled as to where all the leaves had gone. The strangest feeling weaved its way through her. Mystified, she couldn't seem to pull herself away from the cloud. *NeilA!* Angelette couldn't get his name out of her head.

She'd learned all about soul-splits years before. NeilA! A powerful, powerful being! *Was Aedan NeilA's soul-split? Don't be ridiculous!* The thud of her heart pushed the thought out of her head just as a raven crossed her path, squawked, and flew away, satisfied that he'd grabbed her attention. She didn't simply dismiss it like most people would have done. The raven was a messenger who'd come to verify her thoughts—she was on the right track.

"Chandiran, are you busy? I have a few questions." She stared up at the cloud. Chandiran appeared at her side. "Can you confirm the information I'm getting?"

"You met Aedan. At last!" she beamed. "All children are special, but Aedan, he is a little bit different."

"A soul-split?"

"Yes."

"NeilA?"

"That's right."

She gasped. "I knew it! As soon as Maggie said Nay…but why now? What are the reasons behind it?"

"Ah! Too many to go into, Angelette, but the people of Earth, they have been waiting many, many years for his arrival. We hope they are ready to accept him this time…and you."

"Does Maggie know?"

"She does, but she prefers to believe it's a dream. Fragments are being played back to her but she blocks them. She's scared. Remember when you were in Maggie's position? You changed your mind just in time. Conception is daunting to say the least. NeilA understands that."

Angelette remembered it as if it was yesterday. She'd only ever made love with Jacques a handful of times before coming clean about her sexuality yet she'd still managed to get pregnant. But that night— she would never forget it. The fear when she saw him…NeilA! The responsibility…she was just twenty-one…the guilt at the loss of the child. She looked at Chandiran. "I was—"

"We understand," Chandiran assured her.

"I could do it now!" she said, as if trying to convince herself.

Chandiran raised her eyebrows. "Could you?"

"Back then I was just a child, like Maggie. She may be a few years older than I was then, but she's still so young, just twenty-two; so young to have taken on such responsibility."

"Maggie has the power and the knowledge to cope. She's not alone. She has more help than most, despite how it looks. Naturally she's scared, but eventually she will accept the fact that Aedan is no ordinary infant. Angelette, I must go. I have work to do. Is there anything else?"

"No, nothing that can't wait…thank you."

"Stop worrying! We need you to be strong. The sooner you accept who you are, your own power, the better! I know I shouldn't, but I find it irritating!"

As Chandiran left, the raven returned. Its shrill squawks were loud and persistent. Startled, Angelette walked toward a tree a few feet away. She looked up the trunk. The raven flew from branch to branch in an effort to get her attention. "What are you trying to tell me?"

He squawked louder as if to say, You understand! You know what my message is!

She turned her thoughts to that night all those years before. It was still so vivid in her mind. She had to face it. Lose the fear, the guilt. Stop blaming herself for the loss of the child. She'd had enough of feeling like a failure. "NEILAAAA!" Terrified, she cried out his name. She never had been able to face her identity. She knew deep inside that she was one of them but even so it was a strange thought while encased in her human armour. Her brain had a problem perceiving it. She wondered what terrified her the most: the power in NeilA, or the power in herself?

A strong wind whistled up from nowhere, bending the trees southwards towards Gavarnie. Her clothes flapped about her. She hugged herself in an effort to stop her coat from rising to her thighs, and grabbed at her scarf. Its short, sharp slaps stung her face as if trying to knock the fear out of her.

The cloud floated towards her slowly and stopped right above her head. Her neck ached but she couldn't take her eyes away from it. Hypnotised, she murmured, "NeilA." His name gave her comfort, unconditional love, and compassion as she opened up to him at last.

She closed her eyes. A solitary tear trickled down her face as she realised there was nothing to fear. Why? Why had she let fear rule her? She could have had NeilA's love all her life. "I let you down," she whispered.

A beam of sunlight spread from an opening in the cloud and shone down on her. Her eyes remained open, unaffected by its light. She saw him for the second time in her present human life—an omnipotent being, an unimaginable force, like nothing Earth could begin to imagine or comprehend. She realised that the light was coming from him and not the sun. Behind him, masses of colour shimmered and twinkled; some looked like individual orbs while others resembled rainbows. This was her family.

One of the orbs, a mixture of white, golden light, moved forward and positioned itself at NeilA's side. She watched it manifest into a being that resembled him: hairless, with huge dark eyes, and the kindest face. Though thousands of feet away, she could see them as if they were standing by her side.

NeilA smiled, "My dear, I'm past being let down."

She gasped and dropped to her knees. In that moment it was as if she had been released from everything, every pent-up emotion that she'd kept buried inside. And the love she felt from him was sweet, pure, uncluttered.

"Angelette, forgive yourself…please. It saddens me to feel the extent of your distress. At the time you didn't feel ready. You exercised free will as is your right. Being one of our workers on Earth has its challenges. We know this. Try not to succumb to fear. It stifles you and turns you into a fraction of who you really are."

"But the child died because of me! It was me. I took his life through my cowardice!"

His voice was fading. "No, no, no. The soul of the child also made a decision…" His light faded as the split in the cloud closed. It hung over Volonne for a few more minutes before it evaporated into nothing.

Angelette stared, spellbound. The size of the cloud, yet it had vanished in seconds? "Huh!" She smoothed back her hair. Had she imagined it? How could something so huge disappear so quickly and without a trace? "Probably imagined the whole damn thing!" She was already putting the blocks on the experience.

Chandiran's voice soared in and out of her mind like a radio being tuned in. *"An open mind is a free mind, Angelette. Judge nothing, keep what feels right, and toss the rest!"*

She had always felt different, strange…alien. She'd never been one to run with the crowd or fit into society's expectations. Always the rebel, she found many people silly and trivial. Even as a child she could never understand why people seemed to enjoy hounding, tormenting, and bullying each other.

Then there was "the bequest," as she referred to it. A bequest she'd denied for as long as possible in the hope that it would just…well…go away! She had the ability to see things, know things, without being told about them. From a young age she'd been able to read people in a heartbeat, know their life story through a handshake. At school, she could read between the lines and often got into trouble for questioning her teachers. She could see the parts in history that had been rewritten to suit the so-called victors; see the errors and the mistakes that science and religion taught in a bid to outdo each other. Didn't they know that the energy they spoke of was one and the same?

Over the years she'd learned to handle her gift, keep it in check, but there was something buried inside her, something so powerful. It was a feeling not of this world. It terrified her! Why couldn't she just be normal like everybody else?

But it was time. Time to let what she'd known all her life but refused to acknowledge soar through her. She stood for a minute longer breathing in the fresh, crisp air. She felt the cold travel through her insides and freeze them over. The fear was still there. The raven squawked and fluttered above her head. She looked up. "I know! It's not that easy!"

She closed her eyes. Waves of power rushed from her toes to her brain, filled her mind, stretched out beyond it. She swayed from side to side as she tried to keep her balance. Though terrified, she had to know, had to face her fears and know the truth. She staggered over to one of the trees, wrapped herself around it, and slid down its trunk. She let her power override her fear. She let it come through from way down inside her. She was one of them! *Admit it, own it!*

She stayed there a few minutes longer, allowing the realisation to sink in. The raven squawked above her, flew down, and landed at her feet. She held out her arm. It jumped on. With the fear gone, it was easy to see their connection. She wondered why she'd ever been afraid. A soul is a soul, regardless of the outer casing. Human on Earth...but the universe teemed with life. Even on Earth there were species yet to be discovered. The soul could choose to experience all of it!

She smiled at the bird. "Thank you. Now, I must leave. Go!" She flipped her arm gently, watched the bird disappear, and got to her feet using the tree trunk for support.

She brushed herself off, looked up, and smiled at the soul of the empty sky.

20.

David crept into the kitchen, careful not to wake the rest of the household.

The dog, Eriq, squealed over a yawn, stood up, formed his body into an arch, and stretched his front legs. He scampered over to David, tail wagging, happy to spend some of the lonely night with a friend.

"Hello, boy, what's going on in your life?" He stuck his fingers into Eriq's glossy white coat and rubbed both sides of his oversized belly. Eriq responded by rolling over onto his back and spreading all fours in a relatively dignified manner. David laughed. "Oh, it's tickle-belly time, is it? I don't know, you lead the life of Riley, so you do."

It was 3 a.m. and still jet black outside. He couldn't sleep. He walked over to the monitor-topped fridge, grabbed the milk, and gulped from the bottle. The creamy chill iced his bones. It felt good, satisfied a need. He looked down at Eriq and commented, "Marvellous invention, the refrigerator."

David passed through to the grand sitting room where Maggie had lost herself, but he wasn't scared, just angry, that he'd not been there to protect her. Eriq padded in after him and stood staring with his big brown eyes, waiting for an invite. David cocked his head. "Come on then, lie down, there's a good boy." The dog flopped down on David's frozen feet. He worked them through the silky coat, grateful for the fuzzy warmth that penetrated his skin.

He thought about Maggie's dog, Angel. They'd left her with his friend, Father Joseph, the priest standing in for him in his absence. There was no way they'd have left her with Patrick. She'd be dead by the time they got back if they had.

David's mind was in chaos. On the outside he managed to remain calm. He didn't want to alarm Maggie, and he knew that any anxiety from the two of them would rub off on Aedan. He was excited, sad, guilty, apprehensive, and certain, all at the same time. He loved the Church, but there were too many unanswered questions. Why couldn't a priest marry? It seemed so archaic in this day and age. What was so wrong about having a deep and meaningful relationship with someone other than God? Wasn't it one and the same thing anyway? Shouldn't we bring out the God in each other? Why should women like Maggie, who had suffered nothing but misery and violence at the hands of their drunken husbands, stay married to them? And what about some of the scriptures? Hardly appropriate for this day and age.

He pulled a small, worn-out bible from his dressing gown pocket and thought he'd read a few verses in the hope it would put him to sleep. It usually did the trick. As he flipped through the flimsy pages, Maggie's voice echoed through his mind.

'You can live the life of a criminal, and go about causing pain and misery to others as well as yourself, but if you accept Jesus on your deathbed, you'll find your place in heaven. Yet a non-believer, who has spread good, and helped others all his life, but still denies Jesus on his deathbed, is doomed. No place in heaven for that poor sod! And what about somebody that lives in the jungle who's never heard of Jesus? Where do they go? You can't tell me they're all turned away, sent packing just because they don't know who Jesus is! Anyway, why would God or Jesus care less? Why would they condemn you to eternal doom just because you don't believe in them? Talk about ego! Wouldn't that make them the ultimate pair of control freaks? My God would welcome the lot of us! You're listening to the rantings of a few old men who'd set themselves up as the government of the day, and maybe a few younger ones who'd scribed it.'

He yawned. Subtlety had never been one of Maggie's strong points. *'What's the point of being subtle? Say what you've got to say!'* He smiled at her words in his head.

"Why do you bother with church at all?" he'd asked her one Sunday after the service.

"I sit and think about all the things I'm going to do to you after the service," she'd answered, her eyes full of mischief.

"Maggie, in God's house!" he'd replied, genuinely shocked.

"David, God judges nothing, doesn't have to. We never let up on ourselves. You torment yourself and there's no need, so there isn't."

Over the past few months the same old conversations had played out in his mind over and over again. Despite all his prayers for guidance and forgiveness, all his begging for answers: Should I leave the Church? Am I right to give it all up to be with Maggie and my son? He'd failed, in his mind, to obtain a response from God.

"I still don't feel God has forgiven me," he'd said to Maggie, while they were out pushing Aedan in his pram around the grounds of the chateau.

"That's because you don't deem yourself worthy of forgiveness," she'd answered, wisely. "You have to forgive yourself, David. God only wants what you want."

"Well, why won't he give me an answer?"

She'd stopped abruptly and laid her hand on his chest. "What do you feel in there? That's where God is. That's your answer—the love. Me, you, Aedan. We're living in love, David. We're living in God."

His parents had been devout Catholics. They never questioned anything, and had quoted the scriptures constantly throughout his childhood.

"Christ, my parents must be turning in their bloody graves. Oh, for God's sake, I'm blaspheming again…ah, what the hell!" He tossed the bible to the other end of the sofa and gave up on any chance of sleep. He pulled his feet from underneath Eriq, walked over to the drinks cabinet, and filled a shorts glass with whiskey. He fiddled about in his dressing gown pockets for his pipe, put it in his mouth, and flipped open a large, silver lighter. He puffed hard from one side of his mouth until the red embers glowed and blue pipe smoke circled him like the early morning mist circled the chateau.

He sat down again in the hope that his thoughts would nag him to sleep. Of course 'hope' being the operative word! He wasn't looking forward to the lengthy process that would be in store for him when he got back to Ireland. He couldn't simply walk away. He'd have to make sure they had a replacement. He owed his congregation that much at least. And then there was Patrick! What in God's name would he say to him?

"Tell him I'm dead!" Maggie had said bitterly, and she meant it. "As far as I'm concerned, he is. Just make sure you bring Angel back without anyone knowing. Let them think she's gone missing so as not to cause suspicion."

Cause suspicion, he thought dryly. Was it not suspicious enough that Maggie had decided not to return home at the same time he'd made the decision to give up the Church? And then when he leaves, Angel mysteriously disappears!

He couldn't pretend that Maggie had died; there would have to be a death certificate, for one thing. So they'd decided to tell Patrick the truth. Well, half of it at least. Maggie had left him on the grounds of his unreasonable and violent behaviour. She never wanted to see him again. She'd already left France, and David had no idea where she'd gone. He'd begged her to think about what she was doing but her mind was made up.

To say he was worried and uncertain about the future was an understatement, but then there were times in life when you just had to fight for what you loved. Patrick didn't deserve Maggie. He didn't deserve anyone. David felt his anger start to bubble. The times he'd wanted to punch the living daylights out of the man for good when Maggie had trembled, full of bruises, in his arms. She'd always stopped him and begged him not to do anything. "He'll kill me, I know it, if he thinks I've gone running to you opening my big mouth," she'd pleaded.

Without her by his side, it was going to take everything he had not to lay one on the man when he started his barrage of insults. Oh, he knew his type. He'd call Maggie every foul-mouthed name he could think of once he knew that she wasn't coming back.

David knocked back the last of his whiskey and thought about the moment when he'd told her that he wanted to be with her and Aedan for the rest of his life. He read the thoughts in her head by the emotions that flashed across her face. Even Aedan had gurgled for the occasion. It had been one of the sweetest moments of his life. Pure.

He looked at the clock. 3:45 a.m. It was hardly worth going to bed. In a few hours they'd be on their way to England. All the arrangements were made. They'd booked in at a bed and breakfast in Manchester indefinitely while they looked around for a place to rent. He'd get Maggie and Aedan settled before he left to tie up loose ends in Ireland. Angelette had insisted they stay with her at the chateau while he went back to Ireland, but it was too big a risk. Patrick, the parishioners, they all knew that he and Maggie had left for France. What if Patrick decided to come looking for her? No! These things had a way of biting you on the backside and David wasn't about to risk Patrick turning up on the doorstep, especially if he wasn't there.

David decided to try and catch a few hours on the sofa instead of going back to bed. He leaned over to a small table at the side of the couch, extinguished his pipe with his thumb, and left it in an ashtray. He laid his head on the bible accidentally, picked it up and shoved a cushion in its place, then dropped it on the floor. It fell open. Exhausted, he ignored it but something pricked at him. *Pick it up, pick it up.* Grumbling to himself, he reached over and grabbed it with one hand. Some of the words from Matthew 21:9, "The Fig Tree Withers," caught his attention: *I tell you the truth, if you have faith and do not doubt, not only can you do what was done to the fig tree, but also you can say to this mountain, go, throw yourself into the sea, and it will be done. If you believe, you will receive whatever you ask for in prayer.*

He finally started to drift off to sleep with Maggie's voice floating through his mind. *'Whatever you focus on and believe in you'll create, but there's a bit of a trick to it. You have to internalise it, feel it, know it...above all, love it. You have to get past your conscious mind. A lot of people talk about thinking positive, but until you've put whatever you're thinking positive about into your subconscious mind, your conscious mind will constantly question it, and more often than not, reject it. That's why a lot of people fail to get the results they want. It's all about belief, you see. Once you've learned the art of truly believing in yourself, you've cracked it! You can never go back.'*

The bible slid off David's chest. Eriq turned his head to the side and opened one eye in an effort to investigate the sound of book meets floor. Satisfied that all was well, he let out a contented whine, climbed up on the sofa, and fell asleep on David's cold feet.

21.

*D*ublin station was packed. David jumped off the train and dodged his way through the throngs. He sighed irritably. *Just what I need.* Patience was something he worked on, especially in crowds. He wanted to push everybody out of the way and clear a path to walk down in peace. Progress was slow. He fell into the lumber of the crowd, noticing how dark and miserable everything looked. Black suits, black overcoats, black ties, black hats. Some wore brown, some grey. His clothes fit right in but he didn't pay much attention to that.

A sudden hiss from the old steam train made everybody within earshot jump. Clouds of grey bellowed into the air. David closed his throat and nose off to the smell of the smoke even though he liked it. It stirred up all kinds of childhood memories of him and his friends playing around the station, but his lungs didn't appreciate it.

His eyes followed the thick smoke upwards. The station had its fair share of windows; it seemed to David they made up half the building. Blobs of rain crashed onto the panes and ran down the glass in channels. His mood got darker. This was no longer his home. He belonged with Maggie and Aedan. He blew air through his lips just as an unreligious thought crossed his mind—*Pissed wet through, to boot!*

Once he'd made it outside he decided to stop and eat at the first place he could find—hopefully the rain would let up before he started the long trek back to the village. He looked at his watch; 6:50 p.m. and already dark. The rain suddenly got louder. It bounced off the pavement so hard, it looked as if it was being hurled back at the sky. He pulled his hat over his face and made his way to the back streets in search of somewhere empty. He didn't want to make small talk and he didn't want to be recognised.

He found a small, worn-out café on a cobbled side street off the main drag. The yellow glow that shone through the steamed-up windows and old nettings made it look cozy enough on the inside. Besides, anywhere was better than being stuck outside in the damn rain. But something stalled him—a sixth sense. He hovered over the door handle. While he was debating whether to try it or to look for another place, a stranger slammed into him with a force that should have made his mind up for him. Shocked, David turned sharply, expecting an apology.

The stranger, dressed all in black, was huge—full of muscle and tall, about six-feet-five, give or take an inch. The skin on his face was so white it seemed to illuminate the dark, empty street. He almost looked like a floating head. They locked eyes. David shuddered, his expression one of bewilderment and fear. He'd never seen eyes so empty, so black. They looked like two shiny beetles stuck inside the stranger's head, yet the more he looked into them, the more entranced he became. A splinter of fear started to cut through his mind. *Get a grip!* he told himself, not understanding why he was reacting in such a way.

The stranger lifted his hand and pointed. "GO IN THERE." His voice was slow, a gnarly rumble, yet a commanding roar that seemed to hurl itself out of his mouth and invoke the thunder. Or was the thunder the strangers voice? It sent chills through David but he couldn't drag himself away. He turned toward the door just as a beautiful young man, no more than seventeen, appeared in the glass pane. He stared at the stranger. But even the hard expression on his face couldn't override his perfect features. If David had to paint an angel, the boy would have made a perfect model, with sparkling blue eyes that emphasised his tanned, flawless skin and dark curls. Even though he was dressed in a casual open-neck white shirt and black slacks, , there was an overall ethereal look about him.

"Leave, little demon," he said, as if bored. "You're testing my patience."

David had never heard such a musical voice. It sounded like

liquid pureness—hard to describe. Its overtone, like crystal glass, reverberated right through him, its chime fading away slowly. He wanted to fall to his knees but remained on his feet, staring through the glass pane. He watched the boy glare the stranger down until he was no more than a few feet tall.

The boy bent forward as if talking to a child. "Go, little demon, before I turn you into dust." He tightened his lips, pondering. "Hmmm…or will you join Galaxias?" The stranger opened his mouth and snarled obscenities just as a huge clap of thunder shook the empty street. The boy sighed. "As I thought—that's the thanks I get for not inflicting any more pain on your miserable existence!" The musical voice had a face-up-to-it tone. "It would be so much easier if I could crush—" He cocked his head sideways as if listening to something. "Okay, okay!" he relented, raising his eyebrows. He looked down at the stranger. His voice had a disgusted edge to it. "The elders won't let me touch you!" He shook his head from side to side as he spoke. "You should thank them some day!" He waved his hand gracefully, flipping it out just as a bolt of lightning struck the stranger through the top of the head.

Or was the boy the lightning? David was confused but captivated. He witnessed the stranger simply turn into black smoke, as if he'd been extinguished, and disappear.

"Go do something useful, idiot!"

David noticed how immature the boy's voice now sounded despite its pure tone. He turned his head away from the door to look at him.

The boy stood on the street. The smile on his face had a tinge of mischief about it, as if proud of his accomplishment, and the expression served to reinforce his young years. "Don't worry. It's not dead, just out of action for a while. It belongs to the underworld— one of their foot soldiers. There are millions of them always on the lookout to wreak as much havoc as possible." His smile faded into a serious expression. A dangerous edge infiltrated his voice. "It's a constant battle. We have to be one step ahead all the time. We'll let the creature go when we've erased its memory. Just got to make sure it's got nothing left to report back to Evolus."

He rolled his eyes impatiently. "It's the elders. They're always prattling on about being nice—you know, raising their standards instead of lowering ours. If a situation gets too dangerous then we'll fight, of course, but the elders only go in as a last resort. Left to me, I'd kick his—" He stopped abruptly and smirked. "Probably why I have to take orders from them." He nodded at the café. "I'd give that dump a miss if I was you. It's a setup!"

David was dumbfounded. "Foot soldiers? Evolus? What are you talking about? Who are you?" he managed to stutter.

"GALAXIAS!" He was proud to shout it. "Remember? You're one of ours, David Sullivan! The sooner you realise it, the better! We need all the help we can get now your boy has arrived!"

"Galaxias…I've never heard…I don't understand—how do you know my name?" He turned away and faced the glass pane. He turned back. The boy was gone! The only sounds in the empty street were the rain and the gutters working overtime to deal with it. "What in God's name—"

Evolus? He was sure Maggie had called the evil she'd—*No! My mind is playing tricks.* He put the experience down to lack of sleep. He'd read somewhere that sleep deprivation can cause hallucinations—that, and his nerves being on full alert. He looked at his watch. The whole experience had lasted less than a minute. Baffled, he looked up and down the street. There wasn't a soul to be seen. He shook his head, walked the few strides to the café, and struggled to push the door open. He pushed again using a bit more force, until finally, on his third try, it swung open and crashed against the inside wall. *'It's a setup!'* The boy's voice chimed through his head.

A thick Irish accent attacked him. "Like to make your presence felt, do you?" The stout older woman in a flowered apron glared at him from behind the counter. Her eyes were sly as they glanced at the door. "That glass breaks, you'll be paying for it, so you will!"

"Sorry about that," he answered. "The wood seems to have swollen with the damp weather."

She threw the grubby-looking rag she'd been wiping the counter with through the doorway that led into the kitchen. Her aim at the sink was spot on. The sound of water splashed as the rag hit the surface. "We don't usually have a problem with it."

Uncomfortable, he cleared his throat. "Are you still serving?"

She eyed him suspiciously. "As long as the money comes in."

"Do you have a menu?"

"No!"

"Err...I see, well, err...what...do you have anything left?" He smiled, in an effort to remind her how it was done and, hopefully, warm up the sub-zero atmosphere. Dour-faced, she lumbered around and pointed to a large blackboard covered in white chalk on the wall behind her. How could you miss it? her expression said. "Egg, chips, peas, two slices of bread and butter, and a cup of tea, please," he said cautiously.

She opened a warped old drawer underneath the thick wooden counter without saying a word, and held out a worn-out hand covered in age spots. He gave her a few coins and told her to keep the change. She threw them in the drawer, turned around, and tramped through the kitchen doorway. It looked too small for her. Her long, grey braid tied with a brown elastic band swung from side to side, tapping her on the backside as she trudged out of sight. Unintentionally, a picture of the back end of a horse flashed across his mind. He smiled to himself, confirming his thoughts from earlier. *Well! If she's not a sign that I'm no longer welcome here, I don't know what is!*

He looked around. The place was cheap and shabby. He eyed the red Formica and chrome tables. Each table had a set of condiments pushed over to one side: a small glass sugar bowl, two plastic containers—one brown, one red—for matching sauce, a bottle of brown vinegar, and two small glass bottles with silver lids containing salt and pepper.

He hung his hat and coat on the stand provided, and plonked his suitcase down by the side of it. He was the only one in the place so he had the pick of somewhere to sit. He walked midway, pulled out a chair by the window, and sat down. The red PVC made a rude noise as it released the air that was trapped inside it.

He ate slowly and read the various newspapers that were strewn around on the tables. He wanted to kill some time before attempting the last part of his journey. It was a good two hours' walk to Dun Laoghaire if he paced it. It would be at least 10:30 p.m. by the time he got there. There was no public transport running and he wasn't risking a taxi—most of the drivers knew who he was. He didn't look forward to the trek but at least the villagers would be in bed by the time he got there. He wasn't in the mood to answer questions as to Maggie's whereabouts. It wouldn't take long before word got out to Patrick that he was back, and right now Patrick was the last person David wanted to see. No, he'd hide out for a few days. Joseph expected him, but he'd asked him to keep quiet until they'd had a chance to talk. Once he let Joseph know his plans, he'd get the ball rolling with the Church. He knew Joseph loved Dun Laoghaire, and he'd like nothing more than his good friend of many years to take over the parish.

David wiped up the last of the egg yolk and brown sauce with a piece of bread and butter. He wasn't hungry but still managed to clear his plate. The last thing he wanted to do was offend Sergeant Major by refusing to eat every last morsel she'd cooked up for him. But then again, there was something about greasy egg and chips washed down with a cup of hot, strong tea that put it in a class of its own. He wiped his hands and mouth with what he presumed to be a serviette. The tatty white material had definitely seen better days.

The sooner he got back to Maggie and Aedan the better. God, he missed them. He reached into his pocket and pulled a small black and white photo from his wallet. Maggie smiled back at him, holding Aedan in her arms, his huge dark eyes wide open. If he didn't know any better, he'd swear they had halos surrounding them.

A drunken couple arguing outside caught his attention. He shoved the photo back in his wallet, cocked his left side, and shoved the wallet into his back pocket. He thought he recognised the voice and strained to see through the grimy lace curtains that had turned yellow with age and grease.

"Let go of me, you bleeding idiot," the man said, falling against the window before hitting the floor. "There…sno way it's mine."

"Oh, it's yours! Don't think you're getting off with it that easy. Me da and brothers will have your backside for pig swill, they will that!"

"Ahh, shut it, woman! D'ya think I'm scared of them two lumps of lard—let's get something to eat." He crawled up the window and threw an arm around her shoulders. "Come on, darling," he said, slurring his words. He put a hand on the back of her head and pulled her to him roughly. "Let's eat before I eat you." They locked lips and chewed at each other. He pushed her against the wall, fumbled around under her coat and skirts, and shoved his hand inside her panties.

Not quite as drunk as him, she giggled, "Not here. I'm starving. Let's see if Mam's got any leftovers."

The man pushed the door open with ease and the pair of them stumbled in, soaked to the bones. The girl leant over the counter. "MAMMY, ARE YOU THERE?"

Sergeant Major shouted from the kitchen. "Jesus, Mary, and Joseph, child! You nearly gave me a heart attack, so you did!"

The girl went into a spasm of coughing. "Any food left?" she asked, between the dry, hard barks. Makeup ran down her cheeks like two black streams and her cheap red lipstick was smudged around her lips. Her dyed yellow hair was left down, and dripped all over the counter. She looked at David and smiled. She was pretty in a hard sort of way.

The man had his back to him but David recognised him immediately. *Holy mother of God! Patrick!* His heart just about beat its way out of his chest. He jumped up at lightning speed, turned his back on them and knocked his teacup to the floor in the panic. It bounced to the back of the café, spilling its remains everywhere but it didn't break. He chased after it and felt their eyes pierce his back. He knew Sergeant Major had joined them. He could hear the soles of her slippers flip flop across the floor. He picked up the cup, banged it on the nearest table, backed off to the front of the café, and dragged his hat and coat from the stand.

"Oi! Suit Boy! Clean up your damn mess!" Sergeant Major ordered.

Ignoring her, he shoved his trilby over his face, hauled his case over a chair, charged through the door, and raced down the dark, empty street through the brutal rain, struggling to get his coat on as he went.

He stopped, exhausted, underneath a signpost that read "Dun Laoghaire, 7 miles." His breathing was loud and jagged. He put his hands on his knees in an effort to catch his breath and rest for a minute or so. He noticed a small inlet between the shrubs that lined the country road. He walked over, pushed his way through, and looked down the cliff face to the shoreline below. It was like something out of a horror story. Black water underneath a black sky. Bolts of lightning exposed an army of waves, arrogant in their strength as they charged the shoreline in time to the rolling thunder; but within seconds of being out of their comfort zone, the waves were reduced to froth and bubbles and dumped on the beach like used-up eggshells, washed-up remnants of a power gone mad. Their essence was sucked in by their maker who might one day share the power with them again. But only if they proved they could handle it.

He felt suddenly nauseous as an inexplicable feeling of eeriness moved through him—he brushed it off and looked down at his feet. The road was mud. It was going to be a long, lonely walk through the dark coastal lanes…but there was something about the ocean. Even when she was in a foul mood and her temper raged…power was power. It never failed to touch him.

His mood matched the dark, heavy scene. He turned and walked over to his case. He already felt like he'd been back a lifetime. He puffed up his cheeks, let the air vibrate through his lips. Thoughts of Maggie and Aedan gave him an immediate boost but it was soon dampened by his apprehension about the coming months. *It will be over soon enough,* he thought, in an effort to stay optimistic.

He looked up at the black sky. The wind and rain battered him. Undaunted, he threw his arms up, letting them give him their best. "GOD!" His voice was loud and demanding. "WILL YOU FORGIVE ME?" A huge fork of lightning flashed above him. "GOD! ARE YOU

THERE?" Thunder ripped across the sky, shaking the ground below him. "DO YOU EVEN EXIST?" The wind screamed around him and nearly took him off his feet. He was completely downhearted. "What does it take to get an answer from you—to hear you?" He was oblivious to the connection the elements displayed.

David looked like a human drainage system. The rain dripped off his trilby onto his shoulders, and poured down his coat into his shoes. A piece of paper that was stuck on a small bush caught his attention. It flapped angrily as the violent wind fumed around it, but it held fast. He wanted to leave it but he'd always been a stickler for keeping the Earth tidy. He was ahead of his time in thinking about the wildlife and the nature that was being damaged by people's litter and pollution. He sighed and walked over to it. Just as he was about to put it in his pocket, he noticed the scrawny handwriting on the note. He could just make out a few of the words that hadn't run down the page. He knew right away where the words were from: Matthew 13:48, "Only in his hometown and in his own house is a prophet without honour." He shoved it into his pocket but yet again failed to make the connection between the paper and the questions he'd asked of the universe!

He picked up his case and held his collar tight around his neck. Even though it was wet, it kept the cold night air out and gave him some sense of warmth.

He set off on his journey. The wind and the rain backed off a bit.

22.

David was cold, weary, and soaked through. He put his key in the lock gently, hoping not to disturb Father Joseph, but as soon as it turned over Angel charged the door. David jumped back, startled, as ninety pounds of black and tan mongrel warned him to stay put. "Good God almighty!" It took a few seconds for his brain to register that the snarling monster with its fur standing on end was Angel.

He opened the door slowly to give her time to recognise him and whispered through the crack. "Only me, girl. It's alright, there's a good girl."

Within seconds, her snarls turned to happy yelps and her tail reappeared from between her legs and wagged furiously in time with her oversized backside. "What's this?" He rolled her head between two hands. "The Angel four-step."

Her yelps got louder along with her panting, as she expressed her affection for David with no holds barred. "Calm down, calm down, you're not getting any younger, you know, and I've strict orders to take you back to your mammy, so I have."

The light clicked on, filling the hallway with a dim, yellow glow. Father Joseph's portly figure paced from the sitting room doorway, hand outstretched. "David, at last! I was beginning to wonder if you'd changed your mind."

The two men patted each other on the back and shook hands vigorously.

"Good grief, man—you're soaked through!" Joseph still held on to David's hand. "Get yourself dried. I'll fix us a couple of stiff ones.

Are you hungry? Angel girl!" he admonished. "Leave him alone while he gets changed." She ignored him completely. Exasperated, he shook his head and tutted. "Rules the place, that damn dog; doesn't take a blind bit of notice of me!"

David smirked, squinting at Joseph's vibrant fleecy stripes. "Snazzy 'jamas! I could do with some sunglasses. Did you borrow them from Joseph, Joseph?"

"Very funny!" He rolled his eyes. "My mother. She keeps sending me things, telling me how cold it gets in Dun Laoghaire during the winter months. As if I didn't know!"

David unbuttoned his coat. "Are you tired?" He threw it at the stand in the corner then spun his hat through the air. It landed on top of it. "What a shot!"

"Not particularly." Joseph walked over to the coat and arranged it so it would dry quicker.

"Good. There's something I need to talk to you about." David's long strides took the stairs four at a time with no effort. "I'll just go dry off first."

Angel bounded after him. Joseph grabbed her collar. "Let him get changed; he'll be down in a minute. David!"

"Yes?" He stopped at the top of the stairs.

Head bent, Joseph looked over the top of his glasses. "Are you hungry? I made stew with a pie crust earlier today."

"Bloody hell! You're getting adventurous."

"I love to cook! There's a real art to it, you know. I escape from everything when I'm surrounded by onions and potatoes. Any problem will be solved, or at least reduced to a mere triviality, by the time I'm finished. A dab of this here, a drop of that there; beats being down on my knees when I'm talking to the head honcho. Some of my finest inspiration has come from a few carrots and a pound of sprouts!"

David laughed out loud. Joseph had always been one of the more contemporary priests. Probably why he wasn't that popular with the higher ranks; a rebel, they called him. He'd seen life, that much was true. Brought up in a mining town in Wales, Joseph had had a rough life to say the least. His parents had done their best with what little they had, although they made sure Joseph and his five siblings were taught values and respect. Even so, it was a big shock for them and their immediate community when Joseph announced that he was going to join the priesthood. His parents couldn't understand where he'd got it from. It was not like they'd ever rammed religion down his throat, and it was expected that he'd go down the mine like the rest of 'em. Always had ideas above his station, that one.

"I'm starving," David answered. The long walk and battle with the elements had brought on his appetite, not to mention the aroma of the meat, onions, and pastry as it made its way up his nostrils.

Angel's nails tapped lightly on the hardwood floor. She was still dancing the four-step, though to some extent her initial excitement had subsided. Joseph held her by the collar with one hand and clamped the other over her snout. "And you! Would you like some stew?" He let go of her. She jumped three feet in the air and spun around a couple of times.

David laughed. "So much for loyalty. No wonder she's put on weight since we've been away."

Joseph walked toward the kitchen with a devoted Angel following eagerly behind. "She's been spoilt rotten, but she'll be back with her owner soon enough. I'll miss the old girl."

"Adopt a stray. There are enough of them running around."

Joseph looked at him puzzled, and cocked his head. "Ay, some day, when I've got my own place."

David hesitated. "Well then, I'd better dry off."

><

The huge fire burning in the grate welcomed him into the cosy sitting room. Its orange and yellow flames spat and quivered, and threw off enough warmth to heat the rest of the house. A solitary candle glowed on top of a small writing bureau, which was placed underneath the large bay windows to the right of the fireplace. Every now and again its smooth flame would flicker as a sharp gust of wind battered the rain against the small bullet-glass panes.

David looked around. Nothing had changed apart from four months of dust that had settled on the furniture. He turned and used his index finger to sign his name across the bookcase that was set back in the recess to the side of him. He grinned, "You didn't bother to hire a cleaner, then?"

Joseph sat in an old, deep burgundy leather armchair, and Angel lay spread-eagle on the rug in front of the fire, with not a care in the world. "No, I never did get around to it. I should have done because I'm the world's worst for housework—can't stand it! Rather be out communing with nature, reading, cooking, hiking, anything!"

"I take it this is mine?" David walked to a small round dining table and picked up a bowl of steaming hot stew.

"Yep, help yourself. No formalities, I'm afraid. I get sick to the back teeth of 'em." He nodded at a small wooden tray. "There's a tray there."

"Ahh…my damn fingers!" David slammed the stew on the tray and shook his hand in the air. "Idiot!" He blew on his fingers.

Joseph slurped his stew and didn't look up. "Be careful. It's hot," he said drolly.

David shook his head. "Thanks," he said, laughing. He eyed the tablecloth. "New tablecloth? I guess that's one way of keeping the dust at bay." He added a good helping of pepper to his stew.

"What's that?" Joseph strained his neck backwards. "Go easy on the pepper, there's plenty in there. Oh, the tablecloth." He jerked his head and stretched his eyes. "I'll give you three guesses!"

"Your mother!" David said between mouthfuls. "Umm, umm… very good! Very, very good! He sat down. The old leather sofa squeaked in indignation. "What's your secret?" He dipped a piece of bread into his bowl.

Joseph smirked. "Guinness, with a touch of Guinness, garnished with a large helping of…"

"Guinness!" they said in unison.

David pulled the bread, dripping with stew and butter from the bowl, and stuffed it into his mouth. "No wonder Angel is flat out!" She lifted her head at the mention of her name. With a fake sternness in his voice, David demanded, "Are you drunk, lady?" She grunted at him as if to say, So what if I am? and flopped back down.

"So. David." Joseph leaned over the back of the chair and placed his empty bowl on the table. "I know you're tired but there's something else. You've looked decidedly troubled since you arrived."

David's dark eyebrows frowned. "I'm that obvious?"

"To me." He took off his glasses and rubbed his eyes. "Look, whatever it is, spit it out. You know you can trust me, and I'm beyond being shocked."

David let out a sarcastic sigh. "You think so?"

"I know so!"

David thought for a few seconds but the relief at being able to speak truthfully at last about Maggie and Aedan made the tremors in the pit of his stomach erupt, along with the words which gushed from his mouth at lightning speed. "I've been having an affair with Maggie O'Connell going on six years. As you know, we took off to France on the pretext of a mysterious illness, which was really a baby. She gave birth to a boy—Aedan." He smiled as Aedan filled his mind. "He's beautiful, a miracle. The adoption was all arranged—anyway, that's another story." His tone was now adamant, protective. "We're keeping him!"

He stared into space and took on a wistful look. "When I held him in my arms for the first time it was as if the Earth had stopped turning. All the plans, everything…it all went to pot." He leaned forward, looking deep into Joseph's eyes. "There's nothing like it, you know… holding a child in your arms…a tiny person that you've made. I felt like a king, a god—it's as close to God as you're ever going to get." His voice went quiet. "It would have ripped my heart right out of my chest to give him away. I couldn't do it."

Joseph was stunned. "Bloody hell! Where are they now?" were

the only words he could come up with.

"I've left them in Manchester while I wrap things up with the Church." He paused, and for some reason, probably nerves, he wanted to laugh out loud at the startled expression on Joseph's face. He let out a half-hearted chuckle instead. "Welcome to Dun Laoghaire, one of the most beautiful places the world has to offer. I know you'd love to take it over." He was silent.

Joseph massaged his failing hairline. "You're not joking, are you?"

"No." He felt strong. His voice was firm. "Joseph, over the years, I couldn't have asked for a better friend than you and no matter what happens I shall carry that friendship in my heart always. I hope you can find it in yourself to forgive me someday. It will break my heart to leave the Church, but it would kill me to leave Maggie and my son. I can't do it. If that means being shunned for the rest of my life and dragged to the gates of hell, they're worth it!"

"Holy—I'll be damned, David!" Joseph was visibly shaken by the news. He shook his head. "After this, I can honestly say that nothing else could shock me! Sorry, I'm still reeling!"

"Do I still have your friendship? Do you think you can find it in your heart to forgive me?"

Joseph looked puzzled. "Forgive you? For what? It isn't up to me to forgive, it's up to you…but are you sure? What if you give up the Church only to realise—"

"I've no doubt in my heart. I love the Church but compared to what I feel for my fam—" He broke down as the relief of being able to unburden himself became overwhelming.

Joseph looked at his friend. Concerned, he bent forward and rested his arms on his knees. "Then that is where you should be—that is God." He got to his feet, glass in hand, "Refill?"

David nodded and turned to pick up his glass but Joseph was already pouring two more large whiskeys from the half-full bottle on the dining table. "Here. I know alcohol's not the answer but it will help you sleep, if nothing else. You look done in." David looked at him, a perplexed expression on his face.

Joseph sighed. "What?" He sat down and shrugged. "A few whiskeys aren't going to turn you into a raving alcoholic."

"No, no." He shook his head. "It's not that…what you said about God and love, Maggie more or less said the same thing when we were out walking one day."

"She's right. The love you say you have for her and Aedan is the love that I feel for the Church. When you feel love like that, you're in God. That is where you should be, even if it doesn't fit into society's expectations. Only the heart counts."

David dragged a hand though his hair. "Huh…coincidences."

"What are?"

Bemused, David looked at the floor. "Maggie more or less said that as well." He lifted his head, looked at Joseph, and half smiled. "Only the heart counts."

"It all depends on how you look at coincidences," Joseph said casually. "I believe coincidences are messages from God!"

Disbelief removed all traces of David's smile. He rubbed the top of his head vigorously, messing his hair up into different-sized tufts. "She said that as well! Only she calls them messages from the universe."

Joseph laughed. "Well, then! It seems you've had that message reinforced."

The candle flickered and died suddenly, leaving them with a few glowing embers from the dying fire. A strange feeling passed between the two men. "Maggie would view that as confirmation, or a bloody message of some kind." David got up and threw a few cobs of coal into the grate. "Any more candles?"

Joseph walked over and relit the old one, which still had a way to go. "What are you going to do about Patrick?" he asked. "Will you tell him?"

"Good God, no!" David answered, alarmed. "We've decided to tell him that she isn't coming back and that's about it. If he finds out about us, he won't just sit back and let it go and I can't risk him finding her, especially if I'm not there."

"You might be surprised. Rumour has it he's been seeing Bridget

MacNamara. Been going on for a while apparently. Her parents run a farm on the outskirts of town and own a small café in Dublin."

"I can confirm the rumour. I stopped in the café unawares for a quick bite, and bumped straight into them. High-tailed it out of there before Patrick had a chance to recognise me. Then again, he was falling-over drunk, so it was unlikely that he'd have recognised me anyway, but I wasn't about to take that chance." He pulled his face to one side making the skin taut and scratched his cheek. "Judging by the conversation they were having, she's pregnant."

"That's the other part to the rumour. So with any luck, Patrick will be happy to see the back of Maggie.."

In a momentary loss of control, David felt the creature move inside him. In his mind he grabbed Patrick by the throat and rammed him against a wall. "No, not him," he said, his expression sinister. "If he thinks Maggie has let another man into her bed and birthed a child from that union, his rage won't rest until he's hunted them down like vermin." His eyes were intense as they looked into Joseph's. "And wiped them out. There's no way he'll let it go. Maggie belongs to him like the shoes he walks in." He could barely contain his anger. "Promise me that you'll never mention any of this to anyone. I know I've no right to put this on you, but you've got to promise me that much, otherwise there'll be blood spilt. In a mind like Patrick's, murder is justified."

Joseph signed the cross against his chest. "You have my word." But something chewed at his insides. A dark feeling crawled through him, twisted itself around his spine, and spewed its evil through his mind. He broke out in goose bumps. Something terrible was about to happen. He said a silent prayer for his friend. *God, please protect David, Maggie, and the child. Amen.*

23.

David woke to somebody hammering on the front door. He sat up slowly, with no clue as to his whereabouts or what day it was, but the slats of light creeping through the curtains gave him a rough idea of the time—early morning. He looked around the half-dark bedroom and soon realised it was *his*.

It was a miserable room. The skirting boards and trimmings were dark brown, and the walls were covered in a mustard-colored patterned wallpaper. If he looked at the huge interlocking spirals for too long they'd twirl inwards, giving him a sense of unbalance and hazy vision. He wondered why he'd never decorated or cheered the place up a bit. Even the furniture was heavy and dark. The only highlight was the beautiful hardwood floor. But at least it was a highlight. *There is always a highlight.*

He could smell mothballs and rosewater. He didn't mind the rosewater—Maggie and her concoctions. She'd given him a mixture of rosewater and glycerine cream for his rough, itchy hands. Swore it would do the trick. It did! But mothballs always gave him a creepy feeling. He associated the smell with death. Probably because it was often present in the homes of parishioners he'd given the last rites to. Joseph must have supplied them, thinking he was doing him a favour.

The hammering got louder. He threw the covers off, swung his legs around, and sat on the edge of the bed for a few seconds, trying to gather his wits. He rubbed his eyes. They felt gritty and didn't want to stay open. He'd tossed and turned all night. Sleep had evaded him yet again. He made a mental note to see Dr. O'Riley about getting

247

something to help him rest. He didn't want any more hallucinations. The one he'd had yesterday was still playing on his mind…*Galaxias?*

Exhausted, he wanted to snuggle back down inside the thick, warm blankets—"RIGHT, RIGHT, GIVE ME A CHANCE!" Whoever was banging on the door wouldn't give up, along with a dog barking wildly in the distance. Both were starting to grate on his nerves.

The bedroom was freezing. He picked out his dressing gown from the pile of clothes he'd thrown onto the floor, then raced barefoot from the bedroom down the stairs. "Alright! Alright! Let up, you'll have the bloody door off its hinges," he shouted, fastening the belt attached to the gown. He was getting more wound up by the minute.

He rubbed the stubble on his chin and shoved a hand through his messy hair hoping that he looked half decent, then dragged the door open—"Patrick!" *NO!* His heart gave one solid thump. He could only stare in disbelief.

Patrick's left eye twitched. "Where is she?" He pushed David out of the way. The smell of alcohol and cigarettes trailed after him like dutiful soldiers.

In the four months since David had last seen him, Patrick had gone downhill fast. His skin had taken on a yellow tinge which didn't go well with his beady, bloodshot eyes and red hair. His face had lost its plumpness, and the skin hanging from his cheekbones gave him a hangdog, miserable expression. He'd always been on the stocky side but he'd lost weight and now looked thin and wiry. He stalked the hall, sniffing and digging. His new skinny frame wrapped in a shabby black suit that looked too big for him put David in mind of a spider monkey, only Patrick's temperament was a lot more dangerous, more like a wolverine. He was small but had given out many a hiding—any excuse to beat the life out of someone, Maggie included.

He looked at David, a dangerous glint in his twitching eye. "Where's my wife? Why didn't she come home last night?" He opened the sitting room door, paced in, paced out, rushed to the bottom of the stairs as if looking for evidence of…*something*, his instincts telling him that *something,* wasn't right. "MAGGIE O'CONNELL! GET

OUT HERE NOW, YOU DIRTY, CHEAP SLUT!"

David visibly cringed. "She's not here!" His fists clenched. He wanted to beat Patrick into the ground then stamp the life out of him.

Patrick leered. His nicotine-stained teeth spread across his face. "Then where is she, Father?"

David couldn't hide his contempt or the coldness in his voice. "I don't know. She told me to let you know that she won't be coming back to Dun Laoghaire, that she'd had enough of your violence, your…filth." He broke off. His expression told Patrick exactly what he thought of him. "I tried to reason with her but she wouldn't listen. Said I was to tell you not to bother looking for her because she will have already left France by the time you got this message. She wouldn't even tell me where she was going. She thought it best; decided the fewer who knew of her whereabouts the better." He enjoyed lying to him and didn't feel one ounce of guilt. He wondered why it felt good to lie and then realised that in some cases lying had a positive side to it, like the power to save lives. Not everything was black and white. Besides, he wanted to hurt the bastard as much as possible. He deserved it.

Patrick stared, unable to utter a word while he digested the news. He didn't believe Maggie had the guts to leave him, to make it on her own. "Left me?" he whispered. "She wouldn't dare." He coughed violently. The phlegm wheezed and rattled in his chest. David thought how easy it would be all around if Patrick would just collapse and die. He opened the door without saying a word in the hope that he would leave quietly and take his germs with him.

"I get the feeling something's going on here," he said between coughs. "You know more than you're letting on." He pulled a creased-up handkerchief from his pocket and spat into it.

David felt the creature inside him stir and start to creep about. He pushed it back. It settled down and lay in wait, ready to pounce. "I've told you all I know. Now if you don't mind, I've a busy day ahead."

A cunning glaze varnished Patrick's eyes. His voice was a dangerous whisper. "Attractive woman, Maggie. Many a man would like to do her.

I don't mind as long as they're willing to pay a good price."

David felt the force of Patrick's words as if they'd physically punched him in the gut—*Don't take the bait!* the small voice ordered. *Don't do it!* "Don't talk about Mag!" He hesitated. "Get out!" he hissed. "Get out before I put pay to you myself, you filthy piece of shite!"

"My, my, Father. Are such words allowed in the Catholic Church?" Patrick paused, realising he'd touched a nerve. "You seem overly protective of my wife."

David felt the creature inside him crouch, ready for the kill. It was desperate to rip Patrick in half. It took every ounce of will he had to keep it restrained. David leant forward and spoke through clenched teeth. "O'Connell, whatever's in that warped mind of yours, I don't want to be a part of it. Get out, man, before I call the police."

"Seems I should be the one calling the police." He squinted at David suspiciously.

David shook his head. "You, huh! I'm sure they'll come running at your beck and call," he said sarcastically.

Patrick's breath came out in short, sharp rasps. "My wife takes off to France with the village priest who comes back alone armed with some trumped-up story that she's not coming home. I mean, anything could have happened to her, and you expect me to leave quietly and do nothing about it. Well, let me tell you this much, Father: I hold you responsible for her. So go ahead, call the pigs."

David decided to bluff it. He walked over to the small console table at the side of the coat stand and picked up the black receiver. Patrick was well known to the police. They wouldn't put the words of a known drunk before his. He looked at Patrick, receiver in hand. "I'll give you one last chance to leave."

Patrick's intuition worked overtime. Incensed, his eyes bulged with hatred. He moved forward, hissed the words out. "You've been sleeping with my wife, Father! I wonder what the Church will make of that!"

David banged the receiver down hard. The creature stalked, circled. "I can't believe...I've not got time for this, this pathetic..."

He struggled to find words. "You've accused me, of all people, of sleeping with your wife! You're out of your mind, man. GET OUT! GET OUT BEFORE I THROW YOU OUT!" He gripped the door handle, a substitute for Patrick's throat, and squeezed hard.

Livid, Patrick walked menacingly toward him. "Don't play the high and mighty with me," he spat. "I don't give a shit about the Church or your fucking position. You're no different than the rest of them—hypocrites, the lot of you! Was it worth it? Or did she lie there as usual like a bag of rotten spuds while you banged the life out of her—"

David couldn't control it any longer. He felt sweat break out all over his body and heat sear through the top of his dressing gown. His eyes turned black, flipped upwards, and drilled into Patrick. He looked possessed, crazed, like he'd stepped outside of himself to let some evil entity move in.

Patrick stepped back, terrified, but it was too late. David lunged at him, put his hands around his neck and squeezed as if his own life depended on it. "You're disgusting!" he spat. "No wonder Maggie doesn't want to be anywhere near you, you low-life piece of scum!"

Patrick fought for his life but he didn't stand a chance against David's adrenaline-fuelled strength. He flayed and kicked helplessly in midair, gasping for breath.

Overcome by blind rage, a barrage of obscenities spewed from David's mouth, landing spit and bubbles with every word. He held Patrick by the throat up against the wall and reveled in the power he had over him. He wanted him to feel the same fear that he'd subjected Maggie to for years. "Not such a big man now, are you?" He smashed Patrick's head into an antique mirror that hung above the console table, creating an oversized hole. Pieces of glass dropped to the floor like spears. The table broke in half, and sent the phone hurtling to the other side of the hallway. Its bell rang out a pitiful chime every time it bounced off the floor.

Speaking into Patrick's cheek, David hissed, "You're only good for beating up women, you foul-mouthed coward. Do you know how much pleasure it would give me to snap your neck in two, take you out for good?" David lost all control. In this one small moment, the evil he'd campaigned against most of his life had completely taken him over.

Patrick's eyes were wild with fear. Shocked, he couldn't believe a priest would retaliate, would have a temper like this. Frantic, he tried to break free but the priest was too big, too strong for him. His hands grasped desperately at David, then at the wall behind him but it was hopeless. This was it! He was about to die! Beside himself with fear, he peed his pants. The urine trickled down his legs onto the floor, along with his last remaining remnants of life. As the last bit of strength seeped out of him, he gave up the fight and stopped struggling. His head flopped to one side like a doll with a broken neck.

"Let him go! Let him go before it's too late!" the small voice urged. But the creature inside him was enjoying its newfound freedom. *"KILL HIM! KILL HIM!"* it snarled.

The dog in the distance had never let up. It was as if it were barking at David—

Angel! She rained on all the negativity in his head. He looked around as if trying to work out where he was. He looked into Patrick's terrified eyes. They were still wide open and staring, even though the rest of him, lifeless, hovered on the edge of unconsciousness. It was the eeriest thing David had ever witnessed. Patrick seemed to be dead, in a living body, his eyes asking, Are you really going to take the last bit of breath from me? *"Let him go!"* the voice in his head insisted.

Shocked, he slowly removed his hands from Patrick's neck. He couldn't believe they were his hands; that he'd got that close to taking a life—even if it was Patrick's! Bent double, Patrick gasped and coughed. His throat made loud, croaking noises as the oxygen pumped life back into him.

David looked on disbelievingly. He'd always had a temper, but nothing like this. "Get out, Patrick. Don't come back." His voice was quiet, wary. He was afraid that if Patrick said one more word, he'd lose all control and finish the job.

Pushing from his knees, Patrick stood to full height unsteadily. He rubbed his neck. "Call yourself a man of God?" he coughed. "You're a madman!"

Patrick walked toward the front door. A mixture of fear and anger still simmered in his belly. He knew without a doubt that something was going on between the priest and his wife. He felt the anger start to boil again, override his fear. *How dare the priest act all high and mighty, treat me like a piece of shit when it's him who's in the wrong—"KILL HIM!"* A voice in his head flew in from nowhere. *"DO IT NOW!"* He looked around for the owner of the voice—nobody! *"KILL HIM!"*

Just as he was about to leave, the sun shining through the stained glass that surrounded the front door reflected off a large spear of glass which caught his eye. It sparkled like a diamond; it drew him in, entranced him. In a split second it was in his hands as if put there by some unseen force. His anger turned to fury. He swung it forward and jabbed it hard into David's thigh. "What were you saying about big men, Father?" He threw his head back and spat in David's face. "The bigger they are, the harder they fall." With a flip of his hand, he pushed the spear deeper, upward, then twisted for an extra helping of crazed pleasure. "Screw my wife and you're a dead man, and she'll be joining you soon enough." He pulled the glass out, pushed it back in and twisted again and again.

David's tortured screams pierced the walls of the house. He collapsed to his knees, holding the wound, his face contorted in agony. He knew he had only minutes to live. Patrick would finish him. It was a strange feeling—meeting death for the first time. He thought he'd have felt...fear, joy, love, expectation? But it was none of these. All he felt was an uncontrollable eagerness to end the pain that stormed his body. He craved the release, desperate for it to end—until Maggie's face came to him, smiled, then passed him Aedan. "I can't die!" His words were barely audible.

Patrick grabbed a fistful of David's hair and held him upright with it. A slow smirk spread across his face. He looked evil, demented. "What's that, Father? One final request?" He raised his foot and kicked

him hard underneath the chin, sending him reeling against the wall.
"I'm not really a charitable man." His voice was suddenly pleasant. It
didn't match the evil grin it accompanied.

David's skull cracked open. Blood gushed from his head—he
heard his heartbeat grow fainter and fainter. He lay in his own
blood, staring into space. His breath got weaker, slowly inhaling his
consciousness, but not releasing it. "I can't die…" His voice was a
mixture of sad and feeble.

Using his foot, Patrick turned David over onto his back. "You
have to die." The madness slipped inside his mind, spurring him on
but still his voice sounded polite. "You have to die." He lifted the glass
in the air, and aimed straight for David's throat.

⚔

Less than a quarter of a mile up the lane, Angel barked and pulled
on her leash viciously. She'd run Joseph ragged and never stopped
barking for the past half hour.

"ANGEL, BEHAVE! What on earth's got into you this morning?"

She stopped dead in her tracks and turned around. Froth dripped
from her fangs, and her fur formed a Mohawk down her spine. In no
time at all she'd changed from a docile and loyal pet into some kind
of rabid monster. Joseph's heart skipped a beat. He stopped walking
and yanked on her leash in an effort to restrain her, but to no avail.
She squirmed and twisted on the end of it, all the while snarling and
growling viciously.

Terrified, he wanted to let go but hung on. Something must have
snapped inside her brain and he couldn't risk her attacking anyone. He
wound the leash tighter around his fist so that it would act as a choker
around her neck. The thought of having to put her down broke his
heart, but judging by her behaviour he didn't have a choice; the sooner
the better. He'd make his way to the neighbouring farm and get one of
the workers to shoot her through the head. Tears filled his eyes. She'd
been his trusted friend for months, and a sweet and gentle old girl at

that. "Angel girl, I'm so sorry."

As if reading his thoughts, she jumped up and bit him on the hand before he could wind the leash any tighter. He yelled out in pain and instinctively pulled back, letting go of her in the process. Tail between her legs, she ran as fast as she could toward the house with Joseph screaming after her.

⤳

Patrick was just seconds away. He couldn't wait to twist the eight-inch spike into David's throat. "Time to meet your maker, Father. I don't think he'll be too pleased to see you. What the—!" He looked up into the crazed eyes of a demon. Its huge fangs dripped saliva all over the floor, and it seemed bent on plunging them deep into him—

Angel dived, fastened her teeth around his wrist, and dug in. He screamed out, opening his fist. The glass fell to the floor.

"Fucking dog!" Infuriated, he tried to beat her off but she only dug her teeth in deeper. Hanging from his wrist, she dodged and wriggled from one side of his body to the next.

Patrick panicked. He knew that Joseph couldn't be far away. He looked around anxiously, and decided to take off from the back of the house—if he could just shake this fucking dog! He ran into the kitchen with a growling Angel still attached to his wrist, and yanked at the back door in the hope that it was open. He got lucky.

As soon as she realised he was leaving, Angel let go and ran back to be with David. She licked his face, his neck, all the time whimpering as she tried to revive him.

Outside, Joseph could hear her pitiful cries. *What the hell's going on...the door's wide open?* Confused, he raced in but stopped dead at the carnage. His outstretched arms held onto either side of the doorframe. He looked around at the broken furniture and glass that was strewn everywhere, then his eyes rested on what he thought was some kind of crumpled-up baggage soaking up...blood? For a few moments his brain couldn't fathom... *What? Who? David!* "DEAR

GOD!" he cried out in shock and horror.

Angel wouldn't let up. She nudged and licked David in the hope that he'd wake up. Her sad whimpers tore at Joseph's heart. He'd take them to his grave, that much he knew. He tickled her ears briefly. "It's alright girl, calm down, calm down, let me at him…well done." He knew now, without doubt, that animals were anything but dumb. He'd always had respect for them, but this experience had opened his eyes much wider than anything he'd read in scripture.

He felt David's pulse. It was faint but still there. He jumped up. "Where's the phone?" Looking around, he realised the phone was useless, ran to the front door, then turned back. He looked at Angel. Her huge, dark eyes pleaded with him. There was a connection, he didn't know what it was…telepathy? Sixth sense? Whatever it was, it was there, and it was this same connection that had linked Angel to David. "I'm going for help." With that, he raced from the house and prayed that Dr. O'Riley wouldn't have already left to do his morning rounds by the time he got there.

There was no doubt in his mind that Patrick was responsible for David's condition, whether he could prove it or not.

≳

Hundreds of miles away, Aedan let out a blood-curdling scream. Maggie paced over, her heart pounding, and picked him up off the sofa. "I'm here. what's the matter? Shh, shh, Aedan. It's okay." She checked his nappy. "You don't need changing; are you not feeling well? Is it that nasty wind?" She threw him over her shoulder and rubbed his back.

Aedan wouldn't let up. His screams chilled Maggie to the bone. His face bright red, he balled his fists and kicked his feet, as if fighting for his life.

She'd never heard him scream in such a way. It was as if he were frightened of something. He was rigid in her arms, stretching his small body to the limit. Horrified, she snatched her handbag and checked for her keys. Something was seriously wrong with her baby. "We're getting a doctor!"

But then suddenly, the screams stopped. Aedan looked behind where Maggie stood with him in her arms. He chuckled, talked baby talk at something. Bewildered and relieved, she turned. "What are you seeing, little one? You've just put the fear of God in me. What's going on?" Aedan continued to laugh and talk but his eyes became suddenly sleepy.

"It's painful, that old wind." Maggie paced the room, softly singing "Galway Bay." She marveled at his blue-purple eyelids and little rosebud mouth that was sucking gently at nothing in particular.

David's spirit hovered over them both, making funny faces and cooing at his son. Aedan gave one last chuckle before he surrendered to sleep. She looked over her shoulder as she sang. "If you ever go across the sea to Ireland…"

David touched her shoulder, his face tormented with sadness, with loss. "I can't die," he whispered.

She felt a sudden chill and heard a faraway whisper. She shuddered. "It's this horrible house, so it is. We're getting away from here as soon as possible."

24.

*D*r. O'Riley was already way behind schedule. He stood up, stretched his athletic frame, and let out a long breath. He picked up a picture of his dead wife. "Here we go again, Nola, next round." He paused for a few moments. Besides Gael, his secretary, Nola had been the only person who could slow him down. His green eyes glistened with tears. He blinked them out. It was three years now but the pain of losing her still had the ability to destroy him. He'd worked hard to numb the heartache, but it certainly was the source of the splashes of grey in his dark brown hair and the lines furrowing his forehead. He smiled a dashing smile at Nola and put the picture back on his desk.

"You know, a good-looking man like you could have your pick!"

He turned. Gael winked at him. His voice was soft. "I could never replace her."

"You don't have to replace her. Just move her over. Find somebody else to give all that wonderful love to. Don't let it go to waste, Gearoid. Nola wouldn't want you to be living like a monk—to be lonely for the rest of your life, now would she? The heart is big enough to accommodate more than one person, so it is!"

When he smiled he looked ten years younger than his forty-seven years. "What about yourself? I need a mother-hen type!"

"If I was twenty years younger maybe. Now, less of your cheek. You're at least an hour behind, so you are." She held the door open.

He dashed from his office and slammed his brown, worn-out leather bag on the reception desk. "An hour! Jesus!"

"You'll be needing him at this rate!"

"Very droll! When are you going to retire anyway, old girl?" He loved teasing her.

She raised her eyebrows in disgust. "I'm not a horse, I'll have you know! I'll never retire! It would send me around the twist, so it would. Make sure you have lunch." she ordered flatly.

He rolled down his shirtsleeves. "Go do the things you've always wanted. Enjoy yourself!"

"I enjoy working. Besides, who's going to look after you?" She handed him his appointment sheet and, her expression stern, commanded, "Lunch!"

"Lunch! I'll be lucky if I'm done this side of Christmas."

"You can't work on an empty stomach. I'll see to it that there's something here when you get back—what time?"

"God knows!" He looked at his watch. "Let's hope I make it for afternoon surgery."

"3 p.m.! Well, in that case, I'll just have to explain to your patients that you're running behind. Now be off with you."

"Okay, anything to stop your nagging," he joked, hurrying towards the door.

"Your jacket!" she shouted after him, jumping up to run into his office.

"Oh, for God—"

"I'll get it!" She rolled her eyes. "Slow down!" She passed the coat to him.

"Thank you, Gael. I don't know what I'd do without you."

"Nor do I."

He bunched the jacket up in his right hand and jumped the few steps that led down from the surgery door.

"Put it on, it's—" The door slammed shut. "—cold!" She shook her head. "That man! He'll be the death of me, so he will." She leaned down, took her handbag from a small compartment inside the reception desk, and fished through it until she found her face powder. She flipped the silver container open, eyed herself in the mirror on the back of the lid, then took out the soft cotton pad. She dabbed the tan-coloured powder onto her forehead, cheeks, nose, and chin. "Hmm…not bad for an old bird," she said, impressed at how few wrinkles her skin had. "Maggie O'Connell's creams work wonders, they do that!"

Ten minutes later he was back at the office. Gael was in the process of applying cherry-red lipstick. "Well! This must be a record! Did you run out of patients?"

"I forgot my bloody bag!" He fumed with himself, "Like I've got time to piss about like this!"

She rubbed her lips together and gave herself an approving once-over in the mirror. "Oh, no! And I didn't realise you'd left it, and it's staring me in the face." She was appalled at her lack of observation.

Dr. O'Riley shook his head. "They say there's a message in everything but Christ knows what the message in this is, other than incon-bloody-venience—"

They shot around to see Joseph burst through the surgery door.

"Dr. O'Riley, please…you've got to come with me!" He trembled from head to foot. He pointed at Gael, "We need a hospital…I mean an amb…we have to get to hos," he paused, in an effort to act rational and keep his wits about him.

Dr. O'Riley rushed towards him, put his hands on his shoulders, and stared into his eyes. "Who needs a hospital? What's happened?" He looked at Gael. "Get him a cup of tea. Fill it with sugar! He's in shock!"

"No! There's no time. It's Father David, he's dying!" Joseph tugged at O'Riley's arm. "I have to go, we have to go now—oh, dear God!"

O'Riley's voice stayed calm. "Gael, cancel all my appointments for this afternoon—and call an ambulance. In the meantime I'll probably get there a bit quicker myself!" He picked up his bag automatically, and raced through the door after Joseph.

25.

The Rectory
43 Marine Road
Dun Laoghaire

December 19, 1931

My dearest Maggie,

It is with deep regret that I have to deliver such heart-wrenching news. Father David O'Sullivan has slipped into a coma and is on the critical list in a Dublin infirmary. So severe are his injuries, doctors hold out little hope for his recovery and have given him only days to live.

It seems there was an altercation at the rectory on the morning of December 17 while I was out walking Angel. We have a good idea who is responsible, but as of yet are unable to prove anything.

I will continue to take care of Angel, and if there is anything more I can do for you, now or in the future, I will be more than happy to help.

Due to the culprit still being at large, I feel that it would not serve your best interests to try to visit Father David. I urge you to take care of yourself, and to get on with your life.

Yours,
Father Joseph Bevan

Glossop, England.
July, 1938

*M*aggie sat motionless in her living room with the letter in her hand. Over the years, she'd read it time and time again in the hope that the information might change, that Father Joseph had got it wrong. It wasn't David he was talking about. It was somebody else.

She looked at the date. Seven years had passed. She wondered where they'd gone? Where he'd gone? Where he was buried? Did anyone tend to his grave? One day she would go and see him, take him flowers, let him know how much she'd loved him...still loved him. Not that she needed a grave to do it.

"Our son, you'd be so proud of him." Her expression was wistful, her voice longing. "He's the spit of you, like a mini David running around." Her voice cracked on a sob.

Funny thing, grief. Some days she could talk to Aedan about his dad with a smile on her face, some days she'd break down. She left the details of him being a priest on the back burner for the time being, choosing to wait until Aedan was old enough to handle it. Many a time she'd overheard him explaining to his little friends that his dad had died when he was a baby. The last thing she needed was news getting out that he was the son of a priest.

She knew David was alive in the spirit world yet they'd never connected. Not once had he been back to visit her. She talked to him all the time in the hope that he'd come through, but nothing. Even White Eagle clammed up on her when she asked about him. She couldn't understand it.

She closed her eyes and drew a couple of deep breaths, hoping to contact her guide. It was like making a telephone call with the mind. But instead of using telephone lines and a phone, she used her thoughts to tune into White Eagle's frequency until she found him. As a rule he turned up, but sometimes if he was busy with other things she had to wait. "White Eagle, are you busy?"

He appeared at her side. "I detect sadness, sweet Maggie." He looked at the letter in her hand and half smiled. "Ah, you're with David..."

"I wish...God!" She shook her head in frustration. "What I wouldn't give. I just...if only I...why did it—we were so happy! I know it was Patrick, I know it!"

She leant back, removed the elastic from her hair, combed it through with her fingers, and twisted it into a knot again. "Why can't I find him? I can talk to spirit at the drop of a hat but not him. Can't you do something—bring him to me?"

"I'm sorry, Maggie, my hands are tied. Contrary to popular belief on Earth there are some things that even we guides are not privy to."

"But why?" she asked, frustrated.

He shook his head. "Things are not always as straightforward as you'd like them to be. The reasons at play here are very...complex."

She jutted her chin forward, a hurt look on her face. "So you do know what's going on."

His eyes narrowed, a sign of caution. "Remember that your life is a result of every choice you've ever made. In other words, where you are now is your own doing."

"I didn't make this choice. I wanted David with me—still do!"

"But you did make this choice, Maggie: personal responsibility, free will, and all that. Things are not forced on us. Maybe somewhere inside you, you didn't believe that you and David would be together, that it was all too good to be true."

She reacted like a spoilt schoolgirl. "Oh, yes. Make me responsible for David's death!"

He smiled wisely. "Come on, Maggie, you know better than that. Nobody is responsible for the death of another unless permission has been given somewhere along the line."

"Permission from who, the victim?" she scorned.

"Maggie, you went through this scenario with Marguerite. Did she seem like a victim to you? Someone with no choice in her destiny? Only on Earth do we consider ourselves victims. Now, getting back to choices. What about David and Aedan's say in the matter?"

She looked deflated. "So deep down David didn't want to be with us?"

"No, that's not what I'm saying. But everything happened so fast. He was in the frame of mind that Aedan would be adopted. The pair of you would leave France without him and that would be that. You would go back to Patrick and he would go back to the Church. Not for one minute did he think he would leave France with the both of you, find a home, and go back to Ireland to take the necessary steps that would lead to his resignation from Sacred Heart. It was a big shock to his system in more ways than one. Oh, deep down, he'd always wanted to leave the Church to be with you, but he refused to let those feelings surface."

White Eagle paced the room and picked up a photo of Aedan that stood on the windowsill. "But when Aedan was born, and David saw him for the first time…well, the love he had for you intensified. And to add fuel to the fire, he was walloped full force with a tornado of love for his new son—all at one sitting, I might stress. It's enough to blow the earth from under any man. He was quite simply overwhelmed. Overwhelmed with love."

She glanced at the photo in White Eagle's hand. "Isn't that a good thing? How can you be overwhelmed with love?"

He carried on looking at the photo. A childish grin beamed back at him…but a chill ran down his spine. *Once the dark find out about Aedan, they'll stop at nothing to make his power their own.* White Eagle wondered what the next step for Earth would be. "It's a good thing as long as you can handle it. Love is the most powerful force in any universe. Nothing can match it. But it is a force, and believe it or not, it's the driving force behind the whole of creation—good, or not so good."

"How can love be the driving force behind something that isn't good?" She was getting more and more confused.

His voice was controlled but soothing. "All depends on your perspective. A jealous lover will eventually turn the love of his life against him with his unreasonable behaviour. In his mind, he will love his partner with all his heart yet treat her badly. Jealousy is a form of love. Distorted, but love just the same. We could also use war as an example of distorted love. A politician may order the country he loves to go to war on the premise that he is saving his people from suffering. He will justify the untold misery he inflicts upon them, as well as those who he considers his enemies, by putting his hand on his heart and declaring his love for his country and his people. His is a distorted love fuelled by fear—fear of losing control, power, money, prestige—which he also loves! He doesn't realise that true love, the love of the heart, is the true power, true wealth." His voice was now a whisper. "But when distorted, such power can and will turn against you." White Eagle put the photo back on the windowsill and folded his arms. "Putting it simply, it is all about thoughts and where your focus lies in relation to those thoughts, and once you believe them... Well, you know this, Maggie. Why do I repeat myself? You have a mental block where David is concerned," he admonished.

She ignored him. She just wanted to talk about David. "So David loved us but just couldn't see himself leaving the Church...or was he too afraid?"

"Both! Even when thoughts of you and his son warmed his heart, and he thought about spending the rest of his life with the two of you, there was always that What if? niggle: What if the Church won't accept my resignation? What will people think? What if I can't get work? What if! What if! What if! He focused more on the what ifs that surrounded his love for you and Aedan than he did on being with the pair of you. And then there was the confrontation with Patrick, which he knew would come. Note the words 'confrontation' and 'knew.' It never entered his head that Patrick's response might not be that bad, that other factors going on in his life might help foster a more subdued or reasonable reaction from him—"

"White Eagle, come on. We're talking about Patrick! Reasonable? You must be joking!" She all but spit the words out. Her loathing for the man who was still her husband, at least where the law and the Church were concerned, was as strong as ever.

White Eagle smiled and shot her a shrewd glance. He thought

about how many times he'd had this conversation with her, and how many times she had explained it to David and others. *How soon we forget.* "The law of attraction, Maggie! Make it work for you, not against you. Concentrate on what you want, not on what you don't want. The law isn't biased. It doesn't differentiate between the wants and the don't wants, or the haves and the have-nots. If you are always concentrating on what you don't have or what you don't want, it will give you more of what you don't have or don't want!"

"Oh, don't start that again—it's only Monday!" she said, agitated.

"What you focus on gets bigger. Try and focus on Patrick being the frightened, insecure person you once knew instead of some kind of monster you have to live in fear of. Focus on his good points—"

"He has none! Besides, I can't dictate his reactions or his choices. He has his own independence."

"That's true. But you can focus on not being afraid of him. Or better still, focus on never seeing him again. Or even better, don't focus on him at all! Get off his wavelength! Tune in to a different frequency. It's amazing what you can do."

She burst into a fit of hearty laughter. "White Eagle, if bullshit was music, you'd be a brass bleedin' band, you would that!"

"And if brains were dynamite, you wouldn't have enough to blow your nose, so you wouldn't," he joked, mimicking her soft Irish accent. "I've learned a few of your Irish phrases over the years, b'jeysus!"

Hearing him, a North American Indian chief, try to speak with an Irish brogue never failed to put a smile on her face.

"Good! The dimples are back—that's what I like to see. Anyway, Maggie, I must go. Remember these words, there's magic in them..." His voice started to trail off with his image. "Hocus-pocus what's your focus...hocus-pocus what's your..."

"Hocus-pocus what's your focus...eh, White Eagle, you're a character, you are that."

She stood up, picked up the heavy wooden chair, and struggled through to the kitchen with it. She set it down, climbed up, and took an old sweets tin from the shelf above the pantry door. The door also led to a small cellar underneath the stairs where she kept milk, eggs, and other perishables. The chair wobbled on the uneven stone floor. She bent forward, palms flat on the wall. When she felt safe, she stood to full height and banged her head on the underneath of the shelf. "Bleedin' shelf!" she cursed, picking up the old tin and snapping the lid open.

The few coins she'd saved for a rainy day jangled about inside. She put the letter back. Just as she was about to close the lid, the afternoon sun streamed through the kitchen window and reflected on the Celtic cross David had given her years before. She picked it up and rubbed it between thumb and forefinger. She thought back to the time he'd placed it around Aedan when he was just a few hours old. She smiled at the memory and fastened it around her neck. After supper she would explain to Aedan how important the necklace had been to her and his dad, and ask him if he thought he could look after it. She felt that he could. But then again, even though he was wise beyond his young years and held powers far beyond the typical seven-year-old, she'd seen to it that he still held all the childish traits of a normal youngster. She wanted him to have as normal a life as possible—

NeilA! Always there to remind her. That night years ago swamped her mind. Her heart went into spasm, firing palpitations around her chest. She felt dizzy, nauseous, and clutched her stomach—*Don't be stupid! It was only a dream! He is a normal child,* she scolded herself. She took slow, deep breaths in an effort to calm down. *I'm going mad. I'll end up in an asylum—stop it! Stop it! I have to look after Aedan.* She continued to deep breathe until the bout with anxiety started to subside. She would have to explain to Aedan that if there was the slightest worry that he could lose the necklace, they should wait a few years longer until he was old enough to look after it.

She picked out the only photograph she had of the three of them together in an effort to numb NeilA's presence in her mind. David smiled back at her. *He's your child, David! Yours!* "I'd better get tea prepared before I go and pick Aedan up from school," she whispered. She held the photo to her heart and closed her eyes. "What I wouldn't give to be getting it ready for the three of us." She put the photo back in the tin and climbed down off the chair. She struggled through to the living room with it, and slid it back underneath the table.

She looked around proudly. She loved her cottage. She realised how lucky she was in many ways. It was rare in the 1930s for a single woman with a child to own her own home.

After the letter from Father Bevan, she'd lasted six weeks at the house in Manchester. She couldn't wait to get away from there. Just walking up the path towards it for the first time had put the b'jeebers up her. She shuddered at the memory—the cold chills that had raced up and down her spine, and the disturbing scream Aedan had let out as she carried him over the threshold—she'd never forget it. She held him to her breast so tight that David had told her to be careful not to suffocate him. She smiled a watery smile and told him that there was no way she was moving into such a dismal hole. "Just don't like the energy, something bleak about it, it's jinxed!" David had assumed it was something to do with her just giving birth and told her not to be silly. "It's just a house. Besides, rented accommodation is sparse. We can take it for now and move as soon as I get back," he had reassured her.

David had reckoned it would take at least three months to finalise everything, that's if the Church went easy on him. What if they couldn't find a replacement? What if Father Joseph didn't want the parish? So he left her with his savings, £1,517, to make sure that she and Aedan would be well looked after while he was away.

Maggie had stared open mouthed at the small, blue, leather-bound bankbook, shocked by the amount written in black ink on the bottom of the page. She'd told him to keep some of it for himself. His words swam through her head to this day. *'I'd rather make sure you and Aedan were looked after. Besides, I'll have a few pay packets waiting for me when I get back. It's easy to save when you don't have to pay rent and most of your expenses are covered.'*

The money had enabled her to buy the cottage. No. 7 Geraint Place was nestled in a private cul-de-sac off a quiet country lane that backed onto farmland in Derbyshire's Peak District. A steal at £1,295, the man selling it had assured her. And she believed him. At night she lay in bed and fell asleep to the sound of the river behind the cottage as it snaked its way through the Pennines. In the mornings, regardless of the weather, she ran to the window, threw back the curtains, and looked out onto green fields with stonewall borders, some of them built by the Romans. The sheep and cows grazed lazily together, and every now and again, if it was early enough, she'd spot a herd of deer chewing away on the hedges. Sometimes Farmer Bailey's horses stared up at her accusingly, as if to say, "Where's Aedan? We feel like a ride."

She smiled to herself. Aedan called them "his" horses! Farmer Bailey had used cunning tactics when he'd said to him and his best friend, Derrick, "Muck 'em out, lads! Look after 'em and help me now an' again round t' farm, an' they're yours!" By the time they'd turned six, Aedan and Derrick "owned" five horses!

Maggie loved all the seasons but summer was her favourite. Her garden was always filled with colour and birdsong. She'd stand there and breathe in the fresh country air and smells, and always find time to sit amongst her flowers and herbs to meditate once she'd got Aedan off to school. Given her circumstances, buying the cottage was one of the best things she'd ever done. At least she and Aedan would always have a roof over their heads. She'd given no thought as to how they'd survive. She just knew that they would.

Most of the locals had accepted her by then but at first it was difficult to win them over. A single woman with a child didn't go down very well, and rumour had it she was one of "them witch types." But over the years, she made some good friends who helped her out whenever they could, by doing little things such as giving her clothes for Aedan when their own children had outgrown them. Being a proud woman, Maggie would do small favours in return, like babysitting after school if one of the mothers couldn't make it, and giving out herbal medicines here and there, as well as hands-on healing for the more open-minded.

She also earned a few bob by cleaning for a few of the higher-ups in Old Glossop, and selling her own herbal concoctions, something she'd always been interested in. Over the years she had made up hundreds of elixirs, creams, rubs, and oils. White Eagle helped her by explaining which ingredients to mix with what, what their uses were for, and the correct dosages to dispense. She also did the odd readings for those so inclined, despite the vicious criticism from a few narrow-minded ones who wanted her burnt at the stake.

All in all, with her many occupations she managed to keep herself and her son fed, warm, and clean.

Oh, it was hard work, but worth it, she thought to herself contentedly, as she looked around the front parlour. It was sparse in furnishings. A dark red sofa with white trim was pushed against the wall separating the kitchen. She'd become accustomed to arranging herself around the springs which were ready to protrude through the upholstery at any time! The centrepiece of the room, a thick wooden table with six matching chairs, had many uses. She scrubbed clothes on it, baked on it, prepared food on it, ate off it, helped Aedan with his homework on it, and prepared remedies from the herbs she grew in the back garden on it. She even had people laid flat out on top of it when they came for a healing treatment.

On the rare occasions when the table stood idle, a couple of candles placed on old saucers graced its middle. Between them stood an old blue vase with a missing chunk from the rim, which she always managed to hide with an assortment of flowers, also from her garden. Lavender was one of her favourites. Its smell often drifted throughout the cottage and created a calm and healing atmosphere. Beneath the window stood a small bookcase she'd picked up for half a crown at the local second-hand store. She'd rubbed it down and painted it white to cheer it up a bit.

She walked over to the bookcase and ran her index finger along the row of books. She'd start a new one that night. Maggie had always been an avid reader, and in the evenings after Aedan went to bed she loved nothing more than to settle down with a good book, a cup of herbal tea, and some classical music. David had introduced her to the masters years before. She looked over at the alcove in the corner of the room. The small built-in cupboard made for extra storage, and provided a place for the gramophone and her collection of records. David had bought them for her as a leaving present when he left for Ireland. His gentle smile flooded her, rushed her with goose bumps. She thought back to the day when he walked in with them. *'So you won't forget me…and I'd like our son to be introduced to the classics as soon as possible.'*

The emptiness never left her. It was a permanent hole in her chest. She smiled sadly. "I love you so much," she whispered. She turned on the wireless that stood on top of the bookshelf, her latest second-hand purchase. Not many people had one. She'd touched lucky—it had only just been put on the shelf when she walked into the store. Alf got the full asking price out of her. "It'll go like a hot cake! Cost you at least twenty quid new an' I bet it's only six months old, if that!" So she'd paid nine pounds for it—it'd skint her at the time but it was worth it. She'd felt a bit guilty, breaking into her rainy day money that often ended up reinforcing her housekeeping, but what the heck! Music brought joy, and the news kept her abreast of outside events. Besides, just looking at it was a pleasure. She could see her face in its shiny cabinet, and the wooden lattice that protected the golden speaker reminded her of a Tibetan mandala she'd seen in one of her old books. She watched the black dial inside the tuning window move from side to side. Sometimes when Aedan was around, the thing would go off the scale and all the frequencies would jam together. The familiar feeling of anxiety curled her stomach. She blocked it before it had a chance to make an impact. *David's his dad!*

"I'd better do some dusting!" She opened the door to the small cupboard and pulled out some beeswax and an old rag. She hadn't dusted for a week and the place was getting on her nerves. She rubbed a small amount of beeswax into the top of the wireless, and planned to later pick some yarrow and make tea with it. She could feel a bit of a cold coming on and it would help with her menstrual cramps. She wondered if she should treat herself to a jug of mild instead—*No, better not, it's only Monday.* Now and again she would take her old pot jug to the pub ten minutes up the road and get them to fill it up with the dark beer—*Only on a Saturday night, mind.* She smiled to herself as she thought about the expressions on the faces of the locals when she'd first moved there and gone swanning into the pub by herself. It was unheard of. But she was through being told what to do. She had put up with that shite for long enough! Everyone in the place had stopped talking. The women in particular sat all prim and proper with their men, looking down their noses.

Olive Reids had broken the silence. "May God forgive you!" she'd said, disgusted.

Maggie looked her up and down. "Forgive me? He told me to have one on him!" The stunned look on Olive's face never failed to put a smile on Maggie's.

She removed the dry clothes from the wooden maiden that stood at the side of the oven. Ginger, their black cat—Aedan rebelled against everything—managed to lift his head up and give her a dirty look. "Yes, I know, I've disturbed you." She removed her foot from the tiny space between his sprawled legs.

She was about to run upstairs to put the clothes away just as Charlie, the coalman, banged on the back door and pushed it open. He and his wife, Eileen, were two of her most treasured friends. "Half a bag, Maggie?"

She set the clothes down on the wringer and nodded. "I think that'll do it, Charlie. I'm not burning as much in this weather. It's basically just for the hot water and cooking."

"That goes for the rest of us." He opened the small grid that was off-set to the side of the door, and emptied the full sack of coal into it. Dust flew everywhere.

"By Jesus, Charlie!" She ran over to the wooden pole that held up her washing line, and thrust it high into the sky. "My bloody sheets will be rotten!"

"Sorry, Maggie—never gave it a thought." He emptied the whole bag into her bunker while she wasn't looking.

"That's the problem with men. If it was you that stood scrubbing them sheets, you'd think about it!"

Charlie grinned to himself. He admired her, a woman on her own with a kid to bring up. Most of the locals had accepted her but there were still a few small-minded sods who tried to make her life a misery. They didn't like the fact that she wasn't married, and rumour had it she was one of them spiritualists who talked to the dead and what have you. Didn't bother him none, but it put the fear of God up some of em. Daft beggars! He folded the woven sack into a perfect square.

"Cuppa." She dashed past him. It was a statement, not a question.

"That'd be nice."

She dashed through to the living room and picked up the heavy iron kettle that simmered on the fireplace. She always kept a coal fire burning to heat the huge cast-iron oven that took up most of the wall on one side of the room. It was her only means of hot water and cooked food. When the weather was warm she kept the fire down a bit and opened a window.

"I'd love an electric oven, or gas for that matter, and one of them gas water heaters—luxury." She hurried back into the kitchen and plonked the kettle down on the small draining board by the sink, then spooned loose tea into an old brown teapot from an orange tobacco tin David had left.

Charlie smirked. "Only the nobs can afford them things, not the likes of us."

She sighed, "Aye," and put her nose to the rim. "Hmm, I love the smell of—" she jumped back as the strong leafy fragrance rose up with the steam and burnt her nostrils. "OW!" She rubbed her nose with the back of her hand.

"Be careful!" Charlie warned.

"Let it brew for a few minutes." She covered it with a multicoloured tea cosy that she'd knitted, and nodded at a tall cupboard in the corner of the kitchen, adjacent to the sink. "Pass me some cups and saucers and a couple of plates—although forget it!" She noticed the muck on his hands. "Give your hands a wash." She gestured he come in and nodded at a large wooden scrubbing brush with nasty looking bristles that stood on the windowsill above the sink.

He did what he was told and picked up a slab of pink carbolic soap that rested on the back of the brush. When he'd finished, the soap and its bubbles were full of coal dust. He ran the soap under the water until it was clean, then picked up a small towel that hung on the side of the wringer. She handed him a cup and saucer that was too dainty for him, and sliced him a chunk of coconut cake. "Here. Baked it myself yesterday but it's still good." She sliced herself a piece, took a bite, and spoke between mouthfuls.

He looked at the sink. "Your sink looks as if it's seen better days."

They both glanced at the white stone fixture. The rusty old legs buckled underneath it, resembling those of a drunk carrying a slab of concrete. Charlie's grin spread across his face. His teeth seemed whiter than they actually were due to the coal dust smattered on his face, and the lines at the side of his shiny blue eyes looked as if a fine paintbrush had been used to white them in. His curly hair was strawberry blonde, but on his coal round it changed to a dark ash colour. His rough looks matched his personality. He was harsh if he thought a situation warranted it, but his heart was kind. "The legs remind me of old Mrs. Dyer's down the road. Look like they're ready to give way any time." They both broke into fits of laughter.

"And wrinkles to boot," Maggie added, referring to the dark lines where the paint had worn away into cracks all over the sink's shiny white surface. "Yes, wrinkles," she whispered, "no doubt caused by all the hard work over the years—" She clutched her chest unexpectedly. The familiar feeling of spirit energy flooded through her like an electric waterfall—provocation for the hairs on the back of her neck and the goosebumps erupting all over her skin.

Charlie grabbed her arm. "Are you alright?"

His voice was a faint background noise. "I'm fine." She held up her index finger to signal silence. The vision on the inside of her forehead rocketed in, out, in, out. It was like watching a movie in fast-forward. "They have a message for you."

"Who?" Charlie was startled.

"The spirits…"

Charlie's down-to-earth persona was taken aback. Eileen talked about this stuff all the time but he never paid much attention. "The spirits! What the hell do they want with me?"

"It's your parents—Agnes and Donald. Be careful, they're saying. Be careful."

"What of…what—"

"Shh, shh," she gestured impatiently. Her words came out like a freight train. "Your mother, Agnes, she's tiny but a force to be reckoned with. A bossy woman, always wore her grey hair scraped back into a tight bun; caused a bald spot on the back of her head…" She paused. "Got a mole on one side of her lip; quite a looker in her day. And your dad, well…he's as broad as he's long. I can see who you take after. Nice man, smiley eyes just like yours. Worked the coal round too, never wanted you to do it. Hard work, hard work, he keeps saying, freezing in winter. Hard getting old Betsy…," she looked at Charlie and frowned, "to climb the Snake Pass. She didn't mind it in summer but hated the winter rounds—oh, it's his horse!" Maggie raised her voice, as the realisation of who old Betsy was finally hit her.

Charlie was mystified. There was no way Maggie could have known such details about his parents.

"She's singing…your mother… 'Ave Maria.' She's telling me it's one of her favourites, and how much she loved the Church. She wants you to know that she still goes to church over there." Maggie raised her eyebrows and tipped her head, just as Agnes used to do. "She wants to know why you don't go?! 'I disapprove,' she keeps saying, 'I disapprove.'"

"They have churches over there?" He took his cap off and scratched the back of his head. "Well, God help me then. I thought religion was a load of cock 'n' bull, to be honest."

Maggie threw her head back and laughed out loud at the look on Charlie's face. "It's all about what you believe. Your mother was a staunch Christian while she was here. She had absolute faith in the afterlife and what awaited her—coinciding with the teachings of her religion, of course. When you depart this Earth, what you believe you'll create for yourself…for a while, at least. She's met like-minded thinkers over there and lives a contented life, but when the time is ripe, when she's ready, a teacher will appear to plant seeds. Give her something new to ponder on." Maggie closed her eyes, concentrated on keeping the connection with Charlie's parents. "They're already trying to change my views,' she's telling me, but I'm having none of it,' she's saying." Maggie smirked. "She's stubborn!"

"Well, I'll be damned!" Charlie exclaimed.

"No, you won't!" Maggie joked, before continuing. "Your dad, on the other hand, is already open to change. He doesn't go to church anymore. Your mother isn't impressed with his decision but she accepts it. He goes rambling through the countryside, and communes with nature for his inspiration."

"You can do that over there as well?"

"You can do anything you want over there. Habits you formed while on Earth, things you were attached to here, will stay with you until you make the decision to change them and move on. Nothing is forced or judged."

"What if you don't know what to believe, like me? Will I be left hanging…in a state of limbo, like?" He sliced himself more cake, seemingly not too worried at the prospect.

"No. In some respects it will be easier for you because your mind isn't bogged down with dogma. It will be open to new ideas." She turned her head to the side, agitated. "Yes, yes, I'll tell him, have some bloody patience." She looked at Charlie. "Your mother, she's saying there'll be trouble—terrible times. She's worried you'll get hurt."

"That's her, alright! Always bloody worrying about us! Tell her to pack it in before her nerves get the better of her and send her to the bloody grave!" He laughed loud and hard at his own humour.

Maggie grimaced. "I don't know…she's pretty agitated." She tried to keep the connection going at the same time as answering Charlie's questions.

Agnes appeared in Maggie's third eye like a living, breathing slideshow. She pointed her finger at the planets, at Earth in particular, and then at a bunch of planets not in this solar system. Maggie's brows furrowed in concentration. *I don't understand.* Agnes pointed at a huge planet. To Maggie it looked a trillion times bigger than the others. It was a startling vision, golden and glowing, very beautiful. It teemed with life. Then a most extraordinary thing happened. All the other planets in the vision blended into it, adding to its beauty. They were all one and the same, yet she could still see the individual planets inside the—*the mother planet!* It looked familiar, then it hit her. "It's mine! Charlie's! David's! Aedan's!" The words came out fast and weak. She just about collapsed with shock. She grabbed the sink, and held onto some semblance of composure.

Agnes kept pointing, shaking her head, "Yes! Mother planet is a good description, but some over here call it the God planet. I don't know what to make of it. I think it must be heaven."

Maggie felt like she'd cave in at any moment. She knew it was something to do with NeilA and the strange ones. *Was she one of them? Charlie? Aedan?—No! Stop getting carried away! Calm down!* She swallowed, tried to moisten her throat. Charlie's voice brought her back to a sense of normality. Whatever that was?!

"What happens then, when you first pop your clogs? Is somebody there to meet you? Do you know the person, ghost, spirit—whatever you want to call it?"

She grabbed an upturned glass from the cupboard and filled it with tap water. *Stay calm, stay calm.* She wouldn't go to pieces in front of Charlie! A thought in her head rushed her with fear—*Is Charlie an alien?* She felt her mind start to lift off, ready to escape with her altogether—*Stop it, Maggie! It's Charlie—you've known him years, you idiot!* She scolded herself in an effort to calm down, deal with her nerves.

"Oh, you'll know them, alright! It all depends on the love. Where love flows, Charlie goes. Love holds the strongest connection. Those held dear in your heart will be there to meet you." She knocked the water back in large, hard gulps, turned to Charlie, an excitable expression on her face. "Imagine the joy and celebration when you first arrive in the spirit world." She thought about David. "I mean, imagine the excitement you must feel when you see those who you thought had gone forever—your loved ones, who made the transition before you...Water?" She gestured with the empty glass.

"No, thanks." Charlie looked at her, fascinated. *Why did people call this work evil?* He could feel the fear of death lifting from him. "What about people who don't have anyone to take them over?"

Her movements were swift with an air of avoidance. She was having a hard time blocking the vision Agnes had showed her. The huge glowing planet invaded her mind like a pulsating migraine. She ducked underneath his arm—he filled the door frame—walked over to a rosebush, and lifted the yellow flower to her nose. She communicated with White Eagle telepathically. She knew the answers but wanted to make double sure that she didn't give out wrong information. "Just a minute, Charlie. I'll ask White Eagle."

Charlie followed her to the rosebush. "Who the bloody hell is White Eagle!?" Charlie's down-to-earth reasoning was being challenged big time.

The look of bewilderment on his face matched her mood. "He's my spirit guide. An Indian chief. He helps me with my work. We all have a guide...a being that has evolved through countless experiences. Can be an aspect of your own soul, but it can also be an aspect of another soul—you know, somebody...something else independent of you."

Charlie was puzzled. "Why an Indian? What could he possibly have to do with an Irish woman?"

Maggie sighed. "Wellllll...when we get down to the nitty gritty, he's about as Indian as I'm Irish! Such labels are mere descriptions... experiences...for the bigger part of ourselves." She shot Charlie an amused glance. He was utterly flummoxed. "In a nutshell, they're very spiritual beings and way beyond the teachings of any one society." She paused in an effort to conjure up a simple explanation. "This is why many people, not only the likes of me, have an Indian guide." She cocked her head and raised her eyebrows. "Who better?" She remembered asking David the same question years before—

"We can give him a demo if you like," White Eagle cut in. "Don't be too easy on him. Sometimes it's better to be dragged out of the comfort zone kicking and screaming! It's not always practical to wait. Our experience in the underworld comes to mind. There was a lot I should have prepared you for instead of worrying about whether you were ready or not. At soul level, he knows the answers but at Charlie level, he's focused his attention on providing for his family, football, and a few beers on a Saturday night. He gets his inspiration delivering coal to his customers. He's a great man, living out his soul purpose, but a very small part of it—which is about to change!" He paused. His mind ticked over as he thought hard about how to conjure up ways to get to Charlie without Maggie's involvement. "It's time he was introduced to a bit more of our world. I think he can handle it." He sighed, "And you! My dear Maggie! Must get over your fears!"

She ignored the comment. "Why?" She felt perplexed. "I don't think he's got a blind bit of interest in it. I'm only doing this because his mother is worried!"

Unbeknownst to anybody else, White Eagle had brought Charlie's parents in as a ruse. All over Earth, Galaxians like Charlie were getting a rude awakening. It was time. Something was stirring. It might be years yet, but they had to be ready, Maggie included. She was next. He couldn't allow her to block out her heritage for much longer. It was too dangerous. She'd have to be armed and ready to use her powers. As Aedan's mother, she'd be at the forefront of the dark's agenda. His tone was sharp. Sometimes it was the only way he could get Maggie to listen. "Because he's a player—an influence in Aedan's life. He needs to get ready for…Look! It would be better if he had more info on the lad." He didn't want to say too much in case she blocked the connection. Any mention of Galaxias and she'd do just that. The elders had asked him to rope Charlie in, start getting him ready. "It doesn't matter why! There are reasons for everything, you know that. I think it's a good idea to start introducing Charlie to a few things, so let's get on with it." *When the battle begins, we'll all have to be ready!* He felt her uneasiness but was unperturbed. She had to start acknowledging Aedan's spiritual blueprint, along with her own. They were all in it together. The day wasn't too far away when she would have to communicate with NeilA directly. She wouldn't be able to wake up from any damn dream!

Maggie felt concerned. Something was going on. Her heart bounced around in her chest. She felt anxiety start to sneak about inside her as if getting ready to go in for the kill! It was the worst feeling. "But I don't understand—"

"I'm interested!" Charlie looked confused.

Maggie's eyes rested on him. The interruption took her mind off the uneasy feelings. "Sorry, I can't remember your question." Her expression was empty, as if she were somewhere else.

He wondered what was up with her today. "What if we don't have anyone to take us over...after we die, like? Are you alright, Maggie? You seem edgy."

She tried to produce saliva to moisten her dry mouth and throat. "Oh, yes, I'm fine—it rarely happens. There is always somebody there to meet you." She looked away, distracted. "Come inside for a minute." He followed her to the kitchen door and hung about just inside the frame. "Come in, come in," she gestured, walking toward the sitting room.

"I can't! I'm filthy!"

She looked him up and down. "Wait in the kitchen. I'll get a couple of chairs." She rushed to the sitting room, picked up the chairs, one in each arm, and struggled through to the kitchen with them.

He rushed over and took the chairs from her. "Shall I close the door?"

Maggie gave a slight jerk of her head, saying, "Please. Charlie, I must have your word that none of this will be repeated. Eileen knows—she's developing her skills—but nobody else." She knew that she could trust him but still preferred to stress the fact that her antics had to stay behind closed doors. Talking to the dead was not mainstream behaviour! People have been locked up for a lot less!

"You've got it."

"White Eagle will talk through me. It's nothing to be afraid of. I've been doing this work for donkey's years, from being a small child, in fact. All I ask is that you listen with an open mind." She sat down. "I'll explain it in a nutshell. You might see him manifest through me, or you might not. This happens through a process involving ectoplasm—a white, misty-looking substance that will appear to exit from my nose, mouth, ears, eyes, and umm…other, err, various unmentionables." She noticed a faint smirk cross his face but ignored it.

"Sit down! Sit down!" He sat opposite her. "I will go into what mediums call a trance. To you, it'll look as if I'm sleeping but that isn't the case. I'm well aware of what's going on. It's as if I'm standing behind myself watching myself talk, while allowing a train of inspiration to run through me unrestricted—"

"But it's safe?"

"Yes. I'm in control at all times regardless of how it looks on the outside. You can ask all the questions you want in the time allotted." She shot him a serious look. "It's up to you. If you're at all worried, we won't bother. It will be like nothing you've ever experienced before. Like I said a minute ago, there's a good chance that spirit will manifest through me."

"I'm not worried about it, just as long as it's safe for you."

She shrugged. "It's safe. I'm naturally protected, and so are my sitters—that's you, you're the sitter. White Eagle will act as gatekeeper—"

"Gatekeeper?"

"That's right…it's up to him who comes through. With it being a short session, he'll probably keep it down to himself and your parents."

"You mean there could be other spirits wanting to come through?"

"Oh, yes. Most of them harmless, but we do get the odd mischievous ones, and undesirables. It's the gatekeeper's job to keep them out. This is why people who don't know what they're doing shouldn't play with Ouija boards. It's like living in a rough part of town and leaving your door wide open. Not that you're in any danger other than psychological—fear, that is. It's your own fear that causes the problems." She leaned forward, stared intensely, and whispered, "You have to be psychologically tough to do this work, Charlie. Can you handle it?"

He nodded even though he felt unsure.

"Anyway, Charlie, time is moving on." She smoothed down her skirt. "All I ask is that when the session is over, you leave me to come out of my trance gently. There's no need for you to wake me. I've already set the precedent with White Eagle, and I was right. He's decided to keep it short with it being your first time, and only your parents will be invited, so if you have any questions for them now could be a good time. Right! Anything else before we start?"

Charlie puffed his cheeks up and shook his head. "Err, no, no." He was eager and a little apprehensive…just a little. His heart thumped out a slightly erratic beat. He didn't know why. He wasn't scared!

"Okay, then, let's get started." She closed her eyes and started to deep breathe. She was so used to this aspect of herself that it was as natural as using any of her other, usual, earthly senses. Within seconds she was in deep trance. Her head slumped onto her chest and her breathing was so quiet that Charlie strained to hear it. Once her spirit met up with Charlie's parents, White Eagle entered her body. He wasted no time—

"GREETINGS, CHARLIE!" Maggie's head shot up, and the booming voice of White Eagle belted out of her. "LISTEN! WHAT I'M ABOUT TO SAY IS VERY IMPORTANT!" His shadow superimposed itself over Maggie. His expression was intense, his voice firm. "WE DON'T HAVE MUCH TIME. MAGGIE WILL WANT HER BODY BACK SOON ENOUGH. CHARLIE, CHARLIE! I KNOW YOU'RE SCARED BUT SUCK IT UP AND LISTEN!

Filled with terror and shock, Charlie shot back in his chair. He grasped the underneath of it so hard he could have left indentations of his fingers in the wood. He felt every hair on his body stand on end. It was the most alarming thing he'd ever seen—Maggie seemingly possessed by an Indian chief! He could still see her physical body underneath the black shadow—spirit—of White Eagle. It wasn't like a normal shadow that the sun gave off. It had features, clothes, hair— everything. It was a replica of how the Indian chief would have looked during his time on Earth.

"Go gently, White Eagle!" Maggie said, mortified. "By Jesus, you'll have him in the nuthouse at this rate!"

"Oops! I forgot he was new to it all," he lied. Truth was, he didn't care. Charlie's time had come—time for him to get the message. "Charlie, am I too loud for you? Would you like me to turn the volume down a bit?"

Charlie sat rigid, jaw clenched. Not a word came out of his mouth. He could hear the thud, thud, thud of his heart, and the sound of his own erratic breathing. No thoughts were in his head. He was literally frozen into the moment, terror-struck!

"Let me talk to him!" Agnes ordered, pushing her way through.

The only voice Charlie could hear was White Eagle's.

"Err...not so fast, lady!" The force field given off by the chief's energy stopped Agnes instantly. "Nobody gets through without my say-so!" He looked at Maggie. "What do you think?"

"Well, he sure as hell isn't going to talk to you!" she answered, with an amused look on her face. "And who can blame him?"

White Eagle had to deliver his message to Charlie as soon as possible. Agnes could calm him down and make it easier for this to happen. He turned to Agnes. "Very well. Let's hope you're better at it than me."

"Of course I am," she said in a huff. "I'm his mother!"

White Eagle stepped sideways and disappeared from Charlie's sight.

"Charlie, you great lummox! What are you afraid of?"

Charlie's jaw dropped as he watched the spirit of his mother manifest from some white, misty-looking queer stuff coming out of Maggie's mouth. "What in God's name!"

"Charlie!" his mother nagged. "Are you going to say something, or just sit there like a stuffed dummy?" She levitated above Maggie's head and hovered off to the side, but remained attached to her by the misty, milky, queer stuff.

"Mother…," he said weakly "I, err, how are—"

His mother chuckled. "Is that all you've got to say after all these years?" She was overjoyed at being given the opportunity to talk to her son in the flesh.

Charlie smiled. "I'm a bit overwhelmed. To be expected, given the circumstances."

"Of course, sweetheart, but I haven't really changed much, apart from giving up the physical armour. Now, you asked what it was like over here. I'll give it to you in short, too much to go into at one sitting—"

"Err…hold off a minute there!" White Eagle cleared his throat. "I'm sorry, Agnes. You've not been given the clout to advise on the afterlife." Charlie looked on as the two engaged in heated conversation but he could hear and see only his mother.

"What do you mean? I have every right. I'm his mother," she retaliated, dander up again.

"You haven't evolved enough psychologically to advise on such matters—"

Agnes was furious. "How dare you! I'm just as evolved—"

"Agnes! It is up to me who talks to Charlie and right now you are at risk of losing that privilege."

"Agnes," Maggie interrupted gently, "I don't have the authority to advise on the afterlife either, unless it's a subject I've already covered with White Eagle. That's why I asked him to assist me with the sitting. With Charlie being new to it and all that, I didn't want to say something that could scare him, put him off, like. All White Eagle means is, is—"

"I mean, Agnes, that your psyche is somewhat slanted…you lean towards the Church. As you already know, not everybody in the spirit world goes to church, they are…open to other—oh, Jesus!" he said, frustrated, trying to find words that wouldn't offend her. "To other experiences."

"How dare you blaspheme—"

"Agnes!" Donald interjected. "It's important that we get the message to Charlie. Stop wasting bloody time!"

Charlie saw his mother turn indignantly, and shout at the sink. She was ready to do battle. "Don't you talk to me like that—"

White Eagle pulled rank. He wouldn't tolerate this lack of restraint at one of his sessions. His tone was lethal. "Agnes! I'm taking over the sitting. Let Charlie know that he has nothing to fear. If he's still too afraid to talk to me, we'll end it now!"

Agnes felt White Eagle's energy push her sideways and he wasn't even trying. Reluctantly, she let Charlie know that her time was up. Her brashness evaporated as the love for her son took over. "Sweetheart, I'm not able to answer your questions. White Eagle can, but if you're too afraid to talk to him we understand. I promise you, there is nothing to fear. Will you talk to him or would you like to try another time?"

The presence of his mother had reassured Charlie somewhat, helping him become more receptive to the calm, healing atmosphere permeating the room. He felt his clenched jaw slowly start to relax. "I'd love to talk to him," he whispered.

"Goodbye, sweetheart."

He watched his mother disintegrate into the ectoplasm and disappear back through Maggie's mouth. The whole experience was surreal. Maybe he'd wake up in a minute! He unfurled his fingers from underneath the chair, and clenched and unclenched his hands several times to remove the pain from his muscles. "Bye, Mother." There was a faraway expression on his face.

26.

White Eagle's approach was a bit more subdued…but only a bit. He was running out of time and the elders had specified that Charlie's initiation must begin that day. He entered into another reality—a probable reality—without the others having the slightest suspicion. Being a master manipulator had infinite uses! Maggie thought she was in absolute control—she was, to a certain extent, but only at his say-so!

In the probable reality, Maggie had no fear of Galaxias, of her true identity, for this was her ultimate reality. But Charlie still needed to be coaxed. Maggie was used to probable existences. White Eagle had used them many times, dreams being a favorite tool. For her, these worlds were alive in her subconscious, but for Charlie they were buried deep under the surface. It wouldn't be productive to awaken them in a full-scale attack. White Eagle didn't like being so deceitful but he knew that if he stayed with Maggie's usual reality, just a slight mention of Galaxias would send her into a blind panic and bring the session to an abrupt end.

It was a minor glitch for White Eagle. Charlie had been a coalman since he was fourteen! Younger, if the years delivering with his father were taken into account. Charlie's psychic channels were dormant for the most part, so it was easier on him if the first meeting were initiated with Maggie's help.

White Eagle understood how traumatic it was for any Galaxian living as a human to suddenly be told of their true identity and purpose on Earth—that Aedan was power beyond human imagination, and that their job was to protect him and save Earth and, ultimately, creation as we know it! It was a lot to swallow and Charlie had only just been given an infinitesimal snippet into the spirit world—a temporary stopover for everybody including Galaxians. It was a period of adjustment and reflection. Galaxians didn't usually stay long, although there were no time constraints. There were countless spirit worlds, planets, universes, all infinite and without creative limits but Galaxias was the ultimate power that they all strived for, including humans. Once consciousness had been elevated to this level there was no going back except in rare and exceptional circumstances: Evolus had been a Galaxian worker who had fallen from grace, which was why he was so lethal. He'd been trapped in the underworld much like White Eagle and Maggie had been, but he had fallen for the trickery of the dark elders and made the choice to stay.

Galaxias had its ranks. A Galaxian worker still had much to learn. A council of elders oversaw everything. White Eagle and others were under their guidance but NeilA answered to nobody other than the Originator. G.U.N. were a separate concern—a United Nations of planets. Earth's governments had declined countless invitations to join. They were in contact with G.U.N. but had so far denied extraterrestrial life to the masses. Earth also denied the fact that G.U.N. could disarm them at the drop of a hat and greeted contact, for the most part, with military force.

NeilA was high up in the ranks of G.U.N. Though he didn't have to, he consulted with them on all matters. He remained humble and took nothing for granted. White Eagle was a Galaxian worker. He worked mostly between Earth, the spirit world, and Galaxias. His mainstay was the spirit world because that's where he was needed the most, for the time being. His mission today was to awaken Charlie to Galaxias. Once he mentioned the name, Charlie's thoughts would arrive on their vibration. They'd be able to pass on knowledge and start his training via his dreams and intuition. This would get him ready for the ultimate meeting with his true identity.

White Eagle's image remained superimposed over Maggie's physical body. He didn't need it, but decided that for now it would be easier on Charlie if he didn't manifest as his full-blown, Galaxian self! Letting him believe Maggie was in control would be a lot less daunting for Charlie. Galaxias advocated fear as a last resort. "Hello again, Charlie. Sorry if I gave you a bit of a shock earlier. Are you feeling more relaxed now?"

"Err, somewhat." Truth be told, he was still feeling a bit overwhelmed by the whole experience. He looked on with utter amazement as he witnessed the black shadow of White Eagle take over Maggie for a second time, and Maggie mimic his exact mannerisms, right down to his voice. His mother, on the other hand, had appeared to be separate from Maggie, apart from the white stuff, which was now nowhere to be seen.

"Good grief, man, what are you scared of? We don't grow two heads when we cross over into the spirit world, you know!" An odd expression crossed White Eagle's face. "Although…we could if we so desired! Manifestation comes a lot easier on this side. We more or less remain identical to who we were on Earth, until we choose to move on, that is." White Eagle stretched his neck and scratched underneath it. "Hmm…what would be different here? Oh, yes! We're able to fly around, levitate, that sort of thing. Oh, and we can eat what the hell we like without getting fat—if we want to eat, that is! Hmmm…what else might you find interesting? Oh, yes: the ability to see all our past, probable, and—I use the word lightly—future lives. Imagine that! Trying out a life before you live it!?" His laughter bellowed from Maggie's mouth. "Ha, haaaa…you can have a go at being anything while you're over here, even a woman! How would you feel about that, Charlie?"

Charlie looked appalled. He was all man! No way did he ever want to be a woman! "A woman!?"

White Eagle realised the thought didn't sit well with him. "Right, yes, sorry! Now. Charlie. I need to hear your voice in order to tune into your frequency," he said, changing the subject.

Charlie didn't have a clue what he was talking about. "Tune into my what?"

"Your frequency, Charlie. Turn it up, turn it up—your voice, man. Repeat your question."

Charlie still felt edgy. He could feel every pore in his body sweating. After all, it wasn't every day he saw the spirit of a dead Indian take over the body of a living woman, not to mention his mother, who'd been dead for years. He had a right to be scared. He shifted in his chair, rested his foot on his knee, and inhaled deeply in an attempt to psych himself up and ask the question again. "I was wondering what happens to people who don't have anyone to take them over? Would they hang about in limbo? You know, stuck between worlds, like? And how do you communicate over there?"

White Eagle, always the diplomat, questioned, "Is your voice shaking, Charlie? My God! It's years since I've had that effect on anyone! Back in the day, I had them shaking in their boots—"

Charlie felt irritated at White Eagle's attitude. "Look, man, it's not every day I talk to an Indian, especially a dead one!"

White Eagle smirked and shook his head. He'd intended to get Charlie's back up. "That's what I want to see—some fight! Right! Where were we? Oh, yes. What happens when we first cross over, how do we communicate—that's two questions! Hmm...do you realise how many times we're asked these questions and how many different answers there are? What do you believe happens? Be careful: your beliefs can be a hindrance!"

"Hindrance!? Why?"

"I could do with more time to explain, really. In short, it's our thoughts, beliefs, feelings, and focus that attract the frequencies that make our world go around."

Thoughts! Focus! Feelings! Frequencies! Charlie was baffled. "Well...I...I don't know what to believe."

"Actually, that's not a bad thing! It leaves you open to new ideas. Now let me have a think."

White Eagle wanted to make his explanation as straightforward as possible. It was hard. The language tied him. Where he came from, there were many ways to communicate. He thought about musical mathematics—no! Too difficult to explain its simplicity! Besides, Charlie would probably think he was talking sums. He looked up at the ceiling…soul notes, vibrational momentum, frequency manipulation, energy manipulation…and that was just a pinhead of what the universe was about. It was like walking along a beach and picking up a single grain of sand. The grain is infinite. It has multi-dimensional, inter-dimensional, inner-dimensional, and probable aspects to it that even White Eagle hadn't touched on. He decided to play it down and wrap it up under the heading of "telepathy" to save confusion for now—or maybe ignore that part of the question altogether. When Charlie arrived in the spirit world, communication would be a lot more natural. He screwed his face up. "Hmm, how to explain," he said slowly before he began.

"On the whole, we go easy on new arrivals. It can be a bit of a shock at first, so we see to it that they will have somebody there to meet them, somebody they're familiar with, like a relative or an old friend. Failing that, a guide of some description will ensure that they reach their destination. Rest assured, nobody is left hanging around."

"If that's the case, how come some places are haunted?"

White Eagle chuckled. "Ah yes, hauntings. Many reasons, the most common being that those doing the haunting haven't realised they're dead. But even under such circumstances, their guides are never far away and they will see to it that the spirits cross over sooner or later. In spirit, Charlie, there is no time as you perceive it, so even if a place on Earth is rumoured to have been haunted for years, the spirits doing the haunting are experiencing only a moment."

Charlie blew air from his lips. "Sounds like a right rum carry-on, that! How can you not know that you're dead? I've never heard the like! You're having me on, White Eagle!"

"Having you on? *Ich verstehe nicht!*"

"Beg your pardon!"

"Granted—you don't have to beg!"

Charlie laughed quietly to himself. Feeling a lot more relaxed, he lifted his arms in the air, stretched, and crossed his hands behind his head. "A regular joker, eh?"

"Now, where were we?" White Eagle said to himself.

"I'm wanting to know how people don't realise they're dead!" Charlie repeated. He didn't know what to make of White Eagle!

"Too many reasons to get into at one sitting but I'll give you a few examples. Could be shock. The person has passed so quickly that they haven't had time to prepare for death, such as with an accident where they've died instantly, that sort of thing. Murder is another reason. A person might hang around hoping to avenge the killer. But such cases are rare because death is set in stone long before you incarnate. I will even stick my neck out and say that, in most cases, a haunting isn't actually the spirit of the person. It's more than likely to be a residue of old energy left behind by the previous occupants—dead or alive, Charlie!" White Eagle's voice boomed out through Maggie once again. "DEAD OR ALIVE!" He laughed out loud.

Charlie laughed with him, more at the sight of Maggie lifting her arm in the air and scratching underneath her armpit. It was comical to see her behave in this way. Always the lady in her daily life, here she was acting anything but.

"So our death is predetermined before we're even born?" Charlie was intrigued.

White Eagle paused. "Oh, yes! Death is a choice just like birth. Before you incarnate into this life, you will have made the arrangements for your death. Most of us will have at least three," he cocked his head, "sometimes a few more dates in mind, but when on the brink of death we'll be asked if we're absolutely sure that we want to make the crossing. This is why some people beat the odds and survive an incurable illness or an accident. They survive under the most unbelievable circumstances and are labeled a walking miracle. Putting it simply, it was a change of mind. They've just decided to stay a bit longer. So you see, most don't bother with haunting a place because by the time death turns up, they are more than ready to leave

Earth and get on with the next part of their journey. Does that answer your question, Charlie? It really is very easy to die. It's like walking through a door into another room."

"Well, it's food for thought, I can tell you that much."

"It's good to keep an open mind in life. Don't take anyone's word for it. Listen to new knowledge, new ideas, but then listen to your own inner voice on the matter. The answers are all in there—what does your gut say? If you go with your instincts, you'll be on the right track." He let out a loud burp. "Oh, excuse me!"

Charlie had to laugh. He would bet his last penny that Maggie would be horrified to be seen burping like that in public. *Aren't these guides supposed to be holy? They broke the mould with this one!*

"For God's sake, White Eagle! Stop behaving like that or I'm ending the session." Maggie was furious. "I don't know what Charlie must think of me, I really don't!"

White Eagle turned his head to the side, "Maggie." He looked back at Charlie. "Excuse me a minute. Maggie is getting upset with me." He turned away from Charlie and shook his head. "Stop worrying about what people think, it's just a natural bodily function. Anyway, it could be worse."

"What do you mean?" she asked, irritated.

"Could be coming out the other end!" White Eagle roared with laughter.

"Don't you bloody dare or that's it!" she fumed.

"Ahh…humans. You worry about the most trivial of things. My sweet Maggie, it's not me who's got wind. The spirit body does not contain such bodily toxins and so has no need to release them. I must say, though, it brings back memories!"

"Well, don't be letting it out like that! You have to be more discreet."

"Squeeze the old cheeks, you mean!"

Maggie burst out laughing. "You're impossible!"

Though Charlie could hear only White Eagle's part of the conversation, he had a good idea of what Maggie was feeling. He started to laugh. "Tell her not to worry about me." He bent down, picked his cup up off the floor, and slurped cold tea. "So what happens when you first get there?"

White Eagle turned his attention back to Charlie. "It varies, but for the most part your guides, because we all have them, usually stay in the background. Having spoken of your arrival with your loved ones, all the necessary arrangements have been taken care of. Your loved ones will be very excited in much the same way as it is on Earth when a newborn arrives, and of course they are expecting your arrival and will have gone to great lengths to see that everything is ready for you."

Charlie found it hard to contain his excitement. "Well, I'll be! Sounds like a good old time!"

"Oh it is, Charlie, it is! If you knew how good it was here, you'd never fear death again. And your senses are more acute once you've shed your physical body, so the wonderment and excitement is a lot more intense."

"Is it as exciting for everybody?"

"It is. But for those who died with no family or friends to speak of, which is rare, it will be a lot quieter until they get acquainted with their new surroundings. I guess you could compare it to emigrating from one country to another, but a guide of some description will be there to greet them and ensure a gentle transition. Of course, they'll meet up with family they may have lost touch with soon enough, but not until they're ready, especially if animosity surrounded their Earthly circumstances—theirs is a far cry from our celebrators whose arrival will be taken care of for a while by the same relatives and friends they knew on Earth who passed before them. It is understood that much joy and love will increase the overall excitement and wonder at this level."

All of a sudden Maggie flung her arms up in the air and White Eagle's voice exploded out of her. "LET THE PARTIES AND CELEBRATIONS BEGIN!"

Charlie visibly jumped. "Christ, man, keep your voice down! Neighbours will be wonderin' what the hell's goin' on!"

"There is much merrymaking here, my friend, much merrymaking with the new arrivals in many, many ways. Your mother might decide to show you off and take you to see your old grandparents, aunts, etc., for cups of tea or coffee. For her, it is very similar to giving birth to you all over again. You will be protected, nurtured, and reared in much the same way as you were on Earth, and as guides we are happy to remain in the background and leave your arrival to the good intentions of your family—"

"Do they live in houses?" Charlie butted in, realising that it was hard to get a word in edgeways once White Eagle was on a roll.

"Your home will be a reflection of your Earthly experience. It may be that you love to be surrounded by nature and live in a cottage with a rose garden. You may choose to live with your family or parents as you always did on Earth, or you may prefer to live alone. Your home will be ready and waiting for you, and your loved ones will be only too happy to introduce you to it. This is very much a part of the whole pleasurable experience for them and for you. By new home, I am not only talking about a house or an apartment."

"It sounds similar to here." Charlie felt comfortable. He wouldn't have a clue what to say to St. Peter anyway!

"In some respects. It all depends on what you were attached to. Eventually the needs you had on the physical realm will wear out. There is so much for you to learn and explore here that you will give little thought to your old life on Earth. Too much fabulism here, Charlie; it's absolutely fabulistic and I'm a right old fabulist!" White Eagle narrowed his eyes. "Are those words in the English language? I think I'm making them up as I go along. Oh well, always room for a few choice words, I suppose!"

Charlie looked at his watch. He was half an hour late with his round, but couldn't bring himself to stop asking questions. "Isn't there some sadness at leaving your loved ones behind?"

"No, no, no, no!" White Eagle scoffed. "Because you realise that you haven't lost them. Someday they too will enjoy the same beautiful surprises as you. In these early stages, you're too busy loving the ones you thought you'd lost all those years ago—and that brings me to the time phenomena we spoke about earlier. Many years may have passed on Earth, but your loved ones will look and act younger, as will you. Life in the spirit world is not bound by linear time, you see. Years that pass on Earth do not pass in spirit—"

"White Eagle, our message! Galaxias must be instigated now! You talk too much!" Roman butted in suddenly and disappeared just as quickly.

White Eagle answered him out loud, "I'll give it to him right now." Charlie wore a confused look on his face. White Eagle could feel the connection fading as the Earth time he'd allotted came to an end. He jumped up to full height. "GALAXIAS!" He was proud to shout it out. His intense glare captured Charlie's eyes. "You're one of us, my friend. Be proud of who you are! GALAXIAS!" His voice shook the foundations of the cottage.

Charlie jumped up in terror, missed his step, and fell backwards. The chair skidded across the kitchen floor. "What the hell!" He looked around the shaking kitchen. Some kind of white energy force lit everything up. The pots and pans rattled inside the cupboard before the doors were forced open and the contents crashed to the floor. The light above him crashed against the ceiling from one side to the other, smashing the light bulb into a hundred tiny pieces.

"Galaxias, Galaxias," Maggie repeated, as she came out of trance. "You're one of us," she said drowsily.

She opened her eyes to find Charlie staring back at her. "Charlie, what are you doing on the floor!?" she asked, startled.

Charlie leaned towards her but didn't attempt to stand. He looked around the kitchen and shook his head. "Don't you remember…like an earthquake." His words were barely audible, his expression one of complete bewilderment. "The pots, they—" He stopped short. Not a thing was out of place?! White Eagle was nowhere to be seen—thank God! "Maggie, what was that?" He was still having trouble getting his words out.

"What? Are you alright, Charlie? You look really pasty. Don't you feel well?"

"Didn't you…how can you not remember…the house, it shook…
it—!" He sighed. The room felt calm again. He looked up. The light, in
one piece, hung stock-still above him. It was clear to him that Maggie
had no idea of what had just happened. *Did I imagine? No!*

"Oh, I rarely remember what I've said when I come out of trance.
It's because my consciousness is in a different place to the one I'm
in most of the time." She winked. "Oh, I'm parched. Could do with
a drink of water," she said, talking through a yawn and stretching.
"What are you doing on the floor anyway?" she asked again.

"It's…err…I missed my footing. I'll get the water!" He got up
and walked over to the tall cupboard where she kept her crockery. He
still felt shaky.

"Bottom," she said, as if reading his thoughts, "but don't bother
with a clean one. Rinse my cup out, that'll do."

He did as he was told, and filled her cup from the tap. The old
pipes shook and clanged loudly. "What a racket!"

"I know," she said, taking the cup from him. "We've got used to
it. What time is it? You lose all track under trance."

Charlie looked at his watch. "Twenty to."

"What, two?"

"Three—"

"Three! By Jesus, I'll be late for Aedan!" She jumped up out of
the chair, ran over to the under-stairs cupboard, and yanked the door
open. She pushed her slippers off with her heels and slipped into a
pair of open toed, soft blue wedge sandals with a white straw top. She
kicked her feet up behind her, and pulled the worn ankle straps over
her heels, not bothering to unfasten the buckles.

"Slow down!" Charlie said, putting his cup in the sink. "You can
jump on the cart."

"On the cart?!" she responded, taken aback.

"Don't knock it! It'll get you there quicker than your feet."

They looked at each other while she thought about it. She
remembered White Eagle's words from earlier: *'Stop worrying about
what people think.'* She smiled. "You're right." She turned to close the

door but stopped abruptly and looked over at the shelves where she kept her remedies. She picked up a small brown bottle and held it out to Charlie. "Here, take this. It'll line your lungs."

He took the bottle from her. "What's in it?"

"Herbs—cat's claw, violet leaves, periwinkle." Reacting to the look on his face, she decided to do away with the rest of the ingredients. "Don't ask! Shake it well before you take it. A tablespoon a day should do you. And keep it up. When you run out, come and get another bottle. It'll keep all that shit off your lungs!"

"What shit?"

"Coal dust and what-have-you!"

He dug into his pocket, pulled out the few coppers he had left until payday and offered it to her. She clasped his hand, the one with the bottle in it. "Now don't insult me, Charlie. Seems half a sack of coal these days keeps growing." She kept hold of his hand, closed her eyes for a few seconds, and visualised white light going into the bottle, and blessed the remedy to work for Charlie's highest good. "Let's go. Aedan will be wondering where I've got to, and you're going to be in trouble with your customers."

Charlie felt the heat from her hands but said nothing.

They headed out. "I'll meet you around the back in a jiffy," she said, securing the door behind him. "Don't forget to bolt the back gate." He was tall enough to reach over and close it from the outside.

She ran through the cottage, picked up her faux leather shopping bag from the table, and headed out. She slammed the door behind her and raced down the front path. The old wooden gate had slipped one of its hinges and, as was the routine, she picked it up and struggled to slide the rusty bolt in place. "I must get this damn thing fixed!" she said, then turned and banged straight into Olive Reids! Nearly knocked her flat on her back, shopping and all.

Of all the people! It had to be old Big Gob! "Sorry, Olive, can't stop. I'm in a rush to pick Aedan up from school, running late."

"I wonder why?" Olive said sarcastically.

Maggie ignored the comment but wondered what she meant by

it. "Sorry—haven't got time to chat." She raced around to the back of the cottage.

Charlie stood next to his horse, Sadie, gently running the back of his hand down her face. "You're such a good girl," he said, giving her mints from his pocket. He looked up at Maggie and offered his hand.

She grinned. "No, thank you."

He swapped hands and wiped the first one on his trousers. "More germs on us," he said.

"I'll take your word for it." She climbed up onto the seat behind Sadie.

With one great stride, Charlie sat next to her, flipped Sadie's reins, and said, "Let's go, girl. Only a few left." Sadie snorted. The clip-clop of her hooves and the creaky old cart could be heard for miles around.

Maggie looked up and saw Olive jump back behind her twitching curtains. "Nosey old sod!" she muttered under her breath.

Charlie cocked his head in Maggie's direction but kept his eyes fixed ahead. "What was that?"

She couldn't keep the irritation out of her voice. "Bloody Olive Reids and her twitching curtains."

Charlie looked directly at Olive's bedroom window and took off his cap. "AHOY, OLIVE!"

"CHARLIE!" Mortified, Maggie dug her elbow into his side. "How could you!?"

"Well," he scoffed, "these people get on my bleedin' nerves. Always lookin' to make some poor sod's life a misery with their filthy gossip. You watch—it'll be all over the neighbourhood that you and me have been havin' it off all afternoon. Not that I could care less, it's you I'm thinkin' about." He looked at Maggie and smirked. "Just send her to me if she starts—Eileen will kill her!" They looked up at the window and laughed. Eileen wasn't one to mince words.

Maggie looked defiant. "Oh, I can handle Olive, don't you worry about that." Then, as an afterthought, "You don't think...do you really think she'll stoop to that level?" She wondered why she'd bothered to ask the question. Of course she would. Olive had made a career out of being nosey and gossiping to all and sundry. It was her life's purpose. *What the hell, I'll cross that bridge when I come to it.*

Charlie couldn't get White Eagle's intense glare and words out of his mind. He was still unnerved by the ordeal but managed to hide his feelings—*'GALAXIAS!'* A lot of the session had faded into the background but he was haunted by the words *'GALAXIAS! YOU'RE ONE OF US!'* He turned to Maggie. "You heard of Galaxias?" he whispered. The words seemed to come out of his mouth of their own free will.

She was still eyeing Olive's damn curtains. "Sorry, what did you say?" She yawned the words at him.

He realised she was tired. "It'll keep. Journey will give you a bit of time to relax before you pick Aedan up."

He steered Sadie out of the back alley and onto the street. He always found the clip-clop of her hooves and the squeaks of the old cart meditative. A sense of calm started to drift over him. Charlie couldn't shake White Eagle from his mind, but he started to find the glare in his eyes and the words "Galaxias, you're one of us" a little less daunting. Something deep inside seemed to connect…it was as if Charlie knew exactly what the words meant.

27.

The school was old and drab. Its thick walls were built from slabs of stone that turned grey in the winter drizzle, but turned beige and sparkled like a million fairy lights during the long, hot days of summer. The playground was surrounded by green, spear-shaped, wrought iron rails with matching gates, and was situated adjacent to a field with goal posts at both ends and white lines that marked out a football pitch.

The long corridor walls inside the school were broken up by a shiny wooden dado rail; the upper half was painted a bland shade of bottle green, while the lower half was conker brown. The hardwood floors were polished to perfection. The smell of beeswax, disinfectant, and dusty books hung heavy throughout the building—except in the vicinity of the boys' toilets!

An awful mood of subservience mixed with sadness had been created by the young minds that floated around in that atmosphere. Subservient because they'd get a good thrashing or a belittling if they didn't behave, and sadness because they were still innocent enough to understand that this was not the way it should be.

Aedan's classroom was filled with about twenty individual brown desks with patterned cast iron bottoms, all highly varnished apart from the various names and symbols that had been etched into them over the years. The blackboard at the front of the room covered most of the wall behind the teacher's desk. The letters of the alphabet were spread across it in "real" writing, and as always, the Ten Commandments were a fixture in the left-hand corner.

Aedan hated the place but his mam insisted that he go there because it was the closest one to where they lived. It was run by nuns who were always complaining about something. If any child so much as opened his or her mouth without an invite to do so, an eraser full of chalk would miraculously grow wings, fly across the classroom, and never fail to land on the head of its target!

Restless as usual, Aedan's expression said it all. How bored, how frustrated he felt…he couldn't wait for the damn bell to ring, signalling freedom into the great outdoors. He could barely keep his eyes open due to a complete lack of interest in Sister Devlin's words. How could they expect young minds to sit and listen to this claptrap? Not only was it dull, but a lot of the information was wrong. Religion, science, history—they had it all cocked up. There was barely a mention of any spirit world or a galactic presence! No wonder people are terrified of death—they think it's real, unless the Church comes to the rescue and the only way they'll help is if you pussyfoot around some demanding and impossible God!

The twenty or so kids sat rigid. Their eyes and ears were glued to Sister Devlin talking about God being everywhere and how you can't get away with anything. Bibles closed, they waited patiently for her to tell them which verse to go to. As was the usual procedure, they were supposed to read the passage that night, write up on what they thought it meant, and explain their perspective to the rest of the class the following day. Then, of course, Sister Devlin would dictate what the verse actually did mean to make sure that they were indeed taught the truth.

Aedan rebelled every time. His connection to NeilA enabled his mind to be far more elevated than his young years but Maggie did her damnedest to maintain his childhood innocence for as long as possible. "The bible is the word of man, not God," he informed the class one day. "This is how I see it. I will interpret what I think the writer means by all this, but I won't put myself in the position of 'God says'!" Then, as an afterthought, he continued innocently, "Anyway, God is nice, but this verse frightens kids."

Sister Devlin's face turned a deep shade of purple. She opened the bible and rapped her fingers against the said verse, Revelation 20:11, "The Dead are Judged." Needless to say, he received detention and three hundred lines: The bible is God's word, The bible is God's word, The bible is… But that was okay. Nobody could take his thoughts away. They were his. His mind belonged to him and nobody else so he'd think what he damn well liked! But he wasn't stupid. When Aedan knew that it was in his best interests to keep his mouth shut he would look at Sister Devlin, smile, and agree with her, but at the same time he'd be thinking, *You can't change my thoughts, and you're full of shit!* It gave him great satisfaction.

He yawned loudly, forgetting where he was for the minute. He thought about the harsh lighting and bland walls. *No wonder kids get tired and lose concentration. They should paint the walls orange. It would boost creativity and keep us awake. A room for fifteen minutes quiet time would help as well—they could call it 'prayers'!* A past conversation with his mother entered his thoughts. *'The nuns prefer it. Don't mention meditation; they'll probably say you're dealing with the Devil.' Purple would be a good colour for such a room, very spiritual colour, purple, nice and relaxing—'*

"O'CONNELL!" Sister Devlin banged the bible down on the desk.

Aedan jumped up straight. She had his full attention. "Yes, Sister Devlin!"

Her eyes narrowed, as if sizing him up. "Concentrate!" she snapped.

She didn't like him. He didn't care. She was frightened of him. He could sense it. He'd marked her card the first time he set eyes on her. Her and everyone else he came into contact with. He could read them instantly.

She couldn't stand the fact that he didn't listen but could always find the answers. He just seemed to pull them out of thin air! He didn't appear to do any studying to speak of either, yet he had the ability to question all her questions—and this was what irked her the most. How could he, at seven years old, question the establishment the way he did? She didn't get it. She tried to give him lower marks whenever possible but he still managed to be top of the class. Cunning, he was. He'd give her the answers she wanted to hear but then had the audacity to write down questions at the side of them! Not questions he didn't have the answers to. Questions *he* wanted *her* to think about! Then again, what chance did he have? No father, and a mother like that! Rumour had it she used herbs and other things like faith healing to cure people. And to top it all, she spoke to the dead! The Devil's work without a doubt. *No! I mustn't dislike the child. He needs saving.*

It was the end of the day. Aedan was finding it hard to stay awake, let alone keep his eyes fixed on Sister Devlin sitting behind her desk, reading from the bible. It was so damn boring. His mind was walking through Manor Park on the way home with his mam, and then beating her at chess before he went to bed. Sometimes their chess games lasted for days. She was good but not as good as him, which irritated her, being as she'd taught him how to play!

Not a sound could be heard. Nobody dared make any. It was nearly home time and they couldn't wait to get out of there. One wrong move now and Devlin would make them stay behind and do lines. Aedan was always made to sit at the front of the class where she could keep him under control and use any excuse to dole him out a punishment.

Today she'd kept him in at playtime for being extra disruptive. He'd made the mistake of laughing out loud when she explained that God knows every thought that you're thinking so you'd better keep them pure. How the hell can you be expected to think pure thoughts constantly? Besides, doesn't she realise that a good thought has a million times more impact than a bad one? He smiled a sympathetic smile to himself. He felt sorry for her. Fear dictated how she lived her life, and a miserable life it seemed to be. She never smiled!

Sister Devlin stopped reading. "What are you smirking at, O'Connell?"

"Nothin,' Sister Devlin." *God! Now it's a sin to smile!*

"Don't lie, child! Is there something in what I'm reading that you find funny?"

"No!" He added, "I wish...," under his breath, never intending that she hear him.

"What was that? You want humour in the bible?" she asked indignantly. The classroom was silent. The children looked on. None of them dared move, not even breathe.

Sister Devlin stood up and puffed out her chest. She was tall for a woman, at least five feet, ten inches. Aedan bet she had muscles more than she had fat underneath her black swirling gowns. She was a frightening figure; she reminded him of some kind of weird sea creature that dwelled underneath the ocean, yet to be discovered. And to make it worse, she stank like a mixture of mothballs and lamb chops!

She poised herself above Aedan, bible in hand. "I asked you a question, O'Connell," she hissed, twisting her bony knuckles into his back. She applied more pressure with every turn, enjoying it.

He closed his eyes and imagined a thick pillow between his back and Devlin's knuckles, and focused on not feeling any pain. From as far back as he could remember, he'd learned that the more you focus on what you don't want, the more likely you are to get it.

"Open your eyes—how dare you ignore me! Answer my question!" she hissed

He turned his head to the side and stared up at her, a terrified expression on his face. Sister Devlin's features, emphasised by her temper, jumped out at him: a long, crooked nose, golf ball eyes, and teeth that could bite through tree trunks. Her steely glare and wagging head put him in mind of a chicken clucking and pecking around. As usual when his nerves got the better of him, the thoughts wouldn't go away, and he couldn't contain his laughter.

He stifled a small laugh by turning it into a cough; but then came to mind an impression of Sister Devlin flapping her arms at her sides, dressed in nun's habit, and behaving exactly like a chicken. He looked at her, terrified. *Don't laugh, don't laugh,* he willed himself.

The rest of the children looked on, amazed expressions on their faces. A low whisper rippled through the room. "Fancy laughing at Devlin!" "He's in for it now." "I bet he'll get expelled, the strap at least—"

Sister Devlin turned to the rest of the class. "SILENCE!" Their response was instantaneous. She looked down at the terrified Aedan and felt the gush of blood rise from her toes to her throat. "How dare you! How dare you laugh at the bible—at me! How dare you," she whispered.

He looked at her helplessly. He preferred her when she was shouting. "I'm not, I'm just nervous—"

She pulled back the bible and swiped him hard across the face with it.

He immediately burst into tears. "I'm telling my mam of you," he bawled.

"Don't threaten me! Do you think I'm worried about your mother?"

"She'll be angry! She never hits me with any—"

"I will ask you one more time. Do you think there should be humour in the bible, O'Connell?" She looked macabre, dangerous.

He wiped his nose and face on his sleeve. He couldn't understand why she wanted to behave in such a cruel way, why she hated him so much. What had he ever done to her? What was it with people that they always wanted to hurt each other? Once again, even at his young age, he realised that the answer to his question was fear. "I think it would be better than fear," he sobbed.

"Oh you do, do you? But without fear, fear of God, you and others like you would be even worse than they are now."

He looked puzzled and his answer was purely innocent. "I'm not frightened of God. Why should I be? God is my friend."

Sister Devlin turned pale, then red with rage. "You're mistaken, O'Connell. How dare you even consider God to be your friend? The Devil is what's guiding you." She stuck her knuckles in his back again, and dug even harder than before.

"I don't believe in the Devil," he said between tears. "My mam says you get what you believe in."

"Well, she would say that, fill your head with lies and filth. She's one of the Devil's closest aides."

Aedan's mood changed immediately; the look on his face slid from terror to calm within a fraction of a second. Fear gone, he turned in his chair and looked straight at her, fixed his eyes into hers. "Don't say bad things about my mam," he warned quietly. Trembling, he tried hard to stop the anger inside his belly from escaping. If she didn't stop twisting her knuckles into him soon, he'd see to it that she did—and when he saw fit! Who does she think she is, talking about his mam like that? Devlin wasn't fit to lick her shoes.

He practised his anger-control breathing technique Maggie had shown him but it wasn't working. The harder she dug in, the more his anger seemed to destroy his insides, scratch them, tear at them, until he couldn't contain it any longer.

Sister Devlin felt Aedan's eyes bore down straight into her soul. She backed off a bit but she wouldn't allow the fear now swarming her to show. "Don't you talk to me like that." A weak tone entered her voice. "I won't tolerate any more of your insolence. Your mother is evil. She works with the Devil, and you are his spawn!"

Aedan jumped up, pushed his desk away, and sent it crashing to the floor. His books, pencils, and a small bouncing ball spilled out. His chair scraped along the floor behind him. Sister Devlin's hand was still attached to his back. He made sure of it.

His best friend, Derrick, got to his feet to clear up the mess. "Aedan, let's go," he said, trying to defuse the situation.

"SIT!" she screamed at Derrick.

Aedan looked over at Derrick and nodded. He wasn't about to get his best friend into trouble. Aedan fixed his eyes back into Sister Devlin's. He didn't say a word; he didn't have to. She saw courage, war, a winner.

As her knuckles twisted and dug deeper, a searing great heat came off the child's back and burned into her fingers. She could see smoke spiralling from her hand, slow and lazy, like the silver strands from a cigarette. She wanted to stop, and she tried her best to pull away from Aedan's back but couldn't. To the children she looked as if she was in spasm. They had no awareness of what was happening. *What the hell's wrong with her?*

"What's that? Where's that smoke coming from? Who's lit a cigarette? Which one of you is smoking?" She looked around, her head jerking from child to child in search of evidence.

The children looked at her as if she was mad. They had no idea what she was talking about. "What smoke? What's she on about?" they whispered among themselves. "She looks like she's doing a funny dance," one child sniggered quietly to another.

She felt strange, as if she wasn't there. Fear flooded every part of her. She started to float somehow, as if losing herself. Her voice was weak with anxiety. "Aedan O'Connell. Stop this immediately or I'll—"

He looked at her with contempt. She wasn't worth the time of day. "Stop what? You're the one digging your knuckles into my back."

Beads of sweat broke out on her forehead. She was burning up. She looked at her knuckles. They were still twisting, deeper, deeper— going inside him. No matter how she tried she couldn't pull them off Aedan's back. She screamed out in fear and pain.

The class looked on. Some of them smirked and giggled nervously. She looked weird, as if she was doing some kind of tranced-out tribal ritual, and she kept howling like the Indians they'd seen in the films at the Saturday morning matinee.

Aedan had no sympathy. "You get what you focus on," he said, wise beyond his years. "Focus on burning in hell, Sister Devlin, and that's what you'll get—"

"AEDAAAAAN!" White Eagle appeared in front of the blackboard, screaming at his young charge. None of the others were aware of him.

Horrified, Aedan jumped back. "Wha…what?" he answered, terrified.

Devlin collapsed over and stumbled into her chair. Wide-eyed, Aedan sucked in a deep gulp of air. Now he was in real trouble.

White Eagle was livid. "WE'LL HAVE SERIOUS WORDS

ABOUT THIS LATER. YOU KNOW BETTER!" He couldn't have this kind of behaviour from him. Wouldn't have it! No matter what the reason.

Aedan stuttered, "Sh…sh…she called me…m…mam names." Frustrated, he brought his fist down on the desk of the child who sat beside him.

The rest of the class, including Sister Devlin, flinched, turned, and looked at the blackboard. *Who was he talking to?*

"YOUR MOTHER HAS PUT UP WITH A LOT WORSE. SISTER DEVLIN IS A PUSHOVER COMPARED TO WHAT SHE'S HAD TO COPE WITH."

But Aedan wouldn't give in. He shouted back, "WELL, I'M NOT LETTING HER OR ANYONE ELSE TALK ABOUT ME MAM—"

White Eagle ran at his young charge, bent down to his level, and shoved his face into his. Aedan was a handful at times. White Eagle knew that if he showed leniency he would be doing Aedan no favours. He spoke quietly but his tone was dangerous. "Sit down, shut up, and deal with whatever punishment she doles out because I'm warning you, it will be nothing compared to what I'll give you if you don't behave."

The two stared each other down. Aedan didn't stand a chance. He was frightened. He'd never seen White Eagle so outraged. Even the flesh on his face and neck shook! The rest of the class witnessed Aedan glaring into empty space until he slowly edged backwards.

White Eagle looked around at the classroom floor and barked at Aedan, "NOW CLEAN UP THIS DAMN MESS, AND SORT OUT SISTER DEVLIN!" before he disappeared.

Aedan looked at his classmates, then at Sister Devlin. He bent down, picked up his desk, its contents, then his chair. Nobody said a word. He sat down, put his face in his hands, and burst into tears. He'd let his mam, White Eagle, and himself down. He knew, he knew, that his power should never be used to control others…*But she must have had a say in it somewhere…mustn't she?*

He looked over at Sister Devlin's hand. It was red, the skin blistered. She hung onto it, her mind still poking around in a private hell somewhere. To the rest of the class she simply looked tired, spaced out. They weren't aware of the burn on her hand. It was visible only to herself and to Aedan. Guilt seeped into his pores like an oil spill: black, slimy, good for nothing.

He rested his hands on his knees and concentrated on sending healing energy to Sister Devlin. Within seconds, he could feel a tingling heat in his palms and fingertips. He turned his hands over. A stream of swirling, white-blue light oozed out of them and headed towards her.

His heart went out to her. He was genuinely sorry for what he'd put her through. The colour of her aura was mostly grey and black, the colour of fear. *What a horrible way to live,* he thought. But there was light there. It lined the shape of her aura—a transparent replica of her physical body, expanding about three feet around it. He looked through, into some of her celestial bodies—etheric, emotional, mental, astral, causal.

And then he saw her soul. It poured out from her heart. It was surrounded by sadness, not only for her, but also for Aedan. In that moment, Aedan realised that Sister Devlin's soul was sending love back to him in the hope that he'd recover from his own weaknesses— let it go, forgive. But forgiveness had to come from the heart.

Aedan felt humbled. Not only had Sister Devlin's soul—the bigger part of her—forgiven him, it was allowing him to heal, through her! It was a two-way street, a joint decision. Her soul had touched him— what an honour—to be forgiven. From now on, he would behave himself for Sister Devlin. Well, he'd try!

His energy intermingled with hers. It twisted, shone, twinkled, through the grey and the black, his light expanding on hers. He watched her energy field grow, fill with light and an array of vibrant colours: red, orange, yellow, green, pink, turquoise, blue, indigo, purple, gold, white—all luminous, all intermingling. He was mesmerised. *She's beautiful...like a great big rainbow!*

He watched her hand heal until she let go of it and opened the bible on her desk. He continued to focus on her energy, sending in more love until her whole demeanour changed. Her facial expressions took on a gentler look and her body lost its rigidity. Mesmerised, Aedan watched her come out of the fog and escape from the fear that had ruled her life up until this moment. Her soul smiled at him. At last! It had got through. She sat up straight, closed the bible, and smiled at the children. She looked nice, even pretty! He breathed deeply, rested his head on his arms.

"Aedan, are you tired?" she asked, as if nothing had happened.

"A little bit," he answered. He knew that she couldn't remember a thing.

She looked at him sternly. "Then I suggest you go to bed earlier." She paused; suddenly seeing something different in him…she rather accepted him. She smiled. "I can't have you falling asleep in my class. Am I that boring?"

The rest of the class thought that Sister Devlin had definitely gone around the twist! *When was she ever nice to Aedan? And he'd given her loads of cheek today!* They thought she'd send him for the strap, or lines at the very least.

Aedan knew it was the universal energy aiding her transformation. It didn't take long once it got through. Oh, you could drag it out if you wanted to but minutes—seconds even—was all it needed. Nothing was more powerful than the force of love. "No, Sister Devlin," he answered, yawning. He looked at her. "Sorry." But he wasn't apologising for yawning.

She couldn't understand why suddenly she could see the goodness, the purity in the child. Something she'd never seen in him before. It wasn't Aedan that had brought this about, but her own light. He'd simply brought her light-to-light, so to speak. Such was the power of healing. Her darkest, deepest emotions—or demons, as she called them—had been touched, released. She felt airy, bright, loved, for the first time in her fifty-two years. She looked down at the bible and wondered why it was so full of pain and suffering. *Did it have to be that way?* For the first time in her life, she questioned her beliefs.

She thought about her parents, how they'd rammed the catechism down her throat, told her how bad she was, and how to always be on the lookout for the Devil. Sweet Jesus, the beatings she'd suffered for the smallest things: singing, dancing, and once just for playing dress-up in her mother's clothes.

'Focus on burning in hell, and that's what you'll get,' some voice in her head said. She thought about all the good in the world that goes unmentioned. *Then I'll focus on living in peace, on good...* She looked up, and smiled at the class. "No homework tonight, children. Enjoy your evening in any way you see fit. Take in the rest of the sunshine. Off you go."

The children remained rigid, eyes glued. *Was it a trick?*

"Off you go," she repeated, dismissively.

George Mellor put his hand up. "The bell hasn't gone, Sister," he said timidly.

"I know, but we've worked hard enough for one day. Now if you don't make a move soon, I'll keep you all for an extra half hour's bible study," she joked. They were up, bags packed, and through the door in less than thirty seconds.

Sister Devlin looked around at the empty classroom, then stood up and walked to the window. The sun shone and so did the sky, and the leaves on the trees were a deep, emerald green. At the far end of the playground the big oak that had stood on the edge of the woodland for hundreds of years beckoned to her. She decided she would sit underneath it for a while before she went back to the convent. Some strange thought came to her about taking her shoes off. *Let the grass tickle your feet!* She shrugged, blew out a small laugh and walked back to her desk, picked up the bible, put it down again. She knew it without looking at it, anyway!

She left the school, walked across the playground to the old oak, sat down, and looked around. There was nobody about. She took off her shoes and wriggled her feet in the grass. The cool dampness felt good. She could feel the life in it. It was as if they were all one, all the same essence...

She stood up and looked around to make sure nobody was

watching. She had an uncontrollable urge to hug the tree, breathe in its bark. She started to sing "Amazing Grace," then stopped abruptly. *Don't sing out here! It's hardly appropriate; assembly was hours ago!* She sat down again, rested her back straight up against the old oak, and felt its energy. She inhaled deeply within the same second that the summer breeze stepped up momentum and rushed by her. It stroked and teased her, like the touch of an imaginary lover—her heart skipped a bit. Should she be thinking such things?

She thought about going back to the cell at the convent. It was dark in there all the time—miserable, really! It seemed a shame to waste such a beautiful day indoors. She'd make up some excuse as to why she was late. To top it all, Mother Superior had ordered a vow of silence for the next three days. She started to sing quietly, "How sweet the sound." *Why did God give us a mouth if it we had to keep it shut all the time?*

The birds joined in with her. The louder she sang the louder they chirped. She sang louder, louder, "…that saved a wretch like me…" She was surrounded by buttercups and daisies; the smell of freshly cut grass lifted her spirit so high, she felt giddy. She could hear the squirrels and other small animals scurrying about in the backwoods. It had been such a long time since she'd seen nature—*From being a child, perhaps.* Sister Devlin heard it, felt it, took in its scents. She ran her fingers around some of the three-leaf clovers, and wondered if she'd ever find a four leaf? But something deep inside her told her that she already had—"I once was lost but now I'm found…" She sang her heart out. What was wrong with singing if she damn well pleased!? "Twas blind but now I see…" She felt as if she'd been released from something…*From what?*

It was as if her soul had popped in to introduce itself again after years of being away. For the first time in her life, she understood what love was—what it actually was. She felt a connection to something. She was cherished. She belonged. Elation ran through her veins. There was no feeling in the world like this…

She'd missed God.

28.

As Charlie brought Sadie to a stop, Maggie stood up, ready to jump.

"Wait up, Maggie. I'll give you a hand."

"I'll be alright, getting the hang of it now." She lifted her skirts and leapt from the cart. Her outstretched arms just managed to save her from ending up flat on her face. "Shi—I nearly broke my bleedin'neck!" She dusted herself off. "Thanks for the ride, Charlie. You're a godsend."

Sadie's reins hung loosely in his hands. "Do you want me to hang on?"

She looked over at the school steps. "No, no, you've done enough. Anyway, I've got a bit of shopping to do, and it's such a beautiful day, I'll take Aedan to Manor Park for an hour or so. Thanks, though. Bye for now." She ran towards Aedan who was in the school playground, kicking stones around.

"See you later, Maggie." He shook Sadie's reins. "Away we go, girl."

She stopped suddenly and waved Charlie down. "Charlie! You're alright, aren't you…after your experience, like? It's not scared you?"

He thought before answering. "No, no, not scared," he lied. "Unnerved a bit. Guess it's only to be expected…given me something to think about."

Aedan looked over and saw his mam just as he was about to kick another stone at the wall. He wondered what she was doing on the coal cart!? Excited, he charged over. "Mammaaa…" he sang, as he rammed into her. "Are we going on Charlie's cart—?"

"Careful, careful, you'll have me flat on my back. No, not this time."

Charlie tipped his cap. "What about Saturday? It's up to your mother, but if you'd like you can do the round with me and our Derrick. I'm taking him out for the first time; paying him—not much, mind—and I could do with the extra hands on Saturdays. That way I can finish a bit earlier and enjoy some kind of a weekend."

Aedan sucked in his breath. "Mam, can I, can I?" his eyes danced.

She looked at the thrilled expression on his face and wondered how riding around on a coal cart at five in the morning could rake up such excitement. "I don't see why not."

"Thanks, Mam!" He jumped for joy with her in his arms. "I've got a job, I've got a job!"

She clasped his face. "Aedan, sweetheart, calm down."

Charlie looked at him sternly. "Sorted then. Gotta be an early riser, though. Five o'clock we'll be banging on your door, and you'd better look sharpish."

He often had Aedan on Saturday afternoons anyway. It was just as easy to keep him for the whole day. He'd sort of stepped in as a surrogate father to the lad. It helped Maggie out—Aedan had his moments. God knows he needed a male influence now and again.

"I'll be up at four!" Aedan was still hopping about.

"Don't wear any good clothes. You'll be rotten by the time you get home." Charlie flashed Maggie a knowing look. "He'll be asleep by six-thirty Saturday night!" He started to laugh, a knowing expression on his face—Maggie enjoyed her Saturday night tipple.

"You can drink your beer in peace, Mam!"

Maggie lifted her chin and shot him a haughty glance. "Be quiet!" She looked around, relieved that nobody had heard him other than Charlie. "I only have a glass now and again!"

Aedan laughed, and started to sing in a childish manner, "You drink loads of beeeeer, you drink loads of beeeeer."

Maggie chased after him, the back of her hand raised. "If you don't quieten down you won't be able to sit on that skinny little backside by the time I'm done with it—"

Charlie pointed his finger. "Aedan! Button it!" His tone meant business.

Aedan calmed down straight away. Maggie grabbed his hand roughly, pulled him in the opposite direction to Charlie. "Bye, Charlie, thanks again." She watched the cart and Sadie's hooves fade into the background.

Maggie and Aedan walked toward the park. "Are we going to Manor Park, Mam?"

"Yes! Not for long, mind." She grasped his chin and turned his cheek to face her. "What's that red mark on your face?"

He looked awkward. "Oh, that…" he stroked the side of his face. "It's nothing. I was resting my head on my arms." It wasn't really a lie…just an omission of the truth!

Maggie was having none of it. The look she gave him was an invitation to come clean. "Really, just resting your head? Looks like you've had a swipe across it to me."

A picture of White Eagle saying, *'Clean up this damn mess,'* pounced into his mind and prompted him to spill all. His mam was going to find out one way or the other. Head down, his response was sheepish. "Sister Devlin hit me with a bible."

Maggie was horrified. "Hit you with a bible! What for? Why would she do that?"

"Nothing!"

"Nothing!?" Maggie's eyebrows all but fused.

He didn't stop for breath. "She was upset with me 'cos I laughed when she said, 'God knows all your thoughts so you'd better keep 'em pure,' then she asked me if I thought the bible should have humour, I said it's better than fear and I'm not scared of God and God's my friend and she went mad!" Eyes lifted, voice up in tempo, he continued, "Said I was the Devil's spawn 'cos you worked with him, and that's what made me mad when she said bad things about you, Mam—"

"Take a breath, sweetheart—"

"And now White Eagle's really piss—really mad at me—"

"White Eagle!?" Her expression switched from confusion to

suspicion in an instant. "What was he doing there?" Something major must have transpired if he'd turned up.

Aedan's big brown eyes were full of tears. "I did a bad thing. I'm sorry, Mam, I really am." He threw himself into her and broke into uncontrollable sobs.

She put her arms around him. "Holy mother, what've you done?"

Aedan was inconsolable. "I used my power to make Sister Devlin think her fingers were burning."

Maggie felt her stomach shrivel. *God, no! I hope this isn't what I think it is.* "Sweetheart…you're not making sense."

"She screwed her knuckles into my back, so I made her think her fingers were burning," he repeated anxiously. "I knew she was in pain and she wanted to pull away but I wouldn't let her, and then White Eagle turned up and he—"

"Oh, Jesus, Aedan—you didn't!" She pushed him away, put her hand over her mouth, and just stared at him, a stunned look on her face.

Aedan wasn't used to seeing his mother rendered speechless. It frightened him more than White Eagle's temper had done earlier. "Mam, I'm sorry, I am. I'm sorry, Mam!" He was hysterical. He'd overstepped the mark and he knew it. "I won't do it again, never! I won't, honest."

She walked away from him. He followed her. "STAY THERE!" Her face was a sickly grey colour. But it was the fear in her eyes that terrified him.

He stopped dead. He'd never felt this mood from her. What did it mean? He watched her walk through the black iron gates at the entrance to Manor Park a few yards ahead of him. She sat down on a bench, pulled a handkerchief from her pocket, and dabbed her eyes. *Was she crying?* He ran over and threw his arms around her shoulders. "Mam, don't cry—"

"I'm not, I'm blowing my nose." She pretended to blow. "Why didn't you do your breathing…anything…but to use the power like that…!"

"I did breathe but it didn't work! I don't know why it didn't work—"

"His primal instincts, in particular his protective one, kicked in and overrode his reasoning." White Eagle sat cross-legged on the gravel path in front of them, his face grave. He made no effort to hide his anger. "You are never to use your power to inflict pain and suffering on others, Aedan, do you hear me? Do you realise the seriousness… the, the, gravity of this situation? You left the good energy and entered the dark one. Do you know what that means? What the consequences of that would be if it were to get out of control?"

Aedan just stared at White Eagle, unable to grasp what he was talking about.

White Eagle turned to Maggie. "I need to talk to you!"

Maggie sighed. Weary, she stood up and rummaged through her bag. "Let's walk. Aedan, here." She gave him a small paper bag full of old bread. "Go feed the ducks."

Gingerly, he took it. "Alright." He ran on ahead, glad of an excuse to get away.

"We knew that it wouldn't be easy. A child with power like this," White Eagle said. "The elders are prepared to let him slip now and again. After all, human emotions—his own, and those of others—are something he has to learn to deal with."

She ignored his comment about the elders. "Come on, White Eagle, he's just a child. For all his power, he's still childish! I've kept it that way. I want him to have as normal an upbringing as possible. How many times did you think about putting someone in their place while you were on Earth? Me—I do it all the time! Wish I could fire Olive Reid up the garden path now and again, I can tell you!"

"I understand that, Maggie. But the difference is you haven't got the power to do that, whereas Aedan has. He has the potential to cause havoc in the world, the universe, if he slides over into the lower vibrations. We can't let that happen. It won't be allowed to happen."

"Look, he's a good lad." She shrugged. "He can be wilful, I know, at times—"

"Wilful! Full-Will, more like—"

"Let's not forget that he's only seven years old. He must be allowed to grow."

"Maggie, you don't understand. Unless he can handle his power, he won't be allowed to grow—not on Earth anyway." White Eagle's demeanour was intense. "Do you understand the point I'm making here?"

She felt the bile swirl about in her stomach. It burned her windpipe on its way up to her throat. "You're saying that he'd be taken from me?" she whispered.

"Only as a last resort." His tone was quiet yet ominous. "We can't risk Aedan sliding into the dark. Such a scenario is one of their main goals. Should they get their way, it's hard to imagine the devastation it would bring to…not only to Earth but the rest of the universal—"

"But that's not fair!" Her insides turned to liquid. "It's not even realistic. We all slip now and then—"

"But we don't all have his power—"

"Allowances must be made. You can't expect Aedan to be holier than thou twenty-four hours a day, seven days a week. That's just ridiculous!" She lost her temper. "How do you expect him to experience life on this planet if he has to watch his step all the way? He may as well be on automatic—I will be good, I will not put a foot wrong, I will be good, I will not put a foot wrong," she mimicked, in a robotic voice. "That's no life for a child, for anyone!"

"We don't expect—"

"He's going to play tricks, pranks. All kids do."

"Pranks, yes! But this was no prank. His intention was to hurt Sister Devlin, to make her suffer. For God's sake, Maggie, that's not acceptable. Not from a child like Aedan."

"But from any other child, it's fine," she fumed.

"No! It's not fine! But he's not any other child. At the risk of repeating myself, other children can't do the same damage—"

"Christ, he's just a baby!" She looked over at Aedan. He was surrounded by ducks, and his childish laughter rang out through the park. "He's just a baby!" she said out loud to herself. She turned to White Eagle. "He's genuinely sorry, that I do know."

"Maggie, I'm not saying he'd be taken at the drop of a hat. I'm saying that…" he sighed and looked off into the distance. He tried to find words that wouldn't upset her but decided it didn't matter. She needed to acknowledge Aedan, instead of burying him. "You are the mother of a child who has the power to turn the world inside out, upside down—to make the Earth flat! Do you understand!?" His eyes flashed. He looked dangerous. "Your job isn't an easy one." His eyes became slits. "Do you realise who Aedan is? You can't deny him forever. You took the job on! You have a lot of support! Don't be afraid to ask! Yes, Aedan must be allowed to grow, to experience, and yes, we understand you wanting to hang on to his childhood, but he must be made aware of his responsibilities and the sooner the better. You can't mollycoddle him forever!"

White Eagle understood why she always came to Aedan's defence. She felt she'd let him down, that it was her fault he'd missed out on having a father figure in his life. She'd yet to realise that this was Charlie's job, as well as his own, at least for the time being. The older Aedan got, the more he'd benefit from a bit of tough love, and if Maggie wasn't up to the task, White Eagle certainly was.

She sat down by the flowerbeds and ran her hands amongst the pansies. She loved the feel of their velvety texture against her skin. "I do my best…I explain that he isn't to use his gift to show off, and that the fewer people who know about it, the better. It's hard for a child of his age to be saddled with such responsibility." She stood up. "When he's older, it'll be easier for him to understand, but right now…" She rubbed her forehead with her fingers. "Look! I explain right and wrong. He's not a bad kid."

"No, he's not a bad kid, but he'll be tempted like any other." His stare was hard. "You must acknowledge Aedan. You can start by dropping the word 'gift,' for the word 'power.' It's a more apt description of what's stored within him!"

NeilA flashed into her mind. She felt sick. "No! I didn't choose it. I wanted an ordinary baby." She stormed off. White Eagle appeared in front of her. She stopped dead. For some reason she felt rooted to the spot. She looked at him helplessly. "He's normal!"

"Normal is a state of mind. Can you handle him, Maggie?" His eyes searched her mind…her soul…

"I'm so scared. What if I can't help him? Will I lose him? I won't be able to bear it…the loss."

"Love is the only power. Do you love him?"

Her face contorted with disdain. "Love him!" she spat. "You have to ask me?"

"Then you have nothing to worry about."

Aedan ran towards them. His bag empty, it dropped to the ground.

She gestured that he pick it up. "Hey, hey, pick that up and put it in the bin, young man!" He did as he was told. "Aedan, since when have you littered the Earth with your rubbish? You realise the damage it causes."

"I didn't, Mam, I dropped it. You just thought I'd tossed it. I was gonna pick it up!"

"Right, I'll let you off then." She hugged him to her. "Sorry, darling.'" She looked at White Eagle. "See, he's not a bad kid."

"Nobody said he's a bad kid." He turned to Aedan. "Aedan, you have to understand that this power you have is to be used for good things. It isn't to be used for any other purpose." White Eagle's tone was firm. A tinge of anger was still detectable. "You saw Sister Devlin as a bad person and believed that you had the right to punish her. You don't have that right."

"She doesn't have the right to hit me with a bible, or anything else for that matter," he retorted, attitude huffy.

Maggie jumped in. "Don't be so bloody cheeky!" She was protecting Aedan in a roundabout way. White Eagle was pissed off, to say the least. The last thing Aedan should do was come over all high and mighty.

White Eagle put his hand up. "Maggie, don't interfere!"

She braced herself and opened her mouth, "I was only trying to—"

"Keep out of it!" White Eagle insisted. He looked down his nose at Aedan, his attitude ten times huffier. "That's Sister Devlin's problem, not yours."

"It's my problem when she belts me across the head with a bible!"

"No, it isn't! Your reaction is your problem, as well as your mother's, mine, and a whole bunch of others that you're not yet aware of." He felt Maggie cringe at his words. "Every action sets off a chain of reactions, Aedan, remember that. Look at the upset you've caused your mother, brought her to tears, not to mention Sister Devlin and me."

"It's not fair! You're saying that people can beat me senseless and I'm supposed to just stand there like a twit and do nothing about it."

"No, I'm not saying that. But how did you feel after…after you'd made Sister Devlin suffer? Think of your sadness, your shame when her soul spoke to you—graced you, Aedan, graced you! And what about when you saw your mother cry? Did you get any satisfaction out of it? Were you proud of your actions?"

"No!" He wouldn't look at White Eagle.

White Eagle grabbed Aedan's chin. His tone was razor sharp. "Look at me when I'm talking to you! You were fortunate enough to be given a rare insight into Sister Devlin's life, a life that's endured nothing but pain and misery, and you come along and add to it. What does that say about you?"

Cheeks soaked with tears, Aedan pulled himself away from White Eagle, and buried himself in Maggie's belly.

White Eagle eyed her. "Push him away," he mouthed.

It just about broke Maggie's heart but she knew that the time had come to help Aedan understand his gift—*power!* He had to understand intention, and how easy it was to slip into a branch of the lower energy. She pushed him away, no emotion on her face. "Don't expect me to feel sorry for you. I'm ashamed of your behaviour. I never expected this from you, never!"

The sad look on his face caused a bomb to go off in her heart but she kept her guard up. What he'd done was wrong. *I won't lose him!*

"Aedan, Aedan!" White Eagle called. "Come here. Come sit by me."

Maggie stormed off towards the duck pond. She'd leave them to it.

Aedan's eyes followed her. "Mam!" he cried. "Mam, don't leave!" His voice trembled with fear. She stopped for a second. She wanted to run, scoop him up in her arms. *NO!* She carried on walking.

"Aedan." White Eagle patted the grass.

The boy turned sheepishly, a worried look on his face, but he was determined to act the big shot. "WHAT!" he scowled.

White Eagle remained calm but acted anything but. "What! What! Don't take that attitude with me, young man. I'm not your mother! GET YOUR BACKSIDE OVER HERE NOW!" he fumed.

Aedan jumped, burst into tears, and did as he was told.

Aedan was crying so much that he had to catch his breath between great heaving sobs while sniffing up the shiny snot that covered his top lip. Every now and again he'd scoop it with his tongue, and clear the remainder with the back of his hand, smearing most of it up his cheekbones.

White Eagle produced a handkerchief seemingly from thin air. "Look at the state of you! Here, clean yourself up." Aedan ignored him. "Aedan." His voice was soft. "I know your job isn't easy. You're young, you want to play, be like other kids, but you're diff—they all have the power, you know! But it sleeps for the most part, whereas yours is anything but. It must be nurtured. It's a responsibility that can overwhelm you. Do you think that I don't know that? I want to help you with it, help you use it for great things."

Aedan's words were full of anger and contempt. "It doesn't do anything great! I'm sick of it! I wish I didn't have it! I hate it!" he blurted.

"Calm down." White Eagle leaned forward, wiped Aedan's face, and passed him the hanky. "Here, calm down," he repeated. "Things are never as bad as they seem." He laid his hand, palm down, on Aedan's chest. "Calm down."

Aedan could feel his heart react to the warm healing energy. He started to relax as it spread like a tidal wave of warm water throughout his body.

"Aedan, when you sent love…healing…to Sister Devlin, you did a great thing. Being a son to Maggie is a great thing; so is loving her the way you do. Your friendship with people you care about is a great thing, your love for animals." He looked under his eyebrows at his small friend. "To show love is a great thing…the greatest thing of all. Do you understand? The power isn't there to impress others by playing magic tricks such as turning metal into gold and pulling rabbits out of hats." He paused. "And it isn't there to hurt another or to instil fear. The power is love."

Still catching sobs, Aedan looked up, his expression innocent. "But when people want to hurt me, I can't help it that I have power and I can kick their arse—"

"Err…don't let your mother hear you say that word, young man. There's a time and a place."

"I know there is, and you don't care about bad words!"

White Eagle wanted to laugh but didn't. "Well…it all comes down to the vibration that's attached to them. Humorous, loving, nasty…but let's not get into that now. Right! Getting back to where we left off. When Sister Devlin's soul forgave you, how did you feel?"

Aedan smiled. "It was nice. It made me feel…I don't know… bigger. It was a funny feeling."

"That sensation of bigger is evolution…your energy field expanded because your intention was to do good, to do good from the heart. When you were hurting Sister Devlin, your energy field shrivelled, and caused weakness in you. Your intention to hurt was heartfelt—just the same as your intention to do good, but it caused bitterness, resentment, a need to control. In effect, you were hurting yourself much more than you were hurting Sister Devlin."

Aedan flashed a look of total honesty at White Eagle. "But it felt good at the time. I enjoyed it, making her pay. She's a bully and she deserved—!" He stopped short, a worried look on his face. "Does that mean I'm bad? I don't want to be bad, I don't." He started to get hysterical again.

White Eagle shook his head. "No, no, it doesn't mean that you're bad…shh, shh, let's stay calm. Look! We all feel good about bad now and again! This is natural. We're tempted with all kinds of things in life. You wanted to protect your mother, I understand that." He looked around. "Would you like an ice cream?" Aedan lit up. Mouth open, he just stared. "Well! Do you want one or not?"

"Yep! Are you my friend again?" he asked, shocked.

White Eagle looked away to hide his smile. He pressed his lips together so he wouldn't burst into laughter, then turned back to Aedan straight-faced. "Err, I haven't finished talking to you, if that's what you mean. I just think an ice cream would hold your focus a bit longer. Now, what would you like?"

"A cornet."

"What do you say?"

"Please!"

"That's better!"

White Eagle uncurled one of his hands, palm up. He produced a cornet, top-heavy with hard ice cream and dripping with raspberry source. "Voilaaaa!" he sang.

It reminded Aedan of the sign outside the barber's shop he always went to. "Thank you," he giggled, making a grab for it "You just said we shouldn't use the power for magic tricks!"

White Eagle scratched his head. "I know but it's okay now and again between me and you." How to explain things to a child was always a challenge. He didn't want to damage Aedan by frightening him or saying the wrong thing, yet he had to help him understand his power and the responsibility that went along with it. "Aedan, let's walk over to the sandpit." He picked up a small twig that was lying in the grass at his feet. "Come on."

They walked over and sat down in the sand. A few children were playing on the opposite side of the pit. White Eagle sat in front of Aedan with his back to the children. "Aedan, you understand that every thought has its own frequency, right? We've been talking about this idea since you were a baby."

Aedan looked up at the sky and produced a deep sound from his voice. "Yep," he joked, tipping his head from side to side and singing, "Frequency high, frequency low—"

White Eagle put his hand on top of Aedan's head, an amused expression on his face. "Aedan, it really is important that you pay attention to me. Can you give me, let's say, another five minutes?"

He let out a long, weary groan. "I want to play."

"You can play, but hear me out first, alright?"

He bit into his cornet. "Alright," came the reluctant response.

Using his power to make writing in the sand with a twig quick and easy, White Eagle drew a straight line in the sand. "This is the good vibration, or the love vibration, or the good energy—whatever you want to call it." "These are its thoughts." He said the words but just drew squiggly lines representing the branches "Nice thoughts, pleasant thoughts, humorous thoughts, kind thoughts, happy thoughts. All winners…love-filled thoughts." He looked up to make sure that he had Aedan's full attention, and then continued to draw a few stick people with smiling faces. "These are the people who think these thoughts. They stick together, attract more people like themselves, and attract good things into their lives."

He drew another squiggly line underneath the happy people. "This is the lower vibration, the fear vibration, and these are its thoughts." He drew more squiggly lines coming off the lower vibration. "Miserable, anxious, nasty, pain, suffering, control, fear-filled thoughts, and these are the people who think these thoughts." He drew a couple of miserable-looking faces with clouds hanging over them. "They are not really living. They don't understand that their thoughts are attracting their experiences—they are what they think, and if they could only learn to think, they could get off this vibration." He looked into Aedan's eyes, his stare deep and power-full. "How am I doing so far?"

"Good!" Around his mouth Aedan had sprouted a moustache and beard made of sand, ice cream, and snot.

"So you're still with me, then?"

"Yep!"

"Right, listen hard—this is the most important part." Using his twig, he pointed to one of the stick people. "Now, look at this happy person. Today he had a run-in with his teacher, who lived for the most part in the branches given off by the lower vibration. Here she is—this is his teacher." He pointed to a clouded face underneath the squiggly line that represented the lower vibration. "Cutting a long story short, this happy person let some of his teacher's thoughts influence his. The negative energy that surrounded her got to him, and he slid into the branches of this lower vibration. So in effect, she dragged him down to her level…can you grasp what I'm saying, Aedan?"

"Yep—can I play now?"

"When I'm finished! Listen!" he said, sternly. "Your job on Earth is to try and help pull these people," he pointed to the miserable faces, "up to your level, up here in the good vibration." He tapped the twig in the sand. White Eagle was intense. "Do you understand?" He put his hand underneath Aedan's chin. "This is what your power is to be used for. You work, Aedan, for the good vibration. There are pow…influences beyond our contro…others, that won't have it any other way."

"What others?"

"It doesn't matter yet. We'll get to that another time. Right now, my only concern is that you grasp what I'm saying. Now, have you twigged it?" He held up the twig. "Get it? Twig, twigged it—"

"I get it!" Aedan rolled his eyes. "Corny."

"Drums, please!" White Eagle shouted. He mimicked the sound of a symbol and used the twig and his free hand to play drums on Aedan's head, then made his way under his armpits, to his belly, up his arms, and back underneath his armpits.

Aedan laughed loud and hard. "It tickles! You're ticklin'—stop! Stop it, White Eagle!'' he screamed.

"Tell me what your job is and I'll stop. But if you get it wrong…" He formed his hands into crabs at the ready. "Death by tickle!"

"I help people be happy," he yelled, excitedly.

White Eagle leaned slowly toward him. "And how do you do that, young man?" The tone of his voice had changed to that of an evil old wizard.

"With my power."

"But how with your power?" He kept the wizard tone and his

hands remained in tickle position.

Aedan pointed to the diagram. "I drag them from here to here!" he answered, with a nervous chuckle. He didn't trust White Eagle one bit!

White Eagle looked around. Maggie was on her way over. "Well, I wouldn't say 'drag' exactly; they have to come willingly—but very good, very good." He knew it had sunk in. "By golly, I think you've got it!" He attacked Aedan again, tickling him unmercifully.

"White Eagle, you promised! Stop it! No! Stop it! You're gonna make me wee me pants—stop it!" he begged, between hysterical peals of laughter.

"It's a con! I break my promises to little boys because I'm really a nasty old wizard—"

"Who are you talking to?" a girl about eight years old asked Aedan.

White Eagle backed off. Aedan was flat on his back covered in sand. He stood up quick, like a soldier caught napping on guard duty, and dusted himself off. "My friend," he said, with a don't-you-know-that expression on his face.

White Eagle was about to walk over to Maggie but stopped and put his mouth to Aedan's ear. "Oooo," he teased. "A girlfriend!"

Embarrassed, "No, it's not!" Aedan shot back, seemingly talking to thin air.

"I've got one of them," she said. "My parents think I imagine her."

"I wish I imagined him sometimes!" Aedan retorted.

White Eagle made himself visible to the little girl, being as she'd mentioned having one of them! "Err, excuse me, young man, don't be so cheeky. What's her name? Don't you think you should introduce yourselves?"

She smiled at Aedan. "I like him, he's nice!"

"Come on, let's play on the swings for a bit." Aedan looked back at White Eagle. "Stop testing me—"

Maggie ran over to them realizing the two had finished their talk. "Good God, White Eagle, look at the bloody state of him!" She gripped Aedan's chin, pulled her handkerchief from under her sleeve, and in an effort to remove the dried snot, sand, and ice-cream she rubbed at his face like a navvy sanding down a piece of hardwood. "It's all over his bloody shirt and the lot. By Jesus, I can't leave you in charge for a minute!" She spat, not very ladylike, into the hanky. "You'll have spoilt his tea—"

"Mam, you're hurting me." Aedan struggled to break free from Maggie's iron grip.

"Let up, Maggie, you're going to have the skin off his face," White Eagle cut in. "He looks like a damn tomato!"

She shot back at White Eagle, "Give over!" Then to Aedan, "Don't be so bloody soft!"

"Mam, I'll wash it when I get home. I want to play on the swings with Hilary." He wrestled his way out of Maggie's clutches, and turned to his new friend. "Quick! Let's go!" he shouted. The two of them legged it towards the swings as fast as they could.

"Aedan, get back here this minute!"

"No!"

"Aedan! Do as you're bloody-well told or it'll be bed straight after tea—"

"Give him a break, Maggie. He's had a hell of a day for a seven-year-old!"

She looked at White Eagle. "Changed your tune, haven't you?"

"He was inconsolable so I gave him healing. We had a good talk, but right now I think it would be a good idea to let him play and enjoy the sunshine before it goes down. It wouldn't do you any harm either."

"I've to shop, prepare tea, and get him to bed. School in the morn—"

"Oh, it doesn't matter about preparations! Besides, there'll be more chance of him sleeping if he runs off some of that energy."

"Will he be alright?" Maggie was almost scared to ask. "What did you say to him?"

"Oh, you know: things like how easy it is for us to slip into the lower energy now and again, and what his purpose is and whatnot. I tried not to get too heavy." He winked at Maggie. "He got it! Smart boy."

Her voice trembled. "White Eagle, if I lost him." She felt her throat constrict. "I can't bear to think—" She broke off.

"Then don't."

"But what if he doesn't learn, and loses control again like he did today, only next time it's worse?" She sounded frantic, her words hurried. "I mean, we're all fiery when we're young. We don't mellow until we get older. It's bound to happen again while he's growing up. It could be over a girl, football, anything! He'll have his challenges like any other young person. How can he not have?"

Without touching, White Eagle used both his hands to trace the outline of her body. "He'll be fine. He has a lot of support. And like I said, he isn't expected to live like a monk— Bloody hell! We need to do a bit of welding in your energy field!" He put a hand on her solar plexus and continued talking. "It's all about intention. Today his intention was to hurt, but it was also to protect, so a balance was struck. This is why the result turned out for the better. His need to protect you spoke to Sister Devlin's soul—which, in case we forget, is the power here. Her soul forgave him. His need to hurt her spoke to his own soul, which weakened his spirit—not his soul. Speaking generally, the soul will always be giving off light somewhere, even though it may be buried underneath layers of crap! Believe it or not, he and Sister Devlin have done each other a huge favour. They've shown each other the power of love and forgiveness today."

"So I don't need to worry about it, then?"

"No. Aedan is inherently good like the rest of us." White Eagle closed his eyes as if listening to something. "Got to go!"

"What about Sister Devlin? Do you think it would be better if he moved to a different class?"

"I doubt it! Anyway, this was an experience they would have set up between themselves somewhere along the line. Sometimes those we deem our enemies are, in fact, our best friends."

"How can that be?" she asked, puzzled.

"Our enemies offer us our biggest challenges. If we can't find it in ourselves to forgive or to at least compromise, then they become the biggest obstacle in our quest for spiritual growth." He searched for words. "In releasing our so-called enemy, we capture the essence of the creator. Our soul gives a part of itself to our spirit, and our spirit gets a taste of what true power is all about—soul power, a power that can literally move mountains. "You know all this!"

She made her way over to where Aedan and Hilary were playing. "Ten minutes, sweetheart."

She lay down in the grass, stretched, and yawned. Within a few minutes, she was back in Ireland, back in David's bed. God, she missed sex. She'd not had it since losing him. Time was passing by and taking her prime with it. She was only thirty. Did she have to live like a nun for the rest of her bloody life? She didn't want commitment. No permanent fixtures, thank you very much! She'd never replace David, but that need for physical contact, even a hug now and again… Oh, give over! Who was she trying to kid? She didn't have to fool herself. She got all the hugs she needed from Aedan. She wanted sex! Good, hot, physical sex—*David was on top of her thrusting away hard and fast. She wrapped her legs around his back, dug her hands into his backside, and rocked him harder.* The heat speared her from belly to groin. She felt her genitals tingle, her nipples go erect. A picture formed in her mind—she saw herself bare-breasted, no inhibitions, arms outstretched to the sky, on top of NeilA screaming out his name—Maggie went rigid, and jumped up from the grass. "Aedan, sweetheart, we'd better go. I've still got a bit of shopping to do."

He left Hilary with her mother and ran over, panting. "I know about Charlie. He met White Eagle today, didn't he? He's a bit scared but he'll get over it!"

She smiled. "Yes, he's fine and dandy! Did White Eagle tell you?"

"No!" He answered nonchalantly without an explanation.

She took his hand. She was used to him knowing things. She liked to think he'd got it from her.

29.

Catlow's was small and dark, and packed with every conceivable item you could want. The shelves seemed to burst with tins, perishables, soap, disinfectant, candles, tea towels, aspirins, and creams—some of them Maggie's—for every ailment. It was a post office, newsagents, chemist, and grocery store all rolled into one. More often than not, music could be heard in the background from a small radio that kept the village abreast of what was going on with the rest of the world. The strong smell of baked goods, polish, and firelighters hit you as soon as you walked through the door. Maggie quite liked it.

Cyril Catlow was either behind the counter or stocking shelves. If he wasn't visible, his strong Derbyshire accent could be heard instead. "Won't be a minute," he'd call out, and proceed to finish whatever it was he was doing before attending to a customer. Life was slow in this part of the world. He was a tall, painfully thin man with a mass of wiry ginger hair and hollowed-out features covered in freckles. The few teeth he had were brown and those in the bottom row had visible holes eating away at them; but he was a gentleman in every sense of the word, with a kind nature and a good humour. His wife, Ann, was quite attractive compared to him, but it was obvious to Maggie what she saw in him.

Aedan pulled at her arm. "Mam, can I have something from the penny tray—no!—chocolate buttons, chocolate buttons!?"

"Stop pestering, I'm not made of bloody money! Anyway, you've just had ice cream; you won't eat your tea!"

"For after me tea, then—"

"We'll see!"

"What we having for tea?"

"I've not had time to prepare anything. Any ideas?"

"Egg and chips," he answered without hesitation.

Just like his dad! Maggie never failed to catch her breath at some of the similarities between David and Aedan. "D'ya fancy some ham to go with it?"

"Ham!" he said, startled. "I thought we had no money?"

"Shh, Aedan! Don't be telling the world and its cat our affairs. We can run to a couple slices of ham!"

"And chocolate buttons?"

She rolled her eyes. "Go on, then!"

She put a few groceries—eggs, bread, and a packet of butter—down on the thick wooden counter, which had warped in the middle with age. "Give me a quarter of ham, please, Cyril, and a couple of scoops of them chocolate buttons."

"Right you are, Maggie." He lifted the lump of pink meat from behind the glass, banged it in the meat cutter, and sliced her a few thin pieces. "Ham and eggs tonight?" The doorbell tinkled behind her.

"Yes, something quick and easy—"

"A bit like yerself!" The door slammed shut behind Olive Reids.

She turned around. "Olive, twice in one day." Maggie turned back to Cyril, raised her eyebrows, and said, "Lucky me" under her breath.

Olive lumbered around the store, straining to listen in on their conversation. A few other neighbours, Edith Cullen and June Cookson, were waiting in line. The threat of war hung in the air like a lead weight but made for some lively discussion: Hitler was a madman who wanted to take over the world and it looked like Poland would be one of his first stops before he invaded Britain and the rest of Europe.

Cyril noticed the concerned look on Aedan's face. He cleared his throat. "Uh, hmm, let's not forget the young lad here," he said, winking at the women. "No need to worry him. Besides, you never know, whole thing could blow over before it even starts."

"And pigs might fly!" Olive butted in. "Good job we've got

Churchill to sort the Nazi bleeders out!"

Aedan looked up at Maggie, puzzled. "What's a Nazi bleeder?"

Cyril stretched over the counter and ruffled Aedan's hair. "Nothing you need to worry about, son."

"It's not a very nice name used to describe a soldier from Germany!" Maggie gave Olive a dirty look. "Some of them just babies, young, probably terrified."

"Are we going to war, Mam?"

She felt it was better to prepare him than try to hide it. "It's likely," she sighed. "Probably any day now...but I don't want you worrying about it. You've seen the shelters being built, haven't you?" He nodded. "That's where we hide when the sirens go off. They'll keep us safe until the bombers have gone. Apart from that, we just carry on as normal." She smiled reassuringly. "Besides, our shelters probably won't be needed. The bombers usually attack the bigger cities." She squinted playfully. "They don't even know about us!" She stooped forward and kissed him on the cheek. "We'll be fine," she whispered.

"Would you listen to her," Olive laughed sarcastically. "Don't talk wet! We'll be rationed, bombed—"

"Keep it down, Olive! Boy doesn't need to hear it!" June piped up.

Olive glared at Maggie. "Well, she makes me laugh, standing there all high and mighty when there's all sorts going on behind her front door!"

Aedan was baffled. "What's going on behind our front door, Mam?"

Maggie's lips twitched. She wanted to grab Olive by the throat and ram her head down Cyril's mop bucket. "Watch what you say in front of my son," she said, fist clenched, chest heaving.

Olive looked at the other women in the shop. "Keep an eye on your men, ladies." She looked back at Maggie slyly. "Not fussy, this one. Her best friend's husband was there for over an hour this aft'. Seems she has a problem with her knickers. They won't stay up!" Olive cackled and fished through her bag for a cigarette.

Aedan was baffled. "What do you mean? Me mam's knickers always stay up—"

Maggie's head spun around toward Olive. "Be quiet!" She stormed over, shoved her face into Olive's, and began to threaten, "Shut your filthy…," but she backed off. She wouldn't stoop to the woman's level, especially in front of Aedan.

Olive felt Maggie's spittle attack her face like small hailstones. "I'm filthy, huh! That's a joke coming from the local bike—"

Cyril came from around his counter, his demeanour calm. "I won't have this kind of talk in my store, Olive, and in front of the lad here. You should be ashamed of yourself—get out!" He pointed to the door. "Off you go! Out! Out!" He flipped his hand twice in dismissal.

Hands on hips, Olive looked Cyril up and down. "Don't speak to me like that, Catlow, or my Jim'll come down here and paste your arse all over this shit hole."

Maggie didn't want Cyril getting a hiding from Olive's lump of a husband on her account. "It's alright, Cyril, we were leaving anyway. Come on, Aedan." She grabbed his hand.

Aedan disliked Olive and never made any attempt to hide the fact. He was sick to death of her upsetting his mam. He yanked his hand free from Maggie's. His eyes dug into Olive. "We don't have to run from her, Mam." The energy gathering in his belly gave off small, pleasant waves of heat that travelled throughout his body. He could feel the main mass of it that had collected at his heart start to spurt and strike, like forks of lightning.

Olive was vicious. "That's right, you dirty hoar, run away! I bet you can't wait for war to break out, all them soldiers looking for a poke, but at least then our men'll get some peace. Then again, a battalion won't be enough for—"

The sudden twang of elastic slapping against flesh could be heard throughout the store. Olive let out an almighty scream. Cyril, Maggie, June, and Edith looked up, down, and behind themselves, then at each other, with baffled expressions on their faces.

What the hell's up with her? I hope she's not spotted that damn mouse. Size of her gob, news'll travel quicker than wildfire. Cyril's concern rested purely with his business.

Aedan was overcome with childish laughter. "Look! Olive's big white holey knickers!" He pointed to Olive's massive drawers that lay in a heap around her ankles. Worse for weather, they'd certainly seen better days.

"AEDAN!" Her face tight, Maggie mouthed him to stop laughing. All eyes on Olive, everybody, apart from Aedan, did their best not to laugh as she stooped down to pull up her underwear.

"That's the funniest thing I've ever seen!" Aedan screamed, as a red-faced Olive clung onto her skirts in an effort to stop her drawers from dropping around her ankles again.

Cyril didn't know what to do. Red-faced, he passed Olive a roll of elastic, whispered something to his wife who had surfaced to see what all the fuss was about and then beckoned Olive through to their private living area.

As she scuttled past Maggie and the other women, the sound of elastic slapping flesh was heard again, and forgetting all about her loose drawers, a mortified Olive automatically brought her arms up to her huge breasts, which had suddenly dropped down and landed on her stomach. She felt her drawers start to slide yet again and crossed her legs and grabbed them with one hand. Her other arm remained firmly across her chest.

Cottoning on to what was happening, Maggie wheeled around and fired Aedan a warning glance. He knew her every word even though she never opened her mouth! But he didn't care. He'd pulled off one hell of a trick on big Olive! He started to sing, "Olive's holier than thou knickers, Olive's holier than thou knickers," over and over again.

Mortified, Maggie looked at her son. *I'll kill him.* "AEDAN! IF YOU DON'T QUIET DOWN, I'LL, I'LL..." She didn't know what she'd do to shut him up. "...EAT THESE!" she said, spotting the chocolate buttons and holding them up. *Jesus! It wasn't an hour passed since his last rollicking over Sister Devlin!*

Cocky, he shouted at Olive, "Leave me mam alone, or I'll tell the whole school about your horrible knick—"

"AEDAN! Learn when to keep your mouth shut!" Maggie grabbed

his arm and marched him out of the shop. Exasperated, she threw a hand in the air. "Ahh!" she screamed. "I can't believe you did that, not two minutes since your last talking-to! Why did you…what were you thinking? Go home!" She shoved the few groceries into him. "I'll be there in a few minutes."

Aedan was exasperated. "Why are you mad? It shut her fat arse up—"

She lifted her chin and her index finger and fired him a look. "Aedan, I'm warning you, any more of this and you'll be in bed as soon as I get in. Now do as you're bloody told for once!"

He shook his head in frustration. Like an old man, he said, "I don't know, there's no pleasing you at times—"

She put her hands on his shoulders and gripped hard. "GET YOUR BACKSIDE HOME!"

He about-turned and high-tailed it up the street. Maggie drew back her arm, ready to whack his bottom with all her might but he was too quick for her. He thrust his pelvis forward and avoided contact. When he heard the whoosh of thin air soar past Maggie's hand, he looked at her, grinned, and did the sign of the cross. "Holy Father, thank you for making my mother miss my backsiiiiiide…" He sang the words like a Gregorian chant.

Patience at an all-time low, Maggie ran at him. "I'll give you Holy Father, you cheeky little sod!"

But he was already halfway up the street, running backwards, singing the Gregorian chant. "Holy Father, I'm so grateful that my mother can't run as fast as meheeeee…"

The thoughts in her head were driving her mad. She followed Aedan home at a slow pace. An uneasy feeling settled over her. She closed her eyes and shifted her conscious mind to a state where it was literally split in half. Half of it was aware of her physical surroundings while the other half reached out and dipped into the spirit world.

Maggie had the knack of multi-consciousness down to a fine art, but in general she only used it to communicate with the spirit world. She didn't care to contact any other realm of existence, mainly because she still tried to block Aedan's lineage from her mind. The thought of NeilA being some kind of weird alien father to her son terrified her.

White Eagle, have you got a minute? It didn't take long for him to appear in her mind's eye. "I suppose you know what's happened," she stated.

"Err…no."

She told him the full story as she made her way home. He tried to hold the serious look on his face but failed miserably. "You have to admire his reasoning—"

"I don't know what to think, and don't let him know that you think it's funny!" She was anything but amused.

"Olive insinuated that you have a problem keeping your drawers up so he dropped hers—"

"Oh, Jesus! Is that why he thought that one up?"

"Don't tell me you didn't get that!"

Mortified, "I hope he doesn't believe the tripe she comes out with—"

"Give over, Maggie! He won't understand what she meant by it. He'll have taken it literally! Is Aedan's trick with Olive the reason you wanted to talk to me?"

"Yes, yes. Well, in a sense," she said, irritated. "I'm worried." She paused, a confused look on her face. "How come you turned up at his school, yet you didn't have a clue what was going on here?"

"Give me a break, Maggie! I'm not assigned to Aedan's every mood and whim! He has to call on me just like you do. I turned up at the school because…" He sighed heavily. "Look, before he was born, I met with the elders to discuss intervention. I mean, he has a right to free will just like the rest of us. It would be an abysmal misuse of my position to intrude on his every thought, his every action—even if it were possible, which it's not. And," he emphasised, "believe it or not, I have other things to do. So it was decided long ago that only if Aedan abused his power by using it with intention to do harm would I be notified."

"Notified by whom?"

"NeilA," he answered flatly, deciding to dig at her memory.

"Who?"

"You know who I'm talking about. Why deny it? Are you still that frightened?"

She ignored the comment. "So you don't consider what he did to Olive an abuse of his power?"

"In some respects…I mean, it wasn't very nice but Olive isn't very nice, and her intention was to hurt you, so once again Aedan's protective instinct went on full alert. This is to be admired because it comes from a deep and unconditional love for his mother."

"So because he used it to block Olive's intention to do harm, it's okay?"

"Well, I wouldn't say it's okay, but it did kind of balance things out. That, along with the fact that his *intention* wasn't to hurt her or cause harm is another reason I wouldn't have been notified. His main focus was to shut her up so that she'd leave you alone—and he knew nobody could trace her unfortunate position back to him, so he exercised discretion…though not very subtle. But even so, this is to be commended, along with his love for you."

Maggie still looked bewildered. "I'm not getting it and I need to clear it up. He can use his power in circumstances that will enable him to protect himself and the ones he loves…kind of like a self-defence against the Olives of the world?"

"Yes…," White Eagle hunted for a way to explain it, "…he can, but there are different degrees of how and when. If he came face to face with Evolus or one of his sidekicks, then it's no holds barred! But the Olives and the Sister Devlins of the world are at a disadvantage against his power. As he matures he'll become more and more subtle with his teachings—oh yes! Let's not forget that anyone with power like his is here to teach as well as protect—neither Sister Devlin nor Olive posed a threat to him. They are misguided individuals trying their best to get by." He paused; both his voice and expression were sinister when he looked into Maggie's eyes. "But we both know that there are those who will threaten him, who will put him in a position of danger. His survival instinct will kick in naturally. Remember, his purpose is to show people the difference between light and dark. There are many ways in which to do this." He cocked his head over to the side. "Not all of them are nice. Love isn't always about nice! The light can be so bright that it's harsh!"

She went into telepathy, "So now you're saying it's okay not to be nice, if it helps those concerned?" She nodded at one of her neighbours.

"In some respects, but we try to avoid unnatural fear. Of course, a degree of discipline is necessary in certain circumstances, but on the whole we do not suggest the use of fear-based teachings or actions. Natural fear— an inbuilt defence mechanism—is a different matter altogether."

Maggie stopped, and puffed her cheeks up. "Oh, here we go again with your twaddle! Unnatural fear, natural fear, what's the difference?"

White Eagle laughed. "Twaddle! What a great word. I'm guessing from the vibration it means poppycock, or something similar." He screwed up his face, "Hmm, I still prefer 'poppycock'! Poppycock, poppycock—"

"Answer my question, please. I've not even got supper on yet!" She felt irritable. Her nerves were getting the better of her.

"Well, well! We are testy today. I suggest you lighten up a bit— where was I?"

She rolled her eyes. "The difference between unnatural and natural fear," she said, shaking her head. Sometimes White Eagle was more work than Aedan!

"Oh, yes…what many describe as fear is natural fear. It will stop an individual from bowling head-on into something they're not ready for. You know, that voice, that feeling that tells you something isn't right. Natural fear sets off the instincts. It is an inbuilt protection. You can ignore it, go against your instincts if you want to, but the warning signs will always be there whether you listen to them or not. If your life is threatened, for example, natural fear will let you know that you're in danger. It will kick in your survival instinct. Unnatural fear, on the other hand, is put there by outside influences: government, society, religion, science, that sort of thing. His stint with Sister Devlin is another example. He instilled that fear into her. If we hadn't got involved and told him to sort it out, she could have gone off the rails and ended up in a psychiatric ward. Olive, on the other hand, will get over it." He laughed. "Sure, she'll be embarrassed, probably send her husband to buy the groceries for a while—"

"But how has that helped her?"

"Well, the longer Olive's attack on you continued, the more vicious it would have become. She would have done untold damage to herself by upsetting her own spirit/energy/vibration, whatever label we wish to give to it, via her own words and intention. When the spirit is upset, all kinds of problems can arise and, of course, such cruelty keeps her tied to the lower energy system. Aedan stopped her in her tracks; he stopped her from hurting herself further. He made her think, something she rarely stops to do—"

Maggie grimaced. "Olive—think? That'll be the day!"

"She's a way to go yet, but at least today's events will have registered at some level of her being. The position that she wanted to put you in backfired on her. She tasted isolation, embarrassment, being bullied. Aedan did his job today. Amongst other things, he helped her to realise that what you give out, you get back tenfold."

"How? All I can see is the one-sided predicament she was in."

"No, no, anything but one-sided. When Olive was giving it out, the rest of you in the store tried to shut her up. Nobody was impressed by her bullying. By the sound of it, it took all of Cyril's restraint not to lift her by the skirts and throw her out of his shop headfirst. Nevertheless, she could still feel his hostility and the resentment from the rest of you, so who was the real victim? And then when she lost her undergarments, we can say she was definitely in the position of victim. Not only did she shrink physically before your eyes, her spirit curled up. Have you ever seen Olive that deflated?"

"Well, she is deflated if we want to get to the crux of it."

"That's true. But the point I'm trying to make is this. When she was…err, let's say, humbled, by her position, the rest of you felt for her. Cyril handed her the elastic, you mouthed Aedan to stop laughing, and the other two ladies helped her through to the living quarters with Cyril's wife, all hostility gone. She put it out that she needed help and she got it. The kindness she was shown affected her much more than hostility ever could."

"Well, I guess I should make a move. I've yet to explain the Sister Devlin scenario to the elders." Their connection started to fade. For Maggie it was like tuning a radio but not quite hitting the station.

She stopped at her front gate. "You mean they don't know? But I thought—"

"Oh, they know what transpired but they're more interested in the reasons why he did what he did, how we handled it, whether or not I believe Aedan to be a threat. And I'm sure they'll ask my opinion on the outcome…you know love, forgiveness, balance, and the rest of it." He sensed her dismay. "Look, I'm sure it will all work out fine."

Anxiously Maggie asked, "White Eagle, before you go: Aedan isn't in any more trouble, then?"

He paused, wondering how he could put her mind at rest. "Right, let's get one thing cleared up. Aedan isn't expected to live like some holy recluse! Heartfelt intention is what we're looking at, not the he said-she said-you did-they didn't trivialities that mean nothing in the grand scheme of things. Aedan's intention wasn't to hurt Olive. It was a childish prank. His behavior towards Sister Devlin on the other hand, was just the opposite. He could have caused untold misery for her, and set off a chain of reactions for the rest of us—Galaxias, me, you; the Catholic Church could have got involved. If Sister Devlin had gone off the rails, the Church would have definitely asked questions of the children in the classroom, and who knows what they might have unearthed? We don't want anyone getting wind of Aedan, especially those who are not ready for him."

"So what are you saying I should do?"

"I'm not saying you should do anything. You're a good mother. Carry on as you are."

"But I can't bear to lose him. What if they—"

"Maggie, Maggie, stop! If you're talking about NeilA," he stressed the name, "like me, he isn't assigned to Aedan's every thought or action. This wouldn't be fair to the child. He looks in on Aedan from time to time, that much is true, but he will only interfere in Aedan's behaviour should he be tempted by the lower energy system. This is an automatic response. NeilA's vibration is pure, and as his soul-split Aedan shares his frequency. Should a blip occur, NeilA will be affected."

She dug through her pockets for a key, then remembered she'd given it to Aedan. "A blip?"

"Yes, you know: a dip, a drop." *Damn! How to explain it?* "We're only interested in stopping such power from ending up with the more…primal legions, so to speak. Mischief, pranks, and backchat don't come into that category."

Maggie breathed a long, weary sigh of relief. "Oh, thank God!" She buried her face in her hands then wiped the tears from her eyes.

White Eagle smiled. "Aedan is a good boy. Sister Devlin was a blip. She was there to teach *him* a lesson." He started to fade out but then faded in again. "Freedom of choice is ultimate. We *feel* the difference between what is labelled good or evil, and that will depend on individual perception. Nobody is forced one way or the other. But all experience is *felt* at heart level…karma is instant."

30.

The captain looked at the mountain of paperwork on his desk and thought about starting it. He picked up several pieces, read the first few lines of each, then threw them down impatiently. "Sod it!" he said, just as the wind screamed louder and hurled a heavy spurt of rain at the misty old windows.

The storm hadn't let up all day. It was mid afternoon but the sky was almost black due to the heavy clouds. He turned on the small lamp on his desk without looking at it, his eyes focused on the rain battering the windows. "Damn miserable weather!" The windows rattled harder, as if in agreement.

His pipe rested on top of a silver lighter by the telephone. He picked it up, put it in his mouth, flipped the lighter, and puffed away. It didn't take long to fill the small room with smoke and the strong aroma of leafy tobacco. He sat there for a few minutes with the pipe dangling from the corner of his mouth and both hands behind his head, listening to the wind and rain, and the faint orders from the sergeant outside putting the men through their paces. The paperwork was still there, irritating the hell out of him! He'd have to make a dent in it soon. He shoved it all together into a neat pile, and stuffed it into the wire basket that was already overloaded. "Out of sight, out of mind! What a load of baloney that is!"

He removed the pipe from his mouth, snuffed it out with his thumb, and left it upside-down in the ashtray. He got up, walked to the window, and wiped an eyehole with his fingertips. "No wonder the poor blighters look miserable; it's teemed down on them all day!"

He closed his eyes, sighed heavily, and massaged his temples using circular movements. The pain in his head had nagged away since early morning. He wasn't sure if it was the heavy smell of pipe tobacco or the dismal day that had brought the headache on. *She'd be able to get rid of it,* he thought, looking around the small, cluttered space. The office was so untidy, and stank most of the time. *I should do something about this place. Be good to have a day away from it.* His mood lightened. He was looking forward to the following day in Glossop town, meeting the people and enjoying some of the local traditions and good cheer. Everybody made such a fuss of the lads, especially the young children. The excitement on their faces put joy in the hearts of men. *God knows we need it.* In a mirror that hung on the opposite wall, he saw himself smile. It was a genuine smile. A rarity these days, but it still had an air of sadness about it.

He walked to the door and grabbed his cap and thick woollen overcoat off the hook screwed into the back of it. He dressed in a hurry, took a deep breath in readiness for the assault from the elements, and opened the door. The vicious wind attacked, nearly wrenching the door from his hand. It howled like some angry, legendary creature, "Defy us and suffer! Death is an escape route we don't allow! You cannot win!" A huge figure cloaked in black stretched abnormally from horseback and pushed its face into his. The face was misty yet lit, it seemed, with the light from a thousand lamps. The mighty black steed was just as horrific, with red eyes and a piercing neigh—terrified, the captain wrestled against the force of the wind, desperate to slam the door on the evil creatures. With a final push, he succeeded in shutting out the howling storm and the horrors it protected.

The horse reared on its back legs, turned, and sped off into the wind. The captain could no longer see it but he could hear its great, thundering hooves and the rasping screams from its rider as they faded into the distance.

He stood completely still for a few moments, back against the door. The heavy rise and fall of his chest accompanied the sound of his breath—the sound of the wind. It had triggered something that was buried in his depths. *Perhaps the wind is some kind of powerful creature? What if it is a living power…a monster of some description controlled by a dark force? But there are times when it's gentle, loving even?* He shook his head. *"You're the wind,"* a voice invaded his musings. Some of the captain's thoughts, such as the recurring dream about the colossal, golden planet he'd been having lately, made him question his own sanity. *"You have nothing to fear from the dark ones. You're one of us!"* The voice was like a melody in his head. *"GALAXIAS!"*

Frenzied, the captain shot around. A gentle face, kind of misty and brown with many lines and marks, smiled back at him. It had thin, wispy hair that seemed to flow around it yet it appeared to be ingrained in the door. He collapsed back in fear but somehow managed to stay on his feet. "NO, I'M NOT!" he screamed out. "LEAVE ME ALONE! YOU'RE NOT REAL!" But when he looked at the door again, the face had gone. *It was just the markings in the wood!?* He breathed a sigh of relief. He would have to see the doctor about his nerves, especially given his position. *Can't have a lunatic at the head of an army. The men are my responsibility.*

He yanked the door open as if his life depended on it and ran across the yard, head down, grasping his collar. By the time he got to his men he was as wet as they were.

Hands behind his back, he walked slowly. He took the time to look at the young faces, rain dripping off their noses and chins, and wondered how many of them would make it back to their families before they were blown away, their lives cut short, and for what? All because some madman wanted to take over the world. *Why did we give these people airtime? If somebody would just take him out, a lot of innocent lives would be saved. Why do those closest to him take any notice of the lunatic? Surely there must be someone on his team* with half a brain that could get rid of him?

He saluted. "At ease, men!" The captain turned to his sergeant and ordered, "Take the rest of the day off. Go into town, down a few. God knows we could all do with cheering up."

The sergeant saluted. "Sir, thank you, sir!" He looked at his men. "Meet you down the pub in about an hour."

The men cheered loudly and threw their berets in the air. Forgetting all about the rain, they took off in different directions. The captain walked to his quarters, a sad smile on his face. Thank God his son wasn't old enough to join up.

Once inside, he picked up the phone. He couldn't put the hallucinations off any longer. He'd have to phone the medic—get some pills or something! They'd probably make him go on sick leave.

He stood and pondered for a while. Though he'd been having the hallucinations for a few years, they came only now and then. He could handle them, couldn't he? It's just nerves! He put the phone down. *No! I'll go on record as a mental case. We're all bound to feel a bit edgy—we're at war for God's sake! Get a grip on yourself!*

31.

If they weren't with Charlie or at Farmer Bailey's farm, Aedan and Derrick spent their weekends exploring the Peak District in the Derbyshire hills around Glossop. They'd got to know the vast, rugged moorland and its moods very well. In the winter it was often wild and desolate, dangerous and intimidating. Within minutes, the sky would turn black, the clouds would roll, and forks of lightning would skip across the top of the hills on the hunt for another victim. They usually found one.

In their darkness the moors were at their most alluring. The thunder, the lightning, the heavy rainfall—all touched something deep inside. Was it our own dark, our own madness? Did it make us realise how lucky we were to be able to control it? Or at least think we could control it? Or was it the power that nature represented? The nature we're all a part of?

A lone stranger didn't stand a chance against such dark beauty. The moorland befuddled the mind. Just when a lost soul thought he was on the right path he'd look behind and realise he'd taken the wrong one…or was it the same path with a million different aspects of itself?

But for a few months of the year at least, the peaks gave Aedan and Derrick green hills and sparkling rivers, rocks and hidden caves bordered by woodlands that were filled with birdsong and a diverse mix of trees, shrubs, and wildlife. The sweet scents of hawkweeds, thyme, and spear thistle were often camouflaged by the stronger smell of horses and cattle that were scattered around the neighbouring farms.

347

The heather moorland and the lush valleys were everything one imagined in a strange and magical land. When the boys felt tired, they'd sit for five minutes and lose themselves in the magnificent views. Violets, blues, greens, golds, and reds would fade off in the distance until sky and land merged into one.

After a good breakfast, and with a good packed lunch made up of cheese sandwiches, a piece of fruit, and a slab of home-baked cake, the two would remain outdoors until the sun went down. They had no thoughts of the war that raged everywhere in the British Isles except for Glossop, unless the bombers flying overhead roared at them to take cover.

"BOMBERS!" they'd shout as they dived into some rocky crevice or cave. "Da, da, da, da, da, da, da, da!" They'd form their arms into a machine gun, and fire bullets from their mouths.

Imaginations running wild, they were happy climbing the crags, playing soldiers, and catching tadpoles from the marshy bogs that were splattered all around. Covered in mud, the boys would giggle at the tadpoles wriggling about in their hands. When all the water had finally trickled through their fingers they would put the tadpoles back, catch a few more, and the cycle would begin again. They never did keep them even though they had old jam jars on standby. Said it was better to let them stay where they were—that way they'd have more chance of turning into frogs.

When they saw Charlie shaking his fist and looking pissed because he'd had to come looking for them—again!—they knew that they'd stayed out too late and would run as fast as they could towards him, saying how sorry they were, to which every time he'd reply that it's time one of them got a bloody watch because he's sick to the back teeth of having to come look for 'em!

For the tenth time that day, Aedan looked at his new watch, a birthday present from his mother the week before. But his favourite present was the cross she'd given him. He put his hand underneath his shirt collar and rubbed it gently between his thumb and index finger. His insides rippled with a funny sensation. His dad had bought it for his mam, then placed it around him when he was a baby. *'But your dad also wore it for a few days before giving it to me,'* she'd told him. He could feel the energy, his dad's energy, that lingered with the necklace. It was a piece of all three of them rolled into one, his mam had explained. *'That's what the three diamonds represent: me, you, and your dad.'* He'd treasure it forever.

It was a beautiful September day on the peak. A small wind asserted its power now and again, straining out an extra gust. The boys ran against it, arms wide, their heads held up to the sky until it gave up.

"Let's roly-poly down this hill," Derrick shouted.

They threw themselves onto their sides. Aedan grabbed Derrick's shoulder. "Wait, wait, I'll race you!" he said, excited. "First one to the stone wall is the winner. After three: one, two, three..." The pair rolled for their lives, unable to tell who'd hit the wall first.

"Ow, Jesus, my head!" Aedan sat up quickly and rubbed hard. "I'll end up with a lump."

"Will you be okay? Do you want to go home so your mam can put some of her stuff on it?"

"No, I'll be alright." He looked about, sidetracked by the sound of cheers coming from an abandoned farmhouse. "What's that noise?" The boys peeped over the wall. The noise was coming from an old barn about three hundred feet away.

"Can you hear that?" Aedan asked.

"The cheers?"

"No, that other noise."

Heads down, ears toward the barn. "It sounds like growling," Derrick whispered, concerned.

"What do you think is going on?" Aedan asked.

Derrick shrugged. "Don't know."

"Let's find out."

"What if we get caught?"

"We won't! We're spies on a special mission. We'll crawl to that old trough on our bellies, make sure no one's about," Aedan pointed to the back wall of the barn, "and then run behind that wall."

"Then what?"

"We'll stick to the side wall of the barn, sneak up to the doors, and take a look through the gap."

Derrick was panic-struck. "But what if someone sees us?"

"Run!" He narrowed his eyes. "You've not gone chicken, have you?"

Derrick tried to put on a brave face. "No!"

"Are you in or what?"

"I'm in…I suppose."

"Look! You wait here and stand guard. If you see me running, stay hidden behind this wall and scarper as fast as you can in the opposite direction—tell your dad."

"Right!" Derrick was flooded with relief.

Hidden in the long grass, Aedan wriggled down the hillside on his stomach. Once at the bottom, he crouched down, tiptoed over, and hid behind the trough. Just as he was about to run to the back wall of the barn, whistles, cheering, and shouts of "Go for the kill, rip its head off!" and various other such sentiments rang out to the pitiful yelps of a dog in pain. His instincts on over-time, Aedan knew there was something evil going on inside the building. Bypassing the back wall of the barn, he ran straight over to the old doors, both of which were barely hanging on, and peered through the gap.

What he saw inside punched a hole right through him. About fifty men jeered and shouted at two dogs, both covered in blood, going in for the kill.

Shocked, Aedan fell back and stumbled against the wall. Feeling the urge to throw up, he crouched down, put his head between his knees, and gasped for breath. *Get out of here!* But the horrific scene, which seconds ago had wrung a piece of energy right out of him, now only served to inflame his anger. Sister Devlin came to mind but soon left! "Bastards!" No matter what happened he'd have to get those poor dogs out of there.

He looked up and saw Derrick peep from behind the trough. "What are you doing?" he mouthed. Derrick ran over. "Are you okay?" He looked worried. "You've gone white. Don't you feel well?"

Aedan remained with his hands on his knees, breathing heavily. "I'll be alright. Just need to stop feelin' sick… Look, Derrick, stick with our plan and stay behind the wall. It's safer."

Derrick jumped at a sudden outburst of cheering. "Why?" He looked worried.

"The shitheads are fighting dogs so I'm going in to get them. If I don't hurry up, one of them will end up dead." His eyes filled with tears. "I can't let that happen."

Derrick was shocked. "How can you do anything about it? Whoever owns the dogs won't let you just waltz in there and take them. And what about the dogs? They'll rip you apart."

"They won't!" he said, a determined look on his face. "The owners won't come near me either."

Derrick had seen that look on Aedan's face many times. He knew that his mind was set, so there was no point trying to convince him otherwise. Besides, Aedan had pulled off some stunts in the past! But mad dogs?! "If you rescue the dogs, what are you gonna do with them? They'll be too dangerous to keep as pets."

"Dunno yet. The only thing on my mind right now is to stop their suffering."

Derrick looked through the gap in the doors. "I think we should leave it alo—" and did a double-take just like Aedan had done moments before. His face strained, he looked at his friend. "God! How can they enjoy that?" he said, through gritted teeth. "I wish I was big enough; I'd throw them in the pen, the bastards! How can they do that to animals?"

Aedan shook his head in disgust. "Apart from being savages, bets are going down." He looked at Derrick. "I thought it would knock you sideways like it did me."

"No! It's just made me mad. I was ready to run but now I just want to kill the bastards!"

"Right! Wait here and cover me then. Make sure you stay out of sight until it's safe."

Aedan slipped through the old doors, dropped to his belly, and slithered towards the pen in the middle of the barn. There were only a few seats at the front so most of the men stood, some with caps in hands, some smoking, and others swigging beer from bottles. The place reeked of urine and old blood and the floor was covered in straw which started to stick to Aedan's hair and clothes. He knew that the fights had been going on for a long time…but all that was about to change.

The men were so wrapped up in the violence that they didn't notice Aedan buried in the straw behind them. He stopped suddenly and took some deep breaths. He could see that both dogs were exhausted, in particular the Staffordshire bull terrier. If Aedan didn't get to him soon, he'd be dead without a doubt.

He weighed up the fence that surrounded the pen—a cheap wire thing about two feet high, held up by vulgar pieces of wood. He'd leg it as fast as he could, jump the fence, grab the dogs, and get out of there as soon as possible. He gave no thought as to how he'd pull it off. The only picture in his mind was of himself and Derrick walking out of there with both dogs in tow.

He looked back at Derrick's terrified expression one last time before focusing solely on the dogs. He took a few more deep breaths, his mind set on his mission. *This is it!* Suddenly, the whole scene went into slow motion. The men, their cheers, the barn—everything disappeared into the abyss of Aedan's mind. All he could see was the dogs. All he could hear was their pathetic whimpers. All he could feel was their pain. It was the strangest feeling; like he was outside of the situation in a different timeframe watching the goings on from afar, while at the same time being well and truly there.

1, 2, 3—like a flash of lightning, he jumped up, charged the crowd, ducked through legs, slammed through bodies. The men, too intent on the end of the fight, were used to the jostles and general roughing of the crowd. They never took their eyes off the dogs—it would be over any minute. The ones with their money on the pit bull were quids in.

The heartbreaking yelps coming from the Staffordshire spurred Aedan on. Derrick was right. He'd put these pieces of scum in the pen with the dogs and see how tough they were then!

By the time Aedan catapulted over the fence and made it into the centre of the pen covered in mud, straw, and an alarmed expression, he resembled a living scarecrow. The jeers and taunts turned into a stunned silence at the scary sight that had suddenly appeared in the middle of the pen with the dogs. When the men realised it was just a boy that had invaded their fight, they were furious. Heckles of "Get out of there, kid!" and "You've ruined the fight!" mixed with various profanities erupted.

But silence took over again as the two dogs stopped fighting each other and turned their attention on Aedan—his back to them, fear crawled up his spine like a lizard, and made the hairs on the back of his neck stand on end. The dogs were ready to pounce at any given second. Saliva dripped from their mouths through blood-covered teeth. Their snarls told Aedan that they were intent on killing something that day.

Aedan had no time to think. He spun around and faced the dogs. He waved his hand above them and visualised the force that infiltrated the universe pouring from it. "Down, down, calmmmm," he soothed. "Down, down, calmmmm." The sound of his voice was like the tinkle of a bell. "Down, down, calmmmm." The chant infiltrated the barn. The men, mesmerised, looked on. None of them uttered a word. "Down, down, calmmmm." Using both hands, he stroked the air above and around the dogs, manipulating their energy fields—White Eagle had taught him loads of tricks with the force—*Thank God!*

"Down, down, calmmmm." His voice got more commanding as the chant gained in strength. "Down, down, calmmmm. Down, down, calmmm. Down, down, calm." His emphasis on the word "calm" got shorter as the dogs relaxed. "Down, down, calm." He pressed his palms slowly towards the ground, crouched down slowly to their level. "Down, down."

The dogs sat, gently pushed by the unseen force. He looked into their eyes, normally a sign to fight. But all the dogs felt was love, compassion, and peace; and after suffering nothing but fear and brutality since the day they were born, they weren't about to give it up. "Lie down. Rest."

The dogs flopped down, tongues out. Their stomachs pumped fast and hard but their cries and pain had ceased. The pandemonium of the past half hour turned into an atmosphere of silent questioning. The men couldn't believe what their own eyes had just shown them; they thought it was some kind of weird trick the boy had pulled off.

Derrick walked slowly towards the pen, awestruck. He knew there was something different about his friend…there was some sort of odd thing going on with him.

"GET HIM OUTTA THERE!" one of the men yelled, breaking the silence.

"FINISH THE FIGHT OR GIVE ME MY FUCKIN' MONEY BACK!" another jeered, setting off the rest of the crowd.

The owner of the pit bull, Dick Spencer—or Spence, as he was known—jumped into the pen, with a crude-looking stick with a wire loop at the end of it in his hand. "Get the fuck outta here boy, or I'll have Grip here rip your gizzard out."

Grip jumped up. The only gizzard he wanted belonged to the man he hated. Fur up, teeth itching to get stuck in, Grip charged at his owner. Palm towards the dog, "NO! SIT!" Aedan ordered. The dog immediately heeled.

Spence shot Aedan an agitated look, and ran a hand through his dark, greased-back hair. "Look lad, you've got no right being here. Now piss off!" His twisted features revealed a gold tooth on the right side of his upper row.

Grip stood up slowly, his growls coming from way down in his belly. Spence looked down at the dog, lunged with the pole, and wrapped the loop firmly around the dog's neck. "Don't fucking growl at me, you piece of shit. Finish the fucking fight or I'll kick you from here to—"

Still crouched, Aedan got up slowly. His face white with fury, he stared Spence down. "Let him go," he whispered. His lips, drained of colour, had set into a thin line across his face, almost to the point of disappearing.

Grip struggled against the pole but was helpless. Spence hung onto the dog and backed him into a corner. His eyes bulged with rage,

"STOP YOUR DAMN GROWLING!"

Aedan grabbed the pole. "Let him go or you'll regret it," he whispered, menacingly.

Spence didn't know what it was about the kid. He'd never been scared of anyone in his life, but there was something eerie about him. Even so he was just a kid. He wasn't about to be cowed by the little bastard! "You're trying my patience," he spat. "Let go of the pole and fuck off outta' here, or I'll serve you up as dog meat."

Aedan felt his fury shift into a higher gear. He wanted to kill the bastard! But he kept it back. "Look, mister, let me keep the dogs. I'll pay you," he said, naively.

Spence wrested the pole from Aedan's hand and laughed out loud. He turned and shouted at the owner of the Staffordshire. "He wants to buy your dog!"

The other man, Hopper, limped over and leant heavily on his walking stick. He was short, skinny, with a mass of wiry, unkempt, dirty-blonde hair. His face had a yellow tinge to it, and was full of wrinkles and bristles. His small neck seemed too small for his shirt collar. It put Aedan in mind of a tortoise poking its head out of its shell. He was just as despicable as Spence. "Sure, I might as well make something out of him today. Looks like it's gonna be his last fight." His eyes, like two slits, pierced Aedan. "Tell me son, what do you plan on doing with a dead dog?" he sneered.

The Staffordshire, too exhausted to move, rolled his head in the direction of his master's voice. When Hopper limped towards him, Aedan noticed the dog's eyes fill with terror. "GET UP, YOU FILTHY GOOD FOR NOTHING WASTE OF SPACE!"

Even though the dog was dying, so intense was his fear of Hopper that he did his best to stand but only managed to remain on his front legs for a few seconds before they collapsed underneath him. Aedan's heart shattered into a million pieces at the dog's pitiful attempt to obey.

"I SAID GET UP!" Hopper rested on his walking stick, and pulled back his leg ready to kick the dog hard in its belly. The dog would be dead within a few minutes of him landing it. Aedan panicked. The only thought in his mind was to stop contact between Hopper's foot and the Staffordshire—the only thought that came to mind was a brick wall. Though the wall was visible to no other person in the room but Aedan, its energy was strong and ready to manifest into matter at any given moment, and so to all intents and purposes it was a brick wall—bar the physical manifestation.

Hopper got a twisted pleasure out of making things suffer. He used all his might to kick the dog as hard as he could. Aedan nodded at his foot. It stopped dead just before it hit the dog's stomach, hitting the energy of the wall full force. His perverted pleasure turned into an excruciating pain that shot up the whole right side of his body. He was thrown backwards against the fence, screaming and grasping at the wires. Unable to hang on, he bounced from the fence and hit the floor hard. Frenzied, he begged for help, clutching and rubbing at his foot, and using every swear word known to man. The pain pierced his brain, took his mind to a new level. A level that might make him think some day.

Spence and the rest of the men looked on. *What the hell's up with him?* To them, Hopper seemed to have kicked at thin air and thrown himself to the ground. He was rolling about like a man possessed!

Aedan walked over to him and offered his hand. "Here, get up," he said, a disgusted look on his face.

But Hopper stayed down and whimpered like his dog had done throughout the fight. "The pain, please, get someone…I'll never walk on it again!" he cried.

Even though repulsed by the man, something about his suffering… touched Aedan. "Now you know how the dog feels. What you give out you get back, tenfold," he said, like an old man! "Not such a big man now, are you?" He held out his hand. "Get up!"

Hopper stared at him blankly. Something passed between them, he didn't know what. He gave Aedan his hand and the child, though small, had no problem dragging him to his feet. What's more, the pain that was so unbearable just a few seconds ago had disappeared on contact with the boy.

Aedan's voice cut through Hopper. "Go home, Jimmy Ogden, and look after your animals."

Hopper stared in disbelief. It was as if only he and the boy existed. "H, h, how do you know my name?" he stuttered. He never gave his birth name to anyone.

Aedan lifted his chin, his expression hard. "I just know."

Hopper felt the kid's words go through him in the same way a dentist's drill did. He headed for the doors, apparently cured of his limp, but his mind was so intent on getting as far away from Aedan as possible, he failed to notice it.

Aedan watched, a half smile on his lips. He picked up Hopper's stick. "Hopper!" He threw it at him. "You forgot this!"

Hopper caught it, a stunned look on his face. "My sti…" Petrified, he couldn't get the words out.

Aedan pointed his index finger at Hopper. A red light flew out of it, stopping dead in front of the man's face, then formed into a humanoid head and gawped at him with an intelligence of its own. The rest of it trailed back to Aedan's finger. Its body looked like a red snake with a radiance that followed it, lighting up the barn and everything in it. It was frightening, ugly. Its huge mouth bared red teeth. "DON'T YOU WANT ME, MASTER!?" It screeched like an angry whirlwind and pushed its face within half an inch of Hopper's.

Hopper was almost numb with fear. "What's that? What's that red stuff? His voice quivered as he watched the red glow slowly slither around him.

"What red stuff? What you on about?" Someone in the crowd shouted.

"Can't you see it?"

"See what?"

Aedan stared at him coldly. "Your anger. I'm throwing it back at you." He made sure that nobody but Hopper could see it. The red light coiled around the walking stick, warping it into a semicircle. Aedan flashed him a warning look. "It's a C, for cruel. Perhaps you can devote your time to…," he glanced at Hopper's now healthy leg,

"...stamping out animal cruelty."

Hopper threw the stick down like it was contaminated. "My stick!"

One of the men picked it up. "What's up with it?" he asked, puzzled.

"It's bent...bent!" Terrified, Hopper staggered backwards.

"There's nothing wrong with it!" The man tried to give it back to him.

Hopper knocked it out of his hand. "It's bent, I'm telling you!"

"You're off your fucking rocker, man!"

Hopper clutched his stomach. He felt sick. He looked around at the silent faces and backed out of the barn slowly with Aedan's words piercing his mind.

Aedan looked at the stick, flipped his head slightly, upon which it flew into Hopper's hand. "Keep it as a souvenir!"

The rest of the men could only see Hopper pick up the stick and limp out of the barn. To them nothing had changed. Hopper's cure wouldn't become apparent to anybody else for a few months, whereupon he'd make up some fanciful story about a new surgery he'd had done.

Aedan knew that Hopper would never talk about the strange occurrences—his leg being miraculously cured, the red stuff, the warped stick. Even if he did, nobody would believe him, and he wouldn't want people making a joke out of him.

≍

The silence that had descended on the rest of the barn was suddenly broken by the sound of Spence and his nervous laughter. "The dogs fight to their deaths, son; it's what we breed 'em for. Looks like it's the end of the road for Bruiser here."

So far, Aedan had done really well at keeping his anger in check—or so he thought! He wanted to let Grip have some fun with this excuse for a human being, but Sister Devlin kept interrupting him. But some people only understand fear; and if that's all they give out...

Aedan condensed the heat that seared from his anger into a ball underneath his palm, and clenched his small fist tight around the middle of the pole. He focused his attention on the area he gripped until he'd built up enough energy to snap it in two—but he didn't. He remained in control. He glowered at Spence. He'd give him one last chance.

The men jeered to get on with the fight. They wouldn't be satisfied until they saw the Staffordshire ripped to pieces! Spence loomed over Aedan, his voice quiet, intimidating. "You're upsetting my punters and getting right on my nerves." The corner of his mouth and his right eye twitched. His words came out slowly. "Get outta' here or I'll tie you to a chair and beat you within an inch of your life."

Aedan was scared but he wouldn't back off. "Let Grip go. The fight is over."

One hand still controlling Grip, Spence grabbed Aedan's arm roughly. "I'm not taking orders from you, boy! Get your sorry arse outta here before I—" Crack! The pole snapped cleanly in the middle. Grip was free.

Spence stopped dead and started to sweat. He thought about running but the dog would chase him down before he had a chance to take a breath. He turned sideways and started to retreat slowly. The two heavies he employed to take care of him sneaked through the barn doors while nobody was looking. They weren't about to jump into the pen with a dog like that just to save Spence's arse; he didn't pay them enough. They'd tell him they must have been outside having a smoke when the pole snapped. Besides, they didn't see any reason to go in; they knew he could handle a kid…couldn't he? A dig at his ego would do the trick.

"Before you what? You ugly big bully!" Aedan could feel his anger punching and kicking against him. He wouldn't be able to control it for much longer. Sister Devlin popped into his mind again but he didn't care! He'd yet to fathom why people like Spence existed. All they did was make life miserable for everybody else. Wouldn't the world be better off without criminals and their tormenting of innocent people and life? Why won't they do something decent for a living? There are loads of poor people. They don't go around abusing and murdering, and using poverty as an excuse for it.

Unknown to Aedan, White Eagle, Roman, and NeilA looked on. NeilA could feel Aedan's anger but had so far refused to intervene. It was a natural emotion on Earth and there were times when it had to be released. He was impressed with the way he'd controlled it so far, and even more impressed by the child's courage. He was interested to see how Aedan would get out of the situation he'd put himself in, and hoped he would show the same compassion to Spence as he had to the dogs…although he knew he was pushing it a bit there. This was a child. He'd yet to…grow!

≥<

Spence looked into the eyes of the dog that couldn't wait to get its teeth around his neck. Cold sweat oozed from every pore in his body. He could feel it trickling down the side of his face, causing his skin to itch. Now at the mercy of the dog, he was terrified. He swallowed hard. Too afraid to move his head, he looked from dog to boy using only his eyes.

Aedan removed the damaged trap from around Grip's neck and clamped his hand around his mouth. "Give him a break," he whispered, and let the dog go.

Grip lunged at Spence, froth and fur flying, teeth ready to chew through the man he hated…on one command. Within seconds, Spence lay flat on his back, not daring to move, with Grip attached to his neck. The dog snarled darkly. One word from Aedan and his teeth would slice through Spence's flesh with no effort, but so far Grip had managed to control the incision.

White Eagle moved forward. "I'd better stop it—"

"Not yet." Roman put his arm across White Eagle's chest. "We have to know how far Aedan will go. You said yourself that he isn't on Earth to play nice all the time, and so far his intention is to save the dogs, not to hurt anyone."

"Tell that to Hopper."

"Aedan acted on impulse. His intention wasn't to hurt Hopper. All he wanted to do was stop his foot from making contact with the dog, and to get him to think about his actions. Granted, Hopper did endure a certain amount of pain but sometimes allowances must be made. We can't have the child afraid of his own shadow." He turned to White Eagle and shrugged. "Or what good would his power be? Think intention," he said quietly. "Think intention…the law of attraction responds to what's in the heart. It will respond to Aedan's love for the dog, not to his action—the brick wall. The wall is a symbol of his intention. It symbolised love in this case. Had Aedan intended to hurt Hopper and the wall been a symbol of hate, the law of course would respond to that. You know this. Try to relax with Aedan. Enjoy him."

But White Eagle was worried. "Enjoy him! He seems to have a knack for getting himself in situations that make enjoyment difficult."

"Because you're not thinking about the situation at a deeper level. You're seeing it in black and white. Aedan doesn't think in black and white terms—neither do you most of the time. Relax! Be yourself with him instead of getting wrapped up in the guardian role. What's come over you, White Eagle? Stop worrying!"

"It's the episode with Sister Devlin. I don't want him making the same…" He frowned. "Look—it's Maggie. She couldn't bear another loss."

"It's not for you to say what Maggie can and cannot bear, though I understand you're trying to protect her. As for Sister Devlin, there is a huge difference between her and the men we are dealing with here. Aedan will learn, will adapt to situations and people in different ways. It's all part of his development."

White Eagle was puzzled. "But Sister Devlin was cruel. She never treated anyone with any affection. How is she so different from these men?"

Roman paused for a moment and just stared at White Eagle. "Think intention!" He repeated. "She thought she was doing the right thing. She'd been indoctrinated from birth with the right thing, brainwashed with it, in fact. The right thing being taught by parents who were void of love and affection. She'd never been shown any, so how could she give it? Her intention was to spread the word of her God, even if it meant hitting Aedan over the head with a bible!" Roman cocked his head to the side, smiling crookedly. "One way of doing it, I suppose!" The two of them looked at each other and burst into laughter before he continued. "There are many complex reasons for Sister Devlin's behaviour. These men, on the other hand, know. They know that what they're doing is cruel, is wrong. They do it out of greed, out of disrespect for animals, themselves, or anyone else who joins in with this barbaric practice."

"And the money!"

"Money! There are other ways to earn it. Charlie doesn't rob, doesn't fight dogs for a living, and he has four children to provide for. Greed, White Eagle. They want as much money as they can get their hands on without having to get out of bed in the mornings. The pittance Charlie makes on his coal round is beer money to these people." He looked pensive and softened his voice. "But Charlie is the richer man by far. Hopefully some of him will rub off on Aedan." He looked towards the pen. "The child has yet to learn discernment between situations and people. After today he should see a fundamental difference between Devlin and these two. In her mind she was being cruel to be kind. These men are simply cruel. They get a sadistic pleasure out of the power they exert over the animals and the rest of the thugs who pay them to do it."

Roman looked around the barn. His eyes flickered with all the colours of the moods and emotions around him: grey, red, and an empty muddy brown, but they turned black like two shiny insects when he said in a calm voice, "Aedan would have to sign an allegiance with the dark for us to take him, and even then it would be at the discretion of the Originator."

When he looked at White Eagle, the colour of his eyes turned into a piercing mixture of green and pink, representing love, compassion, and healing—a reflection of the entity staring back at him. "When we asked you to be his guide we knew it wouldn't be easy but we did hope that you'd enjoy him. A child like Aedan is a challenge…we know this," he shrugged nonchalantly. "He could literally fire Earth into another dimension. Even so, we don't want you to worry about every decision he makes. This isn't helpful to his growth, or yours, and regardless of what happens the child will be looked after. So will his mother. Remember that."

White Eagle smiled and nodded. "Yes, of course, Roman. I know that."

No matter what, they'd all be looked after. They weren't alone. Nobody was. This was the golden thought that brought comfort in the form of elation to his heart.

⤳

The barn was deadly silent apart from a few pigeons cooing in the rafters above. The men looked on. None of them dared move. What they'd witnessed with this boy and the dogs was nothing short of a miracle. He was barely out of the crib yet still in command of the situation. And what about Spence? A hardened criminal at the kid's mercy? Jesus, heads are gonna roll for this!

Aedan ran at them. They all jumped back a few paces. "Is this what you call fun?" Watching animals suffer, die?" He shook his head and clamped his lips together in an effort to calm down. "You're filth, the lot of you!" he spat.

He looked back at Grip and for one small moment he wanted to let the dog finish Spence. He didn't deserve to live. The world would be better off without a worthless waste of space like him. But the small incisions caused by the dog's teeth on Spence's skin seemed to stretch before his eyes. Even though Grip could have killed him within the blink of an eye, he hadn't. His jaw remained clamped around the neck of his tormentor, but he exercised perfect control. He'd go easy on Spence, just like Aedan had asked, unless instructed otherwise.

In that moment, Aedan realised that if the dog could exercise restraint like this, so could he. He remembered White Eagle's words.

'It's not your place to punish Sister Devlin,' or something like that, he'd said. *'Her life has been filled with nothing but pain and suffering and you come along and add to it.'*

He walked over to Grip and put his hand underneath his jaw. "Thank you, boy. Rest." Grip released Spence's neck, yawned, as if to say, "All in a day's work," and flopped down beside Bruiser.

Aedan looked down on Spence. *What if he's suffered for most of his life? Maybe he has no idea of what love is? Then again, maybe he's just plain evil—'It's your reaction that counts.'* White Eagle's words invaded his thoughts again.

"Go if you want," he said flatly. "Grip knows more about love and compassion than you do. Maybe you should think about that."

Spence's relief was visible. He jumped up, leapt over the fence one-handed, and ran from the barn. He looked back and shouted, "I'll be back for my dog," before hightailing it through the doors.

"He's all wind and piss," Derrick said, jumping the fence. He immediately went over to the Staffordshire bull terrier and stroked him gently. One by one, the old barn emptied. The men left a piece of their spirit behind in its darkness. They would have to work hard to get it back.

Aedan looked at Derrick. "Promise me you won't say a word about what you're about to see."

"What do you mean?"

"Promise! It's a secret."

"One of the weird secrets?"

"Yes!"

"Alright."

"I have to make Bruiser better or he'll die in a few minutes." Aedan stroked Bruiser up and down his body and put his free hand on top of the dog's head. "Come on, boy, you can make it. Everything's gonna be fine. No more suffering for you...come on, come on," he soothed. Tears ran down his cheeks, and he felt his heart blow up like a balloon as he sent a silent message for Bruiser's healing out to the universal intelligence. He turned to Derrick and shook his head. "I don't understand…how they can do it…not for any reason."

The dog whimpered and let go of all stress and tension as the energy flooded through him. He stopped trembling almost immediately and his breathing became less rapid as an atmosphere of calm and tranquillity took over. Derrick watched, awestruck, as the dog's wounds knitted together and healed before his eyes. The blood, cuts, saliva, everything, just disappeared.

Bruiser lifted his head and looked at them both as if to say, "What's going on here, then?" And within less than a minute, apart from a few scars, he was a different dog. He jumped up and moved from one to the other, licking Aedan and Derrick all over their faces. His happy yelps echoed throughout the barn, drowning out the cooing pigeons.

"Okay, okay, we have to make Grip better now," Aedan said, laughing.

"How did you do that?" Derrick asked, taking Bruiser gently by the collar. "Calm down, Bruiser." The dog did as he was told.

"Like that."

"What?" Derrick was clueless.

"The way you've just got Bruiser to calm down."

"I just told him to," Derrick said puzzled.

"But there was a knowing point—"

"A what?"

"A feeling…a knowing point. Something inside that tells you something is going to happen." Aedan picked up a piece of straw, snapped it in two. "You get to a point when you just know. Get it?"

"Kind of," Derrick answered.

"You asked Bruiser to calm down and he did. There wasn't a shred of doubt in your mind that he wouldn't do as you asked—that's the knowing point. When you jumped the fence and walked over to him, you weren't scared. You had no fear of any of the dogs and they had no fear of you. You knew you'd be okay and you were. Your knowing point, the feeling inside, told you so. Nobody else dared to get in the pen with the dogs because their knowing point told them the dogs would tear them apart—"

"But the dogs would have done!"

"Because of fear! The dogs would act on fear and so would the men. The knowing point in both cases would be fear. You get what you focus on. The more intense your focus, the more intense the knowing becomes. It sounds easy, but that's how it is for everything, any situation. You just have to get to that point where you just know. It doesn't matter how big or how small a thing is, we set those margins." Aedan's face held wisdom far beyond his years. At these times his connection with NeilA fuelled his inspiration. He stared at Derrick. "Do you think we can do the same for Grip?"

"You can!" Derrick answered flatly.

"What does your knowing point say?"

"That you can and I can't!"

"Then you won't be able to heal Grip because you've told your knowing point that only I can do it. You have to realise that you have the same power as me. Until you do, it will stay asleep—give me your hands."

Grip had got up and was standing at the gate to the pen, as if on guard. Aedan called him over. "Grip, come here, boy. Let's get you cleaned up a bit. Lie down."

Grip flopped down on his side and laid his head in Derrick's lap. He whimpered quietly. "It's alright, boy. We'll stop your pain." He turned to Aedan with tears in his eyes. "He must be in a lot of it with rips like these."

"He is." Aedan took Derrick's hands, placed one on top of the dog's head, and the other palm down on his belly. He kept his own hands on top of Derrick's. "Think about how much you want to make Grip better. Focus on nothing else. You have to feel it in your heart—but just so you know, you might get a funny feeling like your heart's gonna blow up."

Within seconds Derrick could feel a light buzzing sensation coming from Aedan's hands into his own. He looked at his friend wide-eyed, and opened his mouth ready to talk.

Aedan shook his head. "Shh, don't talk! Just go with the energy so Grip gets the full benefit. It's easier with animals 'cos they're more accepting."

Derrick fought to stay calm as he let Aedan hold his hand and run it up and down the dog's body as if scanning it. He felt the energy take him over, almost consume him. Suddenly, spurts of silver-blue light fired from his hands. He panicked, pulled back, and shouted, "I'm getting an electric shock! Let me go! Let me go!"

"Relax, you're safe!" Aedan nodded. "Put your hands back."

"No! What's that shit coming out of me?" Derrick looked at his hands. Because of his fear, the energy retreated. "Where's it gone?"

"It doesn't want to scare you."

"What doesn't?"

"Look at Grip. Do you want to help him or not?"

Derrick stroked the dog's head and looked at the rips in his skin. Like Aedan, he felt sadness flood his heart. "Course I do."

"Then don't panic! You know you can trust me, don't you?"

"Yes, yes, but it's weird...it feels funny."

Aedan laid his hands on top of Derrick's again. The silver-blue lights spurted out and entered the dog in small waves. "That's what me mam calls the universal energy. It's going to make Grip better."

As Derrick relaxed, the energy pulsing through him got stronger and stronger. He thought back to a few occasions when he'd been to the seaside with his family. It reminded him of being sat in the ocean, only it was a weird kind of electrical current washing over him and not water—and this current seemed to come from everywhere! Inside, outside, it swam over him, under him, through him, around him! It was as if he was surrounded by a magnetic field that spun faster and faster depending on his level of comfort.

A light breeze wafted about him and he could feel a nice tickling sensation throughout his body. Then the strangest feeling engulfed him, like his body had gone off someplace else and left him with just his head...or his mind! Like he could only think, but the thoughts were as real as the body parts that had faded away. At this point, the barn, Aedan, the dogs, everything, seemed to have disappeared into him. Like he was one with everything! Nothing was separate from him.

He felt himself merge into some kind of living energy that had no physical description, but it had an intelligence just the same! It didn't take long for him to realise that he liked it.

Grip bouncing about and wagging his tail in much the same way Bruiser had done brought Derrick back down to Earth—literally!

Aedan rammed his head into Grip's neck. "Grippy, Grippy, you big hairy baby!" he said before turning to Derrick. "There! Grip is your dog. You healed him."

Derrick looked at his friend, shocked. "No! I couldn't have done it without you."

"I only helped you to release your potential." Aedan didn't realise he sounded like a college professor—the NeilA connection was inspiring him again. "It was a joint effort between your energy and the universe that healed Grip. That makes him your dog."

"Where are we going to keep them? My mam won't let me keep him at home."

Aedan thought hard. "We'll sneak them in tonight and work on our parents tomorrow."

"I can't sneak them in, not in our house. There's always someone about."

"Okay, I'll take them to ours tonight but you'll have to distract Maggie while I sneak them under the stairs."

"Under the stairs! Your air-raid shelter, you mean? What if the Germans come? Your mam will find them when you go down there."

"We'll just have to hope the Germans don't come tonight. Anyway, my mam won't throw them out on the street with fighters flying over. She always makes sure that Ginger is in the shelter with us. She's dead soft when it comes to animals."

"Ginger, yeah! But she won't bargain for these two." Derrick looked worried. "I don't think we'll be able to keep Grip."

"Don't think like that. Focus your feelings on keeping him. The knowing point, remember?" Aedan said incredulously. "Just know that when you take Grip home he'll be welcomed into the family. Anyway, your dad loves animals. If he says you can keep Grip it won't matter what your mam says."

Derrick looked at him wide-eyed. "You must be joking! It's mam who's the boss in our house. If Grip wants to stay it's her he'll have to soft-soap."

"And you don't think she'll let you keep him?"

"Doubt it. She's got enough to feed with the four of us, she'll say."

"Tell her you'll buy his food with your coal-round money."

"I'll try, but I don't think it will make any difference."

Aedan felt frustrated. "Look at all the problems you're thinking up and you've not even got Grip home yet. With all the negative energy you're feeding it, you're telling your knowing point to rule in favour of not keeping Grip. Go to bed tonight and see Grip and yourself exploring the peaks with me and Bruiser. Visualise him sitting with us on the cart when we're on the coal round. Whatever you do stop thinking you can't keep him, because thoughts turn into belief, and once belief sets in it gets harder to change things—not impossible, just harder."

"So when I go to bed I'll just pretend that Grip is lying at the foot of it, pretend he's my dog already-like?"

"Yep, that way you're feeding your knowing point the result you want. But start doing it right now, not just when you go to bed."

"Right!" Derrick leaned his head into the dog's face. Grip responded by licking him all over and grunting happily.

Aedan reached over and patted Grip on the backside. "Do you think we should change their names?"

"Why? They're used to the names they've got."

Aedan mimicked Spence. "Yeah, like Shithead and Good-fer-nothin.'"

"But they answer to Grip and Bruiser."

"I know. But it will be harder to convince your mam and mine to keep them if they're introduced as Grip and Bruiser." Aedan laughed out loud. "I think we should give them gentlemen's names." He clamped his hands over Bruiser's nose who responded by snorting and rolling over onto his back. "No, it's not tickle time. Come here,

Bruiser. Be quiet, listen." He laid both hands on top of Bruiser's ears. "Quiet," he soothed, using his thumbs to stroke between the dog's eyes. "From now on your name is Julian!" Bruiser yelped in protest, spun around at one hundred miles an hour. Aedan turned to Derrick, a huge smirk on his face. "He says, 'It'll be a cold day in hell if you think I'm answering to a nancyfied name like Julian!'"

Both boys lay flat on the floor screaming with laughter. Aedan glanced at Bruiser. "Look at his face," he said, commenting on the cantankerous expression the dog had taken on with his new name. "You'll get used to it. Come here." Aedan sat up and spoke to the dog, knowing that it understood every word. "You've got more chance of convincing Maggie to let you stay if you've got good manners. The name Bruiser will tell her that you've been a rude, mean, bad boy in the past, so from now on your name is Julian…right?" The dog looked at him, sighed, and buried its head in his lap. "There, he doesn't like it but he'll put up with it."

Derrick looked at Grip, who in turn was looking at him with a don't-think-you're-gonna-give-me-a-stuck-up-name-like-Julian look on his face. "Now, what gentleman name can we give to you?" Derrick said, reaching out and pulling Grip over by the collar. Derrick thought for a few seconds. "Got it!" He put his hand on top of Grip's head. "Grip," he said, mimicking Father Frank, the village priest. "In the name of the Father, the Son, and the Holy Spirit, I now name you Am…A…" He couldn't get the name out for laughing.

"What? Tell us his name!" Aedan said, laughing at his friend's laughter.

Derrick laughed so hard he couldn't catch his breath. "Ambr… Ambrose!" he screamed. Once again, the boys lay flat on their backs unable to do anything but laugh, before Derrick finally regained control and sat up. "Poor Ambrose," he said, wiping his cheeks with the back of his hand. "Aedan's right. You've got to have good manners or my mam will have your arse in the chopper!" The dog whined back at him several times. "He says, 'You've got another think coming if you think I'm gonna respond to a pansy name like Ambrose; your mam can whistle!'"

Aedan raised his eyebrows. "He's not met Eileen!" He looked at his watch. "We'd better go before your dad comes looking for us."

The boys jumped up, not bothering to clean the straw, mud, or dirt from themselves or the dogs. Julian and Ambrose ran on ahead. Aedan noticed that they were both agitated and took hold of Derrick's wrist. "There's someone out there." He called the dogs back and watched the barn door open slowly. The long, moaning creak it let out added to the eeriness—or was it because Spence had returned with his two heavies, each carrying a pole with a wire loop on the end.

"I've come for my dog," he said, his face twisted with evil. "This time, I've brought a spare trap just in case one of 'em snaps."

Ambrose snarled as convincingly as he'd always done but remained by Derrick's side.

"He's not your dog. People like you don't deserve animals," Aedan shouted.

"Is that right? I've fed him, kept him, paid good money out for him. In my book that makes him my dog."

Julian stood, teeth bared, in front of Aedan as the three men edged closer, ready to charge the dogs.

Aedan knew that he had to scare the men, make them too afraid to come after them again. He could feel his anger start to simmer. He did his best to remain calm, not to let it take over, but still it started to spit and bubble. *Why wouldn't Spence let it go? That seemed to be the man's problem, letting go.* He crouched down, pulled both dogs towards him and whispered in their ears. "Time they learnt, but don't harm them."

The two heavies charged, hooking the loops around both dogs with ease. The dogs simply stood there not bothering to fight. The men couldn't believe it.

"What the hell!" Spence said, mystified. More than that, he'd only just noticed how healthy Grip looked…and Bruiser? *Still alive?* He'd brought the pole just in case, but thought they'd be removing the dog's body!

Aedan Walked over to Spence. "He won't fight anymore. Grip is useless to you now."

"Oh, he'll fight alright, when he realises his life depends on it."

"Be careful what you ask for," Aedan said, losing his temper.

"I never ask—Eddy, pass me that!" he hissed, referring to the trap and never taking his red-rimmed eyes off Aedan.

On contact with his old owner, Grip attacked the end of the pole knowing that his life did depend on it. Teeth bared, fur standing on end, he wrestled and snarled at Spence as if to say, "I'd rather be dead than live another minute under your control." Aedan bent down, put his arm around the dog's neck protectively. "Ambrose, manners," he said softly. The dog instantly calmed, stopped struggling, and flopped down. Spence stood with his mouth wide open, dumbstruck.

Aedan's expression and mood was darker than the bleakest day on the Derbyshire moors. "Get out. Don't come back." His voice was calm but inside he was furious. "The dog shouldn't have to fight for his right to live in peace, and without fear or torment from a lowlife like you!"

The two heavies looked from one to the other, then back at Spence.

"I'm not taking orders from a jumped-up little shit like you." Spence had never been spoken to in such a way, though he had to hand it to the kid: he had guts—could even end up on his team some day. "Look kid, why don't you come and see me in a few years? I could find plenty of work for someone with bottle like yours."

Aedan glared. "You must be joking! Work for you? Finish you, more like!" His indignant expression told Spence just how insulted he was.

Spence reached out, grabbed Aedan by the throat, threw his own head back, and spat in the boy's face. His eyes seemed to expand and fill up with an empty blackness. "I've buried men for a lot less than I've let you get away with."

Ambrose and Julian snarled and wriggled on the ends of the poles but were helpless in their attempts to protect Aedan. Spence pulled Aedan off his feet with one hand, and wrestled Ambrose with the other. He turned to Dan, the other heavy, and nodded at Julian, "Get that in the car." He looked at Derrick. "Eddy, take that one with you. I can deal with these two on my own."

Terrified, Derrick started to scream and cry. "Shut it!" Eddy ordered, wrapping his arm around him, and clamping a hand over his mouth.

Aedan swung and flayed helplessly in the air. He knew that he'd better do something quick or the dogs, at least, would end up dead and Spence would soon knock the living daylights out of him and Derrick, teach them to keep their mouths shut. He didn't want Derrick scared shitless for the rest of his life by these thugs.

The anger inside him burned…what he wouldn't give to bring this whole blasted barn down on Spence. *'Only your reaction counts!'* White Eagle's words again! *For God's sake! Even when he's not around he haunts me!* Impulse mixed with panic, Aedan looked over at the barn doors and with a jerk of his head, slammed them shut. Everybody stopped dead!

Spence spoke first, screaming at Dan and Eddy, "WELL, WHAT YOU WAITING FOR?"

Eddy let go of Derrick and walked over to the doors. They weren't locked but he couldn't budge them.

"What the hell is up with you? Here, get hold of this damn dog and keep your eye on him." Spence tossed Aedan to the ground like he was a piece of rubbish, passed Ambrose over to Eddy, and marched to the barn doors. "If you want something done, do it your fucking self," he said, going red in the face in an effort to force the doors open. "For Christ's sakes!" He kicked the doors several times in temper, then looked all around the barn for another way out. "One of us can climb out through there," he said, looking at a hole in the roof. "The doors will probably open from the outside."

Aedan used his sleeve to wipe the spit from his face. "They won't!" He'd had enough. What's more, if they didn't get home soon, Charlie would come looking for them and he didn't want to get him involved with these scumbags. They weren't fit to kiss Charlie's arse. "They won't open unless I open them."

"Oh, is that right?" Spence ran at Aedan. "Well, get over there and open them, then." He gripped the back of Aedan's neck and ran him towards the barn doors, his feet barely touching the ground.

Incensed, Aedan closed his eyes and took deep breaths. He had to control his anger, he had to. He could feel it welling up inside him like a hurricane, desperate, ready to knock Spence out of existence if he didn't take his hands off him NOOOOOOWWW!

Spence plonked Aedan down in front of the doors, turned him around, grabbed his shirt, and twisted the material. "How do you suppose you're going to open them if I can't you stupid little bas—"

"Take your hands off me." Aedan glared at Spence. "Let go of me or you'll be sorry." His voice was calm.

Spence felt his blood run cold, so cold it felt like it had turned to ice inside his veins. But he couldn't let his men know that the boy was putting the fear of—the fear of what? What the hell was he scared of? He looked down at Aedan, who barely came up to his elbow but seemed to be enjoying a casual stroll around his soul. "Listen, boy—"

"No, you listen! Let us go. I'm giving you one last chance to do the right thing." Any fear Aedan felt had long since departed. He wasn't about to let Derrick or the dogs put up with this crap a minute longer.

Enraged, Spence grabbed the hair on the top of Aedan's head, forced him to the ground, and rubbed his face in the straw. "Do you know who you're dealing with? I've had a lot harder than you served up for breakfast, dinner, and tea!" He looked at the dogs. Both were desperate to get off the poles and help Aedan. "SHUT THE HELL UP!"

Derrick lunged forward, and burst into tears. "Don't hurt him, mister! Don't, please, mister!" he blubbered. He looked from one face to the other, down at Aedan, and back at Spence. "He's my best mate! Please mister, please—"

"BE QUIET!" Spence was getting more and more agitated. Derrick was getting hysterical. Aedan knew he had to act fast. Pinned down and desperate, he pictured Spence flying through the barn wall but quickly brought him back again. He didn't want to be responsible for a death. Not that he cared whether Spence lived or died but it wasn't his place to pop people. Besides White Eagle would have his arse on a plate! But he had to defend his friends as well as himself…didn't he?

The energy was like an electrical storm inside him: the heat, the power, the feeling of getting bigger. It branched off from the main mass collected in his solar plexus, and fired through him. It was as if he had stretched, expanded, grown too big for his physical body. There was nothing else for it. If he didn't act now, they'd all be dead. He'd suffer the wrath of White Eagle later.

Managing to turn his head to the side, he saw two rusty old meat hooks hanging from a beam above him. He smiled to himself and visualised Spence floating upwards like a lost feather, until he hung, like an old carcass, from one of the hooks.

Spence was in the middle of removing the leather belt from his trousers. The kid needed some manners whipped into him—he stopped dead! Put a hand to his forehead. He felt light, dizzy, all of a sudden. He did his best to cling to Aedan's hair but found that he couldn't control his hand. It released Aedan despite Spence doing his best to hang onto him. What's more, his whole body had levitated and was hanging around just above ground level. He tried to claw at the ground, at the air, but carried on moving towards the roof of the barn, doing slow somersaults.

Aedan started to laugh at the terrified look on the hard-man's face. "Up, up," he ordered. With each waft of his hand, Spence floated nearer to the meat hooks.

The two heavies looked at each other, terrified, and ran! Desperate, the pair of them scrabbled and clawed at the barn doors, but they wouldn't budge. Eddy turned to Aedan. "Let us go, kid, and you'll never hear from us again."

Aedan folded his arms, lifted his head in the air like a Roman emperor. "You'd better mean that!" He nodded at the doors. The pair fled through them, falling over each other in the frenzy to get out.

Petrified, Spence reached into his pocket and pulled out a gun. "If this is some kind of trick, you'd better put an end to it right now!" He pulled back the trigger and aimed it between Aedan's eyes—

White Eagle shot forward, only to be stopped by Roman again. "Leave it! The Originator has not yet advised us to intervene."

Aedan couldn't believe that Spence had a real gun! He acted purely on instinct. As Spence pulled the trigger, Aedan formed his fingers into a gun, twisted them around as if drawing a circle, and fired them at the roof. When Spence looked down at his gun, to his horror, he found that the barrel now resembled the braid on a crusty cob, the kind seen in a baker's window. What's more, he was still floating upwards towards the barn roof.

Spence's heart pounded in time with his thoughts: *Witchcraft! Devil worship! Demons!* There was something going on with this boy. He wasn't normal! Spence had no clue that it was his own ability to hurt and spread fear that was coming right back at him.

He was about to toss the gun at Aedan but stopped suddenly, his hand in mid-air. He looked down at the two boys, then at the dogs, both growling and snarling, itching to get at him... There was a gap. For the first time in his life Spence stopped! And thought! About his actions! He tossed the gun hard at the barn wall making sure that it didn't land near any of them.

Derrick turned to Aedan. "What are you going to do with him?"

"Leave him up there until we're well clear." He put his arms out in front of him, and raised them slowly, palms up, towards the roof. A deflated Spence moved with them until he found himself hanging like dead meat from one of the old hooks. In this moment, Spence experienced some of the fear, degradation, and helplessness that he'd put others through, those that had been unfortunate enough to cross him.

"What time is it?" Derrick asked. "I don't want my dad to find us with the dogs."

"We've got time yet." Aedan looked up at Spence. "See ya, dirt-bag! Don't hang about too long—gets cold on the peak!"

Spence was in shock. He could barely speak, and when he did the words sounded slow and drawn-out. "Look, boy, you can't leave me up here. How am I supposed to get down? You'll be sorry—you'll be responsible for my death. The police will have you for murder!" The more his nerves took over, the more he spun on the meat hook.

Derrick giggled. "He looks like he's doing the doggy paddle in midair!"

A half smile crossed Aedan's face. "Let yourself off the hook—"

"How do you expect me to do that?"

"Unbutton your jacket."

Spence looked at the floor below. "I'll break my neck!—"

Aedan smirked, shaking his head, "Let go, Spence. You've just got to let go!"

The two dogs were getting acquainted with the barn. "Eh!" Derrick called. "Don't do that indoors! Let's go!"

They raced from the barn and through the craggy, green terrain of the peak district. It felt good to be free. Dogs bounding at their heels, they didn't stop running until they collapsed, breathless, onto the grass by the banks of the River Etherow. Their hearts pounded not only from the run, but a little piece of fear that did its best to cling on. They lay quiet for a few minutes and let the sound of the water and the feel of the breeze gently ease away their anxiety.

The dogs splashed and played in the water. All they'd ever known was a cold, dark space in a rundown shed. They'd never tasted the outdoors or freedom. They didn't know what it was to run with the wind behind them until now.

"The dogs look as if they're laughing." Derrick hunted through his backpack, pulled out a sandwich, and munched heartily. "We're gonna get it for taking these dogs back with us."

Aedan bit into a cheese sandwich. "There you go again! Don't say that! The knowing point! Try to remember! From now on, it's gonna be me, you, and the dogs."

"Are you gonna tell the police to get Spence?"

"Naaaa!" Aedan said with disgust. "He'll let himself down. It's what he's done all his life."

Derrick laughed. Forgetting all about Spence and his dilemma, he looked over at the dogs. "I wonder if they'll get used to their names?"

"Grip, Bruiser!" Aedan shouted.

The dogs were oblivious to his calls until he used their new names.

⊃⊂

Back in the barn, NeilA nodded slowly at his two companions. "Hmm, Aedan's starting to think before he reacts…good, good. Let's hope this continues as life deals him!" He looked at Spence who was oblivious to them, and with a sharp nod of his head released the man's jacket from the meat hooks. Spence screamed on the way down, landed with a thud, but was pleasantly surprised at the lack of pain. Apart from a bit of a crack to the shoulder, he was fine. He stood up slowly, rubbing his shoulder, and put it down to a lucky escape. NeilA had slowed him down just before he'd hit the floor.

"That's the hard part isn't it? Getting them to think!"

32.

*A*edan and Derrick turned into St. Mary Street just in time to see Maggie run across to Eileen and Charlie's place. Just before her fist hit the door, it opened and a grinning Charlie said, "I'm just about to go looking for 'em."

Eileen handed him his jacket. "Tea will be ready in half an hour, Charlie, so don't dawdle." She looked at Maggie. "I thought you bought Aedan a watch for his birthday."

"I did!"

"And I still have to go look for 'em!" Charlie butted in. "They're going to get my foot up their backsides."

Maggie narrowed her eyes. "The little buggers will have got carried away in their imaginations as usual…but you know, I've a funny feeling something's not right."

"Now, stop your worrying. They—" Charlie saw the pair duck behind the wall of The Prince of Wales, farther up the street. "I think you might be right. Give me a minute or two." He ran full pelt towards the boys. "AEDAN! DERRICK! GET HERE NOW!"

Panic-struck, Derrick turned to Aedan. "Jesus, me dad's seen us!"

Anxiety registered all over Aedan's face. "Dammit! We'll have to make something up—we can't hide the dogs in time—"

"What the bloody hell are you two up to? What the…! Who do them dogs belong to?"

Eileen soon caught up with an irate Maggie not far behind her. "God bless us and save us! Look at the bloody state of you both. You look as if you've been dragged through a hedge backwards." She

379

knelt down, grabbed both boys, and inspected their hands. "Look at
the bloody colour! You'll never get the dirt from under them nails.
Where the hell have you been?" She rummaged through her cardigan,
pulled a handkerchief from her pocket, and spat into it. The boys cried
out in pain as she rubbed at the dried mud on their legs and pummelled
the dirt from their clothes. "Clean on this morning and you're rotten
already; cause more washing than the little ones put together! Honest
to God, I've a good mind to make the pair of you stand at the sink
scrubbing clothes for a week!"

"What are you doing with these dogs? Who do they belong to?"
Maggie hunted for a name disc on their collars.

Eileen stopped beating the boys clean and looked up. Up until this
moment she'd been oblivious to the dogs. "Good God!" She jumped
to her feet. "They look a right rough pair of buggers!" She put her
hands on her hips and shot the boys a warning look. "Where the hell
have they come from?"

It was one of those rare occasions when Aedan and Derrick were
lost for words.

Charlie looked the pair in the eyes, his face stern. "We're waiting
for an explanation. Now. I won't ask again. Where have these dogs
come from?" The boys looked at each other and opened their mouths
but Charlie held his hand out to silence them. "And it better be the
truth that comes out of your mouths," he said menacingly.

The dogs lay a few feet behind Aedan and Derrick, heads resting
on front paws, eyes following the adults.

"We found them on the peaks," Derrick said, looking at Aedan. It
was true. They had found them on the peaks!

"Found them where on the peaks? They must belong to one of
the farmers. You've no right to just take them! We'd better get up
there and try and find their owner. I'll ask Tommy Harrison; he's been
farming the land around here for donkeys' years. If anyone knows
who they belong to, it'll be him. Come on, you two." He turned to
Eileen. "Looks like I'm going to be eating my tea cold!" He looked at
the boys and stooped down to their eye level, shouting, "AGAIN!"

The boys shrunk back. They knew the difference between so far and too far where Charlie was concerned, and they were nearing that difference.

Eileen ran her hand through Charlie's hair. "Hang on, Charlie." She looked at the boys. "Come clean, the pair of you." She narrowed her eyes. "You're telling a pack of bloody lies! Now, come clean!"

Aedan blinked rapidly. There was nothing he hated more than being put on the spot and having to lie. Sometimes, especially when it came down to the matter of life and death, it was necessary to lie and this was one of those times. If they told the truth about Julian and Ambrose being fighting dogs, the adults would panic and have them put down, and he couldn't bear that. The dogs had a right to life. It wasn't their fault they'd been bred to fight. "They were tied up in an old barn. I think they'd been abandoned."

Maggie knew Aedan was lying but refrained from saying anything—with four children, Eileen and Charlie were experts at getting down to the nitty-gritty.

Eileen folded her arms across her chest. "Now why don't I believe you, Aedan O'Connell?"

"I don't know—"

"Oh, yes you do!" She cocked her chin in the air. "Because you're telling pork pies, that's why!" Her voice was hurried and filled with irritation. "That old farm you're talking about has been empty for years." She looked at the dogs. "These two hardly look neglected to me, so they couldn't have been abandoned for long."

Charlie looked thoughtful as well as suspicious. "Are you talking about old Peacock's farm up on Higher Shelf Stones?"

"Err, I think so." Aedan shifted nervously.

The look on Charlie's face told Derrick his dad was onto them. Charlie dug his hands into his pockets. "Rumour has it that dog fights are going on up there."

Aedan laughed self-consciously. "What do you mean?"

Charlie bent down again and put his face into Aedan's, his voice low. "What I say."

Aedan swallowed, then looked at his mam. She gave him a you'd-better-start-telling-the-truth-or-suffer-the-wrath-of-Charlie look. He glanced back at Charlie. "Dog fights?"

"That's right," Charlie answered, his nose nearly touching Aedan's. "I'd say a Staffordshire and a pit bull are prime for fighting, lad." Without taking his eyes off Aedan, he reached out, took Derrick's arm, and dragged him over. His voice was quiet, a low hiss. "Spill it! The pair of you, or your backsides will be red-raw by the time I'm finished with them."

Between their hurried words, sideway glances at each other, and a lot of twitching, the boys related a short version of the story. Spence, Hopper, the rest of the men, bets going down; how they'd healed the dogs; even Spence left hanging on a meat hook!

Maggie gestured nervously. "Shh, shh! Look, we'd better go indoors and talk. I can't risk anyone overhearing this."

"What about the dogs, Mam?"

She raised her eyebrows. "Well, we can hardly leave them here, can we?"

Aedan and Derrick looked at each other and half-smiled. So far, so good.

"But don't go getting any ideas, the pair of you." She nodded at Aedan. "Run on ahead and put Ginger underneath the stairs before we get there." The boys charged, dogs in tow. "Leave the dogs here while you get Ginger out of the way," she shouted.

Derrick bent down and took both dogs by the collar. "Behave for the adults," he whispered. "We've yet to argue your case, especially you!" he said to Ambrose. "My mam is no pushover." The dog whined in agreement. Both boys ran on ahead. "I don't think Ambrose will be giving my mam any trouble!"

"He won't," Aedan agreed. "Animals are quick learners!" The pair chuckled together. It had been an eventful day.

Eileen ran over to her next-door neighbours. "I'd better see if Ada can keep her eye on the kids for a while."

Charlie knelt down between the dogs. "Have you got something to tie these two up with, Maggie?" The dogs leaned their heads into him while he tickled their ears. "I mean, they seem okay now but you can't put fighting dogs with a family…you never know. They'll have to be put down unless one of the farmers wants them."

"Let's not worry about that for now, Charlie." She knew the dogs would be fine. Aedan would have seen to that!

As Eileen made her way back, she waved at Ada. "I shouldn't be more than half an hour."

In the five minutes it took them to reach the cottage, the boys were busy organising cups of tea and being overly concerned about the comfort of the adults in general. As a result, the grownups' suspicions were raised even further.

"Well, this is very nice." Charlie pulled out a chair from underneath the wooden table and sat down. "Makes me wonder what you boys are after—get from under my feet." He gently tapped Julian on the backside.

"You pair! Lie down over there." Maggie pointed to the armchair by the side of the fireplace.

Aedan looked at his mother. He could feel her anxiety and felt bad that he'd upset her, again! He hugged her tightly. "Mam, the men…they didn't realise anything. They thought it was just a trick going on."

Maggie was livid. Her thick Irish accent returned tenfold, and her head jerked on certain words. "Trick, by Jesus!" She slammed her palm down hard on the table. "Jumping in a pen with fighting dogs and living to tell the tale! Taking control of them? Lifting some bloke off his feet and hanging him up in the rafters!" She looked at Aedan, exasperated. "And, and, healing the dogs! How many times have you been told? You can't let people see you use your power like that."

Her words came out so fast that Aedan thought she was talking in a foreign language but he still got the gist. "Spence won't question any of it, Mam. He's a bully. He'll be too scared to show his face around here, and how could I let the dogs suffer?"

She threw her head up at the ceiling, grabbed his shoulders, and shook him hard. "Aedan! So help me God, if you do anything like this again—don't you understand? What if he talks to the newspapers, tells people what happened? Before we know it, all sorts of undesirables will be knocking at the door." She looked at the shocked expression on her son's face, clasped a hand over her mouth, and sighed deeply in an effort to calm down. Her voice softer, "There are others that can't know about you."

"What others?" His face was a picture of innocence.

Mother and son looked into one another's eyes, sharing a pause while she tried to find simple, gentle words which could explain to her eight-year-old that there were others with power like his who used it to do harm...but she came up with nothing! A cocktail of thoughts attacked her. *Underworld, G.U.N., Patrick, Evolus, NeilA*—her defences went up. Aedan was David's son!

Charlie interrupted. "Don't get too carried away, Maggie." He was more concerned about Spence. He knew of the man. He'd never met him in the flesh but he was notorious around the area. "If he did decide to go to the papers, which I doubt, they'd laugh him out of the office, and a man like Spence doesn't like to be made a fool of."

"You know him?" Eileen turned to her husband, a quizzical look on her face.

"I know of him. Nasty piece of work by all accounts. And that's what puzzles me." He looked at Aedan and narrowed his eyes. "How can a man like Spence be threatened by a boy?"

The room went silent. Eileen and Maggie shared a glance. There were no secrets between the two women—not even David. Eileen knew all about Aedan and what he was capable of, though she'd never witnessed it. But true to her promise, she'd never said a word to anyone, not even her husband.

"Well?" Charlie looked from one woman to the other. "What's going on? What's the big secret?"

It was Maggie who spoke. "Charlie, what the boys told us out there. It's all true...Aedan has powers—"

"A gift!" Eileen interrupted.

"Yes, yes, a gift...power," Maggie whispered. "He can do anything with it. Heal, maim, create...destroy." She looked at her son. "We have to keep it secret—for obvious reasons."

"Wait a minute here! You're telling me that this story the boys made up—"

"It's not made up, love!" Eileen cut in. "I believe Aedan has abilities beyond the understanding of most people. I also believe that we've chosen to be in a position to help nurture and protect him." She reached out across the table and took Charlie's hands. "There's a few of us that are…close to him for a reason."

Aedan wanted to show off. "Mam, let me demonstrate for Uncle Charlie," he said, with the typical enthusiasm of an eight-year-old.

Maggie shook her head in dismay, sat down, and looked at Eileen. "He doesn't listen!" Turning to Aedan, she admonished, "After all I've just said?"

"It won't go outside these walls, Maggie, I can promise you that," Charlie winked.

"It's not that. I know I can trust you, Charlie. It's just that…well, I don't want Aedan getting ideas in his head that it's alright to be doing tricks left, right, and centre for all and sundry to see."

Wide-eyed, Aedan promised, "I won't, Mam! I just want to show Uncle Charlie."

All eyes were on her, even the dogs. Maggie stared from one to the other. "Oh, alright! But make it snappy. Derrick, do you realise how important it is to keep this secret for your friend?"

"Course, Aunt Maggie! Aedan's already shown me loads of—" He stopped dead when he saw Aedan's eyes nearly touch his hairline.

Oh, God. Maggie wondered just how much and how long Aedan had been doing private demonstrations for his friend. Her heart sank. *I'll have to explain the underworld to him the sooner the better—but how?* The last thing she wanted to do was scare him to death. She'd talk to White Eagle. Perhaps it would be better coming from him.

"Shall I start, Mam?" Maggie ignored him. "Mam! Shall I start?" Aedan repeated, shaking Maggie out of her anxiety.

"Yes, yes, start! Can I stop you?" She had that warning look on her face.

Aedan looked at the assortment of yellow roses in the old vase.

"See the flowers?" Everybody turned their attention to the vase in the centre of the table.

"They look a bit worse for weather," Charlie commented.

"I know. It's my job to change them when they start looking ropey, but I forgot." Aedan stood up. "And now, ladies and gentleman, a lesson on how to change flowers so that they can live forever." He bowed deeply, threw out a pretend cloak.

"Stop clowning and get on with it!" Maggie felt irked. "And don't leave the flowers this long again!" She shuffled the flowers and carried on talking. "Did you find Ginger?"

Derrick walked around the table and sat on his mother's knee. "Yep, he's under the stairs."

Eileen kissed him. "Give me a bit of room, love, so as I can see." She wanted to be left alone. It wasn't often she got time out from the kids, especially the smaller ones. Derrick got the message and ran around to the opposite side of the table and stood between his dad's legs. Charlie put his arm around his son's middle.

Aedan knelt down on his chair at the head of the table and stretched toward the roses. In a single motion he waved his hand over the top of them. Within seconds they lifted. Their brown, dry leaves turned moist and green, and their withered heads opened in full bloom. Everybody but Maggie sat awestruck as they saw with their own eyes the flowers return to vibrant health and colour.

"Jesus Christ!" Charlie was flabbergasted. "I've never seen the like!"

Eileen had tears streaming down her face. "Isn't it wonderful…the power?" She turned to Maggie. "Maggie, thanks for letting us witness it. I always believed you, but to see it with my own eyes is, is…" She wiped her cheeks with her hand. "I'm lost for words. I feel humbled." Her brash manner returned as soon as she looked at Derrick. "You'd better keep your mouth shut about this! Say nowt to anyone, do you hear me?"

"I won't, Mam. I've already promised."

Aedan was in full show-off mode. Pretending to be a conductor, he chanted out "The Blue Danube" by Johann Strauss, to which the flowers took on a life of their own. Levitating from the vase, they danced in time to both his singing and conducting. Derrick giggled at the stupefied expressions on his parents' faces as Aedan made the flowers bend and curtsy in front of them. Aedan clapped his hands and the flowers immediately stood to attention. "Follow me," he said to his audience.

"Make sure nobody is about," Maggie warned him.

Maggie and the dogs stayed where they were, unimpressed. But Charlie, Eileen, and Derrick followed behind Aedan, who was still singing and conducting "The Blue Danube." The kitchen door opened by itself and the flowers danced through it. In the backyard, Aedan's audience watched, bewildered, as the roses attached themselves back to the bush they'd come from, while others plucked themselves from it and danced past their noses into the cottage. Eileen and Charlie pushed and shoved each other as they raced behind the flowers—Eileen won—but they were both in time to see the flowers plonk themselves into the vase.

A million thoughts went through Charlie's mind but not one of them doubted what he'd seen. After all, he'd seen Maggie turn into an Indian, so what's a few flowers replanting themselves between friends? But one thing was certain: the fewer people who knew about Aedan, the better. He looked at the boy protectively. "Son, be very, very careful, who you show this to," he warned.

Aedan felt his anxiety. Charlie was disturbed. "Do you have any idea of the responsibility involved with something like this?" Charlie's immediate thoughts were with Aedan's welfare. Maggie was right. There were far-reaching consequences at stake here. Some good, but some of them could result in…Charlie didn't want to think about the downside of it. "Aedan, promise us now that you'll use this power only as a last resort."

Maggie looked on and noticed the love between Charlie and Aedan fill the space between them. She smiled. Charlie had taken it upon himself to be a father to Aedan, and Aedan viewed him as such. Why had she only just realised it?

Charlie looked from one boy to the other. "Look, you two. From what you've told us today, it was a matter of life and death. You had to use the power to get out of a scrape." He turned to Aedan. "But you have to think, Aedan. Maybe you shouldn't have gone in to save the dogs. Maybe you could have got them out of there without being noticed. In future try not to go in with all guns blazing. There are loads of ways to use that power without bringing attention to yourself. Do you understand what I'm saying?"

"Kind of!" Aedan's mind was on asking if they could keep the dogs.

Charlie looked over at Maggie and Eileen, and raised his eyebrows. He knew it wasn't going to be easy. At eight years old, gifted or not, it was hard to think like an adult. They'd have to keep their eyes on Aedan without being overly protective—no easy job. "Derrick!" he glared at his son. "It's your job to watch out for Aedan just as much as it's his job to watch out for you. Nobody is to know about this, nobody! Right?"

"Right."

Charlie put his hand on Derrick's shoulder. "Aedan could get into a lot of trouble, get hurt by people that don't appreciate…you have to look after him. Understand? Tell nobody!"

"I won't, Dad! I've seen him do loads of stuff and never said anything—"

"Right!" Aedan wanted to shut his friend up. Maggie would kill him if she found out about some of the pranks they'd pulled off. A few seconds of silence infiltrated the room. Aedan psyched himself up to ask his mam if he could keep Julian. "Mam?"

Here we go. Maggie knew what was coming. It was nothing psychic, just the tone of Aedan's voice and a mother's intuition. "Yes?"

His words rushed out of him. "Let me keep Julian. He'll be no trouble, I promise. I'll look after him, you won't even know he lives here, he's had a rotten life, Mam. Never been outside until we rescued him, made to fight, beat up by his owner from the day he was born—"

Maggie heard the pleading in his voice, felt for the poor animal herself. "Alright!"

Aedan didn't realise she'd agreed to let him keep the dog. "He needs love and kindness, Mam, and he's got good manners, I've already taught him some—"

"Aedan, calm down. I said you can keep him."

"I can?" Shocked, he ran at his mother and peppered her with kisses; he threw himself at Julian and did the same to him. "You can stay, this is your new home!" he squealed breathlessly.

"Hopefully you'll be too tied up with the dog to get into any more trouble—but what about the other one? We can't keep the two of them, Aedan." The room went silent, all eyes on Derrick.

"He's my dog!" he said, sheepishly.

"Is he now?" Charlie said, looking at his wife.

"Absolutely not!" Eileen said. "I've got enough to do with four kids and you!"

"Mam, please. You won't have anything to do. I'll do it…and me dad."

Charlie looked at his son, his expression one of fake indignity. "Oh we will, will we?"

"He can help us on the coal round, Dad, and you love animals—"

"Throw a sack of coal on his back, will he?" Charlie dipped his head and looked underneath his eyebrows. "Clever dog, that!"

Eileen looked at the dog. "We don't have room for a dog like that, son—"

"He won't take up much room, Mam, only a corner, and he can sleep with me."

"I'm not having him in the bedrooms—"

"Does that mean I can keep him?"

"No, it bloody well doesn't!"

Charlie stretched over and clasped Eileen's hand. "You know it might not be a bad idea given how far these two seem to travel when we're not around." He looked at the boys. "You've no right being as far up the peak as Higher Shelf Stones! How many times have I told the pair of you?"

"Sorry, Dad, Uncle Charlie," they said in unison.

He turned back to Eileen. "Dogs will look after them."

Derrick looked at Ambrose. "I told you you'd have to get past my mam."

The dog stood up, walked over to Eileen, and plonked his head in her lap. Shocked, she said, "Would you look at that?" She stroked him softly along his back.

"He knows the decision is yours, Eileen," Charlie said, letting her know that he was on side with Derrick and the dog. "His life is in your hands."

"Don't think you're setting me up to feel all guilty!—" The dog whined, his head still in her lap. She looked down at his eyes rolling about in their sockets. "You know, Charlie, really! You don't half put me on the spot at times."

"The lad needs a dog and I'd like one myself. What's the problem?"

"Feeding it, room, cleaning up after it!"

"We'll take care of it! Derrick's right—he'll only take up a corner somewhere."

"Damn it!" she said, aggressively. "Dog like this needs a lot of exercise and I don't have time to look after him." She turned to Derrick. "That means you'll have to be up an hour earlier in the mornings to take him out, and you, Charlie, will have to take him at lunchtime when you've finished the round, before you have a nap!"

"I'll just take him on the round with me; that way, Derrick doesn't have to get up any earlier on a school day and the dog will be out getting plenty of exercise. I can take that one as well." He nodded at Julian. "But you two will be responsible for changing their water, feeding them, brushing them, and taking them out for their evening walks—no ifs, no buts, no maybes."

"Looks like you've already got it sewn up." Eileen fidgeted with the chain around her neck. She felt dejected by Charlie's lack of support in the matter.

"Come on, Mrs. Gelsthorpe…you'll feel better when the boys are out on the peaks if they've got the dogs with them," he said, appealing to her mother instinct. "You know you will…come on." He stood up, walked around the table, and stood over her. "Come on." He bent down, wrapped his arms around her, and whispered something dirty in her ear. She smiled despite herself. "Dog won't be any trouble. In a few weeks he'll be just like one of the family."

"I suppose."

Derrick beamed. The light coming out of him made his blonde hair and blue eyes shine even brighter. He jumped up and charged his mother. "Mam, I'll never ask for anything again. This is the best present I've ever had!" Tears coursed down his face.

"Don't be so daft!" She turned to Charlie. "Have you got a hanky on you? Mine's still full of mud!" He dug one out of his pocket and passed it to her.

Eileen wiped her son's tears away with the creased-up cotton and squeezed it around his nose. "You're too sensitive for your own good." An inquisitive look rippled across her face. "Have these dogs got names?" Derrick and Aedan looked at each other and immediately burst into hysterical laughter. "Did I say something funny?"

"I'd like to introduce you to Ambrose." The dog let out an irritated yelp.

"Ambrose!" Charlie almost choked on his tea. "No wonder he's complaining! If you think I'm going to be shouting a toffee-nosed name like that up and down the bloody street, you've got another think coming!"

The boys were helpless with laughter. Maggie and Eileen smirked at each other. "Well, at least you two are having fun," Eileen said.

Aedan struggled to name his dog between laughs. "And thi, this is Julie...Julian!" he blurted. To which Maggie's cottage erupted in laughter.

"You can't call ugly buggers like these two lovely names like Julian and Ambrose," Maggie insisted.

Aedan was mortified. "They're not ugly, Mam! Don't say that—you'll upset them." He hugged the dogs to him. "They're beautiful."

"Well, at least with names like that they don't seem as scary." Eileen winked at the boys. "Good choice!"

Charlie laughed. "I'm going to feel a right Richard, shouting Ambrose and bloody Julian after rough-looking sods like these! I don't know which one is worse—"

"CHARLES!" Aedan and Derrick blurted out together, sending Maggie and Eileen into fits of laughter again.

"Don't be so bloody cheeky, the lot of you!" Charlie dragged Ambrose by the collar and pried his mouth open. "Let's have a look at your teeth…not bad, not bad." Then he did the same with Julian. "Obviously been well fed to keep them in top condition…and I don't know where you get them locked up in a cold, dark, space, Aedan. Look at the muscles on them."

"Well…I think they've only been let out in a small space. They've never had the freedom of the peaks!" Aedan knew it was the healing that had filled in the gaps that Spence and Hopper had neglected.

"Is that a fact? The freedom of the peaks!" Aedan was a clever little sod, he'd give him that!

"Yep, and their names reflect their manners," Aedan said, like an old man.

"Well, I hope that's right because they've still got one more test to pass," Maggie said, looking at Julian. "Ginger! If he doesn't like them, you've got a problem on your hands."

Charlie cocked his head in the direction of the kitchen. "You'd better go and get him, son, while I'm here."

Aedan ran down to the cellar and picked up a disgruntled Ginger, who was more than comfortable on the makeshift bed that Maggie had made up. Aedan held the cat out in front of him, and spoke like the cowboys he went to see at the Saturday matinee.

"Time for a talk, Ginger, man to man. We've got a new member in the family—well, two really, but only one will live with us full-time, and I'd appreciate it if you were nice to him. He's called Julian and he's a dog!" Ginger's superior and cranky expression let Aedan know that this Julian had better be worth waking him up for, and he'd also better understand who was boss. "The other dog is called Ambrose. He's going to live with Derrick, but he'll be around here a lot, visiting."

Ginger wasn't impressed. He yawned and looked at Aedan as if to say, "Well then, let's get on with it, if we must." Aedan walked back into the front parlour with his arms circled around Ginger protectively. Nevertheless, all hell broke loose! As soon as the dogs spied the creature in Aedan's arms they went right back into killing mode.

Ginger sprang from Aedan's arms as if on a piece of elastic, body rigid, claws out; his legs seemed to have sprouted an extra two feet in length. He ran full pelt across Maggie's table, knocking her flowers, candles, cups, saucers, and teapot all over the place—hot tea poured into Charlie's lap—"Jesus!" He jumped up, brushed at his trousers. "I'll kill them fu—stupid dogs!" The two dogs, on the table now, charged past him, jumped off the table, and stood barking and snarling at the bottom of Maggie's curtains. A terrified Ginger clung for dear life to the top of them.

Maggie looked at her wrecked parlour, paced over to the dogs, grabbed their collars, and dragged them away from the curtains. "Look at the state of this bloody room! Leave the cat alone or I'll knock the pair of you into the middle of next week!" she fumed. "GET IN THE CORNER AND BEHAVE, OR ELSE!"

No questions asked, the dogs eyed her shamefacedly and did as they were told. She looked at Aedan and Derrick, one eyebrow lifted. "Is this an example of their manners?" The pair remained quiet. "Well?"

"I'll sort it, Mam!"

"You'd better!"

She walked over to the curtains. "Ginger, come here, sweetheart. Come on, it's alright," she coaxed. The cat cautiously slid down the curtains into Maggie's hands. The dogs inched up, low growls coming from deep inside them. Maggie lifted her index finger and glared at the dogs. "Stay there and be quiet!" she snapped. She passed Ginger to Aedan. So far, so good. Julian went to get up. She looked at him, a dangerous expression in her eyes. "You just dare, boy, and you'll be cat meat on next week's menu!" He whined back at her. Maggie shot the dog a look that told him he'd better get out of the habit of answering back! "Don't give me your attitude! It won't wash!" Julian stayed in the corner, not daring to move.

Aedan crouched down; Ginger struggled to break free from his arms. "Shh, Ginger, it'll be okay. I'm going to make sure they know who's boss." He looked at the dogs. Both had guilty expressions on their faces. "This is Ginger; you treat him nice at all times. He was here first, so what he says goes whether you like it or not! Understand?" The dogs grunted and snorted under their breath. Aedan emphasised his words. "And that goes for any other creature or person you come into contact with unless your life, or the life of someone you love, comes under threat. I expect impeccable manners at all times," he admonished. "You're not fighters anymore so you'd better behave like gentlemen." Maggie turned her head away to stifle laughter.

He looked at the cat. "Shall we let them stay?" He tried to release Ginger to the floor space in front of the dogs but he felt the cat's back legs start to kick against him. "You'll be okay. They know you're the boss," he whispered, setting the cat down and stroking the length of its back.

Ginger held back a bit, not quite sure. His back arched and sunk underneath Aedan's hands before he finally decided that the dogs knew their place, and edged a bit closer. Dogs and cat sniffed each other with Ginger circling and inspecting them, like a sergeant on drill duty.

"Well." Aedan squinted at the cat. "Have they passed the test?" The superior expression on the cat's face seemed to say, "I think they know their place." He settled down on Julian's belly and fell asleep.

33.

Aedan awoke to the sound of his mother's muffled singing, a few cows mooing on the neighbouring farmland and the smell of baking. It was Saturday morning. An excited feeling filled his belly—no school!

Maggie's voice singing "Oh, Danny Boy" got louder, bouncing on certain words as she ran up the stairs. Aedan threw back the covers and bolted out of bed. After they finished the coal round, they were going into Glossop! The market was on, and the Manchester Regiment would be there. He'd been looking forward to it for weeks. If he was lucky he might get to sit in one of the jeeps and talk to the soldiers.

"The pipes, the pipes are calling." Maggie's voice filled the bedroom. "You're up, then! Didn't think you'd be much trouble this morning." She pulled back his blankets. "Let your bed air before you make it." She kissed him. "From glen to glen, and down the mountain side...open your window, don't dawdle! Charlie will be here any minute." She left the room, singing as she went, "'Tis you, 'tis you, must go and I must bide..."

Aedan opened the window and then bounced down the stairs after her. Julian was already waiting at the bottom, spinning about and wagging his tail. Aedan bent down, hugged the dog to him, and rocked him from side to side a few times. "Oh, Danny boooooy..." Maggie's shrill tones belted out the crescendo. Dog and boy looked at each other and Aedan grimaced, "God, that's terrible!" The dog made a small noise as if to say, "You're telling me!"

In the kitchen, Aedan sliced off a piece of steaming apple pie and stuffed it into his mouth hungrily. "Ow!" He shouted, spitting it back on the plate.

Maggie ran from her front parlour and shook her finger at him. She'd done most of the preparing the night before, so that she could just shove them in the oven when she got up. "That'll teach you to keep your hands off. The pies are to share with Eileen's lot later," she scolded. "Get cleaned up. Charlie is going to walk through that door any time now and he won't be too pleased if you're not ready."

Aedan faked a posh voice, and had an uppity look on his face. "Good morning, Mamma! I trust that you are well this fine day?"

She ran over to him, hugged him tightly, and kissed the top of his head, taking in his fruity smell. "Good morning, darling."

"Umm, Mamma, you smell like carbolic soap!"

"Carbolic soap! You cheeky ha'peth! You could have said something a bit more exotic. I was enjoying your fruity smell!"

Innocent expression. "I like the smell of carbolic soap."

She looked into his face. His eyes were shining as bright as hers. "Excited?"

"I've got butterflies."

She spied Charlie walking through the back garden. "Hurry up. I'll have breakfast ready for when you get back. Charlie said he's keeping the round short this morning, only delivering to them who's desperate—"

There was a sharp rap at the back door. Charlie stuck his head through the jamb. "Let's go." He looked down and jerked his head at the dog that was practically doing cartwheels at his feet. "Come on, boy."

Aedan was already halfway up the garden. Maggie ran behind, attempting to get him dressed. "Coat, cap!" She plonked the cap on his head and rammed his coat into him.

"It's not cold."

"It's chilly in the mornings—here." She banged the piece of apple pie in his hand. "That'll do you 'til you get back." She followed them out so she could lock the back gate after them. "Charlie will let you back in." There was a small crevice in the wall left by two missing bricks. Charlie always stuck his foot into it and reached over the back gate to let himself in.

"I'll have him back by eight, Maggie. Eileen said you're leaving around nine."

"That's right. Drop Derrick off as well. I'll see to these two. Eileen's got enough to do with the other three."

Once they'd left, she bent down to look at the flowers and herbs in her garden and spied a patch of dandelions hidden amongst the green spiky heads of her burdock root. She reached forward and held them in her hand. "Well, you would feel at home with old Burdock, wouldn't you? Some say he's a weed as well." She stroked the soft, yellow heads. "Now look: you can stay, as long as you don't make a nuisance of yourselves."

She looked up at the sky and inhaled the clean, fresh air. It was just after five. She loved the early morning. It was so peaceful. It was going to be a hectic day. She decided to take a few minutes meditation time to exercise her mind and help keep her relaxed. She reached behind the door, grabbed her shawl from the hook, and wrapped it around her shoulders. She moved to a small grassed area to the left of her herbs and flowers, sat down on the stone wall, and started to deep breathe. She felt the air revitalise her cells as its coolness travelled down into her lungs. She closed her eyes and felt her mind push her brain aside and open up to the creative force. Inspiration flooded through her.

Ah, the beauty of a weed, she thought to herself. *True spirituality has no inhibitions, no limitations, no barriers, and no judgments. True spirituality means liberation. The spiritual person sees the beauty in all things, even that which may be judged as hideous, for the hideous is divinity at its most beautiful and its most powerful. If you can see beauty in the hideous, you recognise God in all things. To go into a garden full of weeds would be considered walking amongst God's treasures, and to dig them up to save a flower, a false truth.*

Opening her eyes slowly, she stretched, and rolled her neck a few times. She looked at the dandelions. "Now remember what I told you!" She laughed to herself. She'd been talking to nature from as far back as she could remember. If anyone heard her they'd have her locked up for sure. She got to her feet and knocked the soil from her clothes. "Ah, well, better get breakfast prepared."

34.

Maggie walked from the kitchen into the living room. "Right, you two! We'd better get a move on. Get cleaned up. Derrick, you'd better get Ambrose home..." Maggie's thoughts registered on her face. "Unless you want to leave him here with Julian; that way they'll be company for each other being as we'll be gone all day. They stay in the back garden, mind! It's not cold."

"Can we take 'em, Mam?" Aedan wiped leftover yolk and bacon fat off his plate with a piece of bread. By the time he'd done, the plate looked as if it had been given a coat of polish.

Maggie gawped at her son's matter-of-fact request. "You must be joking! Don't you think me and Eileen have got enough to do with the five of you?" She put a huge cob of coal onto the fire and pushed a small mesh fireguard in front of it. "Hopefully, that'll burn all day and I won't have to myther with it when I get back." She turned to Aedan. "You're not going to get another crumb off that plate!" She pulled the plate from under him, then pushed it back into him. "Come on, come on." She flapped her hand in dismissal.

"Please, Mam! They won't be any trouble." He stood up, took his plate, and walked to the sink. Derrick was already drying his hands with a dish towel.

"Derrick! Don't dry your hands with my pot towel—here!" Maggie threw him a small hand towel.

Derrick looked at her, confused. "What's the difference?"

"That one's for dishes, the terry is for hands. You should know that!"

"Me and Derrick will look after 'em."

Maggie felt irritable. She didn't know why. She'd woken up with a funny feeling. "Look after what?" she asked, shaking her head.

"The dogs, Mam!" Aedan said, exasperated.

"It's a busy market, Aedan. You can't have these two running around. We've not even got leads for them. Get your coats on, the pair of you. I don't want to keep Eileen waiting." She shoved their coats into their arms.

"We can tie some string to their collars. Please, Mam. They'll be bored on their own all day."

"Not together they won't." She stopped for a minute. Something nagged at her. For some reason she decided that it might be a good idea to let the dogs tag along. "Oh, alright! I'm just too damn soft for my own good." She put her coat on hurriedly and walked out the front door. "But I've not got any string. We'll call in Catlow's and see if Cyril has got a couple of leads." She gave Aedan a determined look. "But if he hasn't, they don't come. They have proper leads or nothing."

Boys and dogs ran up the path before her. "Get hold of their collars this minute!" she snapped. "Keep hold of them until we get the leads." They walked the five minutes to meet Eileen, who was already waiting outside for them. She looked at the dogs and raised her eyebrows.

"I know." Maggie nodded in the direction of Catlow's. "I'm too bloody soft. I've told the boys if Cyril hasn't got any leads, the dogs are staying at home…" She paused for a moment, then winced. "I don't know what it is but I've had a strange feeling about me this morning."

"What kind of feeling?" Eileen asked. "Good, bad, what?"

"Not good, not bad. More like a dread—"

Celia screamed over their conversation. The two women looked across to see Aedan holding a small rubber ball just out of her reach. "Aedan!" Maggie scolded. "Give it back! Stop tormenting her or you'll be feeling my foot up your arse, so you will!"

They walked a little farther and stopped outside Catlow's. Maggie turned to Eileen. "Won't be a minute." She opened the door. Eileen and the rest of them waited outside.

Inside the shop, Cyril and a crowd of men were huddled around a small wireless listening to some bloke called Lord Haw-Haw ranting on about siding with the Germans. The air was blue with cigarette smoke to which Maggie showed her disdain by wafting it away from her nose and mouth. She felt crankier than ever. "It's like a bloody opium den in here!"

"Maggie." The men lifted their caps, and carried on listening to Lord Haw-Haw.

"Off into Glossop?" Cyril asked.

"Yes, the boys are looking forward to seeing the Manchester Regiment."

"Should be a good day. I might shut shop for a few hours later. Me and Ann could do with a trip out."

Maggie gave him a disapproving look. "Why don't you? Get some fresh air in your lungs!"

An amused expression spread out over Cyril's face. He was used to Maggie's bossy persona. She meant well. "What can I get you?"

"I don't suppose you've got any dog leads?" She looked around.

Cyril pointed. "Over there by the pet food; only one colour though."

She ran over, unhooked two leads from a small nail that jutted out from the shelf, and ran back. "They'll do." She passed him the two leather leads, light tan in colour. "They won't stay that colour for long. I'll take a quarter of mint balls and a quarter of the bon-bons, please, and you'd better give me some chocolate for the baby—white if you've got it."

Using a small silver scoop, Cyril shovelled the sweets out of the glass jars into white paper bags. "Do you want a bag for the leads?"

"No, thanks. I've been cajoled into taking the dogs along with us."

"Good luck!" Cyril laughed.

"Do you want me to leave this door open, let some of the smoke out? Bad for your lungs that lot, you know!"

"You'd better not, Maggie—it's Lord Haw-Haw. There's a ban on listening to him."

She shook her head and tutted. "Then turn him off and let some fresh air in; get rid of all that hot air!"

Cyril grinned. "I'll do that, Maggie. Enjoy your day."

Outside she held the bon-bons up to the younger children. "These are to share, but we expect you to behave yourselves." She gave the bag to Celia, the eldest girl. "You're in charge. Share them with Marion. Don't give Peter any; he could choke on them. I've got him some chocolate instead."

Celia's eyes lit up when Maggie handed her the bulging bag of white, sugar-coated, caramel balls. "Wow! Thanks, Aunty Maggie!"

Maggie turned to Derrick and Aedan. "And you two can share these with me and Eileen." But they were more interested in the dog leads.

"Mam, these are fantastic!"

Eileen and Maggie swapped glances and smirked. "Doesn't take much to please," Eileen said. "A couple of dog leads and they're as happy as pigs in muck!" She pushed on Peter's trolley. "Come on, we'd better make a start. We've a good hour's walk in front of us—"

"Oh, bloody hell!"

"What?" everybody said together.

Maggie dropped her shopping bag and headed back toward the house. "The damn gas masks. Not one of us has remembered them!"

"Damn and blast!" Eileen responded. "Derrick! Aedan! Wait here! Keep your eyes on this lot while I run in and get the masks."

Marion protested. "Not wearing one! They make me feel sick."

Derrick had little patience with his younger sister. "Do you want to live to be six?"

"Yes."

"Then wear it or you'll die—"

"Derrick!" Eileen caught the tail end of their conversation. "Don't talk like that to her! You'll scare her to death! There are gentler words you can use to get your point across," she chided, as she ran back to the house.

It wasn't long before Maggie and Eileen returned with the masks. Marion started to bawl at the mere sight of them. "Pooh! Not wearing it, Mam! It stinks!"

Eileen crouched down and slipped the brown paper bag over

Marion's shoulder. "Your brother is right, sweetheart. The gas mask can save your life." Eileen took her own mask out of the rectangular bag and put it on. "Pooh!" she said, from inside the mask. "You're right, it stinks!" She bobbed her head about and started blowing raspberries. Everybody including Marion erupted into laughter.

"Maybe we should have a trial run before we set off," Maggie chipped in, fitting her own mask perfectly. She put one hand on her hip and pranced up and down the street faking an upper class English accent. "This year's top model, Maggie O'Connell, is wearing the latest in designer accessories. This black rubber mask will add that extra bit of finesse to any outfit and can be worn at the most formal of occasions." She did a small pirouette, blew a huge raspberry, and burst into laughter with everyone else.

"Mam, your head looks ten times bigger!" Aedan said, trying on his mask.

"Come on. I want to see everyone with their masks on," Maggie ordered, still wearing hers.

Marion tugged at her mother's sleeve. "What about Peter?"

"I'll be fitting Peter's, love. He's too young to do it himself. Now! Let's fit yours…there, you see. Nothing to it!"

Marion grinned up at her mother. Only her smiling eyes were visible. "I like it!" she announced.

Derrick pointed. "You look like an anteater," he teased.

"Well! You look like a big fat elephant! Anyway, I don't care what you say!" She turned to her mother. "Can I keep it on?"

"No, sweetheart. It's only for special occasions."

><

The day was crisp and shiny with a scattering of white clouds that floated gracefully through a clear blue sky. Apart from the smell of onions and baked goods, the air was fresh and filled with the healthy smell of changing foliage, typical of autumn. There was a keen nip about but the sun persisted in waving its rays over the market town, as if giving a gentle warning that come the afternoon all jackets and cardigans were to be removed.

A brass band played in Norfolk Square, and a small fair with a few amusements and children's rides had been set up just in front of the town hall. The smell of toffee apples, candyfloss, and fudge added to the vibrancy of the atmosphere, which was charged with the excited laughter of children bobbing up and down on the merry-go-rounds.

Families paced slow and easy up and down the small, winding streets and roads. For most, war and work were a million miles away. They would enjoy the day no matter what. However, better make sure the air raid shelters weren't too far, just in case! It didn't do to become too complacent.

Business thrived in the queer little shops with crooked walls and creaking floorboards. The old witches that emerged from the shadows were more than pleased to show off their wares and hidden treasures. Maggie often dreamed that one day she'd set up a business there herself, selling herbal potions and creams, gems and crystals; offer readings and healing; even hold meditation and development classes—perhaps the odd séance or two! She sighed. *One day we'll realise that what we term primitive is the most advanced.* For now she'd have to keep her gifts behind the walls of 7 Geraent Place, open to the few who accepted them…and her.

She looked down at the gold and brown leaves swirling around her feet. A warm sensation, like the feeling of new love, passed through her. She loved autumn. *Something good is going to happen today. I can feel it, but…* She dismissed the feeling of dread that waited inside her like a serpent on guard, and as she glanced over at the market stalls on the other side of the road she was literally thrown into a different era. Ladies in long, flowing dresses and silk bonnets were being escorted by gentlemen in top hat and tails, and market boys no more than five years old scavenged for food. Angry stallholders chased after them, hurling obscenities as well as their fists. All of them were still there, living and breathing in a different dimension; 1839 happening at the same time as 1939! She wondered if the same people running the market stalls a hundred years ago were the same ones running them right now, in this moment? *Perhaps*…maybe those who still felt that they had something to gain from such an experience. She smiled to herself. Could this be another example of the soul living out two aspects of itself at the same time? And how many other aspects did it have on the go? Past, present, and future, living and breathing at the same time—

Eileen's voice brought her back down to earth. "Just look at the state of him!" She brought the pushchair to a halt and crouched down to clean the chocolate from Peter's face and hands. "You're a messy little beggar." She shook her head from side to side. "Messy little beggar, messy little beggar," she repeated.

Peter chuckled. "Meshy ickle biggie," he said, trying to imitate his mother.

She held his small fist to her mouth and sprinkled it with kisses. She looked up at Maggie. "I could murder a cuppa!"

"Oh, good idea! I'm parched."

"Here, give me your shopping. It'll go on the handles."

Maggie passed her already-bulging bag over. "Let me push him for a bit."

Eileen was happy to swap shifts. "We'll have a walk around the stalls later—"

"Not the market stalls! I'm bored with shopping, Mam. When we gonna see the Manchesters?"

"Typical bloody male, Derrick Gelsthorpe! It's no use going to see 'em yet. Look at the queues. We'll be stood there all day."

"Me and Aedan can go on our own. We don't mind queuing up."

Eileen shook her head. "No! What if you get lost?"

"We'll be alright, Mam. We can meet you somewhere later."

"Do you think they'll be alright, Maggie? I know I don't fancy waiting in line for hours, especially with the little ones."

Maggie shrugged. "We could meet them in the line-up in about an hour. That way we won't have as long to queue. They should be alright, being as they've got the dogs with them." She looked at the boys. "Go and see if one of the butchers will give you some water for the dogs; and see to it that you find a shade for them when you're in that queue." She looked across at the line-up by the side of the soldier's stall. "It's getting hot. Dogs and sunshine don't mix very well. We'll meet you in about an hour, so don't move away from that area even if you've seen the Manchesters—which I very much doubt, looking at them crowds."

Aedan and Derrick looked at each other with impatient expressions. They couldn't wait to get away from the women and kids! "Is that it, Mam?"

She felt the serpent of dread in her gut wriggle up her windpipe. *Don't let them go!* She buried it. "Be careful! You know what to do if the sirens go off?"

"Yep," they answered as they half turned, and were already on the run before she had second thoughts.

35.

The dogs jumped up, lapping at the dish of water before Aedan had a chance to put it down on the pavement. "Manners," he said, holding the dish in the air. "Sit!" Their heads following the motion of the dish, the dogs plonked themselves down on their backsides obediently. Aedan put the water down in front of them while staring over at the Manchesters with a strange look on his face.

Within seconds, the water was gone. "Well, that didn't last long, you greedy buggers!" Derrick picked up the dish and turned to Aedan. "I'll take the dish back…Aedan, Aedan? Are you alright?" Aedan's face had taken on a peculiar blank stare. "Aedan—"

"Yeah, yeah, I'm fine."

"Who you staring at?"

"Him," Aedan whispered.

Derrick looked towards the Manchesters. They were based just inside Norfolk Square, about three hundred feet in the distance. "The captain? Let's see if we can talk to him. Do you think he'll let us sit in his jeep?"

"I feel funny…kinda weird about him."

"Why? He doesn't look weird."

"It's…it's like I know him." He turned to Derrick, puzzled. "But I've never met him so how can I…?"

The sudden sound of air raid sirens pierced the air and screamed at everyone to take cover. It took seconds for Glossop to erupt into mayhem. Women screamed; babies and children cried. Men, frantic, shouted orders at their families—"Don't let go of your sister's hand!"

"Come on, get a move on!" "The sooner we make it to the air raid shelter the better." Fear spread through the crowds well before the bombers got there; it scattered them in different directions like small beetles hunting for cover underneath soil.

Suddenly the only world Aedan and Derrick were aware of was the one wrapped around them. Everything went into slow motion: the noise, the people, even their own movements. It was as if an invisible wall had come down and cocooned the two of them, keeping them confined to their own small area, their own moment. They looked into each other's eyes, and read each other's thoughts. *What do we do now?*

The dogs barked and growled nervously as the crowd panicked and jostled past them. "GET TO THE AIR RAID SHELTER!" Aedan screamed at Derrick, just as Julian broke free from his hand. "JULIAN!" He charged after him, stopped abruptly, and turned back to Derrick. "DON'T COME WITH ME—I'LL MEET YOU IN THE SHELTER!" he yelled before disappearing into the crowd.

Aedan looked up. The German bombers, at least fifteen, maybe more, climbed higher and higher into the clear blue sky, reached a pinnacle, and flipped over before heading straight back towards him. In that split second he saw them: huge demons on the wings. He jumped back, terrified. *Don't be stupid, they're planes!* he thought, reprimanding himself.

It was the most disturbing thing he'd ever seen. He felt the fear move right through him. Like a living entity, it pushed and poked, and curled its tentacles around his heart, his brain, his mind. He felt dizzy and nauseous, and an overpowering heat was coming off his body. He felt alone. "MAAAAM!" he cried out, tears streaming. "WHERE ARE YOU?" Just as he was about to collapse into the waiting arms of fear, the pathetic howls of Julian, desperate to find him, brought Aedan back to his senses faster than any smelling salts could have done.

He forgot all about how frightened he was and pushed and shoved his way through the crowd in a desperate attempt to find his friend. "JULIAN!" he screamed out. "COME BACK, BOY, COME BACK!"

The dog tried to run through the massive crowd, twisting one way then the other, yelping out at people who stepped on his paws. "JULIAN!" The dog turned, saw Aedan, and let out a small whimper. "Come here, boy, you're safe now." He grabbed the dog's lead just as the aircraft released a cluster of bombs over the town. He looked up, terrified, but only for a second before the survival instinct kicked in. He looked down into Julian's face. "RUUUUNNN!" he screamed at him, knowing that they wouldn't make it to the shelter. They raced toward the side streets in the hope of hiding out in one of the many shops. Aedan's heart froze over as the high-pitched whistles from the bombs nose-dived toward ground level—louder, louder. He felt the blood rush through his veins, into his head, and thump in his ears to the beat of his heart. He stopped dead in the madness and clutched his stomach. Not even his run-in with Spence had stirred up a sensation like this! The fear inside him turned into a frenzied rage. It coursed through his body like white-hot lava. The cry of a small child caught his attention. He looked around. There were still a few families trying to make it to the shelters. He knew that only a miracle could save them now.

He looked up at the bombs. He didn't know how close they were but they looked big. Just as the energy inside him reached its pinnacle he shouted at the top of his voice, "STAY UP THERE, YOU BASTAAAARDS!" and almost at once the sound of the whistling stopped. The bombs hung in the air like frightened kites looking for the wind. Aedan's eyes drilled into them, controlling them perfectly. The energy exploded out of him. Strikes of blue-white lightning streamed through the sky until it exploded, white and sparkling, like a million fireworks. It cocooned the bombs, holding them suspended in midair.

Aedan knew that the rage inside him had turned into a lethal power. He swallowed hard. He didn't like it. Where did it come from—this power? Why was he so different to other people?

All around him, people stopped running and stared up at the bombs, then stared at him with puzzled expressions. What in God's name was going on? This small boy seemed to hold the bombs captive. Or was it the lightning that had something to do with it? Why wasn't the boy dead or at least unconscious after being struck like that? Could they believe their own eyes?

"RUUUUUN!" he screamed at them. He felt drained. He couldn't hold on much longer. His body trembled, the sweat poured from him. "RUN OR YOU'LL DIE!"

As the energy wore thin, the bombs started to fall slowly, as if captured by an invisible net that was about to break. Aedan held on as long as he could to give people a chance to get away. The German pilots circled the bombs and radioed back and forth before they shot off back to base in disbelief. The sound of the planes tailing off into the distance disguised the manic screams from the demons. They'd failed to catch any souls with no explanation as to why? What had stopped the bombs in midair? Evolus would inflict untold misery and torture upon them!

Julian whimpered, gently put his teeth around Aedan's wrist, and tried to drag him towards the side streets. *Run or you'll die!* The shrill screams of the bombs, sounding like hungry demons, disturbed the small town yet again.

Aedan saw the small doorway and dived as hard as he could towards it, his hand never letting go of Julian's lead, until the ground and the building exploded into a million pieces around them.

Apart from the rustling of autumn leaves being rolled along the empty streets by the breeze, Glossop was silent.

><

"You can't leave, madam, not until the all-clear is given!" The stout, middle-aged special constable did his best to restrain Maggie.

She grabbed his arms and tried to physically throw him from the exit. Hysterical, she screamed at him, "I have to find my son! Move man, let me pass!"

The constable grasped Maggie's hands, looked into her eyes, his voice firm. "The siren will give the all-clear any minute now and I'll make sure you're the first one out."

Maggie felt Aedan cut through her. "IT'S QUIET NOW! LET ME LEAVE! HE'S TERRIFIED, I KNOW IT!" she screamed.

Aware of Maggie's growing hysteria, the constable knew that he couldn't be too soft in his response. "NOW LISTEN!" The look on Maggie's face stabbed at his heart but he remained firm. "You can't leave until I say so. Sit down and be calm or I'll see to it that you're the last one out of here—"

"But my son. He's just a baby. Just a baby out there with the bombs on his own; please let me go. He's my only son," she sobbed, deflated.

He still held Maggie's wrists. "I understand...I do." He looked at her kindly. "But I can't open the door until the all-clear is given."

"Maggie, come with me, come on." Ashen-faced, Eileen grasped Maggie's elbow. "I can't find Celia," she said. "I've been up and down the shelter...found Derrick...do you remember when you last saw her?"

Time stood still between the two women. The sound of the voices singing "Knick-Knack Paddy-Whack" and "Ten Green Bottles" faded into the background. It was Maggie who spoke. "Celia? She's not here? But I thought..." She nodded emphatically. "She was with us. I remember. We had them all with us, didn't we? Oh God, Eileen!" She looked horror-struck.

The welcome sound of the siren giving the all-clear caused a mass exodus. People, relieved as well as desperate to get out of the shelter, rushed forward to the exit. The constable signalled Maggie and Eileen to get a move on before he was hit with a barrage of complaints.

Outside, the air hung thick with leftover dust and grime. Slowly Glossop filled up with people once again. But there was no merriment now. Families held onto each other and trudged along in shock as they made the sombre journey back home; that was, if they still had a home to go to. Others wailed and desperately shouted the names of loved ones who were missing. The distress signals from the ambulance, police, and fire brigade cut through them like evil spirits, as they feared the worst.

Maggie turned to Eileen. "It'd be better if we split up. I remember having Celia with us at the teahouse when the sirens went off. You and Derrick search in that direction." She looked at Derrick. "When did you last see Aedan?"

"Outside the butcher's, across from the Manchesters in Norfolk Square."

"Right, I'll head that way. I'll take Marion with me; it'll lighten your load a bit, Eileen."

Eileen passed Maggie's handbag to her. "Leave your shopping on the trolley. No use lugging it around. Is there anything else you need?"

"No, no," she said, distracted. "I...I think our children are hurt."

Eileen put her hand to her mouth. Maggie's statement agreed with the feeling that had nagged at her insides since she'd discovered her daughter's absence. "Maggie, if I lose her...I couldn't bear it, I couldn't. I'd rather be dead!"

Maggie grabbed her shoulders. "Be quiet!" She looked at the frightened expressions on the faces of Derrick and Marion. "No matter what happens you're still the mother of these three and the wife of a good man. Do you hear me? We can't fall apart now, Eileen. We have to search for the other two. Don't give up!"

Derrick wiped the sweat from his brow, took off his jacket, and placed it over the handles of Peter's trolley. "Come on, Mam, we'll find them."

Maggie bent down and cupped her hands around Ambrose's head. "Sniff 'em out. You know what's going on, don't you boy?" The dog's bottom wiggled and shook like a plate of jelly.

She smiled a weak smile and stood up. She couldn't stop her tears from escaping, or keep the emotion out of her voice. "Look after your mam." She hugged Derrick, kissed Peter, and clasped Marion firmly. When she looked at Eileen, no words were needed. The two women fell into each other and sobbed. They clung to each other for the longest time it seemed, though only a few seconds in passing. Breaking free, they wiped each other's tears away before heading off in separate directions.

⇌

White Eagle turned to Roman. "Aedan saw them—the demons."

"Yes, yes, we're aware of that. They didn't see him…" Roman's voice trailed off with his thoughts before he snapped, "The sooner you explain the dark to Aedan and his role with G.U.N. and Galaxias, the better. When Evolus finds out that the bombs stayed in midair for three minutes before hitting the ground, he'll know that some kind of intervention happened. We'd hoped to keep him at bay until Aedan was a lot older…Yes, yes, we must explain it to the child," he said, as if trying to convince himself. Roman's voice stayed calm and steady. "We'll protect him, of course, but he must be on his guard. He's no match for Evolus or many of his workers yet.

"The weaker demons are no threat to him…they'd never get near his light. But the child is vulnerable, as we saw with Sister Devlin. The temptation to flex his muscles now and again can bring the power of the dark nearer. You must stress this to Aedan. No unwanted attention. Discretion, White Eagle, discretion. Now is the time to train him… yes." Roman's voice turned into a whisper. "Train him how to use his power. He's young in years but old in soul—he'll get it. Now I must go!" He gave White Eagle a steely glare, warrior to warrior. "Above all, you must train him to fight."

36.

The Staffordshire bull terrier barked and growled in front of the jeep in a frantic attempt to get the soldiers to follow him. Every now and again he'd take off, always in the same direction, but as soon as the engine revved up, he'd run back and stop the jeep in its tracks.

"Bloody dog! We're never gonna get back at this rate." Harrison jumped from the jeep. "Shoo, boy! Go home. You'll get lost if you follow us."

The captain sat stroking the bristles on his neck and chin with the tops of his fingers. His gaze was intense as he watched the men try to move the dog out of their way yet again. "Leave him!" he ordered, jumping down from the vehicle. "He wants us to follow him."

He walked over to the dog and grabbed its lead. The dog responded with high-pitched yelps, and a desperate attempt to drag the officer away with him. "Settle down, boy." The captain knelt down and spun the dog's collar through his fingers. "Any ID? No! Well, we can't take you home, and we don't know your name, but one thing's for certain." He looked into the dog's face. "You're trying to tell us something. Lead on!"

He stood up, turned, and issued orders to the few remaining men. "Harrison, stay with the jeep. Mason, Taylor, Robson, come with me."

Julian pulled on the lead. His tongue hanging out, he panted on ahead with the soldiers running behind him. "Dog can run!" Mason commented.

"He's desperate. What's the betting we'll find his owner dead, or stuck somewhere?" Taylor answered between breaths.

414

They came to a halt at one of the small side streets opposite Norfolk Square. Julian scavenged about, sniffed and scratched amongst the rubble, then ran through an empty door frame into what was once a shoe shop and family home. Its insides had been blown apart and replaced with shards of glass, broken bricks, smashed-up pieces of wood, and hundreds of shoes. Some were melted, others ripped apart, and some were still in perfect condition.

The wall that divided the living quarters from the business was all but demolished, but the rest of the walls stood strong. A piece of green patterned wallpaper was torn across the chimneybreast and hung over a wrought iron fireplace—intact, it stood in defiance. A pair of pink floral curtains flapped about in empty window frames that were now the hollowed-out eyes of the building.

The torso of a doll, books, and the bent frame of a blue tricycle lay by the side of a couch, which also remained in one piece—a small teddy bear sat smiling in the corner of it. The captain walked over and picked it up. From his throat he emitted a small sigh of amazement. "Huh!" He stuffed the bear into his pocket. *If I don't find your owner I'll keep you,* he thought to himself. *You beat the odds.* He pulled it from his pocket and held it up to his men. "Bear beat the odds—"

He felt something tug at his trouser leg and looked down to see Julian attempting to drag him over to a hole in the floor situated in the far corner of the room at the back of the premises; it was about six feet deep, eight in diameter.

The dog ran ahead and began to scratch and yelp painfully. The captain looked down at the pile of bricks and wood. There wasn't a doubt in his mind that the dog's owner was buried somewhere beneath the rubble. "Get over here," he barked at his men. "I think somebody's buried under this lot."

The men threw off their jackets and berets, raced over, and jumped into the hole. Frantic, they dug with their bare hands, throwing bricks, broken furniture, and household items across what was left of the derelict room. Julian barked and paced above them; he even picked up pieces of rubble and carried them out of the way. The soldiers were amazed.

Sergeant Mason clawed through the debris and didn't take his eyes off the task at hand. "I thought animals were supposed to be dumb. We should let this one run Germany. He's got more brains than that fucking prick who's heading it at the moment."

"He loves his owner, I'll give him that," Robson added, not stopping for breath.

The four men, their hands cut and bloodied, ploughed relentlessly through the rubble. Exhausted, their mouths dry, their skin, hair, and uniforms covered in dust, it was Sergeant Mason who interrupted their concentration. "How much further, sir?"

The captain stopped. "We must have cleared about four foot of shit and still no sign of life."

"Shall we call it a day, sir?"

The captain looked at the debris. There was still a way to go but, disheartened, he began to question his instincts. "I think so. Though I'd have put money on finding someone buried amongst this lot, judging by the dog's behaviour."

One by one, the men catapulted out of the hole. The captain turned and looked over at the dog. "Come on, boy. If we don't find your owner we'll keep you as the regimental mascot." He pulled at Julian's lead, but the dog strained to remain by the edge of the hole. He wouldn't budge.

Afraid of hurting him, the captain gave up when the dog's collar jammed around its throat. "You stubborn—" he sighed, turned, and looked down at the rubble just as a sunbeam passed through an empty window frame. Small particles of dust sparkled and floated about in the beam that now shone down into the hole.

As the captain opened his mouth to speak, something caught his eye, something shiny, similar to a tiny gold star. It was minuscule but he saw it. He ripped off his jacket, threw it across the room, and jumped back into the hole. "One last effort," he said, pulling a large piece of wood out of the way. Another sunbeam passed through the window frame like a lighthouse signal and caused whatever it was to glimmer again.

The captain took a closer look. A few gold links stuck out from underneath a piece of wood. He picked them up, rolled them about in his fingers, and pulled on them gently. They were still attached to the rest of the chain. Letting go, he cleared the rest of the debris out of his way and discovered a sturdy wooden tabletop beneath the pile. His breathing accelerated but his heart seemed to slow down. He could hear the beats like the steady thump of a double bass drum.

Afraid of what he was going to find under it, the captain lifted the piece of wood and held it sideways—what he found knocked his heart into his throat. The image would remain with him for the rest of his life. The body of a small boy, no older than his own son, lay crumpled beneath the rubble. He had the most beautiful face—long lashes that almost touched his cheekbones and a mass of dark hair spattered with bits of debris framed the flawless features. Apart from a trickle of blood on the side of his face and a few other cuts and grazes, he looked so peaceful, perfect, as if sleeping. "GET HIM OUT OF HERE!"

But the men were already dragging the tabletop out of the captain's hands.

The captain lifted the child gently and handed him to Robson, who asked, "Is he alive, sir?"

"I don't know," the captain answered, scrambling out of the hole. He put two fingers underneath Aedan's chin. "There's no pulse," he panicked. "LIE HIM ON THE GROUND, QUICK!"

Frantic, the captain jumped onto Aedan's lifeless body. He pulled his head back roughly, pinched his nose, and blew into his mouth. "Come on, come on, come back, lad; we've not gone through this for nothing—1, 2, 3." He counted out loud as he pumped Aedan's chest. No response. Desperate, the captain blew again—nothing. "1, 2, 3." His hands seemed to sink into the small chest. The rest of the men looked on helplessly.

"1, 2, 3! COME ON, COME ON, BOY!" The men shot each other puzzled glances. The boy was dead!

"Boy's dead, sir!" Taylor's tone was wary.

"He's too young to die!" Their leader seemed obsessed, crazed. "1, 2, 3!" He pumped again and again. "BOY, YOU'VE GOT TO LIVE!"

Sergeant Mason touched his shoulder. Was the captain losing his grip?! "I…I think he's gone, sir."

"He's not going anywhere!" Sweat dripped from his brow. "1, 2, 3." Aedan's chest all but disappeared under the strong hands. "COME ON! COME ON!" His tone aggressive, he blew into Aedan's mouth again.

"Sir! Get a grip on yourself—sir!"

He ignored his sergeant. "God damn it, boy—GET UP!" The captain leaned his ear into the thin blue lips and felt underneath the small chin—"WE'VE GOT A PULSE!" He placed his arms underneath Aedan's back and lifted him up. "Get him into the jeep! Radio Harrison to get over here. We can't wait for an ambulance."

The captain raced to meet the jeep with Aedan bouncing about like a rag doll in his arms. He looked back at the men. "Robson, bring the dog! He's a hero like the rest of you." When Harrison skidded to a halt, the captain sidestepped after Taylor into the back of the jeep with Aedan still unconscious in his arms. "Get us to Ashton General. Step on it!" he ordered.

With Robson and Taylor on either side of him, he lay the small body across the three of them. Julian was squashed up on top of Mason's feet in the front of the jeep.

⋈

When they reached the reception area of the hospital they looked a sorry lot! Their clothes, hair, every inch of them was covered in dirt, and soaked and stinking with sweat; even Julian's white fur was unrecognisable underneath the muck.

The lady behind the desk was already on the phone when the captain shouted his name and rank at her—"The boy's unconscious; it's not ten minutes passed since we pulled him from under six foot of rubble!" The next thing they knew, a porter, two nurses, and a doctor were by Aedan's side with a stretcher. The captain relayed the story to the doctor and explained that he didn't know the boy, the dog had taken them to him.

"Give your details to the receptionist," the doctor said, running alongside Aedan. "Until we find his parents, you're the nearest thing he's got to a family."

Julian chased after them. "Whoa, boy!" Mason made a grab for his lead, and crouched down. "You can't go any farther; you've to let them do their job now." He tickled the dog under his chin.

"What is that dog doing in my hospital?" a no nonsense, middle-aged matron demanded. She looked them up and down. Her uniform was impeccable, and her light brown hair was set to perfection.

The captain put out his hand and introduced himself. "Sorry, ma'am. I never gave the dog a thought—he's a hero, you know."

Noting the dirt on the hand being offered, she declined the invitation to shake it. "Is he really?" She raised her pencilled eyebrows and looked at Julian. Julian looked back at her. A guilty expression spread all over his face even though he had no idea of what he'd done wrong. She walked over to the receptionist. "Ask Nurse Conway and Nurse Michaels to come to reception immediately, please."

Within a few minutes both nurses were at her side. "Get these soldiers cleaned up, please, and see that the dog gets a drink of water—then take them to my office. I can't have them wandering about the hospital in this state and I certainly don't want a dog loose in my wards!"

The soldiers looked at each other like a bunch of schoolboys in trouble. "I'm sure you've got more to do than worry about us, matron. We can get cleaned up at the barracks," the captain said.

"Nonsense! Those cuts need urgent medical attention." She looked down at Julian. "And he should be given a bath as soon as possible!" The dog whimpered in disagreement. She crouched down to his level. "Never you mind," she scolded. "Bath! As soon as possible!"

"What about the boy?" the captain shouted as he was led away.

"As soon as I know anything, I'll let you know." She walked over to the receptionist and looked at Aedan's details.

The sergeant glanced back at the hospital doors. "Someone had better have a word with Harrison, let him know what's happening."

Taylor took off and headed toward the doors. "I'll go—"

Matron raced after him. "Young man! Young man!" she called. "Where do you think you're going? Get yourself cleaned up now!"

"I'm just letting my colleague know what's happ—"

"Don't answer back! I've a son older than you. You're not too big for a clip around the ears!" Finding it hard to contain their laughter, the rest of the men and the nurses looked in the opposite direction and started to snigger. "Come to think of it, neither are you lot!" the matron snapped. The group immediately quieted down and the nurses raced the men off in the direction of her office. "Off you go, young man. I'll see to your colleague. I'm sure he's ready for a cup of tea," she winked.

Within half an hour, the men had had their cuts cleaned and dressed and were on their way out to the jeep. The captain told them to wait outside while he tried to find out how the boy was. He walked across to the reception area and was just about to ask after Aedan when someone tapped him on the shoulder. He turned and looked into the face of the doctor who'd raced Aedan into theatre. Despite himself, the captain's words came out rushed and filled with anxiety. "How is he—will he be alright—did you get his name—have you located his parents yet!?"

The doctor lifted his glove-covered hand. "He's okay, he's alright," he nodded. "He'll be fine."

"And his family—his name?"

"We haven't located his family." The doctor snapped off his gloves. "He's only just been taken into a recovery room. He's still sedated, so we don't know anything about him yet."

"But there's no permanent damage?"

"No! He's a lucky boy. By all accounts you and your men got there just in the nick of time."

"It's the dog he has to thank. It wouldn't give up even when we were ready to. Damn dog hung in there, refused to budge." The captain shook his head, a thoughtful expression on his face. "Amazing dog, that!"

"I think you've all played your parts, captain. Now, if you'll excuse me, I'm shattered." He yawned. "It's been one hell of a day!"

He yawned again, his eyes red and weary. "Oh, excuse me!"

The captain took the doctor's arm and stopped him from leaving. "Can I see him?"

"He's still out cold due to the painkillers and sedatives we've given him. Maybe come back later when he's awake—private room, ward seven." He looked at the officer's dirty clothes. "Besides, Matron won't be too pleased if she sees you on her wards looking like that!," he joked.

"Private room?"

"The only bed available. We're bursting at the seams because of the bombing." He headed off, stopped, and turned around. "Where's the dog now?"

The captain tossed his head in the direction of the doors. "Outside with my men. I'll keep him at the barracks until we find the boy's family."

The doctor smiled. "Never judge a book by its cover...true saying. Dog looks a right bruiser yet he's a pussycat by the sound of it!"

37.

"I'm looking for two children—a girl: seven, wavy blonde hair, missing her front teeth; and a boy: dark hair, eight years old—he's got a dog with him." Maggie ran through the town asking everybody she came within walking distance of if they'd seen Aedan or Celia. But most of them shook their heads and rushed on by, too preoccupied with their own problems.

For hours she'd searched through shops, cafés, and buildings, some reduced to bricks and memories while others were barely touched. And when she'd turned and seen the back end of their jeep race away, she'd chased after the Manchesters in the hope that they might hear her screams, or see her desperate attempt to wave them down in the rear-view mirror.

Poor Marion trudged around with her, tired and hungry, her small legs doing their best to keep up, yet she rarely complained. Her face solemn, she looked up at Maggie. "Can we find Mam now?"

"Yes, we'll look for her in a minute, sweetheart. You've been so good. Let's just ask one more person if they've seen Aedan or Celia." *White Eagle, can't you help me? At least point me in the right direction…?* Where the hell was he when she needed him?

"What a damn carry-on!" an elderly gentleman said in passing. "Let's hope this bloody war is over before it starts. Don't happen to have the time, do you?"

"Err, yes." She lifted her arm. "Five o'clock," she answered abruptly. Maggie looked him up and down. He was well dressed, probably an intellectual type. She made sure she spoke properly. "I'm looking for two children. A young girl, seven years old, and a boy, eight—he's got a dog with him," she said, defeated.

"Have you tried the hospital?"

"No! I never gave the hospital a thought!" Her mood lifted with the moment, but sank again with the next one. "I don't know how to get there. The busses, are they running? I doubt it!"

His voice was low, rather mellow. "Keep your spirits up. We can give up too soon sometimes, can't we?" He looked at her as if he knew her, knew everything about her.

He's a strange one, she thought, puzzled by the man's demeanour. "Err, I suppose...I've searched for hours."

"Minutes, hours, days, years, just a spark in the grand plan; but when you let go of hope they seem to last an eternity." He shrugged his shoulders. "But with hope in your heart...well, nothing is impossible."

"Well, thank you." She walked away. "Come on, Marion. Just what I need, a bleeding lecture in philosophy," she said under her breath.

"Bleedin' lecha!" Marion giggled up at her. "Aww, Aunty Maggie! You said a naughty word!"

"Shhh, Marion!" she answered, embarrassed. "Don't let him hear you!"

He looked at Maggie's fleeing back. "I'll take you there if you like."

She stopped in her tracks. "To the hospital?"

He tossed a lively glance over at a 1936 Bentley 4.25 litre Mulliner. "It won't take long to get there in this baby!"

She stared at him, taken aback by his choice of words. Up until now, he'd put her in mind of a slim Father Christmas but without the robust personality, more kind of holy. She expected him to talk more like the pope than a gangster! For the first time she looked deep into the sparkling blue eyes. They were so calm, so big, she almost got lost in them. She forced herself to look away, and glanced over at the "baby" in question. It was a fancy contraption indeed! The sapphire blue body trimmed with silver chrome looked almost ethereal with the late sun beating down on it. Maggie wondered when the engine turned on if the car would sprout wings and fly them to their destination.

Marion's face lit up with awe and excitement. "Huh! Aunty Maggie! It's the queen's car!" She darted towards it.

Maggie lunged after her. "Marion, don't run from me! We don't want to lose you as well!"

Marion jumped about on the end of Maggie's arm. "Please, Aunty Maggie, let's ride in the car."

Maggie turned to the man, her shoulder stooped. "Are you sure we're not taking you out of your way?" She put her free hand underneath Marion's armpit. "Put your feet on the ground, pet, before you have my shoulder out of its socket."

He walked to the car. "Which way would that be? This way, that way, the other way; they all end up the same way, you know." He opened the door for her.

Oh, God, here we go again. She sank into the plush leather seats. *He's probably one of them religious nutters that go around mythering people to join them. I should make it clear that I'm not interested. I don't want him getting the wrong idea just because I've accepted a lift to the hospital.*

Marion had no such concerns. Anyone would have thought it was Christmas morning judging by the look on her face. She looked up at the man, her voice serious. "Is the queen coming?"

His hearty laughter brought a much-needed blast of luminosity to the town square. A funny thing happened as he laughed. All the lights in the square came on! He kept one hand on the handle of the car door. "You're the queen."

Marion gasped! She looked at the lights, mesmerised, then threw herself at him and hugged his knees. "You did that! You're magic!" she said, wide-eyed.

"No, no, m'lady. You're the one who brought the laughter from my belly!" He bent down and tapped her nose. "That means you did that! You're the magic one—"

"Hold on a minute, please." Maggie felt embarrassed but when plain talk was needed she never had been one to mince words. He waved Marion in the car, slammed it shut after her, and waited expectantly.

Maggie lifted her chin and flashed him a huffy look. "I hope you're not a Jehovah Witness or something, because I'm not interested! I've nothing against people's beliefs, mind, but I've got my own—"

He stuck his hand out, a baffled look on his face. "Good God, no!" he laughed. "Norman."

"I'm not interested in them either!"

His hand hung in midair. "In Norman?" he asked, confused. "That's my name!"

Maggie blushed. "Oh, I thought you said…oh, it doesn't matter. Dear me, now I feel a right lemon!"

His hand still in midair. "No need—feel a Norman instead." He winked.

She smirked at his dry humour, took his hand, and smiled warmly. "Maggie! And this little angel is…?" She stretched her eyes and looked at Marion.

"Marion!"

Norman bowed low. "Queen Marion, your gracious highness."

Marion giggled, loud and hearty. "Can I ride in the front seat?"

"I don't think that's a good idea, sweetheart," Maggie butted in.

Norman got into the driver's seat, turned around, and faced Maggie. "She can for me. I'm a very careful driver."

Maggie made a face at Marion. "Go on, then. It looks like I'm outnumbered." She wondered what might be in store for her in later years. At least riding in the front seat of this fancy thing would be a pleasant experience to look back on.

Norman reached into the back of the car, lifted Marion, and unceremoniously dumped her into the passenger seat next to him. "Come here, m'lady." He glanced over his shoulder at Maggie, winked at Marion, and then looked straight ahead. "All settled? Let the ride begin!"

Maggie had become accustomed to riding in posh cars while staying with Angelette at Chateau Saint Esteve. This one was so smooth that she strained to hear the low hum of the engine. She closed her eyes and gave in to the overwhelming sense of fatigue that was creeping around her body. Angelette's smiling face slid into her mind. Another person she'd lost not long after David.

About a week before she'd left Manchester for Glossop, she received a formal letter from the administration office at the chateau explaining that Madame Bertrand had died. She'd gone to bed one night as usual, but the following morning when one of the servants had gone to ask whether she wished to breakfast in her room or in the conservatory, he'd found Madame Bertrand unresponsive. A note on the pillow next to her simply stated—and not without the dry humour that Madame was famous for—that her work on Earth was done and her career was to move forward. The ample raise and string of benefits offered was too hard to resist! The doctor was at a loss as to what to put on her death certificate because there was no evidence of any cause or illness. In the end he'd simply written, "Stopped breathing." The letter went on to say that Madame had treated death as if she were emigrating to a new country!

Maggie smiled a half smile. *Typical Angelette style... Angelette, if you can hear me; can you help me find our children?* she thought half-heartedly.

"Here we are!" Norman crunched on the handbrake, and brought the car to a dead stop outside the emergency entrance. Maggie and Marion jerked forward.

"We're here?" Maggie looked baffled. "But we've only just got in the car!"

Norman was already at her side, opening the door. "Time, it's such a...manipulator, you know!" She walked past him, kept her eyes on his face. He gave her a wry glance. "But then, you know more about that than most."

He's a strange one alright! She put out her hand. "Norman, thank you so much for your kindness."

He grasped her hand, brought it to his lips, and shouted, "WHEN IT COMES TO FAST CARS AND WOMEN, I'VE ALWAYS BEEN A PUSHOVER!" His loud laughter was deep and forceful, and seemed to come from the ground below him. A huge grey cloud above them dispersed into brilliant sunshine.

"Huh! You did that! You did it, you did it, you did it!" Marion hopped about in glee. "You're magic, magic, magiiiiiic," she sang.

Maggie noticed the side-glances and funny looks from the passers-by. Mortified, she kept hold of his hand and ran small steps towards him. "Lower your voice, man! You can't say things like that in public! People will wonder what the bloody hell is going on—Marion! Calm down, sweetheart. We have to be quiet in the hospital."

His laughter went up in tempo and he collapsed into a fit of coughing. "Wonderful thing, laughter!"

Maggie banged his back. "By the looks of things, it's killing you! Shall I fetch you a glass of water?"

"No, I'll be fine." His head in the air, arms outstretched, Norman stood outside the hospital like a town crier. "Wonderful thing, laughter; natural healer in fact. Did you know that laughter rejuvenates cells, reduces stress, and boosts the immune system? Of course you didn't! None of this will come to light for years yet!" He looked at the cynical expressions on the faces of the people desperate to stay away from him. "Take my advice," he said, chasing after a poker-faced woman. "It would do you lot the world of good!" He lunged at the runners, who sidestepped away from him. "Get a laugh!"

"Norman! I must go." Maggie urged, in the hope of shutting him up. "Man's a bleeding lunatic!" she said to herself.

"A bleedin' lunatic!" an exasperated Marion mimicked. "I like him! Don't be mean, Aunty Maggie!"

"Shh, Marion!" she snapped, worried Norman might hear her. "Stop swearing!"

"Would you like me to wait for you, Maggie O'Connell?"

She faltered. "Err…I…" She shook her head. *Did I give him my last name?* "Oh, no, no, I couldn't expect you to wait…I've no idea how long we'll be, or—"

"You won't be that long!"

"No! Really, honestly, but thank you…goodbye…say good-bye, Marion." Maggie all but dragged Marion off her feet, and headed towards the main doors of the hospital.

Marion pulled back, waved frantically. "Bye, angel, bye!" she shouted, a huge smile on her face.

"Hurry, Marion, it's getting late." Maggie stooped down to pick her up but suddenly stopped and looked over in the same direction. There was no sign of Norman anywhere!

Marion screamed with laughter. "See you later, angel."

Maggie looked all around for Norman, at odds as to how he'd disappeared so quickly. "Who are you talking to, love?"

Marion sighed and raised her eyebrows. "Norman, of course! Can't you see him, Aunty Maggie? He's an angel, you know!'' She pointed up at the empty sky. "His car's got wings an' it's flying!"

38.

Maggie burst through the hospital doors with a million thoughts on her mind. Were the kids alive, dead, home, lost…safe with Eileen somewhere? She'd better get some food in Marion's belly. Poor little beggar must be starving as well as exhausted. She'd run around ragged for the last three hours—

"Aunty Maggie, I need to wee!"

Maggie stopped a passer-by. "Could you tell me where the toilets are, please?"

The woman pointed. "Just around the corner there, over by the waiting area."

Maggie forced a weary smile. "Thank you—come on, Marion."

They rushed through the washroom entrance. "I'll be right next door. If you finish before me, wash your hands—and wait for me!" Maggie nodded, and gave her a firm look. "Don't leave this room without me, right?"

"Right!" Marion threw the cubical door into the adjacent wall, then banged it shut behind her.

"Holy mother, child! We're supposed to be quiet in the hospital, remember? You'll wake the dea—" she stopped in mid sentence.

The sense of dread was still pecking away at her insides. Yet something told her Aedan was all right, but Celia—was Norman an angel sent to soften the blow? The blow being that she'd never see the children alive again? There was something odd about the man. A kind of weird charisma that had the ability to keep you calm, yet make you think. *Angel—don't be so bloody daft! Obviously the fantasy of a five-year-old!*

"Aunty Maggie, I can't reach the soap!"

"I'm coming, sweetheart." Maggie flushed, pushed the cubicle door open, and rushed towards the sink. "Did you forget to flush?"

Marion thought for a second. "Oh-oh! I did!" She ran back and took care of her forgotten duty.

Maggie turned on the tap, washed her hands, then bent down and splashed cold water over her face. She felt hot and sticky. It was more down to nerves than temperature. She ran some of the cool water over her neck and felt it trickle down her back and between her breasts. "Here!" She passed Marion some soap. "Hurry now. We've still got to try to find Celia and Aedan."

"Can I wash my face?" Marion wanted to copy Maggie.

Maggie lifted her up so that she could reach the tap and emitted a few fake groans. "Oh, you're a lump, so you are!"

Marion laughed, threw water everywhere, and more or less drowned the pair of them.

"You little monkey! What are you?" Maggie plonked Marion down, stooped to her level, and tickled her belly. The pair of them were laughing and teasing until the room went suddenly quiet and Maggie hugged her little friend. "Thank God for you today. You've kept me sane," she whispered into her silky hair.

Maggie stood up and tried to stretch the towel on the roller down to Marion's level but it was no use. She picked her up, stuck her hip out, plonked Marion on it, and proceeded to dry her face and hair. "Right, we'd better get going!"

As soon as they reached the waiting area, Maggie spotted a nurse over by the reception desk. "Nurse, nurse!" she called as she ran, and her Irish dialect bombarded the nurse with questions. "I'm looking for two children, a girl and a boy. Girl's blonde, Celia; boy's dark, Aedan. He's got a dog with him. We were in Glossop when the fighters came over." She stopped talking abruptly, came over all breathless and worn out. She felt as if she was floating in some strange place and stumbled backwards, clutching her stomach. "Celia!" she gasped. Celia was in every ounce of her being, moving through her. But she wasn't in spirit. She was still here, alive on the Earth plane.

The nurse shot her a puzzled look. "Are you alright?"

Maggie tried to calm herself and ignored the question. "Town erupted…all hell broke loose." She burst into tears. "Jesus! We were separated from them." She smoothed her hand up over her forehead and through her hair. "Holy mother, if we've lost them." Her voice trembled as the pent-up emotions surfaced at last.

The nurse looked worn out. She pushed a strand of grey hair that had escaped from beneath her cap behind her ear, removed her glasses, and rubbed her eyes. "We've a girl who fits your description, but no boy. Are you the mother?"

Maggie felt the stuffing go out of her. She was so sure that Aedan was fine. Was it wishful thinking? Where was he? "Of the boy…the girl, she's like family to me; belongs to my best friend. She's out looking for her."

"Excuse me a minute." The nurse walked behind the reception desk, picked up a wooden file, and clipped two pieces of paper to it. "I'll take you to her. If it's the same girl you're looking for, we need her details."

Maggie's eyes filled with tears. "And you're sure about the boy?"

The nurse clasped Maggie's hand. "I'm sorry, dear. But don't give up hope. Could be that he's not made it here yet. Better still, he could be on his way home as we speak—come on." The nurse about-turned and headed off towards a bright, polished corridor adjacent to the reception area.

Maggie chased after her, never letting go of Marion. Her little legs all but left the ground as she tried to keep up. They flew up several stone staircases with iron railings and a maze of shiny corridors until they pushed through a pair of heavy swinging doors onto the ward.

It was pandemonium. The raw stench of vomit and anaesthetic hung heavy. Marion's eyes watered as she gagged on the stale air. Maggie clung tight to her. "You'll get used to it in a minute or so, love."

The exhausted nurses ran in and out, up and down the ward, taking temperatures, handing out medication, dressing wounds, emptying sick bowls, and the rest. Every bed had a bandaged occupant. One resembled a mummy. Its face was hidden, but vacant eyes stared up at the ceiling through slits in the bandages. Some slept while others recounted their stories to a circle of people who sat by their beds. A few lay alone with blank expressions yet with eyes that were full with a mixture of pain and sadness, relief, and…joy. It was still there.

"I don't like it here!" Marion said, walking into Maggie's legs. "Pick me up, Aunty Maggie." She lifted her arms in the air.

Maggie bent down and picked Marion up, cupped her head against her cheek. "We won't stay long, sweetheart. But I think we should visit Celia before we leave, what do you say?" She slapped a huge kiss on Marion's cheek.

"No! I want to go now. Let's go now, let's go, Aunty Maggie." She started to cry. "It stinks in here, don't like it, it stinks!"

"Just five minutes, Marion, I promise. Then we'll go find your mam—are you hungry?" She fished through her pockets and produced the chocolate bar Peter had left earlier. "Here we are." Marion snatched at the chocolate. Maggie pulled it away from her. "Err… young lady!"

"Please, please." She bounced about in Maggie's arms, her eyes lit and sparkling.

Maggie gave her the chocolate. "Marion, I need you to help me now. Will you help me?" she asked.

"Yes!"

The excited eyes of the five-year-old in her arms gave Maggie a glimmer of hope. It was a piece of light—an energy boost to keep her going and stop her from collapsing into a trembling, terrified heap. She had to look after Marion and get her home safe no matter what. "Right, then. Let's go and find Celia."

"If it's her!" the nurse warned.

"It's her!" Maggie had no doubts.

The nurse stopped by a bed about three quarters of the way down the ward. Maggie's heart slowed with her pace. She placed Marion down on a chair at the side of the bed, looked at the nurse and nodded. "It's her," she whispered, flatly.

Apart from a slight movement of her chest, Maggie would have sworn that Celia was already dead. Her tiny arms lay on top of the covers, bruised and lifeless. Dark patches of blood were visible underneath the bandage that was wrapped around her head, and her hair hung loose about her shoulders. Maggie knew in her heart that Celia wouldn't make it, but her head denied it.

"What's wrong with her? Is, is she sleeping?"

The nurse tried to be as gentle as possible. "She's in a coma. She's suffered a serious head injury. We—"

Maggie gasped, horrified. "Oh my God! Oh my God!" She looked at the nurse and shook her head. "No, no, no, she's only a baby."

The nurse ran to her side. "Try to stay calm," she said urgently. The whole day crashed on top of Maggie. She felt a part of herself start to drift off, a part she had no control over. The nurse knew Maggie was about to faint. She plonked her roughly down across the bottom of Celia's bed. "Deep breaths, big breaths—Lizzie!" she shouted to a colleague tending a patient in the bed opposite. "A cloth, please."

Noting the urgency, Lizzie threw a flannel across the ward before getting on with her own workload. The nurse poured water onto the cloth from a jug that was placed on top of a small cabinet at the side of the bed, and dabbed the back of Maggie's neck and brow.

Marion jumped off the chair, lifted one of her legs up onto the bed, and started to twiddle some of Maggie's hair through her fingers. "Are you poorly?" she asked, concerned.

"No, I'll be alright in a minute, darling." She sat up slowly. "Sit back on the chair, pet. I'm worried about crowding your sister."

"Here, drink this." The nurse held the back of Maggie's head and tipped the glass of water to her mouth.

Maggie took the glass from her. "Thank you. I'll be fine."

"Are you sure?" The nurse looked concerned. "You're back with us, then?"

Maggie looked at the floor. "Yes, yes. It's just...we were all so happy, excited, when we left home this morning—then the bomb, our babies." She broke down. "It was such a glorious day. I never imagined it would end like this."

"I don't think any of us did. Are you sure you don't need anything? A mild sedative?"

"No, no. The water will do me more good." She drained the glass. "I'd like another glass."

The nurse stepped aside so that she could pour her own, and asked for Celia's details along with Aedan's, just in case he was admitted.

Maggie lifted Marion from the chair at the side of the bed and sat down. "There's a comic in my bag if you want to look at it." Marion helped herself and sat on the floor beside Maggie, content for a few minutes at least.

The nurse's voice faded into the background. Maggie was aware of her own voice answering the questions, but she still felt as if she wasn't there, like her voice had taken off and left her. She reached over and stroked Celia's arms tenderly. *Celia, it will break your mam and dad's hearts if you leave.* She stood up. "I'd better find her mother."

The nurse looked at Maggie sadly. "As soon as possible. It could be minutes, hours, days." She stopped herself in mid sentence and half smiled. "Look, try to keep your spirits up. We—"

Stunned, Maggie finished the sentence for her. "Can give up too soon sometimes," she whispered, recalling the conversation she'd had with Norman earlier.

The nurse let out a small laugh. "You took the words right out of my mouth." She looked at the lapel watch pinned to her uniform. "My shift is nearly over. I'll make sure your son's details are handed over to the duty matron before I leave." She took Maggie's hands. "I'm sorry...for your loss." She'd already given up on Celia. She was just being kind, trying to soften the blow. "Come on, I'll walk you back to the main entrance."

Maggie thought back to the conversation she'd had with Norman. *What happened to hope? Maybe Celia could still make it?* She bent down and kissed Celia on the cheek. *Try and hang on for your mam and dad, sweetheart.* "Give Celia a kiss, Marion."

She bounded towards her sister and was about to leap onto the bed when Maggie caught her around the middle. "Gently, Marion!" she said, alarmed. "Celia is feeling a bit poorly."

Marion kissed Celia's cheek, laid her head onto her sister's chest for a split second, and stood up. "I'm hungry," she announced, through a yawn.

Maggie caught up to the nurse and followed her out of the ward. "Is there anywhere I could get her something to eat?"

"Yes, there are a few places along Mossley Road. That's if they're still in one piece." When they reached the main doors the nurse pointed. "Right now you're on Fountain Street; Mossley Road is over there. In fact, there's a quaint little café on the corner of Mossley Road and Hope Street. I sometimes treat myself to lunch or dinner there; depends on my shift."

There's that word again. Exhausted, Maggie stepped off the curb. She had no idea how she would contact Eileen and Charlie—*Phone Cyril!* some voice in her head said. "Do you know if they have a phone?"

"They do. The hospital has called me on it a few times if an emergency has come up." She looked surprised. Most people didn't have a home phone. "Do Celia's parents have a phone? We should phone them straight away." She jerked her head back. "Come on, we'll go to reception."

"No, it's a neighbour's phone. But the day you've had, you must be exhausted and the hospital has got enough to do. It'll be just as quick for me to use the phone in the café; besides, Marion is well past her dinnertime." She sighed. "And I could do with a hot drink myself. Do, do you have all the information you need regarding Aedan?"

"I do, Mrs. O'Connell." She showed her the form with Aedan's details. "I'm going to pass them to the receptionist right now and ask her to make sure the duty matron gets them."

Maggie put out her hand. "Thank you. Maggie, by the way."

The nurse clung to Maggie's hand. "Hope," she smiled, retreating. "Hope Ryder."

≍

Nurse Ryder left the doors swinging behind her and headed to reception. "Hello, Julie," she smiled. "Which matron is due on shift?"

"Edith."

"Is Mavis still here?"

Julie picked up the phone. "I'm not sure. I can try her if you like." She dialled two numbers, stopped, and pulled a face. "On second thought, she's worked a double shift—can Edith deal with it or can't it wait?"

Nurse Ryder thought for a minute. "It can wait, I suppose. Edith should be here any minute." She walked behind the desk, picked up a new file and clipped Aedan's details to it. She then placed both files in Edith's tray. "Make sure Edith is aware of these as soon as she gets here; it's important." She thought about Maggie. "Poor woman is out of her mind, can't find her s—"

"Hope! Before you go!"

Nurse Ryder looked over to see a portly chap running towards her. Puzzled, she took a small step forward but was interjected by a woman who stood a short distance away. She smiled to herself as she realised it was somebody else the man was calling. Funny, not many people shared her name. It was quite uncommon. She looked back at Julie and smiled; she decided not to mention Aedan. Edith would be here soon enough. "I'll be off, then! Pray the evening isn't anything like the day we've had."

39.

Aedan walked through a familiar land—a lush green valley at the bottom of tree-covered slopes surrounded by jagged peaks covered in quartz. Flowers grew with clusters of crystals in purple, gold, red, and yellow. Magnificent quartz temples were dotted about on the hillsides, their colours glistening underneath the light blue sky and orange sun. The air was fresh, alive, and rejuvenated him with every breath. He could see an emerald lake in the distance. White sand edged its shores, and lazy waves turned to foam. A few people lolled around by picnic baskets while others splashed about in the water without a care in the world. Everything was calm. Such a high energy; everything was beautiful.

Crystal City—or the spirit world, as Maggie called it. Here anything is possible. He wondered why people were so afraid of death. They experienced it every time they went to sleep. This is how the spirit recharges. It leaves the physical body and travels back to its roots. When people dream, they travel to another dimension, the spiritual—or astral as it's sometimes termed—but on waking, their astral journey becomes fragmented. This is why dreams can be so confusing, but in effect, they could be described as a dialogue with one's soul.

The deep hidden crevices of the psyche, the quiet whispers, the undeniable feelings…what are they? An elaborate mind activity that is connected to the physical brain? Or an elaborate mind connected to all that is?

Aedan found Celia sitting by the lake making daisy chains with two other girls and an older boy. He sat down next to her, crossed his

437

legs, and rested his arms on his knees. The other children looked at
each other with glances that said they knew why he'd come.

"I know why you're here, Aedan," Celia said, as she carefully
threaded the stem of one daisy through the stem of another. "And I'm
not coming back!" she said childishly.

"What about your mam and dad?"

"I've got new ones."

He nodded his head and cocked his lips sideways. "I see. So your
old ones are no longer any use to you. You can toss them aside like a
pair of worthless old dolls?"

She looked wistful. "I know they'll be sad if I don't go back, but
it's different when you're here." She looked around. "Feel this place,
Aedan. Isn't it beautiful?" Her exuberance, the force—life—fired out
of her. "That's why I don't feel sad for them. Not really," she said,
truthfully. "I know we can't die so I know I'll see them again, and
someday they'll feel…they'll feel…," she threw her hands up in the
air gleefully, "…all this! They'll feel all this, just like me. What a
beautiful day it will be when we all meet up again."

"Weren't you happy on Earth?"

Celia placed the daisy chain she'd made around his neck. "Not
like here. Everybody's nice. There are no bullies, and school is a lot
more fun—they teach you how to fly! I jumped off Mount Amethyst
a while ago with Phillip. It was fantastic, the feeling in your belly,
and do you know the house I live in?" The more excited she got, the
more she waved her arms about. "I have my own bedroom and loads
of toys!" She pointed in the distance at a few houses by the lake. The
houses all had a crystal dome or tower to reflect the colours from the
sun. When residents of Crystal City felt a dip in their energy fields,
they would retire to the crystal room to rejuvenate. "I live over there.
In the evenings we sit outside or sometimes my new dad takes me
out on the lake—we even have a boat, and I'm not scared of water
anymore because he taught me how to walk on it!" She burst into
laughter and jumped up. "Shall I show you how to do it?"

"Later," he laughed. "I have to go back soon." He'd been walking on water for as far back as he could remember. "You've already been to school? They don't waste any time over here, then?" He was surprised at how quickly things had started to move along.

"I'm not sure if it's the same with everybody. Phillip said it's easier for kids to accept this place because our minds haven't been in doctors like the adults—"

The boy looked across at her. "Indoctrinated!"

"Indoctorrelated!"

"In-doc-tri-nated," the boy repeated. Aedan noticed how patient he was with her.

She looked at Aedan. "Yes, that! Some people have to rest—the ones who have a hard time dealing with the spirit world. You know," she nodded, "them who don't believe in it, or religious people who think it should look like heaven. For a while they get what they believe in but then the M.O.s go in—"

Aedan looked puzzled, and then the penny dropped. "Oh, yeah! Mind Openers. Evolved beings, specially trained in the art of opening the creative potential," he said, like a person much older than his years.

Celia was impressed. "You know about them—Peter is a Kidmo!" she smirked.

Peter glanced at her with an amused expression. "Quick learner!"

"Anyway," she continued, twirling around and around as she spoke. The M.O.s help those that are having a hard time believing in all this to open the mind up to new ideas, and release its creativity. When you first cross over, though, you usually find yourself in a place you're used to. That way it softens the blow a bit when they tell you you're dead; or, like in my case, while you make up your mind whether you're dead or not!"

She started to giggle. "When I first got here, I found myself alone in a sitting room like the one in Charlie and Eileen's. I remember wondering where everybody was. I mean, how often is our house quiet or empty? And then there were little things I noticed that weren't quite the same, like our Peter's nappies weren't hanging from the fireplace, and my mam wasn't stood at the sink scrubbing. It seemed weird somehow…there was a funny kind of feeling that was different. I kind of accepted something…I don't know what…then there was a knock at the front door. When I opened it, Jack and Barb were stood there smiling at me. They looked all shiny like angels. Barb asked me if they could come in so I stepped aside and let them. I didn't feel a bit scared, even though they were strangers. I knew they were nice. Anyway, we all sat down together and they told me that I hadn't died yet but I was in the spirit world, visiting. They said I could try it first to see if I liked it. I asked them if I had to go to school—"

Aedan burst out laughing. "Trust you! A decision between life and death rests on whether you have to go to school or not!"

"It wasn't just that," she said sheepishly. "Anyway, they said they could take me to school, introduce me to some of the other children if I liked. They said it's better to go to school as soon as possible here, because things are so different and if I'm going to stay, the sooner I learn the basics the better." She sat down next to him and sighed. "I don't get sad here. If I come back I'll have to feel being sad again." She looked at him, her big blue eyes wide. "Or frightened or sick."

"Like Eileen and Charlie? Your mam's beside herself, Celia, wondering how she'll cope without you, and blaming herself for not keeping a better watch on you."

"But they already know I'm not coming back. The choice was made before any of us were born—me, you, Mam, Dad. We all agreed that I'd die in the war."

"But they won't remember the agreement until their time has come to return here, and you seem to have forgotten that you made more than one choice."

"I like it here."

Aedan sensed her stubbornness but pressed for an answer. "What about the deal between you and me? You must at least acknowledge it."

She clenched her small fists and screwed up her face. "I'm not going back and you can't make me! I've asked my new mam; she says it's my choice, nobody else's."

"Your new mam! Don't you care about Eileen? She's sat by your bed all night praying that you won't go."

Aedan understood everything Celia argued for but he had to be sure that she wanted to stay in the spirit world and not return to Earth. Once he left, that was it. She wouldn't be able to change her mind later.

The other children whispered between themselves and stood up. The boy, Phillip, spoke. "We're going to the tree house. Come if you want."

They both answered him at the same time. Celia said, "Alright." She jumped up.

Aedan replied, "Not yet." He pulled Celia down and shot her a steely glare. "We talk now or you won't have a say in it!"

Celia started to cry. "It's not fair. I want to stay here with my friends. They can stay—why can't I?"

Aedan rolled his eyes. "Celia, stop being such a mard arse! You're supposed to have evolved by the time you get to Crystal City!" The other children giggled at Aedan's expression.

"What's a 'mard arse'?" Zhen, a young Chinese girl, asked.

"A crybaby!" Aedan answered.

The children laughed louder. The youngest, Henrietta, started to sing. "Ring-a-ring-a-roses, a pocket full of mard arse." She giggled childishly at her own humour. "Arse, arse, that's a funny word."

"It's not funny!" Celia shouted, red-faced.

Zhen stuck her hand out. "Come on, Henrietta."

The children said their goodbyes and headed for the tree house. They knew Celia's friend was from Earth because he still had the bluish-silver cord attached to his spirit form like Celia did. Once the cord was severed the spirit was no longer attached to the physical body, and the Earth person would be pronounced dead. This was how full-time spirit residents could tell the difference between themselves and the spirits that were just visiting. Full-timers no longer needed the cord.

"I can run here!" Celia jerked her head in an angry manner. "Skip, dance, sing. Why should I stay on earth with a brain that doesn't work? I'll be a burden to my mam and dad. They've got enough to do."

"You can be honest with yourself, Celia…here especially."

"Right! I don't want to live like that! I don't want to! I know it's sad for my mam and dad…they might not know it now, but I'm sure they'd rather me be free in spirit than stuck in a body that doesn't work anymore!"

"Wow, Celia! Very wise…but you're still not being truthful." His eyes drilled into her.

Embarrassed, she punched him softly. "I love it here, Aedan. My choice is to stay…I don't want you to heal me."

"You're sure about that?"

She sensed his resignation, but felt her energy expand. "I'll never regret it. I've never been so happy. If my mam and dad knew how happy I was they'd give me their blessing, and do you know what? They'd like Jack and Barb, they would!" She stopped talking and looked across the lake, her expression pensive. "I'll visit them." She turned to him. "I'll help with their grief; make sure they know I'm still around. Sometimes they'll smell me or I'll come into their thoughts…sing a song we used to sing together…huh?" She looked elated. "Besides, they'll still have a say in my upbringing. Every night when they sleep, they'll come here to be with me. I know they won't remember most of it when they wake up, but no matter what they're still my parents. They just help to bring me up on the spiritual level now instead of the physical one."

Aedan placed the crown of daisies he'd made on Celia's head. "They'll ask me to help you. I'll tell them we talked and your choice was to stay here so the only thing the healing can do is make your transition easier." A shadow suddenly crossed over his face like a plane blocking out the sun.

"What?" she asked.

"Charlie and Eileen. They'll be devastated. On Earth, one of the worst things a person can experience is the loss of a child. It's them who'll need the healing."

"They've not lost me! Tell them they're just as busy with me here as they were there."

His body puffed up with irritation. "I know, Celia, but it's not the same, is it? It's not like they can hold you, kiss you. They might get a glimpse of you when they wake up from a dream if they're lucky. It can be hard for spirit to get through to someone who's riddled with grief. Their emotions are so strong they block everything else out, especially the spiritual. Me telling Eileen and Charlie you said this, and I did that, means nothing! It's just damn words to them!" He wanted to rip into her. Charlie and Eileen were family, and Celia a sister, but right now he wasn't impressed with her lack of sensitivity.

She could feel his reserve fighting to hold back the aggressiveness of his thoughts. "I know! What about a sign? I'll send them a sign to prove that what you're saying is true!" Her triumphant expression slid into one of love. "That way, my mam and dad will have that proof of the physical me they need, and their grief won't be so bad."

Aedan chewed on a blade of grass. "A sign," he whispered to himself. "Good idea, but you'll have to think of it. It has to be yours." He put his hand on his solar plexus. "You'd better hurry; I'm waking up."

He looked across the lake. A white sailboat tipped up and down on the small waves as it floated toward them. He jumped up and ran toward it. Every so often, Earth's atmosphere punched through into Crystal City and caused the two worlds to clash together like an explosion of energy. "Hurry with that sign, Celia! I'm being pulled back."

"The daisies," she shouted, looking up as she ran alongside him. "Don't forget to mention the daisies." They splashed onto the water. Celia screamed. "Huh, Aedan! You sneak! You never told me you could walk on water!"

"Just another one of my many talents," he said cockily, before he triple-jumped off the top of the water onto the boat. He could see the edge of the waterfall that acted as the dividing wall between Earth and Crystal City.

Celia stopped chasing him. "I'll think about you." The sound of the waterfall overpowered her voice. She lifted the crown of daisies triumphantly. "The daisies are the sign!" she screamed.

Aedan slipped his fingers underneath the daisy chain on his neck. "The daisies are the sign…"

He looked over towards the top of the waterfall. His heart pounded, thud, thud, thud. As the boat speeded up, anticipation powered through him. Any second now he would go over. An uncontrollable feeling of fear took on a life of its own. Twisting and turning, it did its best to suck him in. He screamed out, "HERE WE GO, HERE WE GO, HERE WE GOOOOOO!" as he slid over the top of the falls.

But every trace of fear was obliterated by the power of the water that consumed him. Its strength filled him with courage and the rush he felt as he fell down, down, submerged in the water, was indescribable. His body twisted, somersaulted, over and over…

He opened his eyes to see Maggie, Eileen, and Charlie standing around his bed, looking down at him. "The daisies are the sign," he said sleepily.

"Good dream, was it?" Maggie asked. She didn't wait for an answer. "I've got good news. The doctor said you can come home today." She couldn't hide her elation until the thought struck and reminded her of Eileen and Charlie's position. She closed her eyes. *Damn it! Sometimes I just don't think.* She turned to her friends, pressed her lips together. She was worrying for nothing. Wrapped up in a cloud of torment, they were oblivious to her joy.

"How long have I been here?" Aedan asked as Maggie kissed his forehead.

"Only overnight, pet. You were lucky, no serious injuries, but I'm going to have to go home. I didn't think you'd be out this soon, so I've not brought you any clean clothes to put on. The ones they found you in are ripped to shreds and covered in muck."

There was a momentary pause. Aedan waited expectantly for someone to speak. His mother, as usual, didn't disappoint him. Maggie looked into Eileen's eyes. "Eileen has something to ask you."

A cruel fear hunted through Eileen, like a starved black panther. Her thoughts, riddled with darkness and misery, did their best to stalk, torment, and push her over the edge into insanity. Now and again a glimmer of light would break through, only to be set upon and gobbled up by the depression that was doing its best to drive a stake into her heart, her soul. Thoughts from her darkest depths, relentless, would attack her again and again: *If only it was the other way around.*

Not that she wished anything bad to happen to Aedan, or anyone else for that matter. She loved Aedan and Maggie, but why did it have to be her child that was dying? Why her? What had she ever done to deserve this? She wondered if there was a God or if it was all a load of claptrap. Did the spirits exist or were they figments of her own mind, aspects of herself? All this stuff at the séances that she, Maggie, and the other girls attended! What if she and the other women were just raving lunatics, deluded nutcases? Why do these things happen…Celia seven years old and dying? And even if she recovers, she'd be a cabbage, they'd told her. Did she want a daughter who was a cabbage—of course! She loved Celia! How could she think such things? Yesterday, they were all so happy, a happy family. It was all she'd ever wanted and now this! God can take a hike, for all she cared. Nobody deserves to go through this, nobody! She looked at the relief that was written all over Maggie's face and was alarmed at her own bitterness. *I'm happy for Maggie, I am…*

"Eileen," Maggie said gently. "Ask Aedan."

Eileen didn't respond. Charlie cupped her face in his hands. "Sweetheart, do you want me to ask?" His eyes were red-rimmed, filled with tears that he held back. His own grief was kept down by the weight of his worry about his wife, his childhood love. She was his life. What would he do without her? He had to be strong and protect her. If he showed weakness the whole family would be destroyed.

"Charlie," she whispered. "What, what is it?" She looked demented.

He kept hold of her face. "Aedan, he's awake. Do you want me to ask him to help Celia?"

Her voice sounded like the cry of a savage. "CELIAAAAAAAA!" The heart-wrenching scream that escaped from Eileen's insides sent chills through Maggie and Charlie. Aedan stared. He felt Eileen's fear slice him into pieces.

"Celiaaaaa…no, no!" she collapsed into Charlie. "Don't go! I can't live without you, I can't!" she sobbed. She appeared like a rag doll in her husband's arms. Barely conscious, her eyes rolled backwards and she emitted small, pitiful moans from her throat.

Fear gripped Charlie's heart, wrung it clean. He threw Maggie a desperate glance. "What do I do, get a doctor, drug her up?" he asked. "I don't know what to do—"

Aedan jumped out of bed and tried to pry Eileen from Charlie's arms but Charlie held tight. He knew that if he let Eileen go, the life would drain out of her and she'd crumple to the floor, disintegrate into dust.

Aedan's words were fast and anxious. "Aunty Eileen, come here. Come and sit on the bed. Aunty Eileen, I want to talk to you about Celia."

Charlie laid her on the bed gently and looked at Aedan, his eyes pleading. "Aedan, whatever happens, save Eileen. The other kids, they need their mother...so do I. I can't imagine life without..."

On seeing his grief, Maggie ran to Charlie's side. "Here, drink this, Charlie." She handed him a glass of water. "Let it out, let it out. It'll do you good to cry. Sit down on the chair there." She walked him over to a chair in the corner of the room.

Aedan's heart twisted inside his chest. In his eyes, Charlie had always been a strong, powerful figure. To see him crumble and fall like this because of the woman he loved only reinforced his opinion. Charlie knew love. Love was the only true power. Aedan walked over and held Charlie's huge hand in his small one. "Uncle Charlie, the love you have for Aunty Eileen will cure everything."

The words just about blew Charlie away! And him, no more than a bairn! He grabbed Aedan, squashed him to his chest, and sobbed. They remained there for a few minutes until Charlie released him. Aedan lifted Charlie's hands from his shoulders. "I should look after Aunty Eileen now."

"Thank you, lad; you do that. I'll be fine." He looked over at his wife. She seemed to have wasted away before his eyes in just a few short hours.

Eileen lay on her back, eyes closed. She didn't want to open them. She didn't want to open them ever again. What was the point of life if you had to live it feeling like this? She could feel the physical weight of the last twenty-four hours pressing down on her. It was like there was an invisible something—a physical creature stuck to her, with huge talons that knifed into her shoulders. *No!* She would lie there and die...*What about Derrick, Peter, and Marion? I'll have to carry on for them—*

Charlie will see to them, the thing said.

Charlie can't work the coal and look after the kids—

He's a grown man; he'll pull through...

Children need their mothers. There's something special about a mother's love—

It's not that special. It let go of Celia...

"Aunty Eileen." Aedan sat down on the edge of the bed, ran a hand up and down her body until it finally rested on her head. All the while he spoke to her about his visit with Celia. "She's happy in Crystal City. She'll never get sick there, and she's got a new mam and dad who you'd really like."

Eileen's eyes remained shut. She could feel the energy from Aedan's hand ripple inside her head and spread throughout the rest of her body like radio waves. It was a surreal feeling, like something too advanced for the times...but it brought her peace and made her feel safe. She wanted to stay with it.

"She goes to school there; it's a lot more fun than here, though. You learn how to fly. Oh, yeah, and they have three different sections in history. History past, where you learn all about your past lives and see if there is anything you'd like to change—and they let you! Present day history, that's fun as well! They take you back through your last life on Earth, as well as teaching you about Crystal City life.

"Then there's future history...or making history, as they like to call it. Making history is loads of fun. You get to try out different experiences like things you might fancy doing in the future." Aedan's excitement bubbled out of him. "You can fly a jet, be a homeless person or a king, maybe a singer or a film star...anything, really! But it doesn't only relate to Earth. You get to see other planets and meet the beings that inhabit them. They tell you all about life on their planets— where they fit with regards to the solar system, where Earth fits into it. You know, Aunty Eileen, if the balance is upset on Earth it affects their planets; that's why they're here keeping watch over us. There are loads of universes," he said knowingly. "The beings that live on them can visit ours, but it's not possible for us to visit theirs until we evolve a bit more—"

"Did Celia tell you that?" Maggie cut in. She felt a shudder push her insides out. She'd never once mentioned spacemen, aliens, or that, that Neil being to Aedan. It was just a dream, anyway, so why would she?

He gave his mother a sideways glance. "No."

"Then you shouldn't say things that might not be true, Aedan."

"It's true!"

Maggie blew air through her lips, "In your imagination, perhaps!" she mocked.

"Imagination is real."

"So you did make it all up?"

"No! I didn't!" he answered, frustrated by his mother's attitude.

"Then how do you know such things?"

Aedan raised his voice. "How do you know what you know? I just know! Mam! I have to look after Eileen." *What's wrong with her?*

She stared at him. Such was her anxiety, she'd forgotten all about her friend.

Aedan carried on telling Eileen all about his meeting with Celia; her new friends, Jack and Barb; what Crystal City was like. Eileen didn't respond. She had made up her mind to die. But Aedan knew that it wasn't her time, not yet, which meant that she could go into a depression for years. She must utilise one of her other choices. He knew that the sign from Celia was the only thing that had a remote chance of bringing her out of her depression. In effect, Celia, from the grave, was about to save her mother's life.

Aedan continued to run his hands up and down Eileen's body. "Aunty Eileen, Celia has a message for you. She told me to tell you that daisies are the sign that will prove she's still alive." He felt her energy expand slightly, like a subtle tap on his hand, as he ran it over her heart area. "She said you should look for daisies." In his third eye he saw Celia beckon to him. "And you've got to go now because she's ready to leave at any moment." He stood up and indicated that Charlie should take his place.

Charlie walked over, sat on the side of the bed, reached over, and played with a strand of Eileen's hair. "Eileen, Eileen love, can you hear us?"

Though her eyes were shut tight, the tears spilling from them and down her cheeks indicated that she could indeed hear them. She let out a great, heaving sob. Charlie lifted her to himself and buried his face in her hair. They remained there for a few minutes more, and cried together.

Aedan knew that it would soon be time for Celia to break free from her physical body. He walked over to Charlie and whispered in his ear. "It's time. We must go—now!"

Charlie took Eileen's wrists. "We have to be strong for the sake of the kids."

She nodded. The pain in her was evident by the years that she'd aged overnight while sitting by Celia's bed. She tried to remember how she'd got there. It was all a daze. She remembered some elderly gentleman with a posh car asking her the time. "Five o'clock," she'd told him. She smiled to herself as she thought about her reaction when he'd asked her if she needed any help. "Oh, yes, I do! Could you take us home? I have to see my husband—we've lost our daughter." She'd somehow bundled herself, Peter, Derrick, and Ambrose into the car, and God knows how they'd got the pram in! She remembered Derrick clinging to it so it wouldn't jiggle about or get in the way of the driver. The car looked like a rag and bone man's paradise by the time she'd finished with it. He was such a kind man, beautiful eyes…

"Bye, angel," Peter kept shouting after him when he'd dropped them off at home. There were angels on Earth. What would she have done without that kind man? Then there was Cyril. He'd not hesitated when Charlie had asked him for a lift to the hospital, and he and Ann were only too happy to take in her other children, as well as the dog! When Ann realised that Marion was missing, she'd asked, alarmed, if both girls were in the hospital, and had looked equally relieved when Eileen told her that Maggie had taken Marion. "Bring Marion back with you, Cyril. We'll look after her. Hospital is no place for a child—" She'd stopped abruptly when she saw the look of devastation on Eileen's face.

They were good people, Ann and Cyril. Angels on Earth. Her thoughts moved along to the present moment…the moment she didn't want to be a part of.

Something inside told her that this was it. She was about to stand by helpless and let her baby leave. She would look for daisies until the day she died but they'd never mean anything to her other than superstitious ramblings. She stood up but collapsed back down and sunk her head in her hands. "I can't do it!"

Charlie put his arms around her and pulled her to her feet. "You can! You have to!"

Ravaged by bitterness, she screamed at her husband. "Let go of me! I don't have to do anything! Why do I have to watch my baby die? Why do I have to do that? Answer me that!" She pummelled Charlie's chest, over and over. "Answer me that! Answer me that!" She begged him, over and over, "Answer me that!" until the glare on her face collapsed into heartache and uncontrollable sobs.

Charlie crushed her to him. "Calm down, calm down. Everything's gonna be fine…shh, shh. You're right. You don't have to do anything," he said, softly. She tried to escape but was helpless. "You don't have to do anything," he crooned, not letting her move. He felt a tug on his jacket sleeve and looked down.

Aedan looked up at him. "We have to go now if you want to see her before…before…"

"It's all right, lad. Eileen, do you want to wait here, sweetheart? I'll get a nurse to sit with you."

"I'll stay with her," Maggie interjected.

"Where are you going?" Eileen was panicky.

Charlie fought in vain to keep his tears back. "I have to go to Celia. I can't let her go all alone."

Eileen was shocked. "All alone?"

"Yes. One of us should be with her."

"Of course," she answered, as if coming to her senses. "I'm sorry…I've only thought about myself…about—"

"It doesn't matter." Charlie took her hand. No words were needed.

When they reached Celia's ward, Eileen's pace slowed considerably. She felt as if her body was walking with nobody in it. What was the rush? The sooner she got there, the sooner Celia would go away. She dragged her hand from Charlie, told him she wanted a few minutes. He obliged and walked a short distance ahead with Aedan and Maggie.

When Eileen reached the foot of Celia's bed she stopped dead, not daring to move any closer. Aedan took her hand, walked her over, and all but pushed her down next to Celia. At first she simply sat, staring at the small figure that used to be her daughter. But this wasn't her Celia, the Celia who was always so full of life, so full of mischief and fun…and love. She'd already gone. She ran her hand down the soft skin, let her fingers slide down her face gently, and was shocked to find that she was still warm, still alive.

"Look for the daisies, Mamma…" A small voice…a thought?

"Look for the daisies, Mamma!" Celia's spirit was above her physical body, screaming at her mother.

Charlie sat on the opposite side of the bed to Eileen.

"Look for the daisies, Mamma." He heard it…a thought in his head?

Maggie and Aedan were the only ones who could see Celia's luminescent form. Maggie gasped out loud. She could never describe in words how beautiful Celia looked in that moment…the moment of death. "Look for the daisies, Mamma," Maggie said softly.

Eileen and Charlie turned in unison and looked at Maggie flabbergasted, then at each other. It was their daughter's voice, alright! Coming out of Maggie's mouth! They could hear Celia inside their heads like a thought that was being accompanied by the sound of her physical voice, which was coming out of Maggie!

"Look for the daisies, Mamma!" Celia was screaming at her mother.

"Look for the daisies, Mamma," Maggie repeated it in a loud, firm voice, over and over again, as Celia screamed it.

Eileen looked all around her. She couldn't see her daughter's spirit, but she could smell her, feel her force, her life. She broke into tears of joy as she felt the life, like a light, snuff out from her child's physical form. She bent down, kissed her cheeks, ran her fingers through her hair. *"Look for the daisies, Mamma."* Eileen started to laugh out loud but was suddenly overwhelmed. "Oh my God, oh my God!" The others watched as she gasped for air and clutched her stomach.

Charlie reached across to her. "What? What is it, sweetheart? I'll call the nurse," he said, anxiously. "Nurse, nurse—"

Still clutching her middle and gulping in air, Eileen managed to grab her husband's arm, a look of pure elation on her face. "No, no, I don't need a nurse, Charlie, our baby…she's inside me, she's inside me again, I can feel her. I can feel her life inside me again, Charlie." She let out a sound that was half laugh, half cry—*"Look for the daisies, Mamma."* Celia's spirit was a part of her! Why hadn't she realised it sooner? "I'll never stop looking, baby, never. Be free, baby, be happy."

Aedan and Maggie remained calm as they watched Celia's spirit place the crown of daisies on top of the head of her lifeless body. It was Charlie who cried out, "Look!" He and Eileen watched in awe as the crown of daisies manifested, out of thin air, onto their daughter's head.

Maggie stood behind them. "An apport."

Charlie shook his head. "A what?"

"An apport," Eileen answered. She removed it from Celia's head.

Maggie was overjoyed. She knew that this was all Eileen needed. She looked at Charlie. "A gift from spirit."

Eileen smiled through tears of joy at her husband. "A gift. Our baby sent us a gift." Overwhelmed, Charlie held out his arm and Eileen placed the crown over his wrist. The two of them, wrapped in the moment, clung to each other. "Charlie, can you feel her? She's saying goodbye."

Celia spread her aura around Eileen and Charlie for a few seconds more. Maggie could see her new parents waiting anxiously just behind her. A rainbow of colours and humanoid in shape, they looked like long, stretched beams of sunlight. Whereas Celia, apart from the luminescent glow around her, resembled her earthly form due to her being on the other side of the dividing grid, which to Maggie looked like a spider's web made of coloured light.

It was the more masculine of the two figures that shouted. "Hurry, Celia, the veil is closing—sorry to have to do this!" He lunged forward and grabbed his daughter. On Earth's side of the grid, he immediately took on the form of his last Earthly life. Stocky, and with a rugged complexion and short, dark hair with splashes of grey at the temples. *Not a bad-looking man*, Maggie noted.

"You'll have to learn to respect the veil, sweetheart. I don't want to have to keep crossing over for you…it's not as simple as you seem to think it is. I'll talk to your teachers tomorrow about you having extra lessons in space, time, and energy travel—"

"No! I hate STET, Daddy, it's dead boring!"

"Boring or not, you must learn to respect the laws that govern it, and it's only boring because you don't understand it yet."

Maggie smirked as she watched the three spirits vanish like a star in the daytime. It was a few moments before she realised that Aedan had already left. Troubled, she thought he was probably tired and had gone back to his room to rest. She put her hand on Eileen's shoulder. "I'm off back to Aedan's room. I've not really had a chance to ask him how he's feeling. I think he's still a bit tired."

Eileen's face had swollen to twice its normal size. Her eyes bulged, and her eyelids seemed to cover most of her pupils. Her nose looked like a big red blob that had landed there from God knows where, and still the tears poured with no sign of any let-up. "Maggie, the day you and Aedan walked into my life, I was blessed, I really was. I know without a doubt that if it wasn't for your help I would have lost the will to live this day..." she broke off, too upset to talk.

Maggie wrapped her arms around her. "Now, now, don't take on. You would have found it again. You've got Charlie and the kids to think about. We just helped you to accept things a bit quicker, that's all."

"The way I felt in that room…I just wanted to die. Without you and Aedan, I'd have been drugged up, sent to the lunatic asylum." She let out a small, sarcastic sound from her throat. "I had no thought for Charlie or the kids, none! How selfish of me!" She turned to Charlie. "I love you all; I do, Charlie, more than anything—"

"It's only to be expected. You'd just been told your child wouldn't make it! Grief, shock…it affects people in different ways, that's all. Don't start feeling all guilty—we know you love us." He turned away and sat down next to his daughter and lifted her to him. He closed his eyes and sat there for a few moments more, clinging tight. The small, lifeless body all but disappeared into his muscular frame.

Eileen was about to say something to him but Maggie placed a finger to her lips to indicate that she should save it for later. "This is his time to let her go." She freed Eileen from her embrace and took hold of her hands. "I should go and see to Aedan. Do you want me to tell the nurse that Celia has gone?"

Still bewildered, Eileen shook her head from side to side. "The nurse?"

Maggie spoke very softly. "Yes, she'll have to come and…look after Celia until the funeral arrangements have been made."

"Oh, yes, yes—course she will. No, we'll be fine now. Go and see to Aedan."

40.

She found Aedan lying down on the bed, staring up at the ceiling. She ran over and put her hand on his brow. "Aren't you feeling well, sweetheart?"

"No, Mam, I feel horrible."

"Why? Are you in pain? I'll get the doctor!" She turned anxiously, and looked at the door.

"No…I just feel sad, that's all." Big tears rolled down his cheeks.

She lifted him to her. "About Celia? It's only to be expected. There, there, you have a good cry." Poor Aedan. She'd never given a thought as to how Celia's death might have affected him.

He looked up at her. "No! Not about Celia, Mam, about Julian! I've tried using my third eye to find him but I can't get anything." He bawled louder. "Mam, I think he's dead!"

She stroked his hair and kissed the top of his head. "You might be trying too hard. Leave it for a few days. Sometimes it's hard to get information on those who are close to us because of the emotional attachment we have to them." She closed her eyes and spoke softly. "Shh, maybe I can get something." She kept her arms wrapped protectively around him. "Shh, it'll be alright, it will…I promise."

They took comfort in each other's arms. He felt secure. She felt blessed by the small jerks he made as his sobs subsided into tiny sighs. Within a few minutes the atmosphere in the room had changed from one of sadness and loss, to peace and acceptance.

"I don't think Julian is dead, Aedan. I think somebody is looking after him."

455

He immediately stopped crying. His expression flashed from sadness to hope. "Really? You think he's alive?"

"Yes, but I've no clue who's got him. There are so many different faces. They all seem to like him. He's happy, especially with one person in particular, a real animal lover." Aedan started to cry again. "What now? I thought you'd be pleased."

"If he likes that person too much he won't want to come back to me, and how do I know where he is? He could be miles away."

"Aedan! Don't give up before you've even tried! I thought you had more about you than that? He might not like this person as much as he does you, but even if he does, just be pleased that he's found a good home."

"I'm going to ask White Eagle where he is."

"Well…you can try, but White Eagle might not know. Our guides can only pass on information they're privy to, and apart from that he will only tell you where Julian is if you are meant to be his new owner. Could be that you were only meant to have him for a short time, that you acted as a go-between. If this is the case then White Eagle won't be at liberty to tell you where he is."

"I thought our guides knew everything," he said, disappointed.

"Oh, they know a lot. The job they do isn't taken lightly. But it doesn't mean that they're at our beck and call, OR," she emphasised, "that they are the answer to everything. We still have to make our own decisions. They can help but they are not supposed to tell us the future. That would be interfering with free will. Imagine if Celia's guide had told her that she was going to die today before it actually happened. In all probability she wouldn't have gone into Glossop and we certainly wouldn't have taken her."

"But she'd have been able to choose whether she went to Glossop or not, so she'd still be using her free will."

Maggie thought for a minute then shook her head. "To some degree, yes. But in a situation like that, her decision would have rested purely on the information her guide had given her instead of her free will. As it happened, she wanted to stay in the spirit world. Would she have been able to exercise that choice if she hadn't been fatally injured yesterday?"

He raised his knee, gently lifted the edge of the bandage, and started to scratch at the scab underneath it. "I suppose not."

"Don't scratch!" she ordered. "You'll make it worse."

He started to unwind the bandage. "It's driving me mad!"

She spotted a flannel on his bedside table, got up, and poured some water on it. "When I get home I'll mix up a cream." She thought for a minute. "Marigold, St. John's Wort, and a bit of lavender oil should do the trick." She placed the jug of water back on the cabinet and turned around. "Put this on it—Aedan!" She said, raising her voice, "How many times?" Exasperated, she shook her head. "How many times do you need telling? What will the doctor think?"

"He'll just think he made a mistake."

"Mistake, my backside! He put fifteen stitches in it!" She grabbed the back of his flawless knee. "Put the scab back this minute!"

"No! I'm not putting the scab back, Mam!"

"Put it back or I'll not be responsible for my actions!"

"No! It'd be like self-abuse!" The expression on his face said, "You must be joking!"

"Self-abuse! Where the hell do you get some of your ideas? Put the scab back! You're not supposed to bring attention to yourself!" She wanted to say, "It's dangerous. We have to keep you away from Evolus for as long as possible. Right now your power is nothing compared to his." *But how can I say such things to him without scaring him half to death?*

"Mam?"

She thought back to a conversation she'd had with White Eagle. *'We will have to tell Aedan about Evolus as soon as he's old enough to comprehend it,'* he'd said. She stared into space. *'And what age is that?'*—

"Mam! Mam!" Aedan tugged at his leg. "Let go of my leg."

"Huh, oh…sorry," she said, jerked away from her thoughts.

Aedan rubbed the back of his knee. "You've left your fingerprints in it!" he said indignantly.

"Well, that's what you get for acting like a big shot!"

"I'm not acting like a big shot! What's the point of my power if I can't enjoy it now and again?"

"Not if it brings attention! The doctor isn't daft; he knows which knee he put the stitches in."

"I'll confuse him!"

"You'll do no such thing! That's the worst way to use the power. You'd get in a lot of trouble for that from the…the higher-ups."

"Who?"

"White Eagle wouldn't be too pleased! Only in certain circumstances, like a life or death decision," she added, thinking that one day he may have to use his power to confuse somebody.

God, there were times when she wished he was just an ordinary boy! Not that she didn't love him for who he was, but the pressure of knowing what to say, what to do, so that she didn't impede his growth, so that he could have as normal a childhood as possible—it overwhelmed her at times.

She looked at her watch. "I'd best be off or I won't make it back in time to catch the late bus. I could do with stopping at the reception and finding out who it was that brought you in; I'd like to thank them, huh? Maybe they know where Julian is! I never thought of that."

The last twenty-four hours had been a living nightmare. Maggie hadn't given the person who'd got Aedan to the hospital a second thought. She'd phoned Cyril from the café, let Marion finish her meal, and raced back over to the hospital to wait for Eileen and Charlie and hopefully get some news on Aedan. When they'd arrived, the three of them had charged through the hospital doors in an effort to get to Celia as soon as possible, and possibly find out some news on Aedan's whereabouts.

As they'd made their way up the steps to the ward, the duty nurse who'd been on shift for just over two hours stopped and asked them what they were doing there. When she realised that Maggie could be Aedan's mother, she told her that a boy fitting her son's description had been admitted several hours before. With all the confusion and the staff changeover, they'd somehow missed the fact that Aedan was actually in the hospital at the same time that Maggie was trying to find him! It floored her to think that her instinct, sixth-sense, whatever you wanted to call it, hadn't alerted her to this fact, yet Celia's presence had come through loud and clear! She comforted herself by realising that all things happen for a reason, and whatever that reason was, it had steered her away from knowing that Aedan was more or less under her nose.

Aedan felt as if his excitement was about to explode from the top of his head. "Mam! I wonder if they're looking after him? You'd better give the hospital our address just in case they want to bring him back."

"Now don't get too excited. Julian could have been anywhere by the time you were found. Whoever brought you in might not have a clue about him. We'll stop at reception later and find out. I can't go now, I might miss the bus."

"Get Cyril to pick you up."

"No! Poor Cyril's got enough to do. He's bent over backwards to help us as it is." She looked at Aedan's knee. "Put that bandage back on. If the doctor comes while I'm away tell him your knee feels fine, and I'll change the dressing when we get home." She bent down and kissed him. "And no more tricks."

"Why can't I come now?" he whined. "I'm bored!"

She rolled her eyes. "Bored are you, young man? Children these days!" They don't know they're born!"

"Why can't I go home in my old clothes? It's daft having to wait here just so you can go home and come back with clean clothes."

"Don't start!" She pulled his trousers out of her brown PVC shopping bag, held them in the air, and pointed at them. "They look like something a navvy would use to rub down with, and then they'd need a damn good scrubbing first! Look at the state of em. You can't tell me you'd walk through the streets in these, Aedan!"

"Just bang the dust off them!"

"Bang the dust off!" she said, exasperated. "The legs are torn to shreds and half the gusset has gone. You'd be showing your backside to everyone."

"Only them I don't like." He burst out laughing.

"Don't be so cheeky," she said, with a stern look on her face. She glared at him in an effort to stop her laughter from filling the small room but failed miserably. It didn't matter how annoyed she was, he always had the ability to make her laugh.

"How long will you be?"

"How long's a piece of string?"

"Mam! Don't say that—it's annoying!" An aloof expression crossed his face. "I'm not waiting all day!"

"Oh! And where do you plan on going in your hospital gown?" She walked over to him. "Stop moaning and give me a break! I've been here all night and I've still got to figure out how to get back home then back here again then back home again."

"Pardon?"

She kissed the top of his head. "I'll be a while; the buses are few and far between on Sundays. You'll just have to be patient, patient," she winked.

She wondered if she had anything with her that could keep him amused for a few hours. She hunted through her bag for the comic she'd given Marion, then realised they'd left it behind. "Damn!" she whispered, just as there was a gentle knock on the door and an older woman with a jolly face popped her head inside.

"Books, magazines, comics, today's paper?"

Aedan's face lit up. "Can I have a comic, Mam?"

"What's the magic word?"

"Please!" He ducked underneath the woman's arm as she held the door open for him, and raced into the corridor. "Wow!" His eyes lit up at the array of books, comics, sweets, and chocolate bars that were crammed onto the small trolley. It looked like a mini newsagents. Maggie followed him out and thanked the woman for holding the door.

"Why do you always have to be reminded about your manners?" She looked at the woman and smiled. "You're a lifesaver!"

"Oh, no, not really. I just like to help out, especially in these times of trouble."

"You're a volunteer?"

"Yes, been doing it since I lost my husband three years ago." She took a pin out of her grey hair and stuck it between her teeth. "This has been my lifesaver." She wrapped a strand of hair around the bun at her nape, took the clip, and pushed it out of sight underneath it.

Aedan pulled at his mother's arm. "Can I have these?" he asked, showing her two comics.

"No!"

"Mam! You said I could have them."

"No!"

"Why? I'm gonna be stuck here for hours bored out of my skull!"

"No!"

"Please, Mam," he begged. He was puzzled as to why his mother had a disapproving look on her face. He went to put the comics back where he'd found them.

"That's more like it! Better choose a book as well, just in case you finish the comics before I get back."

"A book?" God, his mam was weird! Sometimes he just didn't know where he was up to with her!

"Yes...do you know why?" Aedan didn't hear her. He was too distracted by the books.

"Aedan, do you know why I changed my mind?"

"Huh, *Treasure Island*!" He turned to Maggie. "I've wanted this book for ages."

Maggie took the book and the magazines from him, and repeated her question. He looked at her, baffled. "Err...no!"

She shook her head in disbelief. "Because you used your manners without me having to remind you!"

"Did I?" It was obvious he didn't remember a thing about it.

Maggie looked at the volunteer and rolled her eyes in disbelief. "I'll take these, please." She handed her a few coins.

The woman gave Maggie her change and looked at Aedan. "They'll keep you busy for a while, young man. She grasped the handles of the trolley and gave it a hefty push. Aedan noticed the fat underneath her arms wobble.

He smiled at the lady. He liked her. She was kind; he could tell. "I'm a fast reader. My mam taught me from being little, before I even went to school." His smile turned into a look of concern. "You could do with getting some of that fat off before you get poorly."

Maggie simply stood there, opening and closing her mouth like a guppy fish. Her face burned with embarrassment as she looked from the woman to her son, then back at the woman again. "I'm so sorry...I don't know why he would say such a—Aedan! How could you be so rude? Apologise to the lady this minute!"

Aedan was baffled. Why was he rude? To his mind he was trying to help. The extra weight she was carrying was putting a strain on her heart. He looked at the woman, his face a picture of innocence. "I was trying to help Mrs...Simpson"—he read her name badge. "If you went for a walk like you used to do with Des, and stopped trying to replace him with food, you'd lose loads—"

Maggie thrust her purchases into him. "Aedan! That'll do! I've a good mind to give these back to Mrs. Simpson."

Mrs. Simpson gripped the handle of the trolley so hard her knuckles turned white. She was flabbergasted. "Did you know Des?"

"No, Mrs. Simpson, he doesn't know your husband, he's, he's... just good at...good at, guessing." Maggie glared at Aedan. "I'll bloody brain you," she mouthed to him when Mrs. Simpson wasn't looking.

"Don't worry about it." Her voice was soft and low. She gave Maggie a comforting glance. "The lad's right. I know I should stop eating. It's just that...when Des died he took a part of me with him— the will to stop eating!" Her laughter started off quiet, as if being wound up, and gradually increased in volume until it turned into a high-pitched cackle. "Eh, lad! The look on your mother's face when you came out with that statement! I'd have paid to see it, I would that. Eh, by God! But tell me, how do you know Des? I don't believe for a minute the tale about you being a good guesser."

Maggie looked uncomfortable. Des hadn't shown himself to her but she was pretty certain he wasn't hiding from Aedan. Even so,

Aedan needed to learn when he should and shouldn't open his mouth. For all they knew, Mrs. Simpson might be terrified to learn that her dead husband is alive and kicking, and having a conversation with an eight year old boy about her excess weight! "Well, I'd better get a move on," Maggie said, trying to change the subject. Talking to the spirits, for the most part, was received with suspicion and fear. The last thing they needed was for the woman to run from the hospital, screaming that the Devil enjoyed a private room in Ashton General!

Mrs. Simpson looked decidedly perplexed. There was something funny going on here without a doubt. She eyed Maggie suspiciously. "Did you know *my* Des?"

Oh, for God's sake! She can't honestly believe...he'd be old enough to be my bleedin' granddad! "No, Mrs. Simpson! I've never met your husband. Like I said, Aedan is good at guessing things."

"It's okay, Mam. Des said I can tell her about him."

Maggie rolled her eyes. "I don't give a hoot what Des said—"

"Now come on. I think I've got a right to know what's going on." Mrs. Simpson folded her arms across her chest, ready for battle.

"Des is stood there." Aedan nodded over to Mrs. Simpson's right.

"What do you mean?" she looked behind in the direction of Aedan's gaze.

"He's not dead! I can see him, and he's telling me that you need to do more walking and less eating."

Maggie couldn't remember a single moment in her life that matched up to this one for sheer embarrassment. If Aedan persisted in using his medium skills he would have to learn how to use them with diplomacy. The spirits for the most part tell it like it is, but the mediums need to learn discretion. Even so, Des should have realised that any child, in all innocence, will repeat his words verbatim.

Mrs. Simpson looked terrified. "What on earth are you talking about? Des has been dead for three years!"

"I know," Aedan said innocently. "I talk to dead people, but they're not really dead! Des is in the spirit world."

"No, he is not! Des is in heaven—Father Kelly sent him there!"

"I don't think so! Father Kelly has no clout in the spirit world!"

Oh, Jesus, Mary, and Joseph—"Aedan!" Maggie raised her eyebrows in the hope that he'd shut up! "Des is a Catholic!"

Aedan shrugged, and shook his head. "No, he's not! He's a spirit, and he likes it where he is." He turned to Mrs. Simpson. "And he says you should clean your house more often as well; he doesn't understand why you've let everything go to pot, just 'cos he's dead—"

"AEDAN! THAT'S ENOUGH! Tell Des he must leave right now!"

Aedan was defiant. "Why? He's just worried about Dotty, that's all."

As was characteristic of Maggie when she got irate, she ran a few paces towards him, and then stopped dead in her tracks. "Tell him to leave or I'll shift him myself—"

"Dotty…that was his pet name for me," Mrs. Simpson said, trance-like. "How would you know that?" She looked like a frightened bird. Her beady eyes seemed to have got stuck inside her head, which jerked about like a pigeon pecking at corn. "How do you know that? How do you know these things?" She took Aedan by the shoulders and shook him firmly. "You're talking to the Devil—you are! Don't you know that?"

Alarmed, Aedan pulled away from her. "No, I'm not. I'm talking to Des." He couldn't understand why people were so scared of their loved ones just because they'd died! They seemed to think that because a spirit had left Earth, it changed into some kind of demon that only dealt with a devil! "There's no Devil," he said naively, in the hope that he'd reassure her. "Only if you believe in it. Hell can't touch you unless you believe in it. You make your own!"

"Oh, yes it can, child. You need to go and see your priest!" She turned to Maggie and spoke to her in an offhand manner. "When was the last time you took him to church?"

"I don't go to church," Aedan cut in.

She turned back to him. "You don't go to church!? Do you know who the saviour is?"

Aedan's face suddenly lost its innocence to an older, wiser expression. His steely gaze held Mrs. Simpson in a strong, silent pause. "I do! Do you?" he asked, quietly.

The atmosphere in the room was thick. It curdled, like sour milk. Mrs. Simpson couldn't get away quick enough. She raced up the corridor and bumped into a doctor. She placed her hands on his forearms. "Oh, I'm so sorry, Dr. Bannister!"

"Whatever's the matter, Dorothy?" Can I help you? Do you need anything?"

"No, no, I'll be fine, just some fresh air."

"Mrs. Simpson, your trolley!" Maggie shouted.

She dashed back. On reaching the trolley, she slowed down and kept glancing sideways at Maggie and Aedan. "Get him to church as soon as you can. Save your child from the Devil, missus!"

Maggie envisioned the woman coming back with a gang of parishioners headed by a priest, so she nodded in agreement. "I'll do that."

Maggie pushed Aedan back into the room. She sat down on a chair and just looked at him.

"What?" he said to her. "I thought she was kind."

"She is…just frightened. You've got to learn that not everyone appreciates your…your talents, Aedan. And when a spirit turns up wanting to talk to someone, you've got to make sure that that someone is ready to listen. Mrs. Simpson—her belief—doesn't believe you can talk to the dead, nor does it allow it. They believe it's the Devil making mischief." She questioned him even though she knew the answer. "Was your intention to scare Mrs. Simpson?"

"No! I thought it would make her feel better."

"But it didn't. This is what you've got to learn. Exercise judgment." Weary, she closed her eyes and rubbed her temples.

Aedan went and sat on her knee; he put his arms around her neck. "I'll try—"

"Or just listen! When I tell you enough, I'm exercising my judgment, so listen to me."

He looked confused. "I thought we weren't supposed to judge?"

"At a personal level, such as why people do what they do, but this doesn't mean we mustn't use discretion. If you'd known beforehand that Mrs. Simpson thought talking to spirits was the Devil's work, you'd have made a judgment not to mention Des to her, now wouldn't you? You didn't want to frighten her."

"No—"

"Then you would be using your judgment in a positive light." She tapped his nose with her middle finger. "I've got to go. Read your book. Be quiet. Don't be telling people their dead relatives have turned up unless you know they're ready to hear it! We've had enough excitement for one day. I'll be as quick as I can."

41.

The captain inhaled deep, exhilarating breaths. The blue sky, bright sunshine, and clean, fresh autumn air always made him feel good. He decided to walk to the hospital to see the boy. He should be rested up by then and he wanted to make arrangements to give him his dog back. Presuming it was his dog; what if it wasn't? He'd give it a name other than Dog, and keep it as the regimental mascot. In a way, he was hoping that this was the case. It was a nice dog—ugly bugger, but nice temperament.

As he sauntered up the streets of Ashton, he noticed how quiet they were. Yesterday's attack had brought the reality of war too close for comfort as far as the residents were concerned. After all, Glossop was only up the road—when would it be their turn? Though in all probability, some argued, the bombers would have been heading for Manchester. They'd hit Glossop by mistake.

He smiled and nodded at a few children playing hopscotch and kick the can, not a care in the world. Their laughter pierced the quiet eeriness of the day. "Wow! A real live soldier walking up our street!" a little girl exclaimed as he walked by. He wondered what was in store for them. What would shatter their innocence? How precious it was—innocence—how blissful.

He looked ahead at the green and brown hills as they rolled backwards into a sharp blue sky. He never had been able to reach the bottom of them. The closer he got, the farther away they receded. Just like the end of a rainbow, the foot of the hills was elusive. *Yet someone had got there,* he thought, as he looked at the small stone houses dotted

467

about on the somewhat empty slopes. Chimneys blew out grey-blue smoke that weaved seductively along the landscape towards the trees that were huddled together in patches, only to be dispersed by a small flip of their branches, which had much bigger things to worry about. Accustomed to the moods of nature, the trees stuck their branches out like arms, their bony fingers probing, feeling, searching for when the next onslaught would be.

The captain squinted. *What was that moving along the slopes?* He grinned, realising that the tiny white dots were a few sheep that had landed, and not something more exotic like a UFO—*UFO? Claptrap! Amazing, the places the mind visits when it has time to wander.* She broke into his thoughts. *'I find it hard to comprehend, given the magnitude of creation, how this can be the only planet in the universe to have life on it. I mean...what if there are countless universes that haven't been discovered yet? Countless planets not discovered? Countless non-physical places, even?'*

He wondered if she was happy. Had she met someone else? What the boy looked like—who he looked like? Did he call some other man "Daddy"? For years, always the same questions, and—ashamed to say—the same spear of jealously never failed to slice right through him. He couldn't stand the thought of someone else having her, bringing up their child, moving in on what was his. Yet he wished more than anything else in the world that they did have peace…joy. Oh, yes, he did.

The sound of the ice cream van playing a warped, tinny version of "Twinkle, Twinkle, Little Star," The thought, *How I wonder what you are,* brought the captain back to earth.

Up and down the street, a few doors opened as both adults and children headed to the van. He took his place at the back of the queue thinking he'd have a double wafer with raspberry sauce poured all over it, and some hundreds and thousands. His mouth watered at the thought.

People turned and looked at him. They were friendly, asking him questions about the regiment, and making small-talk about the war in general. Even so, the sight of him in full uniform unnerved them. It wasn't normal to see soldiers walking about the streets and, as of yet, the fact that the country was at war hadn't fully sunk in…not fully. It would happen in other parts of the country but not theirs.

He overheard a couple of men talking about the headlines on the front of the morning newspaper—"Miracle in Norfolk Square!" Some of his men had been buzzing about it earlier but he'd not taken much notice. Apparently, despite many people being injured, only one child, a girl, was on the critical list. It was hard to fathom given the devastation of Glossop's town centre. Hardly a building had been left untouched—

"No!" Some woman said, joining in the conversation.

"Yeah! It's right here in black an' white." One of the men had rushed back indoors to grab his paper and was now tapping the headline with his fingernails. "There are reports from eye witnesses that a small boy had been looking up at the bombs and some electrical charges come out of him—like long streamers of light, one woman described 'em as."

"Well, there you have it," another man cut in. "The boy was struck by lightning."

"There was no storm yesterday!" the man with the paper said. "Besides, the woman said the boy looked right at her, told her to run. Said the light, whatever it was, still poured out of him as he spoke! If it was lightning he wouldn't have been able to stand around telling people to run. He'd be dead! And there are no reports of a boy being killed."

"But what's so miraculous about it?" the man asked, a sceptical look on his face. "Could have been light reflecting off the sun or something like that. Naaaa! The woman would have been panicking with all that mayhem goin' on. It's her mind playing tricks."

"According to the paper, the stuff coming out of the boy wrapped itself around the bombs, prevented them from hitting the ground. The woman said the bombs had literally hung in the sky like air ships, while the boy cleared Norfolk Square. She believes without a doubt that if it wasn't for him, hundreds of people would have been killed."

"Give over—bleedin' miracles! It's obvious! The woman was blinded by panic!"

"She's not the only witness."

"Ahh! People believe what they want to believe. One says something, and before you know it, all the lunatics start crawling out of the bleedin' woodwork. Woman's probably a religious nutcase looking for an excuse to make light of the war. Make herself feel better about God, and why he does things."

The captain smiled to himself as he licked the ice cream from around the edges of the wafer. *There's a true believer if ever I've heard one. A believer in nothing!* "Would you mind?" he asked the man holding the paper.

"Not at all." The man handed it to him. Ice cream in one hand, paper in the other, he flipped the paper in the middle and scanned the article awkwardly.

><

Maggie turned the key in her front door at the same time as she pulled the paper out of the letterbox. She looked down at the headlines and flipped the paper in the middle so that she could read it. "Miracle in Norfolk Square!"—"Jesus, Aedan!" She knew without a doubt that it was something to do with him.

She kicked her leg backwards to close the door, looked at the clock on the mantelpiece, and threw the paper, along with her coat, onto the armchair. She had time for a cup of tea before the next bus. She swept the dead ashes from the grate using a small silver brush and shovel from the companion set that stood off to the side of it. Once she'd got rid of the ashes in the dustbin outside, she walked over to the understairs cupboard and took some firelighters from the shelf. She'd make a small fire to take the chill out of the house; at least that way it would be warm when she brought Aedan back later. *Thank God he's okay.*

She lifted the cushion up on the settee and removed an old newspaper from underneath it. She folded the sheets into long thin rectangles, knotted them, and laid them in the grate before placing a few firelighters on top of them. Once she'd lit the paper, it didn't take long for the firelighters to crackle and spit, always a sign that they had no intention of burning out. If she didn't time it just right she'd have to start the procedure all over again. She took the prongs from the companion set and picked a few lumps of coal from a small brass bucket. Within no time, the fire cheered up the cottage and warmed up the kettle. She made her tea, sat down, and read the article in the morning paper. Her smile was a mixture of happy and sad as she read about Celia still being on the critical list. *The miracle in Norfolk Square let one life go.* "Aedan…Aedan, what are we going to do with you?" she said to herself.

She understood that he'd acted on impulse. He was to be commended. He'd saved lives. How could she tell him not to do such things for fear of unwelcome attention? But tell him she would. It was time to talk to him about Evolus. She would summon White Eagle later that night when Aedan was tucked up safely in bed. She knew that Aedan was well protected but they couldn't underestimate Evolus's power. That would be foolish, and she wasn't about to put her son at even the slightest risk. David's voice broke into her thoughts. *'You have no idea of the power you are playing with.'* "Oh, I do, David. I do."

NeilA invaded her thoughts—*But there are those protecting Aedan with powers that the human brain can't even begin to comprehend!* Her heart skipped a beat! *What am I thinking? NeilA…galactic powers…Evolus—they don't exist! And if they did, it would be nothing to do with Aedan. Nothing!* Hands on her ears, she cried out, "STOP, STOP, STOP!"

As usual, she did her best to deny what she knew—who her son was, who she was, why they were here! She was more afraid of the light than she was of the dark. The light brought so much more… responsibility. She felt a sudden urge to get out of the house; her nerves were getting the better of her. The strain of the last few days was catching up. She gulped back a mouthful of tea—*I'd better feed the cat*—and noticed the tea leaves in the bottom of the cup had formed into a perfect circle. Her eyebrows knitted together. "Unusual, such perfection in the leaves." She looked closer at the blob in the middle of the circle. It was an embryo in the foetal position, and off to the side, on the outside of the circle, was something else! A face! It was—"NOOOOOOOO!"

Terrified, she banged the cup down on the table, and shook it from side to side. She knew, she knew, he was trying to tell her something. He was only being kind, but she denied him! "LEAVE US ALONE!" she cried out. Frantic, she stuck her finger into the cup, stirred it around and around in an effort to change the leaves. *I'm seeing things—must be stress.* But terrified, she watched as they formed once again into the same circle, the same foetus, and the same face—the face blew the circle from its mouth as if breathing it out. Breathing life into it!

And then it spoke in a calm voice, "You can't deny me forever, Maggie. Aedan is as much a part of me as he is you. You must accept that his human form is nothing but a guise. He is of galactic lineage, the most powerful there is…sheer power, like none those on Earth can envisage! But then, you know that," he sighed. "You can't scratch me off with somebody else's name, or your own denial—"

"NOOOOO!" She threw the cup against the wall, smashing it to pieces. The dregs trickled everywhere. She jumped up, turned to grab her coat and bag, but instead watched in horror as the symbol from the tea leaves formed in the bricks underneath the wallpaper. The face in the wall spoke. "It's what's underneath the surface that counts."

"DAVID IS HIS FATHER, NOT YOU!"

"He is his father, yes…but I am in his soul, and permanent. In the end, you both belong to me! We're all together, Maggie!" NeilA smiled kindly. Within a blink of an eye, the face and the rest of the symbol had gone.

Maggie jerked awake and clutched her chest in an effort to slow down her heartbeat. "Must have fallen asleep." She grabbed the cup, ran to the kitchen, and eyed the tea leaves just before she flushed them down the plughole. "Nothing unusual there!"

NeilA turned to Roman, tightened his lips, and said, "I can't keep being nice. There's too much at stake. Next time I talk to Maggie, it won't be in the comfort of the dream world."

42.

The captain looked at the crowd around the hospital's reception desk and decided to boycott it. He didn't have all afternoon to hang around. He still had to walk back to the barracks to pick up the dog and reunite him with his rightful owner. Besides, he couldn't stand hospitals: damn morbid places at the best of times, filled with miserable, ailing people. Not that he didn't have any sympathy, it just put years on him. Then again, he always felt good when he walked out the doors with his health intact. *Thank God I'm only visiting.*

He spotted the matron who had been on duty when they brought Aedan in. "Is the boy still here, matron? I want to make arrangements to get his dog back to him."

She smiled broadly. He was a handsome blighter if ever she saw one. *If only I was a few years younger. He wouldn't stand a chance!* Both her tone and manner were the epitome of professionalism. "Hello, captain, present for him as well?" She nodded at the flowered paper bag in his hands.

"Yes, there was a small newsagents open just up the road there. Thought I'd bring him some chocolate—how is he?"

"Apart from being a bit tired and a few cuts and grazes, he's doing very well. His mother left not too long ago, gone to get him some clothes so she can take him home later."

"Oh, good! He's back with his family. That is good news. What's his name?"

Oblivious to the question, the matron signalled him to follow. "Come, I'll show you to his room—"

473

"That's okay, matron, you've enough to do. Just tell me what ward."

"Lucky number seven for that boy." She pointed to some stairs. "Ward seven, room seven."

He thanked her, charged up the stairs three at a time, and walked casually up the corridor to Aedan's room. When he got there, he found the door ajar. He popped his head inside, and tapped on the door twice. "Good book, one of my favourites." Aedan was reading *Treasure Island.*

The two stared at each other. It was a strange feeling, kind of inquisitive with something else thrown in. The corners of Aedan's lips turned up. It was the weird captain he'd seen with the Manchesters, the one who had attracted him. He didn't know why he was weird or why he was attracted to him.

The captain caught his breath, remained half in, half out of the room, holding on to the door. That face, he'd seen it somewhere...

Aedan broke the silence. "You look like a giant!" he said, wondering if he'd grow that big.

The captain smirked. "You're not shy, then?" He picked up the comics lying on the chair and glanced at them, "Desperate who?" He lifted one off the top of the other, threw them on the bed, and sat down. "Can't remember stuff like that to read when I was your age. So! How're you feeling? Matron tells me you're going home today."

"Yep."

"You don't sound too pleased about it."

"It's my dog...I lost him yesterday." He wondered who the man was. What was he doing here? Then it twigged—"Did you bring me here? Have you got Julian?"

The captain grimaced, wondering how such a rough-looking dog had been burdened with such a nancyfied name. "Julian! Well, I'd never have guessed his name, that's for sure. White, full of scars, black patch over one of his red eyes?"

Aedan couldn't contain his excitement. He just about landed in the captain's lap. "Have you seen him?"

"Yeppers...we were going to make him the regimental mascot if we couldn't locate his owner."

"Julian is at the barracks?"

"He is, being spoilt rotten!"

Elated, Aedan threw his arms around the captain's neck as if he'd known him all his life. "Thanks, mister! Thanks for looking after my dog."

The captain held the boy to him, took in his smell, the feel of him, wanted to kiss him, hold him forever—he plonked Aedan on the bed roughly, unable to understand the feelings that were causing him to panic inside. *What the hell?* "Well...err, we'd better make some arrangements to get him back to you. What's your address?" He reached inside his jacket pocket and passed Aedan a pen and a small, brown, leather-bound diary. "Write it in there." Unnerved by his own reaction, he avoided eye contact with the boy.

"Can I have a ride in your jeep?" Aedan was thrilled that it was a soldier who'd rescued him.

The captain cocked his head to the side. "We'd better see your mother about that."

"Did you save me?" He wrote his address in the back of the diary on a clean sheet and handed it back to the captain.

"Not only me." He reached inside his jacket again and passed Aedan a small black and white photograph. "These are the men who helped rescue you. They've all signed the back of it." One by one, he pointed at the faces. "This one's Tommy Harrison, Albert Robson, Mickey Taylor, Sergeant Arthur Mason—nicknamed Art when we're off duty—and yours truly."

Aedan looked down at the smiling faces of the men, and a proud Julian sitting in front of them. He looked up at the captain and noticed that he was watching his every move. He put it down to his training. Soldiers had to watch everyone in case they were a spy or something.

The captain looked away quickly and pointed to Julian. "If it wasn't for this fellow, in all probability you'd have remained under the rubble. He wouldn't give up, not for a minute, even when we were about to walk away."

Aedan's face stretched into a huge smile, white teeth showing, eager to hear the full story. "Tell me, tell me!"

The captain leaned into him, and played to his excitement. He used a fast, dangerous tone to describe the happenings. "I knew something was up because the dog wouldn't budge from the side of the hole we'd been digging. I dragged at his lead but he pulled back, jamming it around his throat. In the end I let him go because I was worried he might choke to death." He paused and looked thoughtful. "Then the strangest thing happened. A sunbeam passed through the window—well, what used to be a window—and shone down into the hole and caught that chain you wear around your neck. I jumped back into the hole and started to dig again, and then the same thing happened. It was as if the sun was pointing me towards you. I picked up the links, pulled on them, and realised they were attached to something." He looked at Aedan. "I didn't think for one minute it would be a boy, not with a rough-looking beggar like that!" He pointed to Julian. "I thought it was going to be an adult we'd find—an older bloke, maybe."

Aedan was mesmerised. "Wow! So even my necklace played a part in it. It's like my dad saved me as well!"

"Your dad?" The captain was puzzled.

"Yeah. My dad gave my mam the necklace years ago but she's only just let me wear it. She wasn't sure at first if she should wait until I was a bit older but I told her I'd look after it." He looked up, smiled, and started to play with the chain. "It's a Celtic cross." He put his hand behind his neck and slid the cross to the front of the chain. "Do you want to see it?"

"Sure."

Aedan jumped off the bed still grasping the cross, stretched his neck towards the captain, and released it into his hands. "I'm never gonna take it off."

The captain rubbed his thumb across it slowly. He stopped, and looked at it closely. His heart gave one solid thump. He dropped the cross as if holding onto a branding iron.

Aedan looked at him bewildered. "Don't you like it!?"

His words were short. "Where did you get it?" David picked

it up again.

"My mam gave it to me. My dad had it made for her before he died."

David didn't want to believe it…*What if he was wrong? Maggie could have pawned it or anything… No! She'd never do that. Though she must have been strapped for cash through the years—but the boy, his face…* And then it dawned, *He looks like me! No! I'm not getting my hopes built up to have them come crashing down on me again.* Over the years, it had happened too many times…a lead, only to have nothing come of it.

But there wasn't a doubt in his mind that this was Maggie's cross. His design! There could only be one of them.

Aedan was frightened. He tried to pull away, and put his small hand on top of David's. "Can I have it back?"

David looked at him and kept hold of the cross. "What's your name?" he asked urgently. Aedan didn't answer. He'd known there was something strange about this bloke from first clapping eyes on him. "What's your name?" David repeated, keeping hold of the cross.

"Aedan—"

The atmosphere in the room was intense. David's eyes burned into Aedan. His voice was a whisper. "Is your mother Maggie O'Connell?" His breathing was jagged. He felt like he might collapse at any moment. *Aedan isn't the most common of names. What are the chances of—don't get your hopes built up!*

Aedan said nothing. "Let go of my cross or I'll tell the nurse." Frightened, he started to cry.

David realised he was scaring the boy and his heart melted. He let go of the cross. "Don't cry, shh, shh." He shook his head and clasped Aedan's face; he just about buried it in his huge hands. "You're the last person in the world I want to hurt," he said tenderly. But he refused to believe that this was his son until he heard him say his mother's name. "Please…I think I know your mother." He smiled reassuringly.

Aedan didn't know if he should tell him that Maggie was his mother or not. He wished she'd hurry up and then she could tell him herself. He looked up at David with tear-filled eyes and an anxious expression on his face, and refused to say anything.

David continued. "She's not in trouble. I know an old friend of hers, that's all…someone she might like to see…that is, if your mammy is Maggie O'Connell?"

Aedan nodded very slightly and tucked the cross back inside his gown. "Yes, she's Maggie O'Connell and I'm Aedan."

David grabbed the child to him, buried his nose in his hair and sobbed great heart-wrenching sobs. "Thank God, thank God." He hugged Aedan harder and harder, kissed his cheeks, his head; he released him, picked up his hands, kissed them, hugged the boy back to himself. Oh, the joy, the joy. It was too good to be true. His belly turned over and over. He'd found them at last. He rocked to and fro with Aedan in his arms, taking in all the years he'd missed. He'd never lose them again! Never!

Though filled with a world of questions, the room held a comfortable silence. Aedan didn't have any idea what was going on, but since being wrapped up in the man's strong arms he'd lost his fear. He felt safe. He kind of liked it and didn't want him to let go. He didn't know what it was with the bloke but he knew he wouldn't hurt him. *Maybe he's just lonely,* Aedan thought, with the innocence only a child could possess—an innocence Maggie had fought long and hard to keep. "What's your friend's name?" he asked, after several minutes. "I'll tell my mam when she comes."

David pushed him away gently but kept his hands on his shoulders. "David." He ran his fingers along Aedan's cheek, noting how soft and new he felt.

Aedan smiled. "That's my dad's name. Do you want to read *Treasure Island* with me?" he asked, thinking it might cheer the captain up.

David wondered if he should tell him that he was his dad but thought better of it. He was sure that Maggie would want to be there to deliver news like that! Besides, it would come as a shock to the boy, not to mention her, when she set eyes on him again. His impatience wanted to ask Aedan if his mother had anyone else but he refrained from doing so. It was inappropriate, to say the least. He wondered how he could soften the shock for Maggie but realised it was impossible. Whatever happened, though, he'd better get out of the hospital before she showed up. That way, at least the boy could tell her the captain was bringing an old friend of hers along with him, give her some kind of warning. He smiled at Aedan. "I'll read a chapter with you before I go."

Aedan jumped back on the bed. "Sit next to me if you want." David crushed up against him and pulled the pillow from underneath his shoulders. "Hey!" Aedan laughed, and tried to pull it back.

David put his arm around his son's shoulders and looked down at him. With tears in his eyes, he said, "You can lean on me."

43.

"Mam, Mam! I can't believe it, I can't believe it! Julian will be here any second running out of the captain's jeep!" Aedan had his arms wrapped around Maggie's middle and was jumping up and down, unable to contain his excitement. He'd even convinced her to let Julian sleep in his room that night—just once, as a welcome home present. Since they'd got home, he'd been up at the window or opening the front door and running down the garden path every five minutes! The sun was already setting behind the hills. Surely the captain would be here soon? Needless to say, he'd forgotten all about the captain's old friend! "You don't think he's lost our address, do you, Mam?"

"No—sit still for five minutes. You're driving me nuts! How about a game of chess until he gets here?"

"Alright! But he said he'd be here at seven and it's already half-past!"

"He's a busy man. Think yourself lucky he's making the effort at all. Put the curtains back—they're split in the middle. We don't want all and sundry peering in. Get the chess set while you're over there."

Aedan looked underneath some of the other board games but couldn't find the chess set. "It's not here."

"Course it's there, it's always there." Maggie stood up and looked underneath the other games. "That's funny," she said, then realised she'd given it to Derrick earlier. "Oh—sorry, love. I let Derrick take it. He called round when I got back from the hospital, said he was fed up! I gave him the chess set to keep him occupied for a few hours. I'll go and get it. If I'm not back when the captain arrives, come for me." As an afterthought, "Tell him to have a seat. Make sure he doesn't sit on the springs. I don't want him leaving here damaged." She winked.

Aedan looked at her disbelievingly. "Mam! Don't be rude!"

She laughed. "Just because I'm your mother doesn't mean we can't share the odd rude joke!"

Maggie had been gone about five minutes when David pulled up in his jeep. Aedan was already outside, running down the path. He'd heard the engine as soon as it turned off the lane into their cul-de-sac.

Julian's high-pitched yelps and barks could have woken the dead, and David not wanting to spoil the fun antagonised the situation by charging the dog, and wrestling its head between his hands. Aedan fell to his knees, hugged Julian, and tickled his belly. He was gifted with big, wet, sloppy doggy kisses in return.

David cringed. "Ugh! Make sure you wash your face and hands before you go to bed, young man."

"Don't say that—he's lovely! I like his kisses, don't I? Yes, yes." The dog emitted small grunts from the back of its throat, and danced about on his front legs.

"Think about the places that tongue's been!"

"What d'ya mean?" Aedan jumped back. "I know where his tongue's been. He eats his dinner with it."

"And?"

"Licks me with it."

"And?"

"Cleans himself with it."

"Yes."

"So?"

David bent down and put his face into Aedan's. "So…where does he clean himself with it?"

Aedan looked puzzled, thought for a minute, and started to giggle childishly. "Oh-oh! His bottom!" He broke into full-bodied laughter. "I don't care; he's got a nice bottom."

David tickled him. "Well, I'm glad somebody thinks so!"

Aedan screamed. "Don't tickle me, don't tickle me, I hate it!" he said, hardly able to get his words out through fits of laughter.

David looked toward the front door. He thought Maggie would have been out by now wondering what all the racket was about.

"She's at her friends. She said you're to go inside and sit down, but mind the springs on the settee; she didn't want to do you any damage. I'll go and get her."

"Where does her friend live?"

Aedan pointed towards the lane that ran along the bottom of the avenue. "About five minutes up that lane. Come on, Julian."

David watched until he was out of sight, a puzzled expression on his face. *Do me any damage!?* He walked up the path and let himself in. He stood for a few moments wanting to take in the ambiance of the cottage. It had a homely feel to it…cosy, but he wouldn't have expected anything less from Maggie. He sensed their happiness—mother and son, a closeness. His heart stretched as he thought about the lost years that he'd longed to be a part of. *'There are reasons for everything!'* a distant voice echoed in his head. "Maybe!" he answered, his voice full of cynicism. He could smell her, taste her…feel her. He closed his eyes. It was nothing new. She'd never left him. He sat down with his back to the door, noticed the springs, and let out a small laugh. "Not lost your sense of humour, then!" He removed his hat and placed it on the table. He spotted the mirror on the wall, stood up again, looked at himself, and ran a hand through his hair. He rubbed the bristles underneath his chin. He'd shaved before he came out but the blue-black, five o'clock shadow was already back at seven-thirty. Maggie used to love it, said it made him look even more handsome.

His stomach was in knots. What would he say? What would she say? Would she still love him as much as she used to? *There's no sign of a man about the place—stop getting your hopes built up*, he chastised himself. Then his stubbornness set in, not to mention a tinge of jealousy. If there was a man around, he wasn't going to walk away and pretend that Aedan wasn't his just to keep the peace. He had a right to his son, and his son had a right to him. *For God's sake! Calm down!*

≍

Maggie was already on her way home, chess set tucked on the inside of her arm. Julian bounded at her, just about knocked her off her feet, and sent the chess set scattering all over the place. "Julian!" she scolded. "Look what you've done." She frowned at him. "Naughty dog!" The dog took no notice and continued to nudge her with his head. He knew the difference between a genuine scolding and a pretend one. "Hello, hello." She rubbed the sides of his belly with her fingertips. "Now let me get on with clearing up your mess." Satisfied with her greeting, Julian walked across to Olive's begonias and peed all over them.

"Can I go and see Derrick for a bit, Mam?"

"Julian! Come here this minute." The dog bounded over. "Don't do that on Olive's flowers again!" She looked at her watch. "It's getting near your bedtime!"

"Please, Mam, just for a bit. I want to take Julian to see him and Ambrose."

"What about the captain?"

"I'll come back before he leaves."

She pointed at her watch. "No more than half an hour, Aedan. I'll be offering the captain a drink so that should give him time to finish it. As soon as he leaves it's bedtime for you; you need to rest up."

"I feel great, Mam!"

"Doesn't matter! You've still had a shock to your system." She raised her eyes. "I don't want to have to come for you."

"You won't, I promise." He raced off, Julian in front.

She stood and watched them disappear into Eileen's. All was quiet. She stood for a few minutes to admire the sun. It peeped over the top of the hills like half an eggshell. The patches of blue sky etched with gold that ran into pink reminded her of some of the pictures she'd seen of the saints and angels in the holy bible. *'Heaven, I'm in heaven, and my heart beats so that I can hardly speak.'* She'd had that damn song in her head for a week now. She started to sing it quietly as she walked home. "And I seem to find the happiness I seek, when we're out together dancing cheek to cheek. Oh, I'd love to climb a mountain, and to reach the highest peak, but it doesn't thrill me half as much, as dancing cheek to cheek..."

She breathed in the evening air. It was lovely, this part of the world. Fresh, clean, something homely about it. She saw the jeep parked outside her cottage and stopped dead! She felt nervous all of a sudden. A thought in her head said, *Is the love of my life waiting for me?* "Give over, you fool!" *It would always be David...it was always him.* But she often wondered what it would be like to have a friend and lover in her life again. She lifted the gate off the path. When the captain left she would sit outside in her garden for an hour and listen to the river. It was a beautiful night and the air was unusually warm for the time of year. A bit of a nip but nothing a warm cardigan couldn't handle. She pushed the front door open and smiled, ready to greet her visitor who sat with his back to her.

He turned around...

She screamed in shock! "GOD ALMIGHTY!" She edged backwards as if being pushed by a rush of energy. The smile fell from her face and got caught in the gasps that forced their way through her throat. Now frozen to the spot, she gawped at him; she felt the blood rush through her body and her heart drop from her chest to her stomach. She grabbed the thick wood of the tabletop just in case her legs gave way and sent her crashing to the floor.

He went to get up but, like her, he couldn't move. She looked like a vision, and if God turned up and asked him if he'd like to swap her for an angel, he'd refuse. He already had one. There was nowhere else in space or time that he would rather be than in this moment. In this moment forever...

And it was just a moment but it felt like an eternity. They looked at each other with blank expressions. Everything had disappeared. The house, the walls, the furniture...the only thing either of them could see was the face of a long-lost love, surrounded by an incandescent golden glow.

It can't be…Is he a spirit? "Da…," her voice was hoarse. "David," she whispered.

At last he managed to stand. She ran at him, threw her arms around his neck, and her legs around his waist and sobbed! Sobbed out all the longing, the sadness, the lost years. "My God, David, David…is it really you? Here? I can't believe…" The moment was so surreal, she couldn't believe—dared not believe! She clung to him desperately, terrified that if she let go he'd disappear in the same way a mirage in the desert disappeared when you got too close. Shaking, she put the palm of her hand on his cheek. It was warm. He was alive! Living! Breathing! Here in her front parlour!

He clung to her, breathing in her scent. "Maggie, Maggie."

She felt his tears, warm, across the top of her hand, trickling through her fingers. She laughed and cried at the same time. She couldn't stop touching him, had to make sure it was really him. Mesmerised, she traced his eyebrows, ran her middle finger down his nose, around his lips, then let her fingertips slide down his chin and along his neck to the perfect knot in his tie. She undid it gently, then undid his shirt buttons. She wanted to feel his flesh, feel his life inside her. Her fingers slid down his Adam's apple. He let out a small groan as she rubbed his chest gently, so gently that her fingers barely touched.

Neither of them could contain it: the lost years, the love, the passion.

"I can't believe you're here." She still clung to him, her legs still wrapped around his body. Her lips, hot, placed kisses on his cheeks, his neck, her fingers gently caressing…

He couldn't stand it. He grabbed her wrists and carried her through to the kitchen as if carrying her over the threshold. Spotting the stairs, he raced up them until he came to a small landing. She nodded towards her bedroom door. He kicked it gently, carried her through, and dropped her on the bed. Frustrated, he got his hand caught in his jacket sleeve in his impatience to get undressed…to get at her. She reached up, pulled the jacket roughly from the shoulders, and pulled him next to her. He ran his thumbs over her breasts, licked her nipples through the blouse she wore. She moaned softly, unzipped his trousers, pulled out his penis. "I want you inside me," she demanded, running her tongue from the bottom of his neck to his ears. The taste of him almost drove her crazy. She cupped his testicles and ran her fingers gently underneath them. But still he held back, sliding his hand inside her blouse and tracing the delicate lace of her bra. Impatient, she started to undo her buttons one by one and pulled his head between her breasts. He sucked and prodded, circled her swollen nipples with his tongue. The throb between her legs made her cry out. He lifted her skirt and ran his hand up the smooth nylon that covered her legs. He felt dizzy; the flesh at the top of her stockings was driving him crazy. He couldn't hold out much longer. He traced his fingers over the soft cotton between her legs; she spread herself and cried out his name. "David, David!" she moaned. "Please, I've waited long enough!"

Their kisses were hungry, expectant, impatient. He ripped off her panties; she lay breathless, and nearly climaxed at the thought of what was to come.

He balanced on one arm, pulling his trousers off with the other, and climbed on top of her. He paused...he looked into her eyes as he entered. She curled her legs around his back and clasped both sides of his face. His thrusts were deep and slow. He wanted to savour her...but he couldn't hang on; within seconds the thrusts were fast and hard—she belonged to him. He grabbed a handful of her hair, breathed it in. It had an exotic, spicy smell. He couldn't take his eyes from her face...he wanted to see her pleasure, her need of him—

"David, David." She panted softly but then her need became more urgent. He felt her nails dig into his flesh, her pelvis circle, her legs like vises tighten around his back. She bunched his hair in her palms and looked deep into his eyes, knowing he loved to see her yearning. She screamed out his name as the throb between her legs and the aching throughout her body couldn't be contained any longer. She arched her back—"I love you, I love you!"—and climaxed over and over again.

He groaned. Sweat poured from him as he released himself inside her. He shuddered over and over and drained himself completely. "Maggie, Maggie, Maggie." He was still inside her, didn't want to leave the sweet, warm moist of her. "Maggie, if you only knew how much I love you, how I've longed for this moment." He kissed her over and over. They cried, they laughed, they loved for a few minutes more until they had to prise each other apart…

"Aedan will be back any minute." She stroked the side of his face.

"When are we going to tell him who I am?" He withdrew himself.

She sat up and buttoned her blouse. "Now!" She opened a drawer in her dresser and passed him a cotton handkerchief.

He zipped up his pants after wiping himself. Their love was as natural as it had always been. "I thought perhaps I should take him out a few times first, let him get used to me."

She sat on the edge of the bed and looked in the mirror of her dresser. The navy blue ribbon that held her hair in place had slipped down to the end of her ponytail. She pulled it out, brushed her hair, and tied it up again. "No!" She turned to him. "I want you to stay the night. I'm not letting you go again—not ever." She couldn't hide the panic in her voice.

"I don't want to shock him…upset him." He turned up his shirt collar and started to fasten his tie.

She took over and fastened a perfect knot. "It's going to come as a shock no matter when we tell him."

"What if he doesn't like me?"

"Tough! He'll have to get used to you." She had butterflies. "I'm just as concerned about his reaction, David, but I don't think putting it off is going to make it any easier. Anyway, I think he'll be thrilled."

He looked hopeful. "You think? He did seem to take to me easy enough yesterday, or is that just his nature?" They walked down the stairs, David behind.

"In what way?"

"Yesterday in the hospital he gave me a hug because I'd looked after Julian." He narrowed his eyes. "How did that dog end up with a name like that?"

She laughed. "It's a long story."

He sat down on the armchair in the corner of the room beside the fireplace. "He asked me to read *Treasure Island* with him. We were so comfortable together. I put my arms around his shoulders and he lay with his head on my chest and fell asleep."

"Really!?" She felt relieved. "No! He isn't usually that familiar with strangers. Funny…he said that he thought there was something weird about you, not in a bad way, just something weird, but he couldn't explain himself. His sixth sense was probably working overtime to prepare him."

He noticed how edgy she was. "Why don't you sit down?"

She stood in the middle of the room with her hands clasped. "Yes, why don't I sit down?" She arranged herself around the springs.

"I think it's time you had a new three-piece. You're right: I might end up damaging myself."

Maggie stared at him until the realisation set in. "He never said that to you! Honestly, I have to watch every word I say to that boy!"

David laughed. "I wondered what he was talking about until I walked in here and saw it." He went quiet, looked at her, frowned. He had to ask. "Why didn't you wait?"

There was an awkward moment before she spoke. "I thought you were dead! The letter Father Joseph sent…it, it said the doctors held little hope for your recovery. They only gave you a few days to live."

"Held little *hope*, Maggie. Where there's any hope at all, there's possibility…" He trailed off when he saw the tears spill from her eyes and run down her face.

"I know. I'm so sorry—" She broke off, unable to finish.

He stood up and clasped her chin. His voice was slightly aggressive, void of sympathy. "Don't cry. You must have been frightened! The responsibility of a child? By yourself? " He lifted her head as if questioning her.

"And the love of my life, dead! David…it's true, I was terrified of so many things. I knew it had something to do with Patrick." She felt his hand tighten around her chin at the mere mention of that name. "And you remember that awful house we found not long after we'd arrived in Manchester. I never wanted to move into it in the first place.

I packed up a few belongings and left six weeks later. Something in the back of my mind told me that if I stayed in that house only bad things would happen. I didn't want to wait for Father Joseph's letter telling me you'd died, and I couldn't visit, not with Patrick on the loose…I, I, feared for Aedan."

"I suppose Patrick is the reason you left no forwarding address?"

She felt as if she was being interrogated. "I left no trace of us anywhere, David."

"I know. I contacted the chateau. They told me Angelette was no longer with us, and that the only address they had was the Manchester one." He jerked her chin roughly. "If you only knew how I searched for you both over the years…if you only knew the heartbreak, the longing, the questions. You'll never leave me again, Maggie, never!" His gaze was hard, intense.

"I know." She started to sob. "We have so much to catch up on… so much."

His mood softened. He ran his thumbs over her wet cheeks. "And years to do it." He bent down, kissed her lips, lingered. Hungry, she kissed him back…the passion smouldered in his belly again.

They heard the gate creak and little footsteps run along the path. David jumped back and sat down in the armchair. Maggie wiped her face with the back of her hands.

Julian bounded in ahead, running first to Maggie, then to David. "That's enough, boy. Go and lie down." Aedan stopped between the chair and the sofa and eyed them, one to the other. He didn't know what was going on but they looked different. "Have you been out, Mam?"

"No, sweetheart, not since I left you. Why?"

"You look all flushed!"

David and Maggie eyed each other. She clamped her lips together to stifle her laughter. "I felt a bit hot earlier." She looked at David. "Under the collar, nothing to worry about."

David burst out laughing. Aedan shot him a look. David pretended to cough. "Sorry, something in my throat."

Aedan felt strange. Something was going on with these two and he wasn't sure if he liked it! They kept looking at each other funny! He'd never seen his mam behave this way. It was as if she'd suddenly grown years younger. Julian nudged his legs, bringing him out of his reverie.

Maggie stood up and made some tea using the hot water from the kettle she always kept by the fire. "Check his food and water, sweetheart." Aedan went off into the kitchen.

She past David a small cup and saucer. "Biscuit?"

He shook his head. "No, no. I can't remember ever feeling so nervous."

"Relax. It's still Sunday, isn't it?"

He looked at his watch puzzled. "Yes."

She laughed. "He doesn't bite. Only on Mondays!"

"Maggie, this is no time for jokes! Be serious!"

She ignored her own panic and apprehension. "Relax! Aedan, can you come here, love? We need to talk to you." She wouldn't lose control now. She couldn't. This was going to be a sweet moment, and she'd be damned before she'd let nerves get in the way.

Aedan recognised the look on his mother's face. Sheer will, determination, and stubbornness. "Don't you want me to go in the jeep?"

"In the jeep?"

"For a ride in the captain's jeep?"

She hesitated and flipped her hand while she tried to find the right words. "Oh, no, no, that's fine."

David wanted to help her but said nothing. She should break it to Aedan before he added his two-penn'orth. He caught her eyes, willed her to say something... *It's okay, I'm here,* his eyes said.

"Aedan, sweetheart...what I'm going to say." She stopped and clasped her hands in her lap. Looked down at them. Looked up at Aedan. "You might be shocked at what I have to say—" *Jesus, Mary, and Joseph! Why couldn't she just say it?*

"Aedan..."

"Are you all right, Mam?"

She felt his panic merge with her own, and her protective instinct kicked in. "You don't have to be afraid...I..." She looked at David.

"We have something to tell you."

The atmosphere felt charged, full with something. He didn't know what. He waited anxiously.

"Aedan, this is David Sullivan." She was still looking at David. "You know who David Sullivan is, don't you?"

"No! But he's got the same name as my dad." It didn't register that they were one and the same.

At last, David's quiet strength had reached her. She held her son's eyes captive with her own. "Aedan, this is your dad. I made a mistake. He didn't die."

Aedan stood rigid. He didn't look at David, only at his mother. "My dad!?" His heart started to race. He felt terrified; he didn't know why. He ran at his mother, jumped in her lap, and buried his head in her chest. He wouldn't look at that man! He wouldn't!

David and Maggie looked at each other, dumbfounded. They'd expected one of only two reactions. Aedan would either be happy or angry to find out that he had a father. As it stood, he seemed scared to death.

Maggie tried to prise his hands from around her neck. "It's all right," she crooned. "You know when you were tiny it was often your dad who you'd stop crying for. He'd pick you up in his big strong arms and you'd fall asleep within minutes."

"Did I?" He still had his head buried in her chest.

"Are you frightened?"

"A bit."

"Why?"

"I don't want him to take you away from me!" His voice trembled.

Her heart melted. She understood his childish concerns. She cradled him to her. "Aedan, I'd never leave you. I love you. I'd never want to live without you."

Aedan was content to stay hidden in his mother's breast. In all his eight years, it had just been him and her. What did it mean, having a dad? Derrick liked it! And at times he'd wished Charlie was his dad as well. But now he had his own, he didn't know if he wanted one or not!

"Aedan, I'll leave if you want me to." David winked at Maggie. "I'll come by tomorrow and take you for that ride if you'd like. We could go up the peaks."

Aedan still didn't move but he pictured himself riding the jeep on the peaks, and telling everyone at school that he had a dad who was a soldier. He did like the captain, but...

"I'll be off then." David stood up.

Aedan turned and looked up at him, smiling shyly. Something inside him said he didn't want David to leave. "Are you really my dad?"

God, the boy was beautiful. He wanted to hug him, kiss him, smell him again, shout from the rooftops that Aedan was his son. But he kept his distance. He knew that Aedan had to come to him. He crouched down. "I am, and I'm proud to say it."

There was a pause. Aedan's lips turned up at the sides. Not quite a smile. He stared at the man intensely, then yawned widely; he didn't bother to cover his mouth.

Maggie tried to lift him off her knees. "Cover your mouth when you yawn! Come on, it's way past your bedtime, young man. Would you like the capt—your dad to come and see you tomorrow?" She felt hopeful but when Aedan turned and clung to her neck yet again, her hopes were dashed but only for a split second. He dotted kisses all over her cheeks, "Night, Mamma. I love youuuuu," he said, rubbing his nose against hers. He jumped off Maggie's lap, looked up at David, took his hand. "Will you tuck me in?"

David scooped him up, crushed him to his chest, and sobbed. "You have no idea how many times I've lived this moment in my head."

Maggie stood up, wiped his tears, her tears, Aedan's tears. "Just look at the state of us." David bent down with Aedan in his arms so that he could reach his mother for one more kiss, and then headed off to the bedroom every bit the proud father.

"Can we read *Treasure Island*?"

Apart from their voices fading as they climbed the stairs, the room was quiet. She sat down, closed her eyes, and enjoyed the silence. Like David, she'd lived this moment over and over again in her imagination…*And people say imagination is fantasy!* She had an urge to turn on the small radio… "Dance with me, I want my arm about you, the charm about you will carry me through, to heaven, I'm in heaven, and my heart beats so that I can hardly speak, and I seem to find the happiness I seek, when we're out together dancing cheek to cheek." It was that damn song that she'd had in her head for the past week!

David walked back in the room. "Do you know where his book is? I said I'd read a chapter with him."

She nodded over at her shopping bag. "In my bag."

David rooted through the bag, took out the book. "I'll be back in a jiffy."

She looked at the clock, 9:10 p.m. She'd nip out to the Prince of Wales for a jug of beer. She needed to wind down. Besides, she would give David the heads up on his son—tonight! It felt right that he should know as soon as possible. A small feeling of anxiety crept around her, an urgent feeling that she shouldn't waste any time. Yes, the sooner David knew the better. The more protection Aedan had the safer he'd be. She wondered how he'd take it. Probably think he'd walked into some strange fantasy. She sighed to herself. He had! But she knew he would believe her. She didn't doubt David for a minute.

She closed her eyes, so many questions. But it was all so clear— *"GALAXIAS!"* the voice boomed in her head; it seemed to come from nowhere. She jumped up, grabbed her coat and purse, and ran from the cottage. "Stop it!" she said out loud. She pulled the door behind her, turned, and pushed on it to make sure it was shut tight. "I'll do it in my time!"

Roman looked at White Eagle, and nodded. "Ahh…at last she accepts Galaxias. David adds to her strength. Good! The elders won't accept her reluctance for much longer."

44.

*I*n the dark, sinister chamber buried in the bowels of the underworld, Evolus sat behind a dusty desk. Small wisps of yellow vapour weaved from his nostrils. He let out a sadistic growl that penetrated the thick stone walls to instil fear into the demons beyond them. *You're never alone! I see everything you do and know every thought in your pathetic, weak little minds! Don't forget that!*

The war raged all over the world. Major cities were brought down one by one. The fear he'd released into the hearts and minds of the human race got denser, more terrifying each day. He could feel their misery, their pain. He sneered, and bared razor-sharp teeth. It wouldn't be long now and Earth would be his! Its people his slaves! Its children his warriors! But there was light coming in from somewhere. Evolus stretched his arms either side. His huge fists gripped the corners of the desk, leaving indentations of his fingers in the thick, solid wood. Where was that light coming from? He growled a low, menacing growl from deep within. Something threatened his plans—a power! Young! Naïve! Weak! No match for him, yet it worried him. Why? *"One day it will mature, gain strength. It will be your downfall, Evolus,"* an inner voice hissed. *"Find it now before it's too late!"*

He slammed his fist down on the desk. His sword bounced into the dank, sulphurous air and released a fork of energy that lit up the room. Particles of dust floated around in the silver-blue light and then slowly settled on years of grime. Outside the chamber thousands of dark souls squealed pathetically, their master's rage filling them with fear. He pushed the table away and stood, chest out, strong, powerful, formidable. His sword had landed upright. As usual, the blade buried itself six inches deep in the stone flags by the side of his chair. Without looking, palm down, he reached out. The sword withdrew from the flags and flew into his hand as if with a life of its own. He flicked his head and directed his wrath at the solid cathedral door as he walked toward it. It opened within seconds, smashed into the wall, then slammed shut behind him.

A battalion of dark ones stood at attention. He looked them up and down. They could feel his fury like a stranglehold around their throats. None dared move or make eye contact. If they did, an abyss of misery and torture would be their fate for all time. Apart from the wheezing of their laboured breath, the only other sounds to be heard was the trickle of stale water as it ran down the ancient stone of the building, and the horrific thud of Evolus's huge feet as he inspected line after line of evil.

He stopped, looked under his bulging brow, and called forth the two demons in charge of the Manchester bombing. "Maphra! Llution!"

The two demons, both high-ranking, formidable warriors, rushed forward, heads bowed, not daring to look up. Both were huge yet insignificant in comparison to Evolus. They had the same deformed brow, scaly skin, and razor-sharp teeth. Their nostrils were set wide apart, and their eyes were large and angled, with the ability to change colour. But most of the time, an inky-black pupil, rectangular in shape, was surrounded by a yellowish sclera—this was where the similarity ended. . Like humans, the faces of demons had their own unique character making each individual easily identifiable.

"Look up, both of you!" Evolus commanded.

Slowly they raised their heads. Quick snorts of vapour left their nostrils, showing shortness of breath and outward terror.

"Did you get lost on your way to Manchester?" Evolus was calm but there was no mistaking the threat behind his eyes.

Maphra spoke: "My lord, we are your humble servants—"

"Shut up! You were instructed to bomb the major city. Why did you divert?"

This time Llution answered. "When we flew over Glossop, my lord, we noticed the locals seemed too happy. They weren't taking the war—you—seriously. We had to do something to command respect for you, my lord…instil the fear."

Evolus snarled. A low rumble could be heard throughout the underworld. "Respect! You've made me a laughing stock! Where are the thousands of souls I expected? The operation was pathetic!" He stared down at the two demons. Under his evil gaze, their skin melted from their flesh, adding a foul mixture of burnt fat and sulphur to the already toxic air. Screaming in agony and begging for forgiveness, they physically shrivelled before him, becoming half their usual size. "You're supposed to be the best! Do I strip you of your rank? Throw you into the pit and let the weaker ones deal with you?"

Horrified, Llution and Maphra unfurled their black wings in the hope of protecting themselves from Evolus's fury. Bowing and pleading, they backed away slowly.

Maphra trembled with terror. "Please, my lord, we'd hoped to please you, but the bombs they, they were right on target, yet they missed—"

Evolus grabbed Maphra by the throat, held him in the air, and waved him around like a piece of flimsy cloth. "HOW CAN THEY BE RIGHT ON TARGET AND MISS? IMBECIIIIILE!" he raged.

"They stopped in midair, my lord!" Llution answered. "For three minutes they just hung there, giving the humans time to seek shelter."

Evolus threw Maphra against the wall behind him. When Maphra screamed in pain, Evolus lifted him to his feet again by slamming a mighty fist underneath the lesser demon's chin. "STAAAAND," he ordered. Maphra did his best to straighten but crumpled in a heap before his master.

Evolus looked over the heads of the thousands of demons before him. "SEE HOW WEAK!" He gripped the back of Maphra's head, dragging him to his feet. "I WON'T TOLERATE IT!"

Evolus curled his hand and with lethal fingernails scratched out a huge circle in the stone flags to open a vortex of unspeakable evil. It flamed red, yellow, orange, and the most alarming screams and voices could be heard coming from deep within it. Maphra cried out. Sheer terror filled his being. His eyes alternated the colours of the flames and bulged from their sockets. He opened his mouth to reveal many other occasions he'd been led astray by Llution in the hope that he'd be freed from a fate that would leave him begging for death. Evolus knew this. He trusted none of them.

Just as Evolus was about to hurl Maphra into the vortex, Llution panicked and shouted out, "MY LORD! Maphra was incensed by the disrespect the humans were showing. His loyalty to you is to be commended. Forgive me, my lord. Maphra would be a great loss, a waste of one of your finest warriors and loyal servants."

Evolus threw Maphra into Llution. He was intrigued by such loyalty. A suspicious grin crossed his face. He'd let the pair live for now. They obviously thought they could beat him. He admired that in his warriors. It showed courage. The vortex was full of imbeciles with no guts! He calmed. "Llution, why do you think the bombs remained in midair?"

Still in agony with his burning flesh, a bewildered, Llution shook his head. "I'm not sure, my lord. Pressure, wind—"

Evolus narrowed his eyes. "Llution, do you think you can beat me?"

Terrified, "Never, my lord! I'm your servant. I have no desire to beat you!"

"Don't interrupt me again! Ever! Especially with a lie!" Evolus's voice was deadly. "You're power will never be a match for mine. It will pay you to remember that. If you think it was pressure or wind that suspended those bombs in midair for three minutes then even I underestimated how weak you are. Intervention, Llution! You were right there! Right where the light is coming in!" Evolus nodded in disbelief. "Yet you failed to recognise it!"

Llution was appalled. How could a demon of his standing have missed the enemy when they were that close? "It, it, must be…a, it must be strong—"

"NO! IT IS WEAK! YOUNG!" He turned to the other demons.

"BUT IT IS PROTECTED BY GALAXIAS!" Shrill screams and dismayed shouts of "GALAXIAS! NO!" filled the air.

Evolus was incensed. They feared Galaxias more than they feared their master!? He marched through the ranks, picked up demons at random, and hurled them into the vortex. "YOU FEAR GALAXIAS MORE THAN YOUR MASTER?"

A hush immediately came over the underworld. The demons stood at attention. Red eyes, yellow eyes, black eyes, all were fixed and staring. They didn't dare move.

Evolus unfurled his massive wings, took off, and landed on a thick stone podium just above them. Two four-columned sacrificial altars made from the same stone stood on either side of hundreds of steps. An ancient world, it had been lost to Evolus through greed and corruption. These creatures before him were once its citizens. But this was only one small unit in underworld circles.

Evolus climbed the last few steps to reach a jewel-studded throne carved from oak. Looking down on the warriors, his eyes alternated from red to black and moved slowly from side to side. He raised his arms in the air, looked up, and let out a mighty roar. "I HAVE NO USE FOR COWAAAARDS!" he raged. He blew on the first three rows of demons before him; his breath was colder and more powerful than the strongest northern wind. Their fear and pleas for mercy made him blow even harder. Thousands of them were lifted off their feet and flung into the vortex. Evolus eyed the rest of them and spat, "None here will ever be a match for me! I can and will finish every one of you within minutes... but death will not be your saviour! DO YOU UNDERSTAND?"

In unison, thousands of demons stood at attention and placed left hands on chests while right hands gripped swords. With legs slightly apart, they stamped both feet hard on the ground. The eerie sound reverberated through the underworld as they raised their chins slightly upwards. They were ready for battle. A formidable might, not to be underestimated.

Satisfied, Evolus reached out with his huge hand and snapped the vortex shut. "MAPHRA! LLUTION!" The two unfurled their wings, lifted straight up off the ground, and landed at their master's side. Both stretched to full height, looked straight ahead, and stood to attention. "Sit," Evolus ordered. They sat in smaller thrones on either side of him. He turned to his legions and let out a terrifying howl. "THIS WILL BE A WAR LIKE NO OTHERRRRRRRR! LET THE BATTLE FOR EARTH BEGIN!"

CPSIA information can be obtained at www.ICGtesting.com
Printed in the USA
LVOW080049090113

314962LV00002B/125/P